THE
ODDS

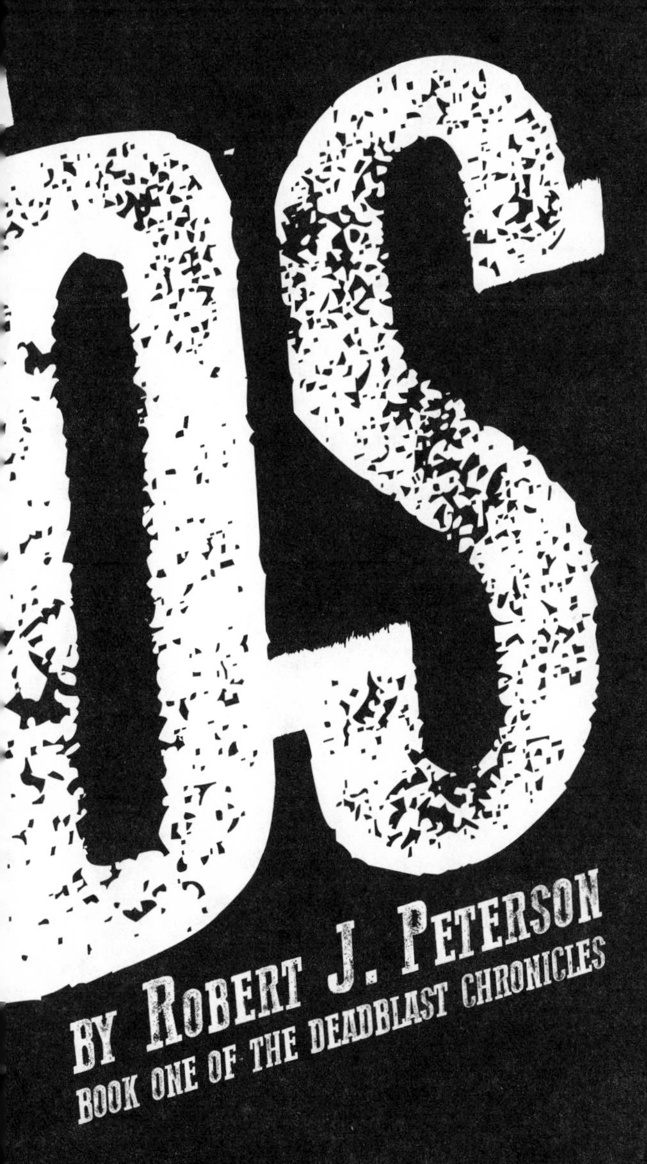

A California Coldblood Book | Rare Bird Books
Los Angeles, Calif.

THIS IS A GENUINE CALIFORNIA COLDBOOD BOOK

A California Coldblood Book | Rare Bird Books
453 South Spring Street, Suite 531
Los Angeles, CA 90013
rarebirdbooks.com
californiacoldblood.com

FIRST TRADE PAPERBACK ORIGINAL EDITION

Eldridge art by Ratna Pappert: curiositydrawsme.com
Landscape art by Nils Jeppe: enderra.com
Author photo by Meeno Peluce: meenophoto.com
Set in Goudy Old Style

Printed in the United States
Distributed in the US by Publishers Group West

10 9 8 7 6 5 4 3 2 1

Publisher's Cataloging-in-Publication data

Peterson, Robert Jason.
The Odds, Book One of the Deadblast Chronicles / by Robert J. Peterson.
p. cm.
ISBN 9781940207810
Series : The Deadblast Chronicles.

1. End of the world—Fiction. 2. Science fiction, American. 3. Apocalyptic literature. 4. Adventure fiction. 5. Black humor (Literature). I. Title.

PS3616.E8475 O33 2014
813.6—dc23 2014904865

Sing, goddess!

"Chess is war over the board.
The object is to crush the opponent's mind."
–Robert James "Bobby" Fischer
World Chess Champion, 1972-75

"Never tell me the odds!"
–Han Solo
Captain, Millenium Falcon

Dedicated to my mom, Wanda Sue Bohon Peterson

Introduction: 10 Reasons Why You Should Read THE ODDS

by Karl Mueller

1. It's generous. There's more invention on a single page of this book than in most novels in their entirety. If books were priced per killer idea rather than a flat rate, *The Odds* would cost roughly $5,124.82.

2. It's funny. Wait'll you visit the mountain base of the steroid-gobbling, weight-lifting maniacs known as the Narsyans.

3. Live chess. To the death. With the entire world as the board. With a Queen who attacks with a rocket launcher.

4. It introduces the concept of "power-fucking" to an unsuspecting world. (Though it leaves just enough of the details of what power-fucking actually is to tantalize the imagination.)

5. Though I wouldn't want to live in the postapocalyptic world *The Odds* describes, I would love to visit—provided I had an indestructible, climate-controlled suit capable of teleporting me through the black markets of the underground cities and the abandoned mines teeming with meth-addled, pineal-glands-gone-thermonuclear "dreens." Reading this book is the next best thing.

6. It's the very satisfying introduction to a series that plunges us headfirst into a freezing cold/boiling hot world gone horribly awry.

7. It's full-bore sci-fi/post-apocaylptic writing where the writing is actually good, not just functional. The dialogue sizzles. The sentences are packed with radioactive imagery and double-barreled zingers. The paragraphs grab you by your eye sockets and scream in your ears 'til they bleed while repeatedly punching you in the face—and you love every second of it.

8. If an underground, unregulated lab run by Project Mayhem fused the DNA of John Carpenter, James Cameron, and Charles Manson and gave the resulting unholy embryo the resources of Viacom and final cut, the movie adaptation of *The Odds* would win every Oscar, render the MPAA's NC-17 rating useless, and cause more home foreclosures than the 2008 economic collapse. Just trust me on this.

9. You know you want to.

10. See number four.

• • • • •

Karl Mueller has been a working writer in Hollywood since 2007, when his postapocalyptic thriller screenplay Shelter *made the 2007 Black List of Best Unproduced Screenplays and launched his career as a screenwriter.* Shelter *eventually turned into* The Divide *directed by French horror auteur Xavier Gens, starring Michael Biehn, Rosanna Arquette, and Milo Ventimiglia. It debuted at the South by Southwest Film Festival and set a festival acquisitions record when it was bought by Anchor Bay Films. Anchor Bay released film theatrically in 2013 in the United States and Canada.* The Divide *was released theatrically throughout the world through Content Media Corporation.*

Mueller made his directorial debut with Mr. Jones, *which he also wrote, It's inspired by real-life encounters he had with a hermit near his parents' cabin in Northern Minnesota while growing up.* Mr. Jones *had its world premiere at the Tribeca Film Festival and was also acquired by Anchor Bay Films. The film was released theatrically in May of 2014.*

Mueller continues to work steadily as a screenwriter selling specs and doing rewrites and adaptations. Mueller wrote the recent The Devil's Hand, *starring Jennifer Carpenter, Rufus Sewell, and Colm Meaney–a horror-thriller set on a repressive Amish settlement where a Taliban-like theocracy searches for signs of the Antichrist in its teenage daughters.*

Interview with Robert J. Peterson

by Barbra Dillon, FanboyComics.net

This interview originally appeared on the website FanboyComics.net. It was conducted by Fanboy Comics Managing Editor Barbra Dillon. You can view the interview online here:

http://tinyurl.com/rjp-interview

• • • • •

Barbra J. Dillon: As the writer of *The Odds*, what initially inspired you to tell this story, and how did you come to develop such an intricate world with a dynamic cast of characters?

Robert J. Peterson: Phew! What a great question. *The Odds* is one of those projects that started out as one thing but quickly morphed into another. I sometimes joke that I'm always trying to write normal, mainstream fiction, but I can't go 10 pages into a novel without introducing some kind of high-concept element. That definitely happened with *The Odds*, which began in my mind as a simple, gritty crime novel set in a dusty, desert town. (I've felt the pull of the desert for many years and could easily see myself landing in the high desert near Joshua Tree in my retirement.)

In any event, I'll probably still write that book, but when I started writing *The Odds*, I very quickly made that wrong left turn at Albuquerque, so to speak. The lead character makes a left turn on his motorcycle early in the story, and it takes him into the subterranean city of Dedrick. I've always been fascinated by enormous indoor spaces like caves, and enormous, man-made indoor spaces are even cooler! So I imagined Dedrick as a five-square-mile city enclosed by a giant, vaulted brick ceiling overhead. I couldn't quite keep all of the action inside Dedrick—quite a bit happens in the aboveground areas, as well—but most of it does, and that was great fun to limit myself to that small region as a storyteller.

Building out the world and the characters came through one of the longest and most challenging development processes in my writing career. I work closely with a lot of trusted editors, but my most trusted editorial voice over the years has been Karl Mueller, a filmmaker and writer. Pretty much, when I grow up, I want to be a writer like Karl Mueller.

The Odds was actually the fifth novel I completed, but it was the first one I seriously outlined. If you can believe it, I completely wung my first four books. Yikes! But when it came time to write my fifth, I decided to plan it out, and I wrote several outlines before I settled on one that I liked. And it's funny—at Karl's behest, I actually wrote one outline where I stripped away all but the most essential story-points, and I wrote another one where I stripped away the science-fiction trappings and reimagined the story as a grindhouse-y Jason Statham vehicle.

Guess which two outlines contributed most to the final product?

When it comes to characters, I've also joked that the heroes in my novels are different parts of my personality with certain eccentric adjustments. The hero of my first novel is me if I turned into the Incredible Hulk. The hero of my second novel is the sad, skittish and very angry fat kid who hides inside me. The hero of my third novel is my "Evil Kirk." (Remember that episode of *Star Trek* where Captain Kirk got split into his good and evil halves, and his evil half included all of his command skills, bravery and womanizing? If that happened to me, my evil side would be the hero of my third book.) The hero of my fourth novel is the lonely part of me that suffers from body dysmorphic disorder. (Body dysmorphia comes up in just about all of my writing.) The hero of my most recent novel is the part of me that retreated into technology to find connections with other people.

But Eldridge, the hero of *The Odds*, is me if I were a superhero. Let me explain:

I feel like all of us have "super" versions of ourselves. They come out in good times and bad. Sometimes an especially wonderful significant other (like my exquisite partner, Lauren Rock) can help you access that super-version more often. But when I talk about a "superhero" version of myself, I'm not talking about a version of me that has super-powers (although Eldridge has a few), and I'm not talking about a version of me that wears tights and a cape.

No, a "super" version of yourself is you at your best. It's all of your best qualities given voice and form. I like to think that Agent Dale Cooper of *Twin Peaks* is a superheroic version of David Lynch. He's intelligent and spiritual, but most of all, Cooper is incredibly kind to everyone he meets. He also has a few superpowers, including the ability to get a full night's sleep after 20 minutes of meditation, as well as a powerful sense of intuition.

When it came to Eldridge, I didn't set out to write him as my "super" self; that's just how it shook out. But when I was rewriting the book, one of my beta readers pointed out how Eldridge's actions—some of which are incredibly foolish—are driven by a deep sense of empathy and an abiding love for his friends. I mentioned earlier that Eldridge has some superpowers; he has superhuman strength and limitless endurance, but he rarely uses those powers in the book, no matter what kind of trouble he gets into. (And he gets into a lot. Apparently the "super" version of me is just as bumbling and clumsy as I am in real life.) No, he always has help from his friends, even if they're not around.

BD: Are there specific creators who have most influenced your work as a writer or, more specifically, your work on *The Odds?*

RJP: Oh, yeah. A lot! The central action setpiece in *The Odds* is the Xiang tournament, a live-action chess battle royale. A couple of old computer games influenced that idea, including *Battle Chess* and *Archon. Battle Chess* was a standard chess engine that portrayed all of the game-pieces as animated characters, while *Archon* was a chess variant that included one of the most important elements I imported into Xiang: battles for the squares.

As insane as this sounds, I actually wrote the first "draft" of the Xiang tournament when I was six years old. No kidding. I used to draw tons of storybooks on notebook paper. Mostly these involved me inserting me and my friends into Saturday morning cartoons. But I wrote one called *Chess* that depicted two men playing a chess game. Every time they made a move, I drew a battle scene. I imagined every piece as a different warrior with different weapons and powers. One image from this storybook—and I'm not making this up—that made it into the novel was a rook-pawn battle. I imagined the rook as someone driving a big-rig with a cow-catcher mounted to the front, while the pawn was on foot, fighting with a broadsword. (In the novel, the battle ends with a decapitation. I don't think I included that in the storybook.)

That basic idea—the live-action chess tournament—lingered with me until I wrote *The Odds.* Given the popularity of *Most Dangerous Game*-style action mayhem in recent years *(The Running Man, Battle Royale,* and later *The Hunger Games),* I was happy to make use of the idea.

Oh, and along with *Battle Chess* and *Archon,* one other 80s video-game influenced *The Odds: The Bard's Tale.* That was an old dungeon-crawl that consumed hours of my time back in the day. It all took place inside one small village, Skara Brae, and there was a huge tower you had to infiltrate to kill the big bad. I installed Dedrick potentate Jeb Goldmist atop a mighty tower in *The Odds*. Skara Brae also included an endless street called Sinister. (I assume the game's creator, Michael Cranford, included it to make level-grinding easier.) I named the main drag in Dedrick Sinister Street.

As for writers, my biggest influences remain Neal Stephenson, Joss Whedon, John Irving, and Barry Unsworth. When it comes to the craft of novel-writing, I'm always trying to be like Irving and Unsworth, who construct these beautifully headlong narratives. Unsworth in particular astonishes me with his versatility. Whenever I pick up an Unsworth title, I feel like I'm reading an entirely new novelist. Of course I try to be like Stephenson, too, who writes with incredible energy. (He also uses hyperbole better than any author I've read.) And when it comes to geek overlord Joss Whedon, I mostly try to emulate his characters. Whedon's characters are good people who are trying to be better people. Whedon also destroys cliches with alacrity, and I try to maintain a similar impatience with cliche.

But more than any one video-game or novelist, the biggest influence on *The Odds* is John Carpenter's *Big Trouble in Little China.* When I try to describe the tone of *The Odds*, I always call it "an extended ode to *Big Trouble in Little China*," which features a wise-cracking, world-weary hero who's also a klutzy goofball, as well as a narrative that mashes up a lot of genres, including martial-arts movies and American westerns.

BD: What do you hope that readers will take away from the book?

RJP: That the greatest weapon any of us can have is a good heart.

BD: Are there any plans to revisit the world of *The Odds* in any further novels?

RJP: Affirmative. It's the first of a four-book cycle—or tetralogy, or "quadrilogy," if you're marketing the *Alien* franchise—called the Deadblast Chronicles. The second book, *The Remnants*, is tentatively set for a 2016 release, to be followed by *The Oceans* and *The Palaces*.

BD: *The Odds* will mark the first publication of California Coldblood Books as an imprint of Rare Bird Books. What led to creation of California Coldblood Books, and what do you feel makes the publishing company unique in the ever-expanding literary landscape?

RJP: I'm a huge fan of the team at Rare Bird—Tyson Cornell, Julia Callahan and Alice Marsh-Elmer. Pretty much, they lead fascinating lives that bring them into contact with interesting people who write books, and that's who they work with. I originally created California Coldblood Books to serve as the publishing label for the Deadblast books—and by "created," I mean, "I built a website."

As for what makes CCB unique, I'll offer this: I want to make CCB into an Island of Misfit Toys. I want to work with kooky authors who want to write novels and who maybe haven't found a home yet. I'll give them a home on this Island of Misfit Toys where they'll get boutique treatment from a goofball editor (me), and where they can develop and write books that excite them, because that's what makes for great fiction.

BD: How did California Coldblood come to find a home under the Rare Bird banner, and how do you feel that the companies will complement one another?

RJP: I'd had a longstanding fantasy to make CCB into Rare Bird's imprint for sci-fi and fantasy. The stupendous Lauren Rock encouraged me to approach them with with idea, and when I did, it was kismet; they'd been hoping to expand into sci-fi and fantasy for a long time.

I plan to expand Rare Bird's reach into the worlds of sci-fi and fantasy, both with a slate of new titles, as well as with outreach to blogs, websites and agents who represent authors in these arenas.

Rare Bird, in turn, provides extensive support in public relations, with years of experience in the literary world, as well as a fantastic distributor, Publishers Group West. The Rare Bird team also just has great taste. I love their design and presentation. I'll be the art director for CCB, but I plan to get feedback and creative advice from the Rare Bird crew. In addition, they've been acting as my mentors in the publishing world for awhile now. I'm looking forward to a long and fruitful relationship with them.

Part One
XIANG

THE REDHEAD CAME TO town to celebrate his deathday.

A bulky motorcycle hummed between the redhead's legs as he passed a green highway sign that hung from one corner and told him he was entering a place called Nevada. Minutes later, he rode into the town at a red dusk. The town was brown, mostly, except for a few flashes of yellow coming from the grimy lightbulbs and neon tubes that remained. No one greeted him because no one was outside. Thermometers in that part of the world had permanent mercury stains around 150 and 50 below. The sun rose hard and set fast, and nothing but desert hot and desert cold followed it into the brown town.

Thermally lined tubes connected the redhead with his bike. They bristled like giant spider legs between the brown leather jacket he wore and the bike's fuel tank, which was about twice the size of a normal tank and resided just below his butt, right in between two heavy leather saddlebags. The engine sat between his knees and sprouted four chrome exhaust pipes that ran the length of the bike. Although the exhaust pipes were covered with dirt, they hadn't seen any exhaust in a long, long time. A small analog clock sat in the engine's housing and ticked away between his knees.

The redhead stopped at the edge of town, removed a black bandanna from his skull and used it to wipe desert dirt off the aviator goggles that encased his head. Wind kicked through his locks of red hair. Another bandanna, this one red, covered his mouth. His hands were green. As he moved, dirt flaked and rained from his clothes, hitting the ground in little bursts of brown. Once his goggles were clean, the redhead rested his hands on his thighs and surveyed the town. It looked the same. Corrugated steel held up crumbling roofs here and there, while adobe-style stucco struggled out of the sand elsewhere. The occasional burst of jagged graffiti brightened up a few of the buildings with the gleefully unholy litanies of the ones who followed the Odds.

The dusk turned from red to purple. The redhead's goggles instantly frosted over. He grabbed the eight tubes plugged into his jacket, four in each hand, and yanked them out. Chilly white gas burst from tips of the tubes. The redhead reached between his bike's handlebars and spun a valve shut. The gas shut off. The redhead stowed the tubes in holding hilts on the side of his fuel tank, then reached into his pockets and produced a pair of thick gloves. He took a few moments to drywash away the green gunk that coated his hands. When only a few bits of green remained caked in the nooks and crannies of his hands, he pulled on the gloves. Steam clouded in front of his mouth. He used the bandanna to wipe the frost from his goggles before he tied the strip of black fabric back over his hair. He disengaged his bike's brake and rode farther into town. He had two stops to make. The first was with an Odd, and for the first time in his life, the redhead wasn't afraid of the Odds.

He wasn't afraid of anything anymore.

His bike rolled up in front of the one building in town that still stood above the drifts of sand that had consumed most everything else. It looked like a temple: Thick marble columns held aloft an A-frame roof. Huddled underneath that roof were a half-dozen windows, all of them blocked out with shiny steel that reflected the sun's rays during the day and stood ready to repel an attack if need be. Years ago, the marble was a mix of green and blue. Now it was the same color as everything else.

Across the front of the roof, blinking lightbulbs said: CASINO. The redhead dismounted his bike and rolled around the side of the building where a series of metal rods arched from the wall of the casino into the ground. There was nothing between them. He opened one of his saddlebags, reached in and used both hands to pull something out of it. A neutral observer might have thought he looked like a mime pulling on a length of imaginary rope. He flexed his bicep and wound the invisible rope around his forearm. That done, he used the unseen rope to tie his motorcycle to the metal parking rod, winding length after length around his bike. Eventually, he ran out of invisible rope and, holding the end of the rope in his fist, he propped a dusty boot against the metal rod and pulled. His bike skidded along the ground and clinked metal against metal. Still holding the end of the invisible rope, the redhead pressed his fingertip against the side of his goggles and detached a small, round ring. Holding the ring between his thumb and forefinger, he gave it a small squeeze. The ring divided into two halves and separated. He slid the invisible rope in between the two ring-halves, which re-fused when he pinched them back together.

The redhead walked around the front of the casino, still bundled up in his goggles, gloves, and bandannas. He climbed three steps up to the front door, a thick slice of heavy oak. It swung open as he approached and expelled a bustling, rotund man who wrapped a heavy animal hide around himself as he hopped down the steps and jogged down the empty dirt street. The redhead walked inside and stopped in a foyer. The front door closed behind him with a *hiss*, vacu-sealing the small room from the elements outside. He opened the second door and entered.

Two rows of video machines sat back-to-back through the center of the room. Their lights flashed in fits and spasms, each spasm accompanied by a corresponding surge in light. The slot machines whined and wailed like a bundle of babies drowning in a well. A few swaddled people hunched over the machines, tapping the touch-screens with their fingertips.

That was the center of the room. Faded green gambling tables stood against the walls, most of them empty. Another lump of rags and dirt straddled a stool in front of one of the tables, playing Blackjack against a dealer clad in black. The dealer wore the only collared shirt in the room. The floor sloped upward as it approached the rear of the room, melting into stairs that rose out of the steel floor. The stairs led farther into the casino, where dark hallways waited.

The redhead removed his goggles and bandannas. Red and gray stubble lined his jaw. His flesh looked like someone had taken a skull, shrink-wrapped it with leather, and then freeze-dried the result. A pair of dimples in his cheeks marked the centers of two twin webs of wrinkle-lines that flared across his face and merged with the crow's feet that clawed at his temples and dipped into the dark sockets that held his eyes. A thin scar bisected his forehead from his hairline to the top of his nose. At the midpoint of the scar, a perfect little circle of scar tissue bulged.

Headgear in hand, he walked toward the stairs at the back. The lone dealer made eye contact with him and stared a moment. The redhead stared back and held up his hands to say, *What?* The dealer looked away.

The action was waiting for him behind the slot machines, up the stairs, at the rear of the main floor. The redhead ignored everyone else and made his way up the five small stairs. On the third, he paused a beat and used his right hand to probe the left side of his chest. Then he did the opposite with his other hand. He made a confused smirk but shook his head and continued up the steps, which flowed together into a hallway with walls of steel. Small light-projectors sprayed green and yellow digital alphanumerics onto the walls on either side of the redhead. Some of the text spilled across his face and negotiated the peaks and crevices of his flesh. He walked soundlessly down the steel hallway to a single featureless wall at the rear.

The redhead patted the wall twice with his palm.

An opening melted through the steel at eye level, filled with two black-on-black eyes. The eyes fixated on the redhead. Then he heard a grunt. The opening resealed itself, only to reopen and melt away until a door stood in the wall. The black-on-black eyes belonged to a man who looked like a giant potato, with arms that rested against rolls of flesh that sagged along his frame and collected near his ankles. Light black fabric semi-floated over the mound-man, who sprouted forests of kinky black hair along the sides of his head. His face was nothing but sideburns and those black eyes. Another steel wall stood immediately behind him.

The redhead turned to face the mound-man. The mound-man looked him over, grunted and stepped back. The redhead nodded and pulled his goggles and bandannas back onto his head, covering his eyes, nose, ears, and mouth. That done, the redhead turned and patted the second steel wall with his palm. Another opening melted through the steel. As the redhead hustled through it, the mound-man pulled a tube out of the wall behind him and stuck it into his maw. Wet, chunky slurping sounds faded behind the redhead as he stepped into the next room and the steel door melted shut behind him.

When that door shut, the redhead knew he was trapped. With an Odd.

An electronic voice spoke from the dark room: "Happy almost deathday, Eldridge. I thought you'd be dead already."

The redhead, Eldridge, smirked and said, "Not yet."

There was no answer. Fingertips tapped on metal, and another green digital readout appeared on a wall on the far side of the room. The text read:

```
Eldridge | Deathday: July 4 03 | 1B
```

A beam of light scooped a face from the darkness. Eldridge never even heard the click that activated the lamp. A desk spanned the middle of the room. Eldridge stood on one side of the desk. Behind the desk sat an Odd: Crius Kaleb.

Eldridge knew Kaleb from way back. Back before Kaleb became an Odd—an elite caste of bookies who accepted wagers based on anything imaginable. Some Odds were big-time. Others were small-time. Kaleb sat somewhere in between, but even so, he still commanded the respect due to any Odd, because if you didn't make odds, you didn't live. Oh, sure, there were normal jobs that people worked to pay the bills, but the only way to get ahead was either to make odds or to *become* an Odd.

Eldridge didn't have the stomach to become an Odd, so he took his chances by making some odds. A few too many chances, as it turned out.

But back to Kaleb. He wore fine fabric—the same kind of light fabric worn by the mound-man, only much, much, much more expensive and 10 times as light. He looked like he was wearing spiderwebs, but Eldridge knew that if he tried to shoot Kaleb, the bullet would crumple against those fine clothes. Kaleb didn't wear any jewelry. Heavy shit against his skin made him go kill-crazy.

Lots of things made Kaleb go kill-crazy.

Kaleb stared at him with no eyes, because his withered, organic eyes hid behind ocular implants that had been wedged into his sockets. His face looked like a slab of milky bread. Skin hung around his mouth in saggy pockets, barely holding up chalky lips that sucked on a black pacifier-looking thing—Kaleb's speechmouth. The redhead knew that Kaleb was sucking on the other end of the speechmouth with orange teeth and a black tongue.

Eldridge had known Kaleb since they were kids. Kaleb lived underground. Eldridge lived in the mountains north of town. Kaleb got sick at an early age—but not sneezing-and-sniffles sick. *Head* sick. *Mind* sick. He started to do crazy things. One day he swallowed something he shouldn't have, and Dr. Enki had to pump his stomach. One time Eldridge and Kaleb met this other kid. And the kid disappeared.

Kaleb didn't care. Eldridge did. The redhead left Dedrick. Kaleb stayed and became an Odd, and somewhere along the line, he had blocked off his mouth and eyes with the speechmouth and oculars, all while his office had gradually become his inner sanctum and permanent address.

Eldridge nodded at the green letters on the wall.

"So?"

"So," Kaleb said. "The wager stands. If you die this July fourth, you win the money. An obscenely large amount of money, by the way. But if you miss the date, you get nothing. Are you sure you don't want to go for a yearly wager? If you die next July fourth, you'd win one-quarter—"

"Forget it. One quarter won't do it. I need the whole kaboodle."

"*You* need? After you've departed? Don't you mean *someone else* needs?"

Eldridge exhaled and kept his expression neutral. Tried to. In response, Kaleb's speechmouth emitted a trio of slurps interspersed with bursts of static. Laughter.

The Odd said, "So the redhead has family after all. Do they know about you and your little gambling habit?"

The redhead's eyes narrowed behind his goggles. "How's *your* kid doing, Cri? I haven't seen him around much."

Kaleb's speechmouth pointed suddenly at the ceiling as his teeth clamped together around the device. He laid his palms on the table.

"You know I haven't seen my son since...since..."

Eldridge raised a palm. "Forget it. Sorry I said anything. The wager's good?"

"Yes, the deathday wager is good."

Eldridge turned to leave. Kaleb rapped his desk with his knuckles.

"Remember, no suicide. It's got to be natural causes, an accident, or murder, and if it's a murder, it's gotta stand up. Tola and Goldmist have to sign off or you won't get paid."

Zora Tola. The local law. And Jeb Goldmist. Another Odd. The most powerful in town.

Eldridge shrugged. "Fine." He turned to leave.

"Where you off to?"

As the steel wall melted open before him, Eldridge said, "Dr. Enki."

• • • • •

BACK ON THE CASINO floor, Eldridge got stopped by Constable Zora Tola—all six and a half feet of her.

"Colder than Luna out there, and you make me write you a parking ticket?"

Eldridge hadn't bothered to remove his goggles and bandanna, but now that Constable Tola had halted his progress with a flat palm to the chest, he raised his goggles.

"How'd you know it was me?"

Tola's big eyes got bigger. She had black rings around them from where a terrormonger had tried to blowtorch them shut. She looked like a mascara enthusiast with a dusting of buzzcut black sprinkles on her head, a round jaw and loads of grade five heavy armor strapped around her torso and covered with the drab-olive duty fatigues of the constabulary.

In response to the redhead's question, she said, "Know it was you? How many redheads do I know who are dumb enough to make a billion-strong deathday wager *and* meet with Crius Kaleb in person? Plus, you walk duck-footed."

"It's a sign of virility. Thanks for the ticket."

Eldridge took the citation and stepped around her hand.

She said, "By the way, I've got a few hundred K on the Fourth."

He turned around and looked at the baby-faced cop. So young, so ignorant.

"That's touching," he said. "I'll do my best to croak."

Eldridge walked to the front of the casino, where the same clot of rags was asking the black-clad dealer to hit his six of spades. Eldridge waited until a face card busted the ragclot's hand, and then he nodded to get the dealer's attention.

"Rooms?" Eldridge asked.

The dealer shook his head. "Not here. Go down, try Yasim's or Fiachra's. Might be one left you don't have to share."

Eldridge nodded and walked to the door. After taking a moment to secure his coldgear in place around his eyes, ears, and mouth, he opened the first door, let it close and listened. The building's insulation system went *sssst*. He paused and reached into his jacket to retrieve a small plastic bottle. A sticker wrapped around the bottle bore black, handwritten letters: 6/28/03. Eldridge held the bottle up to his nose and twisted it open, breaking a seal around the cap. White mist hissed out, and the redhead snorted it, his eyes rolling back to whites. After a moment, his eyes returned to normal, and he stuffed the spent bottle back in his jacket.

"Five days left," he muttered as he opened the front door and admitted an onrush of frozen air that smashed against the door behind him. He clutched his chest again, shook his head and ventured outside, where the wind was calmer. He ran down the steps and around the building to his motorbike, where he stopped.

A smell had killed his foot motion. Not many odors could generate enough molecular chaos to travel that far through the frozen desert night air, but some could.

Dreens could.

Two dreens were chomping at the nanocord—the invisible rope—that Eldridge had used to secure his bike. Both the dreens were naked, as they usually were, with huge, lima-bean-looking growths pulsing all over their bodies in tune with the triple-fist-sized heart-things that powered endless, hummingbird beats somewhere inside their hollowed-out chests.

Eldridge remained motionless. He knew they had heard him but hadn't chosen to come at him. They were too busy trying to boost his bike. Figured. Dreens liked human flesh, but they liked synth more. They'd eat anything man-made that they could force down their gullets and into the deformed, inhuman grinders where their stomachs had once been. Eldridge noticed they were only chewing at the nanocords. They hadn't made any marks on his fuel tank. Good.

But the smell. Pure endocrine. Dreens perspired everything. Insul. Sero. Dope. Prolac. Eldridge tried to ignore the stench and let his hands creep down the fronts of his thighs to where a pair of long cargo pockets bulged. Black straps along the tops of the pockets secured them shut. He ran his fingertips along the straps, and they fell loose, revealing handles underneath. Slowly, he drew his sidearms, a pair of sawed-off shotguns retrofitted with something that glinted underneath the abbreviated barrels.

He gave the shotguns a shake, and two bayonets *flicked* out from under the barrels, business ends at the ready, shining in the moonlight.

The dreens heard that.

Their heads jerked toward him, revealing distended crania that threatened to burst from the inside. All dreens had swollen brains and baseball-sized hypothalamus glands—huge, muscular hormone factories that blasted their systems with juice and kept their body temps somewhere in the mid-100s. These two dreens looked like a pair of experiments gone wrong. Deranged pituitary function caused dreens' bodies to grow in all kinds of crazy ways. The one on the left looked like a walking muscular map, with thick blue and red veins and vessels throbbing all over his body. His plumbing must have grown too huge and pendulous, because all he had left between his legs was a cauterized stump. The one on the right hunched over double, his head lolling on a neck twice too long for his cramped torso. A kidney had grown large enough to burst from his left-rear trunk and scab over with red gunk that festered and flaked.

This all happened too fast for Eldridge to process. Eldridge saw their actions as flip-book strobe-images—one instant they were chewing on his nanocords, the next they were looking at him, the next they had already sprung at him.

Eldridge blasted the hunched one with a good load of scatter-pellets. Its torso disintegrated in a splat of red and yellow bile and pus. The force of the shot sent the sundered halves of its body flying backward. Eldridge spent a second round to shoot the creature's head out of the air. He knew if he didn't neutralize both the head and the heart, the dreen could keep coming.

The redhead moved on to the second one, but it was too fast; it caught one of his bayonets with his long, bony fingers and swatted it aside. Eldridge resisted the impulse to shoot—he didn't want to waste the round. More strobe-images flashed in Eldridge's eyes: The dreen grabbed the barrel of his scattergun. So Eldridge released it. The dreen dropped it. Eldridge palmed the barrel of his second scattergun and rammed his bayonet up through the dreen's jaw and toward its brainpan. Eldridge took a wide stance and lifted the dreen off the ground. It flailed, so Eldridge held it just high enough to keep its claws away from his face. He ran forward a few steps to get the momentum he needed to drop the dreen in front of him and drive his bayonet through its head and into the ground. He pulled the bayonet out of the ground and fired a round into the creature's heart.

It still wasn't dead, though.

Eldridge sighed, yanked his bayonet out of the earth and thrust it through the dreen's neck. As he pressed down, the sawed-off barrels of his shotgun caught on the warped arc of bone and flesh that had once been the thing's mandible. It detached from its head and left its entire upper jawline exposed.

And for a moment, Eldridge froze. Because he recognized its *teeth.*

Or rather, the absence of. As the dreen squirmed and hissed under his blade, the redhead counted the teeth on its left-rear jaw. It was missing three—two back teeth and one canine.

Time telescoped. Eldridge's memorybanks came alive and delivered an image from years past: The image of a young redhead holding a pair of pliers and reaching into the mouth of an old friend. More to the point, this old friend was the *son* of *another* old friend. An old friend he had spoken with not moments before. An old friend who had ascended to the rank of Odd in the intervening years: Crius Kaleb. Kaleb had somehow fathered a son, and years ago, Eldridge had helped that son—Stewart Kaleb—yank three rotten teeth out of his pain-pounding skull.

"Stew?" Eldridge said.

Talons swiped through the air before his face. The creature's eyes continued to roll in its sockets. Eldridge knew that a dreen brain could generate enough electricity to power every light in Kaleb's casino, much less what was needed to animate a body.

"Aw, man," Eldridge said. Then he spent a round to blow off the top of the dreen's head. Its brains spread in a drippy orange circle on the ground. Some of it misted on his goggles and spattered his bandanna. Eldridge stopped and watched the orange fluid coalesce into splintering crystals across his torso and legs.

"Great. Covered in frozen dreenjuice. *Again.*"

He stopped and breathed. His chest rose and fell. He felt his chest. Then his arms. His breathing slowed to normal. He frowned and looked at the corpse of the dreen on the ground—the dreen that had once been Crius Kaleb's son. Its dead eyes stared at him. He looked up at the casino.

Damn, Cri, he thought, and then he muttered something under his breath. Someone standing nearby would have heard two syllables that meant nothing in the years before Deadblast, but after that cataclysm, they meant a lot.

"Urbit," he said.

Eldridge propped his foot on the dead dreen's shoulder and yanked his bayonet out of the ground. Once the excitement left his body, he was instantly freezing again. He jogged down the alley, dropped to his knees next to his bike and squeezed the small circle of metal that locked the nanocords in place. His bike came loose, and he held it upright with one hand as he slid his scatterguns back into his cargo pants. As soon as he had stowed his nanocord, he pressed a button in-between the handlebars of his bike. Without a sound, the bike leapt out of the alley and took him farther into town.

• • • • •

UNDERGROUND. ALL ROADS EVENTUALLY led underground. Some buildings stayed topside for the dregs. Kaleb stayed topside because the very idea of entering a hole made him kill-crazy. If you asked him about underground, he'd pretend like he hadn't heard you. Or he'd fill you with molten lead.

Eldridge's business, though, was underground. The big cities had all moved underground, leaving behind blackened ruins of their skyscrapers like teeth rotting back into themselves.

Smaller towns like this had less topside. Less people, less dregs, less topside. But there was still plenty of underground. Topside travel, like Eldridge used, was fastest–but not for lightweights.

The motorbike silently surged through the town, which grew darker as he put distance between himself and Kaleb's Casino. He clicked on his headlamp. A cone of fading light stretched into the desert and danced across the peaks of distant mountains–mountains that Eldridge knew from his youth. Age-old streetlights teetered on the side of the road, dark. His headlamp flashed red across the occasional fleeing pair of pupils as dregs stumbled out of his way. The bike kicked up sheets of dust, revealing white-faded concrete underneath. He passed a building that looked like it had melted. A red octagon hung on a metal post with a hole blown through it.

Dedrick sat in the southwestern region of a desert basin that stretched hundreds of miles in every direction. About 10 miles to the northeast stood the ruins of a pair of old roadside attractions: the Ancient Sea and the Old Mine. About five miles due north of those sat Constable Tola's jail, and still farther to the north—about 50 miles total—rose the Oasis Mountains, where Eldridge spent most of his childhood.

Within Dedrick proper, there was only the one still-standing landmark: Kaleb's casino. But that was topside, *above* ground. All roads led underground, and from Kaleb's casino, the paved road twisted through the ruins of the old city like a varicose vein on a child's withered leg, winding through clusters of corroded buildings and twisted fencing.

On his way to the perimeter of Dedrick proper, Eldridge passed a turnoff that he knew led to an old rock quarry that had come in handy in years past, but his destination was underground, and that meant taking the ramp.

At the northeastern boundary of the city, a second turnoff—this one paved black—split off from the main road to the north and began a long, slow descent into the earth down a paved ramp. As Eldridge rode his bike down the ramp, walls of earth rose on either side. The only sound was the hum of his bike between his knees, but soon another sound joined it—the thrum of wind ahead. The road ended in a black, flat surface that seemed to be moving. Vertical walls wiped across his sightline and emitted gusts of warm air.

He rode his bike into the giant revolving door, which rotated around a broad stone pivot set in the earth. On the other side, the walls split open with a deluge of light and a stew of stenches that included fried flesh, miscellaneous rot, and the periodic burst of purified air from giant fans that churned somewhere above.

The subterranean part of Dedrick, the main part, hid under the earth and under a giant, vaulted ceiling. The ceiling was made of red bricks, but an elaborate network of catwalks covered most of the ceiling and the walls like a coating of cobwebs. Standing where he was, just inside the giant revolving door, Eldridge was standing at the midpoint of the city's southern wall. He faced due north, looking down the main drag, Sinister Street, which bisected the city from north to south.

Under-Dedrick covered about five square-miles of space. A jagged skyline rose before the redhead, all of it diced into hectic city blocks whose layout resembled an incomplete jigsaw puzzle—crooked alleyways ran into broad boulevards, while the occasional traffic circle swelled here and there, all of it punctuated by open squares and circles. Thousands of dregs bustled to and fro.

The establishments of the Odds dotted the town: A few blocks to the northeast, a red neon sign rotated over the surrounding hovels. It read *Nix's.* (Daniel Gannix, aka Nix, handled all major oddsmaking surrounding sports and games.) About a mile into town, and to the northwest, Eldridge knew that Yasim's joint was hiding inside a warren of old houses. (Yasim handled odds that pertained to the ever-changing appearance of the world's map.) But if someone were to draw a triangle with Nix's and Yasim's as two of its vertices, the northernmost point on that triangle would be the tower.

Jeb Goldmist's tower.

The mighty Jeb Goldmist ruled from on high in his tower, which rose from the middle of the skyline near the very north of the city at the terminus of Sinister Street. His prodigious work as an Odd had brought him untold wealth, which he used to build his stronghold, a cephalopod of jagged stones and tendrils and towers and parapets that swelled out of the under-earth of Dedrick and stretched high above.

Eldridge's bike rumbled over the cobblestone streets as he rode past a few clapboard huts erected just inside the revolving door. Dregs wearing rags and tatters warmed steel cups of unspeakable stew beside the road, which was slicked with fresh vomit and bits of cabbage and carrots that another dreg was scooping back into her cup.

Some dregs got to work underground. The lucky ones. Others lived topside, running from shelter to shelter, hiding from the elements. The lucky ones topside made it underground to work. Others sold themselves. Others started the quick, endless road to becoming a dreen.

A few dregs grabbed at his bike as he rode past. He kicked one in the chest and sped up to leave them behind, but one of the dregs—a withered woman in a hijab and overalls—threw herself in front of him and forced him to lay out his bike. Or at least that's what Eldridge thought she did. Nope, she wasn't trying to stop him so much as she was trying to escape the oncoming rearward rush of a dreg who had draped blue bedsheets over his head and shoulders, holding them secure with a length of bicycle chain tied around his waist. The rest of his body stood out naked, except for his plumbing, which tented up a swath of that blue bedsheet. A years-in-the-making sunburn had charred his flesh until he looked like a silhouette from a nightmare, his eyes and teeth shining amidst his dark, wraithlike form like a demented constellation on a black night.

At the same instant that Eldridge laid out his bike, the sunburnt dreg lunged for the woman's legs. They both fell to the ground in a haze of dirt kicked up from the ancient road. Meanwhile, after the redhead had fallen off his bike, he skimmed on his ass for a few yards until a flophouse built from corrugated steel and soft tissue brought him to a clattering, wet halt. He jumped up, instantly beset by dregs clad in a dark rainbow of tertiary tones—blacks, browns, and scabby reds. He drew his two shotguns and elbowed his way through the crowd back to his bike. As soon as he reached it, the frantic woman in the hijab fell to his feet and tugged at his pants.

"*Succurro mihi, succurro mihi,*" she pleaded through clenched teeth.

Eldridge barely spoke Latin, so he growled something approximating, "*Hog ergo mason*"—an attempt to say he wouldn't help her—but before he could shake the woman loose from his legs, he found himself looking down the triple spires of a mortarchain rifle. He froze.

"*Succurro mihi, succurro mihi,*" the woman continued to squeal.

"Shut the *fuck* up," Eldridge yelled as the mortarchain rifle's owner lowered his weapon and revealed his plaid face. Plaid, because he had a patch of threadbare, faded plaid flannel stitched over his face from brow to chin and from cheekbone to cheekbone. Plugged into the middle of his forehead was a rectangular protrusion about the size of a pack of cigarettes cut in half. A black electronic lens narrowed its aperture on Eldridge. A lipless mouth rustled behind the flannel.

"I thought I'd find you here among the dregs."

"I'm surprised you can find your dick when you pee, Quillig."

The plaid-faced man, Quillig, twitched.

Eldridge smirked. "Oh, right. I forgot you used to be a dreen."

Used to be a dreen. Such words could only be applied to one man alive, and it was Quillig, whose only exposed flesh was the rubbery-red scar tissue that clung to his exposed cranium. A three-piece suit fashioned from dark red Kevlar fiber covered the rest of his frame, except for his hands and feet, which bore black leather gloves and boots.

Quillig's weapon commanded stillness and silence wherever it was seen. When fired, a mortarchain rifle would disgorge a trio of red-hot, luminescent chains that would burrow underneath the target's skin and merge with their nervous system, leaving the rifle's owner in utter control. Only one group of enforcers used the rifles: the bounty-mercs of the Chain of Tears, whose ranks included Quillig.

"Still a wiseass, aren't you? Is it true what they say about the hole you dug for yourself?"

"You're a B-M, aren't you?" Eldridge said, using the common pejorative for bounty-mercs. "Don't you already know?"

"Oh, sure, I *know,* but when I heard the number, I didn't believe it. It sounded like a spook story gambling addicts tell their kids at night. *Be a good little degenerate, or you'll wind up like Eldridge and owe all the jenta in the world.*"

"You gonna fire that thing or are you gonna wait around till these dregs decide to do something?"

Quillig's head jerked with the jagged laughter that rose from his gorge.

"*Do* something? They're not gonna do shit as long as I've got this." He shook the rifle and sent a ripple of backpedaling through the crowd of dregs, most of whom shrank away from Quillig's presence—all except for the sunburnt dreg, who hovered behind Eldridge's left shoulder, his eyes trained on the cowering woman. Quillig jerked his concealed chin to say *Let's go.* "No more time, Eldridge. Let's get you to the Chain."

Eldridge shuddered at the mere mention of the Chain. Thousands of miles long, the Chain of Tears was the shitcan for every deadbeat and delinquent who defaulted on a wager made with the Odds. The Chain stretched across mile after interminable mile of desert, steppe, and tundra, all of its members joined together by the same glowing red mortarchain links. The rumortrysts held that you could see it from space, but after Deadblast, there was nothing left in orbit to look down and see.

Eldridge didn't move. Quillig once again aimed the rifle at the redhead's chest.

"What's it gonna be, El? Are you gonna come easy or hard?"

"I think I'll take it *hard,*" Eldridge said at the same instant Quillig fired the rifle. A slow-motion replay of the rifle's muzzleflashes would resemble the rapid bloom of a triplet of sunspots. It took less than a microsecond for the rifle to implant its fearsome payload into a victim, but Eldridge hadn't waited for Quillig to pull the trigger. He was already jumping out of the way when the red-hot chains lightning-snaked across the divide and impaled themselves into the sunburnt dreg who had been menacing the sorry woman on the ground.

The implantation of mortarchains into a human always evoked a sudden surge of sympathy among everyone present, no matter how loathsome the victim. Many fell to a knee and covered their heads as the sunburnt dreg shrieked like a newborn and shook like the air around him had suddenly become electrified. Others simply looked away and wept. Eldridge ignored the sight and helped the hijab'ed woman to her feet. She spat on the sunburnt dreg's face. Her saliva sizzled off his convulsing body with a *hiss*. She turned to Eldridge and bowed her head.

"Divinus, divinus," she said. *"Gratias."*

"All right already," he said and sent her on her way. Meanwhile, Quillig stood still, his hands hanging at his side, his shoulders slumped. The rifle dangled from his fingertips. Eldridge dusted himself off and smiled.

"That was your last round, wasn't it?"

Quillig nodded.

"How long do those things take to recharge? About a week, right?"

The bounty-merc spun on him and hissed, "I *will* see you around."

With that, he jerked his rifle and yanked the sunburnt dreg along the road out of Dedrick. Eldridge hopped on his bike and rode up Sinister until the dreg shanties ended, giving way to a serrated skyline made from wood, brick, stone, slate, stucco, and steel. Faces glared down from windows at Eldridge as he rode past. A few did double-takes and watched his silent passage.

• • • • •

DR. ENKI'S OFFICE CLUNG to the side of Jeb Goldmist's tower like a leech to an unsuspecting testicle. It looked like a leech because it was a leech, stark red against the dark grays and blacks of Goldmist's lair.

Eldridge steered his bike around a traffic circle and dodged a dreg hauling a rickshaw loaded with squirming white maggots. He aimed his bike at the doctor's office, but before he could make the turn-off, a black-clad soldier blocked his passage with an open palm and the business end of a rifle. The soldier's steel-weave duty fatigues looked like thousands of long, vertical zippers all bound together. A black helmet covered his head. Shining steel spikes bristled on his shoulders.

He was one of Jeb Goldmist's personal standing army. An oddment.

"Where you going?" asked the oddment as he fingered the trigger of his rifle. Eldridge knew the weapon was loaded with splatter-iron—super-hot rounds that would embed themselves in a target and explode into a million molten bits. In response to the oddment's question, Eldridge jerked his chin at the leech.

"Headed for the doc's. Got an appointment."

The oddment remained motionless for a beat, then nodded.

"I'll watch you in."

"You're a doll," Eldridge said as he rode past. The cobblestones faded into steel as they rose from the street and carried him up a right turn that led to Enki's. Dedrick sank beneath him, giving him a look across the five square miles of under-earth sprawl that had taken hold and spread around the tower.

The secondary road led right into the rear-rictus of the red leech that hosted Dr. Enki. Eldridge stopped his bike, engaged the brake and deactivated the engine. Up close, the leech glimmered with more colors than red. Slippery yellows and oranges danced in the leech's highlights like streams of fruit liquefied by the sun, the colors bleeding and pooling in on themselves like a million tiny Mandelbrot fractals.

Eldridge dismounted his bike and removed his headgear. Instantly the murky smell of digestion hit him. The leech drew its sustenance from the ground, as well as from thousands of benign, penta-ped symbiomites that swarmed across its back and deposited nutrients into it through countless microscopic pores that thirsted for sustenance.

Dr. Enki fed the leech, too. Sometimes.

A featureless white door waited in the rear-rictus, wedged in flesh. Eldridge stood in front of the door, waiting. He cleared his throat. The door subdivided into five wedges that retreated into its flesh with audible slurps. Eldridge shook his head and entered.

Enki, his body nothing but torso, head, and arms, peeked out from behind a wall of frayed books that sat on his main worktable. Enki had hollowed out the inside of the leech and made a permanent habitat with some kind of synth-alloy that the leech allowed to live inside it. Eldridge stopped on the threshold and looked to his right, where a picture hung on the wall. It depicted a flowery structure. It looked like someone had jabbed a giant, glowing head of cauliflower onto the top of a ladder. Enki, who had propped himself up on one hand, let the flesh-flat cross-section of his torso come to rest on the table and pointed at the photograph.

"Hello, Eldridge," Enki said. "Have you figured it out yet?"

Eldridge shook his head. "C'mon doc. Just tell me what it is. Don't torture an old guy on his deathbed."

"Be nice if you could crack it before the fourth," Enki said. "You could go into the abyss without that nasty scar on your head."

The doctor indicated the vertical scar on Eldridge's forehead, then flipped himself off his book-strewn desk and onto the floor. He jerked his head at a cylindrical convexity on the wall to Eldridge's right. The redhead nodded and walked over to it, where it rotated into the wall and exposed a seven-foot vertical cavity that bristled with villi and tentacles and wisps of organic filament.

Dr. Enki pointed at the cavity. "Time to get naked."

Eldridge disrobed and draped his dirt-caked clothes over a chair that looked like it had been carved from a giant pearl. The doctor picked up a sheet of smartpaper and a stylus.

"Now, have you been taking your meds as a prescribed?" Enki asked.

"Yes."

"You're sure you've been taking them *exactly* as I laid out? One inhalation per day up until...well, your demise?"

"Righto, doc."

"Very well. Get into the leech."

The redhead looked at his naked body. Dirt darkened his face and hands, but his pale skin reflected the light from Dr. Enki's computers like a pool of milk. He stepped toward the leech's opening, then stopped.

"Doc, something's off."

"What is it?" Enki asked.

"I fought some dreens. Tonight."

"I saw the juice on you. Glad you made it."

"And I had a run-in with Quillig."

"Oh! I hope he's well."

"Uh, yeah, he's great, doc, but..." Eldridge trailed off.

"What is it?"

He shook his head. "Nothing."

Eldridge stepped into the cavity. The cylindrical door enclosed him inside the leech. Luminescent blue medical grids appeared on the inside of the cylinder. A yawn from Eldridge instantly prompted a rebuke from the doctor, piped into the room through an unseen sound system.

"Stay still, stupid."

Eldridge stood still. The leech closed around him, tickling exposed flesh. Tentacles sucked themselves onto the soft spots behind his earlobes. He stood still. Thousands of brittle, jagged hairs wove their way through his skin. He stood still.

"Almost complete," Enki said.

Eldridge saw a glowing blue outline of himself appear on the medical display before him as the leech closed around him entirely and cut off his vision. He stood still.

Dr. Enki was shaking his leg to wake him.

Eldridge blinked and looked down to see the doctor gaping at him with pricks of red on his cheeks and sweat on his temples.

"Wake up. Are you up?"

Eldridge nodded. "What happened?"

"The tests. The tests. How do you feel?"

"Tired. What happened?"

"Three times. Five. Eleven. Tests. You've been out an hour."

"Doc–"

Enki swung himself across the room and climbed a small ladder up the wall and onto a table. A curved sheet of paper-thin glass floated above the table. A fully detailed scan of Eldridge's every physical system floated within the glass sheet's concavity in a haze of blue mist. A keyboard floated in the mist perpendicular to the display. Every system appeared: skeletal, muscular, circulatory, endocrine. Dr. Enki passed a finger through a button on the keyboard, and his full-system readouts were replaced with detailed readouts on each of his individual organs. As each of his organs flashed by, the word "scanning" appeared next to them, accompanied by a progress bar that filled with blue information. And as each progress bar filled up, it was replaced with a glowing green check-mark.

Eldridge exhaled hard. His fingertips touched the desk and slowly spread apart as his shoulders drooped and pressed his palms down flat. He looked at Dr. Enki, who nodded so hard he shook sweat off his brow.

"It's right. It's right. You're going to live."

Eldridge straightened.

"Well, shit."

• • • • •

THE DRY MAN TRIED to remember what came before, but his memory turned to static when he looked too far back. As he shuffled through the streets of under-Dedrick looking for odds to make and marks to mark, he grinned at the surprise he had planned for everyone.

It'll be a coming-out party, he thought to himself, wondering where he had heard the turn of phrase. He certainly hadn't heard it recently, and he suspected that its origin lay behind that wall of static that rose up from the dusty road that led back into the recesses of his memory. Sometimes he got glimpses of what lay behind the wall of static–buildings that no longer stood, or colors that no longer were–but they always vanished behind the wall, which churned in eternal silence.

He wore a black skullcap. His head looked like someone had spun it on a pottery wheel with their eyes closed before cooking it in a kiln for an hour too long. No moisture existed near him. He didn't have expressions so much as various assemblages of cracked skin.

The cobblestone streets gave way to the smooth cement pathways that encircled the biggest building in town: Jeb Goldmist's tower. The dry man jumped out of the way of a speeding four-wheel moped and hunched on the side of Sinister Street. The dry man craned his neck and looked to the top of the tower, which clawed at the darkness of the ceiling above.

The rumortrysts sang high and mighty about Goldmist. Some said his lifespan predated Deadblast. Others said he had figured out a way to live forever. Still another maintained that over the last score years, Goldmist had enlisted a genetic splicer to accelerate his evolutionary development, not understanding that evolution doesn't have a target, and that forcing his body through a few hundred generations of random mutations without any kind of natural pressures to guide his progress might not be the best idea. This tryst went on to say that Goldmist's sedate lifestyle of thrice-daily prostate kneads coupled with a congenital obsession with exotic liquors and tobaccos did not lend itself to a distinguished evolutionary track. Instead, Goldmist melt-morphed into a rigid, dense collection of fat cells and vain proclivities that no longer had joints in the conventional sense and breathed more carbon dioxide than oxygen.

The dry man chuckled deep in his chest. He knew that wasn't true, because he had actually *seen* Goldmist, as well several thousand members of the Odd's personal standing army, the oddments. And that reminded the dry man: *Watch it.* The dry man knew he had to monitor his peripheral vision when he was within striking distance of the tower, not only because of the oddments, but also because of all the jenta he supposedly owed Goldmist.

Supposedly, he thought. *If only they all knew. But they will.*

The metered *clomp* of marching feet interrupted his thoughts. They marched to and fro, the oddments, all of them clad in black and covered with glistening spikes, their splatter-iron rifles at the ready. The circular drive that hugged the perimeter of the tower swarmed with the mighty Odd's terror-troops, one of whom looked his way, then stopped and looked again.

Did he recognize me? The dry man thought as he shuffled across the path in between waves of black and hustled down an alleyway that slashed diagonally across a city block. Buildings hewn from stucco, stone and steel rose up from the cobblestones, all of them dotted with windows that looked down at him, weeping rusty tears. A pair of men, disparate in stature and appearance, stood at the far corner of the alleyway, both of them with the twitch.

The twitch only an Odd could relieve.

"Gentlemen, gentlemen, gentlemen," the dry man repeated as he skidded up before them, his red stylus appearing in his hand over a sheet of smartpaper that he produced from the endless folds of arid burlap that enshrouded him. The "gentlemen" in question had both dropped from different stunted branches on the tree of life. One of the gentlemen hunched over, his huge brow weighing down his head so that it hung between his shoulders. The other man concealed his appearance with dozens of plastic raincoats, only his lips and nose visible underneath a plastic visor.

The brow spoke first: "Clovis Wine, baby. Whatta you got for us?"

The dry man, Clovis Wine, said: "Oh, it's good, Kloot, it's real good. Snuff-odds extraordinaire. Random implantation, full view, plenty of relatives. No heirs. You want some?"

Kloot graced the dry man with a view of his bulging oculars. "Full view?" he asked. "How?"

"The saps still observe some old holiday," Clovis said, twiddling his stylus with a dry glint in his eyes. "Their first-born's a war hero, and she's coming home. To Dedrick. And she's got a ticking clock in her head that's worth a whole lot of money if you can place the time. Bonus odds if you can pinpoint the number of suicides her death'll spark. And all, *all* of this is good, my friends."

The raincoat'ed dreg spoke: "Who put the clock in her head?"

Clovis shriveled. "Who do you *think?*" He hooked his thumb at the tower. "One of Goldmist's goons. The freak's got some old grudge against her, and he wants her whole family to know. A whole *family*."

Kloot shook his head. "So when's this happening?"

"She's having dinner with her family tomorrow."

"What's her name?"

Clovis frowned. "Katrina something."

Kloot wiped his brow. "And we can watch?"

Clovis nodded. "You'll *have* to—to make sure the odds are good. If you predict when the little bomb in her head goes boom, the jenta's all yours."

The raincoater stepped closer to Clovis and whispered, "But we can...*watch*, right?"

Clovis leaned back and nodded. "Oh, yes. You can watch."

"Odds. Odds, *now*," Kloot said. "What's the max?"

"No max," Clovis said. "Lay as much jenta as you want."

Kloot snapped, "How much we got?"

The raincoater: "You know how much."

"Bet all of it. I bet he pops her at...1:23."

Clovis: "In the ante- or the post-meridiem, good sir?"

"The p.m., the p.m."

The two dregs each produced a stylus and scribbled jenta characters onto Clovis' smartpaper—a *lot* of jenta characters. Clovis gave them both a time and a place where they could sit and watch an unknown woman named Katrina die in front of her whole family. They had both made odds as to exactly *when* Katrina would meet her demise—1:23 p.m.

What Clovis *didn't* tell them was that they had both caught the attention of the illustrious Jeb Goldmist. Clovis didn't tell them that some weeks ago, Goldmist had heard them both utter words that impugned his name. Even high up in his tower, he heard them, and so Clovis was forced to forget that he also knew that the charge implanted inside Katrina's head was powerful enough to take out the entire floor of her building. And that included Kloot and his raincoat'ed friend. Goldmist set these events in motion not only to avenge the slight committed against him, but also to dispose of the raincoater—an up-and-coming Odd who Goldmist predicted might one day challenge him.

But Clovis knew that only *he* was destined to return to the top of Goldmist's tower. Soon.

Plans within plans, thought the dry man to himself as he sped down the block in search of more odds to make, and as he ran, he looked back at that wall of static in his memory and tried to remember where he had heard that phrase, *plans within plans.* Maybe he had read it in a book. That pretentious twit Boris Hagan would know. Maybe he could ask the old fool the next time he saw—

"*Him!*" came the voice, followed by the *tromp-tromp* of jackboots as Goldmist's oddments surrounded him in the street immediately past the alleyway. Clovis might have blushed if his cheeks could withstand the influx of any blood. Kloot and the raincoater laughed at the dry man as the oddments made an instant circle around him. Two stepped forward and braced him, one for each arm. Another, as faceless as the rest, stuck his splatter-iron rifle under Clovis' chin.

The oddment said, "No blood. No viscera. Not even any spotting. And what's the date, Clovis?"

Clovis mumbled something. The head oddment rammed his rifle-butt into his chest. The dry man hit the ground, hacking up lungs-full of dust. The oddment used the business end of his rifle to lift Clovis' chin.

Behind his black faceguard, he repeated, "The *date*, dry man?"

"June twenty-eighth."

"And *when* did you say Kira would first bleed?"

Ah. Klara Kira. A bespangled prepubescent sexpot who shook her ass for the hardlines and screeched the occasional set for the masses. As a major Odd, Goldmist made odds in several areas of wager, including bets made on when this or that pop idol would get her first period. The preternaturally nubile Kira had elevated this particular oddsmaking to regional obsession after her *Fuck My BabyPussy* Tour had cut a swath across the eastern deserts.

Again the oddment pressed his case: "*When* did you say she would bleed, Wine?"

"Midsummer's eve!"

The head oddment laughed, and they all joined in. "Midsummer's eve, he says! What day is *that*, Clovis?"

Clovis peered behind the wall of static. "June twenty-one. The day of the summer solstice."

The oddments looked at each other. A few shrugged, but the head oddment pressed on: "June twenty-one. You're seven days delinquent.

That's a lot of jenta you owe Goldmist. A *lot.* Payable immediately. But of course you don't got it on you."

"No, I don't have it, but gimme a few days. *Four* days, to be exact."

"What's gonna happen in four days, Clovis? You gonna kick Jeb out of his tower? Make yourself all high and mighty?"

Clovis grinned up at the head oddment. *This one deserves a reward. Never breaks character.* Finally, the dry man raised a wrinkled finger at a poster that hung from a nearby wall, its corners still damp with glue. The poster depicted four squares that alternated between black and white. Bold text shouted underneath the squares:

XIANG TOURNAMENT
QUADRENNIAL MATCH
STALEDATE JULY 4
ALL COMERS
BIG CASH PURSE
MAKE YOUR ODDS AT NIX'S!

Again, laughter boomed from behind all their masks. The head oddment said, "*You?* In a *Xiang* tourney?" Unwittingly, he pronounced the ancient word properly: *shee-ang.*

Clovis struggled to his feet. "I can win the money. Just give me till the staledate. I've got legerdemain you've never seen in the Zone of 64. Goldmist'll be rolling in jenta."

The head oddment spoke to his men: "What do you think? Give the dry man till the staledate? And *then* let Goldmist rip the skin off his bones? Or send him to the Chain?"

The rest of the oddments said yes, chuckling. The head oddment jabbed his rifle in Clovis' chest.

"You're better off dead, Wine. And if you want in the tournament, you better get over to Nix's. The roster's filling up."

Clovis pressed his palms together and bowed, backing away. "*Gratias,* thank you, thank you, gentle oddment–*you scum-sucker!*" With that, he reached under his arm and hurled a ball of dirt at the footsoldier. It exploded in a cloud of dust against his faceguard. He didn't even flinch, instead joining with his comrades to laugh at the dry man as he sprinted around a corner, intent on getting his name into the Xiang tournament–only Clovis had yet *another* surprise planned for everyone.

The dry man had already snuck a look at the roster for the tournament, and one very interesting name had popped up on it. An early and unexpected entrant from afar, and the moment Clovis saw the name, he knew that the Xiang tourney of '03 would be one for the rumortrysts. He just hadn't anticipated having to enter the tournament himself, and that meant talking with a fellow Odd, Daniel Gannix, aka Nix, oddsmaker for all games and bookkeeper for the past six Xiang tourneys. The spinning neon sign for Nix's rose above the skyline ahead of Clovis, but he adjusted his course *away* from it and made his way toward the blackened edge of the city. The dry man had already dropped by Nix's that morning, and he knew Nix wasn't there, and if Nix wasn't at Nix's, there was only one other place he'd be: Fiachra's.

• • • • •

THE REDHEAD'S BIKE SILENTLY zoomed around corner after corner. Eldridge kept his eyes on the road, not wanting to run someone over while he thought. The bike helped him think, and the underground was warm.

Before today, Enki had worked it all out. He couldn't guarantee that Eldridge would die on the Fourth, but he had given him plenty of meds with precise instructions.

"Administer these inhalants to yourself according to my precise directions, and you just might die on the Fourth. I made the instructions easy, Eldridge, because I know you're an idiot."

That had been more than a year ago, right after got his first diagnosis: He had cancer of everything. Well, not *every*thing, but Dr. Enki didn't want to worry his pretty little head with the details. It was cancer, and it was attacking a particularly important organ. Months ago, Dr. Enki had shown him a full-body scan produced by the same symbiotic leech, and months ago, Eldridge had smiled at the sight of the amorphous black creature that hovered inside his midsection and extended its inky fingers into his guts.

That's when he got the idea to place the deathday wager.

Seemed like a good idea at the time.

By definition, the odds against a deathday wager were astronomical. It was the closest thing to a lottery that still existed. The brains of lotto addicts had flash-evolved the ability to predict six randomly chosen numbers with astonishing accuracy, and in response, lotto-Odd Walter Torsten started asking players to predict the shape of a 4D hyperobject generated by a teraflop-crunching supercomputer so powerful that every time it ran a routine, lights would dim for a thousand miles in every direction.

What lights were left, that is.

But back to Eldridge and his pesky cancer: Earlier that night, when he fought the dreens, he knew something was off. The doctor's scan confirmed it.

"Too easy," Eldridge muttered to himself.

Now it was time for plan B. Months ago, the vague notion that he might not die on his deathday crossed his mind, but like any good idiot, he ignored it, though not before formulating a backup plan that was even stupider than making a deathday wager.

Under-Dedrick's roads drew the redhead's bike around to the western edge of the underground. The pigment of the bricks seeped away until the mortar merged into crusty black walls. Eldridge pulled his bike up to the far wall, next to a door. Fiachra's.

Fiachra's smoke bar hid behind a black door that sank into the western wall of under-Dedrick and right underneath one of the lowest hanging entryways into the network of catwalks that covered the subterranean city's walls and ceiling.

From a distance, the catwalks looked like cobwebs—they infested the walls and ceiling in an irregular pattern—but up close, they reminded Eldridge of an old photo he had seen of an ancient, pre-Deadblast building that was equipped with fire-escapes, except in this case, these fire-escapes covered most of the walls and ceiling of under-Dedrick.

Very few dregs ventured into the catwalks and lived, as they were the home of the psychoskags—fearsome human-machine hybrids. (Eldridge was one of the few dregs who had made it in and out of catwalk city alive. But more on that later.)

The psychoskags and their catwalks would have covered the *entire* ceiling, but Goldmist's tower lanced into the ceiling and caused a permanent ripple in the dense network of steel walkways. A circle of bare, vaulted brick ceiling surrounded the top of the powerful Odd's fortress.

Eldridge secured his bike in place with the nanocord. He had done someone a favor on his last visit to Dedrick. Time to cash in that chip.

He pushed open the door to Fiachra's, which emitted the smoke and the stench of a thousand different types of tobacco, weed, crystal, and a dozen other combustibles. Eldridge inhaled a deep breath of the smoke. Some of it sparked old buzz receptors deep inside him, while other parts of it clawed at his lungs like someone had stuffed petrified dumpster-crust into a pipe to smoke, which was probably the case.

A bar emerged from the smoke like the prow of a ship. A U of finished wood looped in and out of the smoke, its surface long since cracked, faded, and chipped. Eldridge peered into banks of smoke that rolled along the bar, searching for the man who owed him a favor. His eyes passed over a few tattooed roughhousers that clung to their barstools with thick thighs and one anadyne trixie with arms like the legs of a flamingo, a swatch of hot-rainbow fabric caught around her bones. As Eldridge passed, her fingernails hooked in the crook of his elbow like a pitchfork.

"Wanna finger me?" she said, waggling her uvula at him.

Eldridge shook off her arm. She went back to sucking on a hookah with a jagged mouth. He plunged into more smoke. Hazes of color glowed through the murk. Voices made their way through, too, distant and muffled.

But one dry rasp caught his ear, as distinct as a strange cough in a dark room:

"I'm a bishop, not a rook."

Eldridge made a right turn and wove around a waitress who was carrying baskets full of green and black pipe-weed. Another haze of color emerged and quickly coalesced into a neon sign that read SUDDEN DEATH AND BLOODSHED in slashing red letters. The sign hung over a half-circle table that protruded from a black brick wall. Two men sat on either side of it—one of them an Odd, one not.

The Odd was Daniel Gannix, but everyone who made odds with him called him Nix, and if you liked sports, Nix was your Odd. He pinched a pair of hand-rolled cigarillos between his orange fingertips. When he moved, his body sparked and crackled with the static electricity from dozens of multicolored armbands, wristbands, and chestbands, each of which shouted the name of a different team across hundreds of different sports. The Triumph. The Contagion. The Fuckheads.

The one who wasn't an Odd wore a black skullcap and looked like the corpse of someone who had been lost in the desert for a year. Every twitch and shudder of his spastic body kicked up a mini-duststorm.

"Clovis Wine," Eldridge said, looking at the dry man. "You owe me a favor."

The dry man clutched a glass of water in his hands. He gulped it down with both hands, and then his mouth forced apart the islands and archipelagos of bone-dead flesh that composed his cheeks. A smile.

"Eldridge," Clovis said. His teeth looked like filthy yellow fingernails. "Thought you'd be dead already."

"Not yet," Eldridge said.

Clovis made a sound like someone pumping a bellows. Laughter.

"El," he said. "Lemme introduce you—"

The Odd spoke, his words coming in rapid-fire bursts: "Oh, I know Mr. Eldridge. I used to be Mr. Eldridge's favorite oddsbroker for gameplay. But he abandoned me for greener pastures." Nix stuck the cigarillos into nostrils that were as orange as his fingers and snorted a twin drag. He left the cigarillos in his nostrils. "I heard you got yourself in quite a hole, El. How much are you in for?"

"Hey, how about you fuck off, Nix?"

Nix shook his head and laughed. "OK, all right."

Eldridge turned his attention to Clovis and said, "Clovis, you owe me."

The dry man deflated like an ancient accordion, his clothes exhaling dust as he sank in his seat.

"Elly, I can't. I can't help you now. Nix and I, we're, well–"

"It's Xiang, right?" Eldridge asked.

Nix smiled with blue lips. "Yeah, you know it is. And every badass from here to 'here there be monsters' wants in. I just signed up Mr. Wine here."

"Right," Eldridge said. "I'll take that slot, thanks."

Nix chuckled so suddenly that he spat the cigarillos into his palm, both of them trailing shiny filaments of mucus. He fumbled them back into his nostrils and said, "Pardons begged? *Revolvo?*"

"Nix, you're going to take Clovis out of the Xiang match and replace him with me. And, Clovis, you're going to fuck off."

Clovis opened and shut his mouth. He caught a passing waitress and ordered three more waters. Nix ground his cigarillos into the tabletop and ordered something "really fucking strong." Nix then turned his attention to Eldridge and said, "Mr. Wine is already in the pipeline. There's no taking him back now. You'll have to wait for the next Xiang match–"

"That's four years distant, and I don't have four years," Eldridge said. "I don't even have a week. I have 'til the staledate to win a shit-ton of money."

Nix's lips twisted into a smile. "A shit-ton."

"Right."

"To pay yourself out of that big hole you're in."

"C'mon, man–just pull Clovis out and put me in."

Nix shook his head. "Can't pull out now. Trixie's already pregnant."

"And I'm a wire hanger. He's coming out."

Clovis broke in: "Eldridge, you can't *do* this to me."

"You owe me, Clovis. Remember the last time you got yourself into a Xiang tourney?"

Clovis held his head in his hands. Meanwhile, Nix's eyes got wide.

"What're you two talking about?" Nix asked.

Eldridge: "You remember the Xiang match of ninety-nine?"

"What about it?" the Odd asked.

"It was fraudy, and on your tally. Surprise!"

Hands sprang from the haze. Nix and Clovis jumped. The hands set down three glasses of water and Nix's "really fucking strong" pipe-weed, which looked like ground volcanic glass. Clovis immediately started draining the glasses, while the Odd packed the shiny black crystals into his hookah and took a snort through his crusty orange nostrils. He exhaled a snaking plume of smoke that linked his mouth with the endless cloud that filled the room. Black fluid stained the whites of his eyes. He leaned against the wall and puffed.

"Eldridge, that isn't true."

Clovis wheezed—the closest he could get to whimper. "Oh, it's true."

"So what *happened?* I know I signed you up, Clove."

Eldridge said, "You signed him up, all right. As a rook. He knew he couldn't bring the thunder, so I stepped in and rode out the match."

Nix sneered. "You're lucky white resigned so fast."

Eldridge shook his head. "Nope. Not so lucky. Longer matches mean more money. Otherwise I might not be in the legendary hole I'm in now."

Nix covered his ears. "I can't be hearing this. I have to report it to Goldmist."

"No, you don't, buddy," Eldridge said.

"No, you don't," Clovis said, clasping his hands together. "*Please.*"

But Nix was already standing. "I have to tell Goldmist personally."

Side note: Although some forms of radio transmissions were still used after Deadblast, cellular technology had long since been outlawed for reasons that will be made clear later.

Both Eldridge and Clovis grabbed Nix by his sleeves and pulled him back into his chair.

"Ten thousand," Nix said. "Ten *thousand.* Do you know what that number means? I'll tell you. It's the approximate number of blowjobs I receive per year as a product of the money I make as an Odd. But if Goldmist finds out I ran a Xiang match off the rails, then that's how many years he'll keep my brain animated in an acid bath. *Which will suck.* Maybe I can convince him it was an accident—"

Clovis said, "Aw, El-El—be reasonable. I owe Goldmist forever and a day's worth of interest on a bet that went tits-up in the final few."

Eldridge smirked. "Klara Kira?"

Clovis kicked up a dust-storm by pounding his fist on their table. "I was *sure* she'd make it by the solstice!"

Eldridge frowned at the unfamiliar word, then said, "Sorry, Clove, but I need more money, and I need it worse than you."

Clovis shifted gears. His spine crumpled around his clasped hands as he assumed a pose of supplication. His head craned up like a dreg begging for scraps from a sultan.

"But El—if you're going to screw me, at least give me the same gentlemanly screwing you did in ninety-nine. I know we didn't go halvsies, El, but you at least dropped a quarter of your coin in my cup. Can't we work out something like that this time?"

"No can do, Clove. Even if I make it to the staledate with a bunch of notches in my belt, I'll need every cent."

Clovis shot him a hard, cold look and crumpled further into himself. "But Elly-Eldridge, I owe someone *besides* Goldmist. I owe Marko Marinus."

Marko Marinus. Not an Odd, and one of the few power-brokers left who *wasn't* an Odd. Not as powerful as Goldmist, but much more well-liked. Well-respected. Marinus led the Narsyans, an elite order that hid up in the Oasis Mountains north of town. As the Narsyan chieftain, Marinus acted as the moral and intellectual driving force of a fellowship of physically perfect maniacs who burned upward of 20,000 calories a day.

But he wasn't an Odd, and he never made odds.

"Bullshit," Eldridge and Nix said simultaneously in response to Clovis's claim that he owed Marinus money.

"No, no—it's true," Clovis said.

Eldridge shook his head. "Marinus? Playing? *With you?* Clovis, come on. Don't embarrass yourself. If you're in a hole, you're in a hole. Face it like any of us."

"But, but this is *Marko Marinus*, El. You have any idea what they can do to me? Make me one of their fuck blankets or send me up to the mountain's peak or worse."

"All right, all right," Eldridge said. "Him and me haven't talked in years, but maybe I can put in a good word. He and I used to be in the order together."

The order. The Narsyans. Eldridge caught something in Clovis's dry eyes that looked like a ray of sunlight gleaming for an instant on a sprinkling of quartz in the earth. Was it a twinkle? Eldridge didn't have time to process it because Nix was yammering in his ear again.

"Why do you even need all that cash, Eldridge? You've got a deathwish anyway. Just go quietly."

Eldridge scratched his chin. "Hm. I want to die so I can win some money. That wouldn't make any sense unless I still had some kin knocking around."

Nix cocked his head. "I didn't know you had family."

"Right. Now you do. So if I can pull this off, they can inherit *nothing* from me instead of a death-warrant's worth of red ink. So, last chance: You sure you don't want to make this happen?"

Nix made a face. "What? Am I *sure?* Yeah, I'm sure I don't want to put my tick next to *another* fraudy player in a Xiang match."

Eldridge's shoulders jerked. "How about now?"

Nix's eyebrows rose over his black eyes. "I beg your pardon?"

"Ribs."

The Odd reset the hookah in the wall and patted himself down. When he brought his hands away, they were red. Chair legs skidded on the cement floor as Nix's feet kicked out and slammed his back into the wall.

"What–?"

Clovis stood and stole looks around the place, but no one was near their island in the smoke.

"Eldridge, man, what are you doing?" he asked.

The redhead set a handle on the table. Floating in air on the same axis as the handle was a line of red. Blood beaded at the end of the line and dripped on the table. A microblade.

"I pricked an artery. Not bad, but you'll die."

Nix sat back down and leaned forward fast–too fast, and he bent around his wound with a grunt. "Eldridge, you fuckin' gone bugs? Stab an Odd? You're dead."

"I'm dead anyway, I don't get big coin," Eldridge said. "You go to Tola, I'll finish you. You even mention Goldmist's name, I'll finish you."

"Oh, man," Nix said as his lap turned red. "Eldridge, what do you want?"

"Time. Yours."

• • • • •

FIFTEEN MINUTES LATER, ELDRIDGE burst into Dr. Enki's office bearing a bleeding Nix in his arms. Clovis shuffled in close behind, trailing a cloud of dust. When Dr. Enki saw them enter, he jumped onto his worktable and swept it clean with the flat bottom of his torso like a pre-Deadblast acrobat. Eldridge set Nix on the table while Clovis cowered underneath the mystery photograph and the doctor affixed a pair of laser-loupes into his eye sockets and performed a scan on the quickly bleeding Odd.

Enki said, "I take it you need something from this Odd?" He tapped on a small black square printed on Nix's left temple. The mark ID'ed him as an Odd, and although it only looked like a black box, a few hundred levels of magnification would reveal an info-design as dense and intricate as a nanoprocessor.

In response to Enki's question, Eldridge nodded. "He'll bleed out in fifteen, right?"

"Twelve," Enki said, turning his attention to the Odd. "Anything to say for yourself?"

Nix spoke through a wince: "What do you want, El?"

"I want in the Xiang tourney."

"All right already. I'll redo the book, but if Goldmist gloms on, I'm through."

Clovis lurched around the table and stopped, dislodging a sheet of dust that pattered across Nix's chest.

"Doc, can't you do something? I don't want Goldmist or Marinus to find out I was in on any of this."

Enki and Eldridge shared a significant glance.

"The procedure?" Eldridge asked.

Enki scratched his chin, a small grin rising from the corner of his mouth. "I *have* been eager to test it on a willing primate."

Slicked in sweat, Nix said, "Procedure? What's it do?"

The doctor smirked and vaulted off the table over to a stack of books. He pulled one out and flipped through a few dozen pages.

"Mr. Gannix, I can wipe your memory so you won't remember ever adding Mr. Wine to your Xiang roster."

Eldridge said, "That way, if Goldmist ever comes asking, you won't have to lie."

Enki scrambled back onto the table.

"Won't be *able* to, that is," he said. "How does that sound to you, Mr. Gannix?"

Nix clenched his fists. *"Would you two quit fucking around and stop this bleeding?!"*

Enki rolled his eyes. "Yes, yes, quite right." In a blurry series of moves that took less than five seconds, the doctor reached under his worktable, opened a drawer and procured a red sphere the size of a ball bearing. Enki tucked his pinched fingers under his chin and pointed his elbow at Nix's midsection, which was mummified with dozens of shiny, vinyl merch-strips that blinked with green and red numbers—all scores—that were slowly being submerged by the pool of blood pouring from Nix's insides.

But Eldridge stayed the doctor's hand.

"Get me in first, Nix."

"Eldridge, you are a stone-cold fucker."

"Yeah, I'm touched. Get me in."

Nix's red hand plunged into a pocket and emerged with a crumpled, grimy note pad. Its wire spiral binding had come loose and twisted up like an ancient TV antennae, but despite its haggard appearance, the old notepad swarmed with smart characters that spilled from a glowing red stylus that Nix slid out of his forehead. He swipe-erased a few lines from the pad, then scribbled a few new characters in their place.

"You got a hardline hookup in this place?" Nix asked.

"Of course," Enki said.

"All right," he said. "You're in. Now *do it.*"

Enki assumed the same pose he had before: Fingers tucked under his chin, elbow trained on Nix's stomach—a pose familiar to any rambunctious kid who has spun a copper coin at someone's head. Enki snapped his fingers and flicked the tiny red sphere into Nix's midsection, which lit up with an internal glow for a brief moment before returning to normal. The instant he was healed, Nix sat up and continued to scribble away on his note pad.

"What're you doing?" Clovis asked.

"Covering my tracks," Nix said. "*You* try to reverse-hack a hardline-firewall you wrote while drunk." He blinked hard, then swiped a few carriage returns into his code and closed out the wiggly terminal window he had been squinting into. That done, he turned his wrath on the redhead and the doctor: "This procedure had better fucking work."

"No need to fear," Enki said. "It's quite effective."

"Dangerous?"

With glinting eyes, Enki winked. "Oh, yes."

• • • • •

OR MAYBE THE LINE *was "wheels within wheels."*

But the wall of static blocked the dry man's efforts to uncover the source of the adage. Instead, Clovis turned his attention to the present, where the redhead was helping Nix the Odd out the front door of Dr. Enki's office. Moments earlier, Enki had finished his procedure on Nix and given him a quick influx of O-negative. That done, Nix poured himself off the table, slumped over to a hardlined computer station and called over an oddment to escort Eldridge up to Jeb Goldmist's tower, where he would receive his Xiang assignment. Eldridge wrapped Nix's arm around his shoulder. As Eldridge and Nix staggered out of Dr. Enki's office together, Clovis peered at the sight of the redhead's knees bowing under the weight of someone else. Outside the doctor's office, Eldridge deposited Nix on his feet.

Clovis sidled up next to them. "Elly-El. Just listen for a minute."

"I gotta get up to Goldmist's to get my assignment, Clove. What is it?"

"*Gentle. Men.* You and I are gentle-*men.* And gentlemen tell each other the truth about their situations. You're in deep-blue trouble, I know that, and I want to help you as much as you want to help me."

Eldridge gave him a look. "Since when do *I* want to help *you?*"

Clovis backpedaled: "*Maybe* you want to help me? I'm in deep to two of the most powerful men in Dedrick. Surely you can relate to that kind of predicament?"

As Nix teetered on his feet, Eldridge snorted. "Oh, I *wish* I was in hock to Jeb Goldmist, Clove. That'd be incredible if I owed all that jenta to *him* and not..."

He trailed off. Clovis stepped closer.

"Who? Who is it you owe, Elly?"

"Nobody," said the redhead as he walked in front of Nix. He patted the Odd's cheek. "Anybody in there?"

A line of blood trickled out from Nix's hair and ran into his ear. His eyelids drooped, and his head lolled forward. Eldridge caught his chin.

"Wake up, Nix! You've got gigs of hard-earned jenta to swindle!"

Clovis looked at the Odd. "What did Enki *do* to him?"

"Beats me. Up and at 'em, Nix!"

Clovis tugged on the redhead's sleeve and said, "I owe Goldmist and Marinus *big,* El. What am I gonna do?"

Eldridge frowned.

"Did Marko Marinus *really* make odds with you?"

"Elly-El—did he *ever.* Big time. You gotta help me. What am I gonna *do?*"

"Me, I'd get gone, Clove."

Particles of dry dirt crumbled from Clovis' crowsfeet as his eyelids squinched together—the closest he'd ever come to tears—and he maintained the pose. Eldridge focused on Nix, but after a moment of Clovis' arid blubbering, he sighed, turned to the dry man and patted his shoulder.

"Listen. Marko and I go way back. I wasn't planning on going to see him, but I'll make a trip up there and see if he'll waive the jenta you owe him. Now, about Goldmist—I can't make any promises. I need big-time coin. But if I can spare any, I'll pay off your debt, too. OK?"

"You'd do that, El? You'd do that for me? I'd call it a favor to me if you did."

"It's not a favor. It's not even a promise. It'll just be *words.*" Eldridge underlined the word "words" with his voice. Clovis knew he was indirectly invoking an old Narsyan saying about what kind of weight words pulled.

"Multiply 'em by zero," went the adage, but the arrival of an oddment interrupted the moment.

The oddment hurtled out of the innards of Dedrick on a hoverbike that offset its advanced design with a pukey internal-combustion engine that belched a black smoke that congealed into sludge upon contact with the air and rained down toxic night on everyone in its wake. The oddment wrestled the bike down onto the ramp and brought its engine to a wailing idle.

"Who's Eldridge?"

The redhead raised his hand, walked down and climbed on the hoverbike, which lurched into the air and carried him directly up toward Goldmist's tower. Clovis stood beside a swaying Nix, who pointed at the ascending redhead.

"Where's Clovis going?"

"What did you say?"

Nix squinted. "That's Clovis Wine. Where's...where's he going?"

The dry man got that gleam-of-quartz look in his eyes again.

"How very interesting."

• • • • •

ON HIS WAY UP to Goldmist's, Eldridge's knees wobbled. Now that he didn't have a death sentence, he was back to being afraid of the Odds like everyone else.

No one had actually laid oculars on Goldmist since Deadblast, which was what drove most everyone under-earth and turned the world's thermometers into pogosticks that leapt from one extreme to the other depending on the presence of the sun in the sky. That was also when the Odds really started to gain influence everywhere, not just in Dedrick. Eldridge remembered the words of his wise old friend (and pre-Deadblast expert) Boris Hagan:

"Mighty Odds like Walter Torsten, Lilya Hanna, the Creep—after Deadblast, they all scaled the smattering of Ararats that marked the remnants of the old places."

Eldridge didn't know what the hell a "smattering of Ararats" was, but he knew all about big-name Odds like Torsten, Hanna, and the Creep, and he knew that of the Odds of Dedrick, only Jeb Goldmist had earned the right to sparkle in the same constellation as them. Each of the remaining remnants was governed by a neverending succession of overlords, strongmen, potentates, and would-be dictators—and since Deadblast, all of them were Odds.

But none of that mattered as the oddment pulled his hoverbike next to a blind chamber, which was where the redhead would receive his Xiang assignment. The chamber itself teetered at the end of a filament of strongwire that jutted out from the side of Goldmist's tower, which bristled with hundreds of such rooms, all of them seemingly floating on air and undulating on the surges of heat like metallic, rusted palm fronds. The instant Eldridge entered the chamber, which housed roughly 100 square meters of floorspace, his vision and hearing went null. Not black, just *null.* A pair of hands took his shoulders and guided him against one of the walls. Eldridge remembered this dance from his last experience in a Xiang match—each of the players entered the blind chamber to line up on a life-sized chessboard in their assigned positions.

The room was packed with import. Besides the workers (who were outfitted with spinal-tap gizmos that canceled out the chamber's effects), Eldridge knew that all of his fellow Xiang players were in the room, and that included the two Kings. Eldridge remembered most of the rules of Xiang, but he relaxed and waited for the blind chamber to dust off his memorybanks.

Which it did. Digital characters stared to scroll across his line of sight as he formally received his piece assignment:

```
ELDRIDGE: ROOK | BLACK | KINGSIDE
```

"Great," Eldridge said, in spite of himself. His complaint drew an instant rebuke from the match-runners he knew were milling around the room. Even though he couldn't hear it, one of them must have pulled up to a keyboard somewhere to send him a message. In the cybervoid that floated before his eyes, a small yellow box suddenly popped open—a quicktalk:

Shut up and pay attention.

Eldridge shut up. The rules of Xiang started to scroll by.

XIANG TOURNAMENT 03

Xiang echoes the rules and traditions of ancient chess in the form of avatar-warriors who carry out the orders of the competing kings, who play out the match via correspondence.

The normal rules of chess apply, but whenever a piece is captured, the avatar-warriors play out the battle within a 100-mile or 160-kilometer radius of Dedrick.

Each avatar-warrior in the tournament must capture and defend their squares based on rules, which fall into three categories: Notice, Weapons and Vehicles:

Notice determines how much time an avatar-warrior must give before they attack. The stronger the piece, the less time they must give before their attack.

Weapons determines what style of weaponry can be used by a certain piece. Stronger pieces generally have access to more powerful weaponry, though there are some exceptions.

Vehicles determines what kind of vehicles, if any, can be used by a certain avatar-warrior.

Avatar-warriors fight to the death. The remaining Avatar-warrior wins the square.

To the death. Death, or the possibility thereof, always increased winnings in wagers, whether they were deathday wagers or Xiang tournaments. You won more money by playing as a weaker piece, but the odds of making it to the end of a tournament as a pawn were astronomical. That's why Eldridge was disappointed to have been made a rook. Major pieces were easier to play, but won far less money. Based on his own rough estimates, he'd have to survive until the tournament's staledate to win the money he needed, and as long as that was the case, he might as well have been a pawn.

The rules continued to scroll by:

PAWN

Notice: Must give 36 hours notice before attacking, unless they're capturing en passant, in which case they need only give 30 minutes notice.

Weapons: Hand-to-hand weapons: knives, baseball bats, etc.

Vehicles: none.

Tactical atomics are only available to a pawn that has reached the eighth rank and been promoted to Queen. Underpromoted pieces receive no extra advantage.

In the storied history of Xiang, only one man had ever made it to the eighth rank and achieved promotion: The great Qi Li. And every good Xiang player knew what promotion meant. More power in the game. And more money. A lot more.

Some Xiang players who made it to the end of particularly competitive matches could actually retire. Some took their winnings and became Odds. And there were always some who couldn't get enough and just had to enter again. And again.

Like Eldridge.

Qi Li couldn't stop playing either, and his obsession with Xiang (and all its worldwide variants) had made him a legend, although no one had ever found out why he kept playing—and always as a pawn. The rumortrysts said he did it to keep his sword sharp, but then again, they also said he could chop a lightning bolt in half. Eldridge had his own pet tryst to explain Li's repeated appearances.

"He's a degenerate, like me," Eldridge had told his friend Marko Marinus so many years ago. Before they stopped being friends.

KNIGHT

Notice: 12 hours.

Weapons: Hand-to-hand, guns, low-grade ballistics (RPGs, bazookas).

Vehicles: Ground (single-axle), air.

NOTE: Knights are the only players allowed to use aerial support of any kind.

Not every Xiang knight exploited the advantage of flight because players could only call on whatever resources they had—that was partially the point of the game—and if a player didn't have the jenta or the wherewithal to build a flight apparatus that could stand up to a firefight, then they didn't.

BISHOP

Notice: Does not have to give notice before attacking **AND MAY ATTACK DURING OTHER MOVES.**

Weapons: Hand-to-hand, guns, ballistics, poison.

NOTE: Bishops are the only players allowed to use poison of any kind.

Vehicles: Ground (single-axle).

Eldridge always thought of bishops as the deadliest players in the game. They didn't have to give notice of any kind, and a bishop attack could come at virtually *any* time during a match—even if a player had already received notice of another move. The bishop position usually attracted the shiftiest of competitors—two-faced dregs who happily watched from afar while their enemies perished.

ROOK

Notice: 30 minutes.

Weapons: Ballistics, explosives of any kind. No firearms.

Vehicle: Ground (any number of axles).

Having played as a rook before, Eldridge was familiar with the gameplay involved. The ability to use any kind of vehicle imaginable was enticing, but the restriction on using firearms made the piece deceptively difficult to play.

KING

Notice: 36 hours.

Weapons: Hand-to-hand.

Vehicle: None.

NOTE: The king can enlist any other player on their side to carry out his move if he or she so chooses.

A note on castling: The king may enlist either of the rooks to protect him, but if they do, the king gives up their right to enlist other players to fight on their behalf.

Never, never, never, never, never. That's when Eldridge would play a Xiang king. Even though the position called to mind the image of quiet afternoon playing a game over a board, Xiang kings had to play a madcap game of chess in their heads, all while running for their lives.

QUEEN

Notice: 5 seconds.

Weapons: Any.

Vehicle: Any, except air.

The deranged pantheon of maniacs who had played as Xiang queens over the years made the redhead's mouth dry up. The position simultaneously attracted vengeful types with old odds to settle, as well as flying-on-fumes headcases who were looking for a spectacular way to die.

A note on the enforcement of rules.

Ka-chung! The sound echoed in Eldridge's head as a sharp pain lanced into the side of his neck, right in the vicinity of a lymph node. He yelled something that approximated *Fucking fuck,* but the blind chamber silenced his words, which ricocheted around his head.

The sharp pain, he knew, was the insertion of a tiny bomb into his neck. The device had a lot of names, including "nacclemite" and the more common "polycharge," and its purpose was well known: It enforced the rules of Xiang. The device included a microscopic sensor that monitored the competitor's brainwaves and heartrate. If a competitor decided to ignore the rules, the device was equipped to detect the treachery and would, in response, detonate a bomb powerful enough to decapitate the victim. The rumortrysts told tales of Xiang matches of old in which scofflaw players would raise a gun in an attempt to kill an unsuspecting competitor, and their polycharge would blow off half their neck and leave them staggering around with their head dangling on a few strings of tendons and nerve tissue before their bodies collapsed. In the early days of Xiang–before polycharge technology had been perfected–the occasional competitor would meet an untimely demise when they considered cheating on a loved one or otherwise pondered a dishonest action unrelated to the Xiang tournament. And their heads would explode.

Over time, the tech had been perfected to avoid any false positives.

Most of the time.

He felt rough hands around his waist, and he knew that one of Goldmist's lackeys was clipping a device to his belt about the size of a small book. The device was called a jad, and it worked in tandem with the polycharge technology.

More rules scrolled through the void before his eyes:

Moves are divided into two types: **OFFENSE** and **DEFENSE**. An avatar-warrior on **OFFENSE** is attacking the square, while the avatar-warrior on **DEFENSE** is defending it.

Avatar-warriors on **OFFENSE** will receive notice of their move via jad printout. Once they receive notice of a move, they have **24 hours** to in turn deliver notice of their attack to the **DEFENDING** avatar-warrior, also via jad transmission.

NOTE: Once an attack is initiated, the attacker has TWO HOURS to win the square, otherwise it will be awarded to the defending piece.

Avatar-warriors on **DEFENSE** will only receive notices of **impending** attacks.

The jad-polycharge combo was what made Xiang work. The nature of the game demanded that the game-runners deliver notice of moves to players within a 100-mile radius of Dedrick, but they also had to be able to tell the players on offense where their targets were.

Pursuant to the Cellphone Edict of Deadblast, transmissions made over certain high-frequency bands were outlawed, but lower-frequency bands and their associated gadgets—telegraphs, some radios—were still usable. The game-runners would transmit moves to players in the field, and their polycharges would essentially transform their heads into miniature radio antennas.

It hurt like a bitch, but it was still safer than using cellphones.

What a pain in the ass, Eldridge thought as he reviewed the last of the game's rules. Holding a successful Xiang match was the sole purview of powerful Odds like Jeb Goldmist, and even he couldn't run it alone—Nix helped. Together, they organized the competitors, enforced the rules and gathered the intelligence and results of the tournament to disperse to the masses of dregs who obsessed over the results. Successful tournaments took years to organize, hence the four-year gaps between each one.

But for all of the expenditure involved, Xiang tournaments generated 20 times the jenta they cost. And that meant that the Odds made a fortune at the expense of dregs everywhere.

Next the players got the usual notice that the opening moves of the match had already begun. That's how Xiang always worked—all of the initial development moves took place before the collection of the avatar-warriors. That way, the action could get underway as soon as possible. With that knowledge, all players were prepared to receive notice of moves as soon as they got out of the blind chamber.

Leaving the blind chamber itself was a lengthy ordeal because the game's officiants made the players leave one at a time. Eldridge felt his bladder fill up as he waited half an hour to get his turn to ride back down to town on a hoverbike. The oddment assigned to Eldridge made a quick hop down the side of Goldmist's tower to Dr. Enki's leech, where his bike was parked. Eldridge started to climb onto his bike, but the polycharge in his neck *fritzzz'ed* to life and sent an electroshock down to his tailbone. He staggered off his bike and checked his jad. It printed out a small piece of paper. Dot-matrix letters read:

`White Knight captures Black Rook`

Eldridge looked at the oddment. "Are you kidding me? White's got a knight in position to attack a rook already?"

The oddment turned his blank, black face on him, then kick-started the hoverbike.

"You've got twelve hours to prep."

The bike hawked up some exhaust and hoisted him into the sky. Eldridge looked at the note again and pocketed it. The actual moves of the game were always concealed from the avatar-warriors, lest they get an idea of what danger might be headed their way and gain an unfair advantage.

But for now, Eldridge didn't have much to do other than get some rest and think about how he was going to rustle up the firepower needed to hold his square.

Yasim's was calling.

• • • • •

PEOPLE IN DEDRICK SAID Yasim's was hidden because it was only accessible by climbing up three stacked rooftops and into the kitchen window of a dreg named Claude, who had so well resigned himself to being a pit stop on the way to Yasim's that his own home had become a respectable watering hole in its own right.

Eldridge took Sinister south from Goldmist's tower, then hung a right down an alleyway that led to a hectic pile of houses, shacks and shanties. Yasim's lay within, but to get there, the redhead rode his bike up a rickety plywood ramp to the top of the pile of houses and parked his bike alongside a dozen other modes of transport perched atop Claude's home. He walked to the edge of the roof, where Dedrick stretched out all around him.

He kneeled, gripped the gutter and pulled a somersault/flip maneuver that delivered him into Claude's kitchen, where Claude—dressed in a bloody apron—yelled a greeting as Eldridge slid through the crowd and through a few more abandoned buildings all heaped together. After stopping off to take a leak, Eldridge made his way through room after room and door after door, delving deeper and deeper into a warren wrought of steel, brick, and wood until he encountered a simple burlap curtain that hung over a trapezoidal doorway. He pushed it aside and brought Yasim's joint and its legendary hyperglobe bursting into the foreground.

The hyperglobe was the epicenter and source of Yasim's lucrative oddsbroking. It was their planet, naturally, but surrounded with a dozen flatscreens that spat out line after line of data like so many hyperactive tickertapes. Meanwhile, the globe itself displayed the most up-to-date representation of the world's map. Most of the globe was dark, but across one half—Eldridge's half—of its slowly spinning surface, bursts of kaleidoscopic activity marked where feudal borders moved back and forth. The information powering these constant updates was aggregated from thousands of dispatches, news reports, declarations, and treaties, as well as from a healthy selection of the best rumortrysts in operation.

Most of the wagering centered on this half of the world, but a few brave souls ventured guesses on what was happening in the mysterious lands that lay across the oceans, which encircled the planet from north to south like giant rings—all of them many thousands of miles narrower than they once had been. Yasim treasured the idiots who made odds on what happened across the oceans. Disputed bets about those lands always went in favor of the house. If the hyperglobe were a Roulette wheel, those faraway lands would be its double-zeros.

Yasim himself lorded over his hyperglobe astride an easy chair held aloft by a steel arm that gave him full view of the globe whenever he wanted. He wore his usual attire: ancient silks that floated around his torso, silk pants that ballooned around his legs and a headdress that marked him as a member of one of the old religions. He had slowly built his place from the detritus of a thousand old juke-joints and bars. Dark wood beams crisscrossed the ceiling, which was a mere nine feet high. Light emanated from dozens of old lamps—some oil, some electric, some neon. Filaments of pink plasma danced along the inside of a glass tube that ran around the edge of the ceiling. An old buddy of Yasim's had fashioned the glass tube to look like an ancient wood railing.

When Eldridge entered, a dozen heads swiveled his way, most of them dregs and trixies. Most everyone was seated around the circular bar that surrounded the hyperglobe, though a few patrons huddled in wood booths that lined the walls. The dregs gave him bored glances and went back to staring at the globe, but the trixies converged on him like eager white bloodcells attacking a newly inserted splinter. Yasim always kept his place stocked with trixies to bolster business for the inn he maintained in the array of derelict houses that formed a sphere around his bar, all of it tucked deep into the clot of old homes that sat near the center of Dedrick. Trixies naturally enjoyed many of the perks of life near Yasim's, including free room and board. In fact, it was impossible to spend the night at Yasim's inn *without* a trixie in your room. When Eldridge entered, two of the trixies working the bar disengaged themselves from their tollos and sashayed his way. One of them was an anadyne man who had altered his genetic code so he could show off his skeletal system, which glimmered under his translucent flesh. His legs terminated at the ankles and were capped with steel prosthetic stilettos. The other was a female who had installed a chip in her neck that could instantly alter the color of her skin anywhere and in any way. When she approached Eldridge, she had configured all of her flesh to be a fluorescent yellow-green, adding in rings of bright red around her wrists and ankles. Both were naked but for the customary outfit for trixies: one C-shaped plastic cup that clung to the trixie's groin and two strips of latex that held the cup in place and wrapped around their shoulders. The outfit was revealing, but that wasn't the point. The latex shoulder-straps included a small device that scanned the trixie's blood for venereals. If necessary, the device would scrub the trixie's blood of anything harmful, but some of the more highly evolved venereals took time to cure. In those cases, the trixie's overalls would display a bar code near their right collarbone that identified the venereal in question. Tollos were still welcome to retain an infected trixie, but at their own risk. Anything that could infect a trixie for more than a few hours would fricassee your average tollo. Only Narsyans had the kind of brawny immune systems that could handle an infected trixie—but none ever did.

In the case of the two trixies that approached Eldridge, blinking green bars marked both of them as safe. The redhead pushed his way past them and cast his eyes upward in search of the resident Odd.

He spotted Yasim a few yards away, where he had lowered his throne to bar-level so he could scream at a craggy man who was drinking a bottle of something dark and who wore a sleeveless blue vest over a muscular frame that bore thousands of tattoos, one of which he referenced in his argument.

"Yasim, the emir *clearly* took control of the western shores of Mesoplanitia a fortnight ago! The border should be adjusted three seconds south-by-sou'west to the *other* side of the riverbank!"

"Their influence terminates with the river!" Yasim yelled and pointed at a snaky blue line that flashed on the globe next to his head. To either side of the river, a pair of city-states contested the boundary in flashing primary colors. To the northwest of the contested river, Eldridge noticed a creepy-crawly line of red lights that spanned half a hemisphere—the Chain of Tears. Dread welled up in the redhead's chest. Yasim snapped his fingers and called over one of the globe's infoscreens. It slid over next to the Odd's head and output a stream of info that confirmed the distant river as the boundary of the nameless emir in question. The unlucky man wrinkled his nose.

"You fucko."

"I am no fucko!" Yasim yelled. "*You* are the fucko, my friend, and you owe me my jenta!"

The dreg pulled a red stylus from his pocket and scribbled out a transaction on the bar. Yasim unhooked a brooch from his headdress and used it to collect the smart characters that spilled out of the stylus.

As soon as the transaction was complete, smiles resumed their dominion over the exchange.

"You *are* kind of a fucko," the tattooed man said.

"No argument here," Yasim said as he spotted the redhead. "Eldridge! You're not dead!" Yasim turned to the thousands of draught handles that lined the pedestal of the hyperglobe and served Eldridge a mug of something sweet and purple.

"Not yet," Eldridge said, pulling up a seat next to the tattooed man. "How you doing, Yasim?"

"Me? How are *you* doing? I heard you owe so much money you put up a deathday wager! Isn't it coming up soon?"

"Yeah, the Fourth, but it's not going to happen."

"You should have more faith."

"Right. Faith's no match for the Odds. You hear anything about the Xiang tourney?"

Yasim shrugged. "Started this week, as I understand."

A man halfway around the bar waved at Yasim. "Yo! Need some grog here!"

"Keep your hole shut while I talk with my friend!" Yasim yelled back at him, then turned to El. "Did you enter?"

Eldridge looked up and down the bar, then gave one tiny nod.

Yasim: "*Again?* I can't–"

The grog-thirsty man once again yelled, "Yo!"

Yasim rolled his eyes, spun around and grabbed a glass jar rimmed with a broken, jagged lip. He filled it with a draught of grog, which he slammed down onto the bar in front of Eldridge, slopping the deep-amber fluid everywhere. He cast his gaze down the bar.

"This grog won't cure your ass-face, my friend, but–"

A tattooed hand appeared over the jar of grog and in front of Eldridge's face.

"You're Eldridge?" the tattooed man asked, proffering his hand.

Eldridge sniffed, then shook the man's hand. "Yeah, that's me. Who're you?"

Yasim smiled. "Eldridge, this is Paco Cristobal, a man who doesn't know a cadastral survey from a demilitarized zone."

Canyons of pockmarks sank into Cristobal's cheeks. A smile. "Yasim likes to pretend he doesn't cheat so he can keep this dump open."

The grogger yelled, "*Yo!*"

Yasim propped the jar of grog against the glass railing that encircled the bar and slid the drink down to the loudmouth man, who gave him a thumbs-up.

"And fuck you, too!" Yasim shouted just as a dozen new dregs streamed in the front door with accounts full of jenta, all of them convinced of their superior knowledge of geopolitics. Yasim said, "If you'll excuse me, gentlemen." With that, he swept up into the air around the hyperglobe. Cristobal sipped his black beer.

"So what's your story, Mr. Eldridge?"

Eldridge sipped his drink. "Not really worth the telling. Why do you wanna know?"

Cristobal shrugged. "I just took a sip of beer. It'll take my body a few minutes to metabolize it. Help me pass the time."

Eldridge gave him a funny look. "How do you know Yasim?"

"He and I used to be brothers in faith, once upon a time."

"That right?"

Cristobal nodded. "About a thousand leagues from here, we studied at one of the monasteries that survived Deadblast. Brick tower, up on a hill near a river. You wouldn't believe the books they had. Yasim and I studied together. Copied old manuscripts side-by-side. He did the coloring, I filled in the illuminated letters. We had a falling out, but we got back in touch a few years ago."

Eldridge suppressed a sigh. "Is that right?"

The tattooed man nodded and took another sip. "Whoops. That's two sips. I guess I'll need your attention for a couple more minutes while I process this. Have you ever lost a best friend, Mr. Eldridge?"

"Sure I have. A few of them."

"How many?"

The redhead's eyes rose as he did the math. "Four or five, at least."

Cristobal's drink paused halfway to his mouth. He set it down and said, "That's a lot."

"I don't know if it's a lot or a little. Feels like a lot. Sometimes."

Cristobal took another sip. "Look at that. I went and had some more. Guess you're stuck with me for another coupla-few. Any one of those old friends stand out?"

"I guess," Eldridge said. "I used to run with this crew of supreme badasses who live up in the mountains. I grew up with them. Never knew what happened to my real parents. They—the badasses—told me I just showed up in a garbage bag on their front steps one morning. No telling how or why. Y'know—*I* used to live in a kind of monastery, too, but like—imagine the world's loudest monastery."

"That's where you met your friend?"

"He's the one who raised me." Eldridge chuckled. "Feels funny, saying he raised me. He was only two years older. But he raised me, up there in those mountains. Holy Crom, the winters. Well, the *winter.* No seasons anymore, especially not up high. Sometimes we'd get this freezing acid-rain mix a few clicks down below the main compound, and the head honchos would roust us up for a fight in the middle of it. Naked. We'd form a circle, and one at a time, we'd get in the center of it and fight off everyone else. Some of the kids died, but we never did, my friend and me. We always lived."

The redhead's pupils dilated, his eyes going to soft-focus as they flitted across distant, imaginary mountainpeaks that danced with the specters of memories long forgotten. Down the bar, the grog-thirsty loudmouth started screaming for another drink.

Eldridge continued: "As we got older, though, everything got harder. I mean, it got harder for *me.* But it never got harder for him, my friend. I remember days when I felt like I was going to die, and he was just smiling along. The order—Marko *belonged.* I never did. I kept up with them for a while, but that was it."

The loudmouth must have really been thirsty, because he was slamming his palms into the bar over and over, his screams drawing a torrent of blood into his elongated face. Eldridge glanced over his shoulder at the screaming grog-fiend, but Cristobal tapped his knee to bring his attention back around.

"Marko? That's your friend's name?"

"Yeah."

"What happened to him?"

"He became the leader of the monastery," Eldridge said as the sounds of wheezing joined the grog-fiend's screams. Eldridge turned and saw that the grog-fiend's chin was resting on the bar, which he gripped with trembling hands. His face had gone from red to purple in seconds. Eldridge took a tentative step forward, but Cristobal appeared beside him and touched his shoulder.

"I'd keep your distance."

The grog-fiend's body hissed like a tire that had sprung a leak, only it hadn't sprung one leak; it had sprung *millions*. Every pore on his body had transformed into an emitter that sprayed a red mist–his blood, instantly aerosolized–which clouded around him. When the mist cleared, his white body crumpled to the ground. Yasim circled around the globe, looked at the corpse, and screamed at the rear of his joint.

"*Clean*-up! I think someone just got bishop'ed!"

Eldridge looked at Cristobal. "You poisoned the drink when you went to shake my hand."

Cristobal nodded and crossed his beefy arms. "Sorry I had to keep you talking. I needed to make sure I got that square. So what're you? Knight? Bishop?"

"Kingside rook."

"Right on. I'm the black queenside bishop. You're black, too, right?"

"Yeah. How'd you know?"

Cristobal shook his head. "Just a vibe I got. You look like an underdog."

He sat down and returned to his drink. Eldridge joined him.

"So who's the poor bastard you just capped?"

"Some dumbass pawn," Cristobal said. "But word on the street is he was a passed pawn on the queenfile. White's got a knight on D5 and an avalanche coming our way, so watch yourself."

"Yeah, I've got to defend against a knight attack tomorrow."

"You serious?"

"Yep."

Cristobal rolled his eyes. "*Great*. This'll be over in days. I could've used the money from a longer match."

Eldridge chuckled and sipped his drink. "Me, too."

The smell of lightly frying skin filled the air. Cristobal lurched off of his stool, clamping his hand over his polycharge.

"Looks like I've got an incoming move," he said, and sure enough, his jad printed out a small piece of paper. Eldridge got a look at it:

```
White Queen captures Black Bishop
```

Cristobal spent the rest of his life saying, "Dang it."

Eldridge was already hurling himself under a nearby table, which he flipped and propped in front of himself for protection. He heard the high-pitched whine of incoming munition. The next instant, a stream of smoke streaked across the bar and slammed into Cristobal's chest. The tattooed man exploded, showering the bar with blood, gore, and viscera. A crater marked where he stood, and a full tenth of Yasim's beautiful bar hung in bits and pieces of dangling mahogany.

Eldridge knew that anyone playing a Xiang Queen could bring serious firepower, but when he peeked over the top of the table to see who had killed Cristobal, he gasped. It wasn't a who. It wasn't even a *what.* It was more of a–

"Holy. Fucking. Shit."

The hunching creature smashed through the meager doorway. Six-inch-thick scales covered its body like layer upon layer of natural callusing that gleamed like burnished metal. Heaped upon its shoulders was a giant set of padding from an ancient game, all of it augmented with steel-reinforced shielding. More plates of armor covered the creature's massive legs. At eight feet tall, the creature was large enough to hold its rocket launcher like a handgun. Strapped to its back was a giant blade ripped from an old agrarian vehicle. The creature strode across the dumbstruck-silent bar to Cristobal's smoking crater. Miscellaneous wreckage surrounded the hole, and the creature tore through it until it found Cristobal's severed head. The creature slammed the head onto the shattered remains of the bar and reached into a pocket in its leg armor, from which it produced a giant syringe. That in hand, the creature picked up Cristobal's head and jabbed the syringe into his dead brain. The creature depressed the plunger–and Cristobal's eyes sprang open. One of his eyes lolled back in its socket, but the other glared in horrified protest at the sight being forced upon it in death. The creature crushed the syringe, cast it aside and gripped Cristobal's head with both hands so it could speak into his face with a subwoofing voice that made the air in the room quiver and exerted hundreds of pounds of pressure on everyone's chest. When it spoke, Eldridge felt like a fist was closing around his heart.

"I am the White Queen. And I'll kill you all. I swear by everything. Everything. The dark sun. The roiling sky. The seas in the earth. The mysteries of Hecate. I shall rain down horror upon black. Knock your souls to hell in one stroke." The creature's voice rose with its rage. Segments of callus-armor folded together across its wide brow. It bellowed through gnashing teeth: *"You'll never be dead enough! Never!"*

That said, the creature that was the White Queen reached behind its back and pulled out a giant rifle. It stabbed the barrel through the blackened stump of Cristobal's neck, and with Cristobal's impaled head screaming silently at the end of its rifle, the creature addressed the bar.

"Let this be a warning to the Black King."

The creature pulled the trigger, and Cristobal's still-living head exploded. The creature wiped the dead bishop's brains out of its eyes, then turned and smashed through another wall, leaving a callus-creature-shaped hole in its wake.

The remaining bar patrons slowly rose from where they had taken cover. This included Eldridge, who struggled to his feet on a pair of shaking legs. He lurched over to the bar and found his mug of purple beer miraculously still standing on a chunk of wood. He attempted to drink it but wound up slopping it down the front of his jacket. Yasim, his headdress askew, floated over on his throne.

"You picked a helluva game to join, El."

Eldridge's head jerked up and down a few times. "Y-y-yep."

"So what're you going to do now?"

Eldridge managed to drain the drink, which he swallowed with a wince. He slammed down the empty mug and responded with one word:

"Cheat."

Part Two

the TYPHOID MAIDEN

LAWS WERE LAUGHABLE, BUT everyone obeyed the Odds, and everyone obeyed the Cellphone Edict of Deadblast.

Even trixies.

A filter sat between the past and the present, its setting strongest around the time of the Deadblast cataclysm, and through that filter, only discrete bursts of data made it through intact. One of those databursts was a desperate howl from the commanding officer of a space station as it plunged back to earth and burned up in the atmosphere. As he fell to his death, the astronaut made a final, desperate plea into his commlink: "*Disable all cellulars! Burn the towers! Eighteen-fifty to 1990! Burn them now, or–*" A shriek of white noise terminated the message and, presumably, marked the point when flames engulfed his cabin.

The message arrived in the post-Deadblast world as a relic, a time capsule, a fossil. Post-Deadblast scholars puzzled over its meaning and made copies of the message that they delivered to other remnants. Those scholars in turn made copies, and so forth, until the brute fact of its original meaning–cellular technology was *macta*–had leapt into the stream of whispers that ran from remnant to remnant, thereby transforming the doomed astronaut's message into the first post-Deadblast law to arise naturally from the new order.

That meant that everyone who remained had rediscovered how to communicate over long distances via moto-express or, if they were communicating over short distances (inside a city, for example), everyone got used to tracking down a computer with a hardline that could deliver their messages along a physical wire.

But even though no one made cellular phone calls anymore, the devices themselves still existed—and were traded on the blackest of black markets.

Trixies, by their very profession, acted as independent contractors. Legend had it that before Deadblast, trixies used to answer to various middle managers who claimed a percentage of their earnings and kept them in abusive check. The average trixie—male, female or otherwise—would giggle at such a notion, as they maintained their own stashes of jenta, the concept of banks also having been stopped by the info-filter that marked Deadblast. Trixies also thought of themselves as a giant, interconnected family. If one happened to fall ill to an especially virulent venereal, others would take care of the ailing trixie, even going so far as to increase their workload and share their extra earnings with their comrade. They also would occasionally trade off on tollos if one was too violent or unsavory for someone's tastes.

For example, at the same time the White Queen killed Paco Cristobal, a certain trixie named Oksana had traded off on a job with a colleague named Pryor. Hard-up for jenta, Pryor had accepted a retainer from a tollo who enjoyed a cocktail of uppers that drove his heartrate into the 200s and forced him to eat constantly. In addition, he had to periodically moisten his own eyes with drops, because the last time he tried to blink, his eyelids flew off his face.

In short, this tollo was a wannabe rager, and one nudge in the wrong direction would send him down the lifepath to becoming a dreen.

Genetically, Pryor favored XY, but his DNA was scrambled enough to afford him the ability to expand or contract different crucial body parts depending on the tollo. The wannabe dreen-rager client seemed to despise all of them, so Pryor sent word for Oksana to take over the job. Trixies still got attacked by the occasional tollo too dumb to know better, and Pryor himself was still recovering from an attack.

So Oksana the trixie strutted down a narrow hallway that led through the warren of densely packed housing underneath Yasim's joint. The ceiling hung low enough that even the five-and-a-half-foot brunette had to tilt her head to avoid hitting it. She wore her usual outfit: a leather corset that tapered into a skirt that hung to the floor, its conservative length offset by a pair of slits that revealed muscular flashes of thigh every time she moved. She strapped her trixie overalls under her corset, leaving her shoulders and clavicle exposed so tollos could see her venereal scan, which was blinking green. She wore standard, flat hiking boots that crunched on the occasional errant tumbler or glass tube that covered the floor.

Spherical fluorescent light fixtures protruded from the walls at regular intervals and cast sickly shadows into the corners of doorways. Grunts and moans wafted out from inside the doors she passed. She had ventured into a hard fuckzone, three circles below Yasim's and dead in the center of the most eccentric proclivities (and depravities) that Dedrick had to offer.

She rounded a corner and passed the rubberized relief of a man who had been entombed in latex and stuck spread-eagle against the wall. One of Oksana's fellow trixies, a pear-shaped XX named Leteesh, wore a pair of gloves whose fingertips were capped with black blocks. She ran her hands across the form of the man in latex, her movements causing the occasional spark and sizzle. The man's gleaming black form writhed in response.

Oksana bumped fists with Leteesh as they passed, and the contact sent a shiver up Oksana's right forearm, which was encircled with a ring of warped and wrinkly scar tissue. It looked like someone had severed her forearm midway between her wrist and elbow before soldering it back on.

But back to the pads on Leteesh's gloves: Oksana knew that her fellow trixie's gloves were tipped with Heisenperv pads—devices that let the wearer caress single atoms at a time. Presumably, the man in latex was only feeling the sensation of the single atoms that Leteesh disturbed in the layer of latex that coated his body. That kind of specialized work was easy—fun, even—but Oksana had some *real* work to do that night.

The wannabe rager's room radiated heat like a grease fire. She hissed when she touched the doorknob, and the instant she rattled it, the wall inhaled the door like a vacuum had suddenly opened inside. He stood there naked, shining and steaming with sweat, his lidless eyes bugging. His plumbing hung between his legs like a bloodless pinkie-finger, stark white against his sunburnt-red form.

"Get in here," he said.

She did, and the doing of the deed involved a chastity belt-looking contraption that redirected blood from his femoral artery into his nether-regions, as well as a lot of splintered furniture. Pillow talk consisted of various forms of hand-to-hand combat as Oksana was forced to wrestle him to the ground and extract his jenta stylus, which he had hidden up his ass.

"*Give it up, you macta!*" the trixie screamed as she wedged his head under an ancient oak dressed with her knee, sweat cascading down her face.

When she was finally paid, she vaulted to her feet and made for the door, her hands aswarm with red jenta smartcharacters, but before she could reach the doorknob and escape, he grabbed a fistful of her hair and yanked her back onto the remains of the bed, where the sharp points of a dozen broken bedsprings stabbed her in the back. She sat up and started to scream, but instead of sound, her mouth spewed a line of flame across the room. Her temples throbbed. Her head listed. A blinking red light caught her attention—her venereal scan.

"What did you *give* me, you buttwaaaaah—" Her attempted utterance of the word "buttwad" turned into another burst of flame. Fortunately, Oksana's immune system stood among the most powerful of the Dedrick trixies—her venereal indicator was already blinking yellow. The wannabe rager sprang onto the bed and hunched over her.

"I think you'll wanna give me those jenta back," he said. "I've got an offer."

Oksana propped her hand on the wall and drove her boot-heel into his stomach. Bile sprayed from his mouth as he sailed across the room and crashed into the same oak dresser under which Oksana had held him helpless moments earlier. The dresser toppled forward and sent its bottom drawer falling onto the floor, where it spilled forth its contents: a pile of shiny plastic and metal devices, all of them equipped with small numeric keypads.

The trixie gasped. "Are those–?"

The wannabe rager was already shoveling them back into the drawer.

"Slimy cunt! Trying to get us ka-boomed?"

"What the fuck're you doing with all those? You know the edict!"

The wannabe rager walked on his knees across the room to her, the drawerful of cellphones in his hands, his eyes dancing in their sockets.

"The price is all kinds of right, trixie. You know you only need two. One to call, one to go *boom*. What if you need to make a call? A *last* call?"

Pursuant to the Cellphone Edict of Deadblast, the rumortrysts held that the placing of a cellular call would cause a disaster. Some said it would merely spark an explosion. The deep-desert theocrazzies maintained that it would call down some manner of providential retribution. Still others questioned the edict itself. After all, there weren't any satellites in orbit to deliver the calls, and neither were there any towers left to transmit them.

But Oksana the trixie wasn't about to test the edict. She just had to get out of that room, and to do so, she was going to call on the oldest trick in the oldest profession: a trixie bribe. She plucked a stylus from her hair and drew little circles in the air with it.

"I'll take one of those treasures from you, sweetiebuns."

The wannabe rager shuffled forward, still on his knees.

"You'll thank me later, when–"

When he said the word "when," he broke eye-contact with Oksana for an instant, and in that same instant, her arm transformed into a neck-stabbing piston. Her stylus struck jugular on the third stab, and she rolled off the bed to avoid the spray of blood that hit the shattered headboard. As the wannabe rager rolled on the ground, she leapt over his prone form and ripped open the door—but with one foot out of the room, she paused.

In one sweeping motion, she grabbed two of the cellphones and slammed the door. Her venereal indicator was already blinking green again.

• • • • •

AFTER ELDRIDGE GOT A look at the White Queen, he immediately asked Yasim for his usual room and retained his usual trixie, Oksana.

"You sure you want to sleep with Oksana *now?*" Yasim asked as he and his crew cleared wreckage out of his bar. "Don't you have to buy a billion bazookas to get ready for the rest of the match?"

Eldridge nodded. "That's a firm, and I know you're my man for that, but for now I need a room with a hardline, and I need Oksana. Bring her to me."

Yasim nodded and tossed him the key to his usual room, which hid at the farthest reach of his humble inn. To get to it, Eldridge navigated a narrow hallway that stank of mildew. His boots sank into the damp shag carpeting and crunched on old syringes and neck-pumps. The hallway ended in a sharp turn that curved up a small stairway. At the top of the stairs stood a three-foot door embossed with the number 209. Eldridge unlocked the door and admitted himself into a room lined with dark-finished wood that had lost its shine a century ago. Dark red plaster covered the walls. A built-in closet sat to the left of a wrought-iron four-poster bed. A rusty old padlock hung in the air in front of the closet, its crescent-shaped deadbolt secured in place with a dense coil of nanocords.

But most important: An ancient rolltop desk sat next to the window, bearing a hardlined computer. Eldridge knew the computer well, having acquired it himself halfway across the continent from a road-merch named Finnegan. The price: one of his kidneys. The computer had been easy to transport because it was roughly the size and weight of a human head. Plus, it came with a keyboard.

Once Eldridge had locked the door to his room, he took off his coat and revealed a sleeveless gray T-shirt that read: PROPERTY

OF UTAH JAZZ PROFESSIONAL BASKETBALL FRANCHISE. He unstrapped his cargo pockets and laid his sawed-off shotguns on the bed with their barrels facing the door. As he sat at the computer, he glanced through the curtains at his view: a brick wall. He smiled and booted up the device, which was housed in a warped, beige plastic box. Five minutes later he was looking at a black-and-white screen filled with folders and icons. Onscreen a small arrow sat in the corner. Eldridge frowned at it, wondering what the hell it was for. The system's hard drive bore the name Little Darla. Eldridge typed "hard" and highlighted an icon for a program called "Hardline Message." Hardline messages worked more or less like quicktalks, but they took longer to send, and whether your message reached its intended target depended entirely on how often they checked their computers. Eldridge took a breath and composed a message:

```
From: Eldridge

To: Boris Hagan
```

Boris Hagan. Aspiring Odd, pre-Deadblast expert, crusty old crank, and a current underling of Jeb Goldmist. Most important, Hagan was always plugged into the tournament. Eldridge sent a ping out over the hardline:

```
You there?
```

Hagan's response came back seconds later:

```
Hagan here. What the F are you doing back
in a Xiang  tourney?
```

Eldridge responded:

```
Tell you later. I need to see your balls.
In the desert. 0100.
```

At the same instant he clicked "send," the bolt on his door slid back with a *clack*. He jumped up, spun around, and aimed both of his scatterguns at the midget-sized door just in time to see a head of shining black hair enter the room. The head looked up and revealed a face out of a thousand far-eastern toonreels of old: Big, round dark eyes sat at the center of a face whose round cheeks swooped into a tiny chin that hid under a slightly overbiting mouth and a hooked nose. She looked into the redhead's eyes—and hung her head.

"Hey, buttwad."

"Hey, Oksana."

She sighed and reached inside the room, giving Eldridge a look at the ugly ring of scars on her right forearm. The image brought back memories of Oksie as a little girl—memories both good and bad. The redhead pushed them away for now.

Once Oksana had a grip, she pulled her curves in through the small door, pausing briefly as her hips got stuck in the doorway like they always did, and like always, she gave her rump a hard shake that simultaneously dislodged her butt and sent a seismic ripple across her cleavage. Once inside, she stood. As a beauty, Eldridge knew she considered herself curvy but flawed—a "slutterface," as she put it—but Eldridge thought she was feruccio, all the way.

He noticed, however, that she had black streaks emanating from the corners of her mouth. Plus, she was spattered with blood.

"What happened?"

The trixie looked down at herself. "Oh, this? Just a pain in my ass. Can I?"

She nodded at a washbasin that sat in the corner of the room on top of an antique vanity. Eldridge nodded, laid his scatterguns on the rolltop and pulled back the bedsheets. Oksana washed up, then turned and put her hands on her hips.

"Same drill?" she asked.

"Oh, yes," Eldridge said, taking off his pants and draping them over the desk chair with his coat. He drummed his fingertips against each other, eyes twinkling.

Oksana smirked, undid her corset, gripped its waistline and shimmied her hips to pull it off. It flumped to the hardwood floor, leaving her naked but for her trixie overalls, which were stretched to their limit over her chest. She cocked an eyebrow—then turned and opened the closet to reveal an arsenal of steel and chrome. Hanging in the center of the closet was a full set of enhanced titanium-weave

Kevlar body armor—pants and chestplate—which Oksana pulled on. The rest of the closet held a selection of Eldridge's favorite weaponry, including Oksana's usual choices—a nitrogen-cooled, laser-sighted hand cannon that fired red-hot pellets of splatter-iron; and an old-timey .357 Magnum that Oksana kept cleaner than Dr. Enki's operating theater. Once she was outfitted, she opened a small drawer on the bottom of the built-in closet and pulled out a clear brown cylindrical bottle about the size of a shell casing. People used to keep medicine in them. Oksana used this one to hold her remkillers, three of which she dry-swallowed. Two seconds later, her eyelids fled and left her oculars glowing like a pair of twin lamplights in the middle of her trembling face.

Eldridge was already snuggled up in bed, dozing. Oksana gave him the closest approximation to a dirty look her bulging eyes would allow. She punched him in the arm, but he didn't stir.

"Hey, old man. Remember that time when you fucked me?"

"Mm-hmm," Eldridge said.

"Yeah, you ripped off my clothes. Threw me on the bed. Had your way. I can't wait to tell my grandkids about it."

"Murf," Eldridge said as he drifted away.

"Why won't you ever fuck me?"

"Because I'm afraid I'd get you pregnant," Eldridge said, suddenly lucid in his last moments before sleep.

• • • • •

No one really slept in the years since Deadblast, at least not anyone like Eldridge. Only the Odds had enough security—financial and otherwise—to truly fall asleep. Everyone else always teetered on the edge of a psychotic break from long-term exhaustion because they never allowed themselves to fall into REM sleep. REM sleep meant dreams, and dreams meant you wouldn't be able to react fast enough should a threat present itself. Hiring Oksana to stand guard was the only time Eldridge allowed himself to fall into REM sleep, and even those seldom refreshed him because of the bloody, twisted monstrosities that visited him in his dreams.

So when a ruckus woke him that night at Yasim's, Eldridge at first only saw a pair of dreenspawn duking it out in his room. Rare was the dreen whose reproductive organs survived its transformation, but a few of them managed to hyperaccelerate their glandular output while keeping their testicles and ovaries intact. The unlucky result was a daughterson born with ribonucleic helices so warped that their brain and heart would develop as one throbbing mess in the middle of their chest while their cranium would remain empty and sunken. Others would emerge from bloody wombs with teeth for fingernails, their lungs having reverse-evolved into gills so that every breath was a torment. And all dreenspawn shared the same horrible fate: Their bodies wouldn't let them die.

Eldridge was dreaming when the ruckus woke him, and in the few brief moments before he completely woke up, he blinked owlishly at the creatures in the room with him. An instant later, though, his waking instincts kicked in, and he spun off the bed, thinking that the extra person in the room was an oddment or a bounty-merc or that the White Queen was seconds away from exploding into the room and ending him.

Unfortunately for the redhead, his attempt to spin off the bed failed as his legs got wrapped up in the bedding. He wound up face-planting into the wood floor, his lower half cocooned in a duvet.

"Oksana! Run! Save yourself! Run!"

A familiar voice, but not Oksana's, said: "Eldridge?"

Eldridge turned his head so his ear rested on the floor and he could peer up at the six-foot-six-inch woman who had busted into his room in the middle of the evening:

"Zora?" he asked, then pushed himself up and spun onto his rear-end. Constable Zora Tola stood over him, her sidearms drawn, her cheeks red from wrestling with Oksana, who hovered behind the constable's right shoulder with the nitro-cooled hand cannon trained on Tola's head.

Oksana said, "Sorry, El. The big dummy announced herself before she came in, otherwise I woulda popped her one."

Tola flashed: "Of *course* I announced myself, trixie. I'm a cop. That's what we do."

Eldridge, still relieved that a cop had interrupted his sleep and not Quillig (or the White Queen), shook his legs out of the bedding and stood—and when he saw what the constable was packing, he held his breath. In her hands, she held her usual notebook, but attached to her belt was a flashlight-sized scanning gizmo. The redhead had only seen her use it for certain cases.

And he had a good guess what this case was about.

"What's the problem?" he asked.

Tola glared at him. "I think you know."

Eldridge totally knew. "I don't know what you're talking about."

Then Tola said four words she had told him a dozen times before.

"Eldridge, you're under arrest."

He sighed. "What for?"

"Murder."

Oksana said, "That's not legal?"

"Not when you murder the son of an Odd it isn't."

Eldridge raised his hands in protest. "Oh, *come on!* The kid attacked *me*. He was full dreen! What was I *supposed*—"

Tola cut him off: "El, you're lucky I didn't tell him myself. He said he didn't recognize the body, the poor bastard." She crossed to Eldridge's clothes and unhooked the scanning device from her belt.

"You're not going to get a positive," he said.

Oksana: "What's going on?"

Tola: "Quiet, trixie."

Oksana's eyes flared. "You gonna let her talk to me that way?"

But Eldridge was already hovering over the constable's shoulder. "What's it say?"

She deactivated the scanner with a *click* and returned it to her belt.

"It says you killed Crius Kaleb's son. Let's take a ride."

"Wait—let me see that thing. I'm calling *macta* on this bullshit!"

Tola rose over him, saying: "You want me to pull your oddsmaking privileges?"

"You *wouldn't*."

She advanced on him: "How many teeth was that dreen missing, El? The one you whacked outside Kaleb's casino tonight?"

Eldridge crossed his arms. The constable walked forward and bumped him with her armor-clad torso. He fell backward a step.

He said, "Which dreen? I killed two." He dropped his arms and shifted gears: "Zor, seriously—you don't want to revoke my odds."

"If you want to stay in the game, then you're getting even with the house again." She grabbed him by the scruff of his collar and shoved him toward the door. "Should've washed the dreenjuice off your clothes, El. Let's go."

• • • • •

ELDRIDGE WAS WHINING THE second they got out of Yasim's.

"Come *on*, Zora. I've got a big meeting in a few hours. Can I just send him a quicktalk somewhere and let him know?"

"What's the meeting about, Eldridge? I can send the message for you."

This exchange took place beside Eldridge's motorbike, which the constable had locked in place with a gravboot—a credit card-sized device that decupled the weight of an offending vehicle while simultaneously sinking an invisible filament of superheavy matter into the ground 100 feet deep that kept it tethered in place.

In response to Tola's offer to relay his message, Eldridge balked. She smirked.

"What? Can't you tell lil' old me about one of your secret boys' club meet-ups?"

"OK, OK," he said. "Just tell Boris Hagan I need to delay our meeting until I get out of jail."

Tola took notes, nodding and frowning. "Hm. Hm. Yes, an important meeting. Right. An important meeting with Boris Hagan, one of Jeb Goldmist's lackeys." Tola turned her big, dark eyes on him and spoke in the high-pitched drawl of an airbrain: "Doesn't Mr. Hagan help run the Xiang whatzamajigger?"

"Would you fuck *off* already? Just tell him I won't make it this morning. It'll have to be later."

"Later," she said, her voice suddenly deep with mock importance. "Oh, yes, Mr. Eldridge. I'll tell him that your important meeting will happen later at an important time." Her voice returned to normal: "But you're going down for murder. Might be a while."

Tola tapped a few buttons on the gravboot, disengaged its gravitether from the earth, and linked it with her vehicle, a tricycle. Eldridge remembered from his days as a Narsyan that "tricycle" used to be a name for a child's toy, but in the days after Deadblast, "tricycle" had emerged as the name for a new breed of all-terrain vehicle that made use of gyroscopes, nanotech, and lightweight bulletproof glass. From a distance, a tricycle would look like nothing more than three giant wheels rolling along. Closer inspection would reveal that the three giant, deep-treaded wheels were attached via tree trunk-sized axles to a glass sphere that appeared to be empty—but that was where the nanotech came in. As a tech, invisibility was still nothing more than using cameras on opposing axes to deliver an image of what lay behind, but the nanocams on a tricycle swam in an ultrathin layer of silicon soup that clung to the outside of the sphere. That gave the tricycle driver a 360-degree view around the vehicle, all while concealing the interior. And invisibility wasn't the nanotech's only purpose. In addition to the nanocams, the silicon soup also held millions of nanohooks that not only connected the axles to the central sphere but also allowed the axles to rotate around the sphere in virtually any direction. This gave a tricycle incredible mobility over all kinds of terrain.

The vehicle itself had come into the constable's life through luck. Like most people living in those days, she made odds with the Odds, and she got lucky once or twice. She never got lucky enough to leave her thankless job as a cop, but her prowess at guessing the mutation rate for an especially cunning virus that had wiped out a remote sector of the polar continent had scored her the jenta to buy the tricycle off a small-time Odd named Zak Chamberlain, who had left Dedrick for the promise of more lucrative Oddsmanship that beckoned from the coast.

On that night years ago, Tola and Eldridge had toasted her good fortune over drinks at Yasim's, but on the night she arrested the redhead for the murder of Stewart Kaleb, she merely looked at him with dark eyes that were dark from within, too. Gone was Tola's playfulness outside of the bar. They were on their way to the jail.

The constable drove the tricycle down Sinister, out the revolving door, and up the ramp to the aboveground realm. At the end of the ramp, she turned left and headed north up the endless highway that led to the jail and would eventually run into the Oasis Mountains. Once they were on the highway, frost encrusted the tricycle's dome. Tola started asking questions, and they weren't about the murder.

"When did you get sick?"

"About a year ago."

"Why didn't you tell me?"

Silence. Eldridge checked out the back to make sure his bike was still there. It weaved along behind them, the filament of gravitether flickering purple in the night like a laser brought into focus by a puff of talc. A few more miles rolled by, and Eldridge jerked his head to the side as they passed an infamous Dedrick landmark. At a glance, it looked like an old wooden outhouse, but closer examination would reveal a structure thrice as large, constructed from wood that was lined with red veins of petrification. All of it centered around a black doorway that sank into the earth. A fading billboard stood on a man-made hillock to the left of the structure and identified it as just another roadside attraction that existed in the years before Deadblast: The Ancient Sea and Old Mine. A curved wooden boat sailed cartoony blue waves that broke off the end of the sign in three dimensions. A bearded man commanded the boat, shortsword in hand and a spiked helmet on his head. Eldridge forgot the name for these bearded guys, but he was pretty sure they were called spikings. Because of the helmets.

"No, they're *vikings*, dummy," Tola said as they left The Ancient Sea in the darkness behind them.

"What the hell is a *vike?*"

"I dunno. But that's what they're called. Did you ever peek in there to see the mine?"

The constable was referring, of course, to the Old Mine—the sister attraction to The Ancient Sea. Years before, The Ancient Sea was enough of an attraction. People traveled for hundreds of miles to find The Sea, their journey punctuated by a neverending series of advertisements that proclaimed the majesty of The Sea from hundreds of billboards and atop just as many barnhouses. "SEE THE SEA! BRAVE THE MINE!" shouted the ads, which all led into the deep desert and took them down into a labyrinth of natural caves that led to a vast underground lake. Natural wonders filled the cave: stalactites and stalagmites that melted into each other; pools of milky water that rainbow-glimmered from within; passages so narrow that the obese had to turn back; subterranean bluffs overlooking cavernous great halls that nature had hewn from the earth. But as time wore on, the populace lost interest in The Ancient Sea, and so the proprietors decided to sell some snake oil alongside their great discovery and opened the Old Mine. The rumortrysts carried with them stories of what the Old Mine had once been: a horrorshow engineered to terrify wayward children. Eldridge remembered when Marko Marinus first told him the tale of the Old Mine when they were children. They had encamped for the night in a hastily built igloo near one of the peaks of the Oasis Mountains, where the Narsyans made their home. Their mentors had cast them out into the mountains with the promise that they were coming to kill them. Eldridge and Marko held each other in the three-foot-by-three-foot space, not daring to start a fire. Fire meant heat, which meant sweat, which meant the igloo might melt and soak them. And they both knew what that meant. They wrapped themselves in the pelts of two six-legged suprafelines they had slain. Both boys already bore the telltale vertical forehead scar that marked all Narsyans, although neither of them had the small, circular bulge at the midpoint of their scar. Marko held him from behind while they both lay in fetal positions and shook, using a Narsyan-taught technique to generate body warmth. They held hands. Eldridge noticed an inkvine scar that ran along the inside of Marko's forearm.

As they held each other and hoped that their mentors wouldn't discover them, Marko told Eldridge about how the proprietors believed in things called souls.

"What's that?" Eldridge asked, his voice barely above a whisper—both out of fear and bone-frozen exhaustion.

"People used to believe we had magic spirits inside us that *were* us," said his old friend.

"*Were* us? What's that mean?"

"I don't know. It sounds kind of scary. People thought you were two things. Your body was just junk. Muscle and fat and bone. And inside your head, you had this magic spirit-thing that made it move."

"Weird."

"Right, but that's not the end of the story. The proprietors of The Ancient Sea, they met with the eldest Odd, a man named Uzziel, and he got them both to sell him their souls. In exchange, he built them the Old Mine. But Uzziel tricked them."

"How?" Eldridge asked.

"I'll tell you in a second. Just listen. See, the mine wasn't actually a mine. Nobody dug for anything there. It was just a tunnel that snaked through the earth for miles and miles. It made a huge circle that began and ended at The Ancient Sea. A track ran around the edge of the circle and carried customers on a ride through the tunnel. Uzziel, he told the proprietors that kids would love getting scared on the Old Mine, so the proprietors put up signs everywhere bragging about how *scary* the ride was. And they were right. After the first child died on the ride, the legend got bigger, and kids from all around dared each other that they could make it all the way through the Old Mine with their eyes open, because y'see—the only way to *survive* the ride was to close your eyes. If you closed them, you might be able to make it, but even that didn't work sometimes. The ride just went on way too long. Almost an hour. Most kids could make it halfway, but just after the three-quarter mark, the track made a turn down the longest, blackest hallway you've ever seen, but even though it was so dark, you could see someone standing at the end of it. A woman. Naked. Covered in blood and bits of red. You could see all her veins, red and blue. She had her back to you. And all the way down that tunnel, you knew she was going to turn around when you got to her. And as soon as you thought that—as soon as you *knew* it—you lost your mind. Parents got back to the loading station with corpses in their arms, their faces all scrunched up with tears."

"But how did Uzziel trick them?"

"He built them the mine for free. He never collected their souls. Instead, he collected the souls of all the kids who died in the Mine and laughed while he watched the proprietors' souls wither away in shame."

The young Eldridge looked ready to weep. He didn't cry, but he did whisper a few words: "I don't ever, ever want to ride the Old Mine."

Marko looked him in the eye and said, "You won't ever have to. But if you did, you *could do it.* You could make it all the way around."

Both attractions had closed down years ago, of course, and everyone knew to stay away from The Ancient Sea and the Old Mine because of what lived there.

Dreens.

Lots of 'em. Once you went dreen, the desert exerted its pull and brought you out into the cold nights, which was the only place where dreens and their superhot body-temps could survive. But once they made it out into the desert, they invariably gravitated toward The Ancient Sea and its vast, cold underground caverns. As for the Old Mine—well, no one ever went down there, including Eldridge.

"No," he said on his way to be tried for murder. "I never even had a look in the Old Mine."

"Me, neither," Tola said.

Eldridge fidgeted. "I didn't tell you I was sick because I didn't tell *anybody* I was sick. And I had a plan."

"You mean Dr. fucking Enki had a plan. If you needed money, why didn't you ask me?"

He chuckled.

"Oh, right," she said. "Crazy Eldridge, in so deep he's got the bends."

Eldridge was going to ask her what "the bends" were, but he ignored the presumed insult and rode out the last few miles. Soon, some foothills rolled up on the right. Tucked in among them was a hectic collection of brick, stucco, and steel—the jail. Tola pulled the tricycle over to the side of the building and paused a moment while they pulled on their coldgear. Once properly bundled up, she broke the seal on the dome. They jumped out and ran inside.

The jail was at once a jail, the police office, and Tola's home. Inside, walls and staircases followed the contours of the foothills. Two levels straddled the thrust of a hill. Toward the rear, a spiral staircase led up to Tola's apartment, where she kept a single bed and a lot of firepower. Stone and wood covered most exposed surfaces—slate, tile and the occasional burst of mosaic. Tola's desk sat to the far left of the main room, right underneath the giant mounted head of an animal. It looked a little like a horse—Eldridge had once seen a picture of one as a young boy—but this creature, the dead one, had a fatter, heavier snout that hung over its lower lip. The sides of its head were adorned with what looked like tree branches that had been sanded and sharpened.

"What's that called again?" he asked as he pulled off his goggles. "A noose?"

"It's called a *goose,* silly," she said as she pulled up a chair behind her desk and opened her ledger. Despite the presence of a computer to the left of the desk, Tola reached for an actual fountain pen that stood in an inkwell—no smart characters for *this* criminal court. The constable recorded Eldridge's name and offense in a ledger. That done, she opened a drawer. He moaned.

"Zora, come *on*—"

But she already had the wig out. It looked like an arrangement of bone-white eggrolls and emitted a puff of white powder when she plopped it onto her head. Eldridge smiled.

"You look like a moron."

"You look like a moron, *your honor,*" she prompted him. When no correction was forthcoming, she continued, "Eldridge, you are hereby charged with the murder of one Stewart Kaleb, a human homo sapien."

"*Arguably* human," he said.

"Be that as it may. How do you plead?"

"Well, seeing as how *he* was an *it* who was trying to eat my fuel cell and my face, I plead not guilty."

She squinted at him. "You're sure you're not a little guilty?"

He raised his palms. "Zora, the guy had gone dreen! How was I supposed to know?!"

"Dreens used to be people, too," she whispered.

Eldridge swallowed a smart-ass something he had on his tongue-tip. He knew the score. Silent, he produced his red stylus and scribbled some smart characters onto the constable's desk. She collected them and frowned.

"What's this for?"

"As long as I'm in court, I thought I'd settle up my parking ticket," he said.

She dropped the jenta back on her table, where they scurried back into the redhead's stylus.

"Keep your stupid jenta."

Eldridge sighed. "Look, I'm sorry about Milos, OK?"

Milos. Milos Tola. The constable's ex-husband, though "ex-husband" wasn't the right word. In the days after Deadblast, they called the constable a *duata*. In the days before, they might have called her a widow, even though her husband wasn't dead.

"Is that *all* you're sorry about?"

"What else would I be sorry about?"

"How about Cri's kid?"

"'*Cri*'? Are you and Kaleb buddies now?"

"You were friends with both of them, Stewart and Crius, way back when."

"You've gotta be kidding me."

She shook her head. Her eyes dropped to her desk. She mumbled two syllables Eldridge himself had mumbled earlier: "Urbit."

Eldridge winced. "Come on. That was a cheap shot."

"But it's true."

They stood in silence for a moment. Finally, the constable twined her fingers and looked at her ledger. After a moment, she looked up and said, "I find you guilty. Well, partially guilty. Manslaughter. You'll sleep it off tonight." She pointed at the crooked cell that sat on the opposite side of the main floor. Eldridge fumed, stood and walked to the cell. Halfway there, he stopped and considered leaving–but he didn't. Eldridge knew she could eject him from the Xiang tourney if she so chose, and he couldn't risk that. But considering how he had just rammed his boot down his throat, the redhead decided to risk an apology. He turned.

"Look, I'm sorry, OK?"

Ignoring him, she replaced her wig and turned to her computer. "I'll tell Hagan you'll be late. Your sentence is up in the morning. When do you want to meet him?"

Eldridge did the math. The jad delivered the notice about the pawn capture around 5:30 in the evening after he got into town. Knights had to give 12 hours notice, so the attack would come around 5:30 the next morning.

"Ask him to meet with me at five a.m. tomorrow. You think you can let me out before then?"

She nodded and started typing. Eldridge looked at her.

"Hey," he said. "*Everybody* knows a dreen who used to be someone."

Ink slopped onto her desk when she spun on him and said: "Yeah? Well, they *still count*. Now get your ass in jail."

• • • • •

LIKE THE REST OF the jailhouse, the jail cell had been built on great stone shelves that a long-ago earthquake had heaved out of the earth. The surface of one of the shelves made for a nice bed, and Eldridge stretched out for the night. Tola had already retired up to her room. Looking up to the top floor, Eldridge could see her shadows dancing on the walls as she rustled around, disrobed, and bedded down for the night. Faint squeaking sounds drifted down after a while. Moments later, scratchy music sounded above. Eldridge smiled.

"Still got that old thing?"

"You're being punished. Try to get some sleep."

Eldridge smiled. He knew that the constable kept a foot pedal at the end of her bed that she used to power an old music player. Years ago, when they lived together near one of the oceans, he remembered how proud she was to show off her collection of these weird old plastic disks that held music. That had been shortly after Eldridge parted ways with the Narsyans, and at the time, he thought that Tola was setting herself up for tragedy by collecting such rarities.

In the jail the night after he killed Stewart Caleb, Eldridge sighed, remembering another night years later when he and Tola cobbled together a sound system from spare parts they found in a landfill under a mountain. A town called Junktown had sprung up at the foot of the mountain where people could buy and trade spare parts. Eldridge and Tola found a few months of peace working in the landfill. They even built a junkshack with their favorite findings and lived in it for a while—a home with ancient tech on every wall and an empty screen in place of every window. They built a verandah on the flat top of the junkshack and piled high the old stereo speakers they found, all of them wired into a music player they found clutched in the arms of a petrified woman. Tola blasted the music over the redhead's objections. People still listened to live music after Deadblast, but Zora counted on the novelty of recorded music to attract hundreds of eyeballs to their little shack. Eldridge didn't approve.

"What's that fancy word for *stupid?*" he asked.

"Ostentatious?" she grinned back at him, her black hair down to her waist, her eyes undamaged by the terrormonger who would ambush her weeks later.

But no matter how loud she cranked the music, no one cared. No one even *complained.* A complaint or two would have kept her heart intact, but the dregs who haunted the mountain junktown wandered past their place like it was silent. Eldridge, back in those elder days when he wasn't such a charming, sensitive guy, got punched in the face when he squatted before her and asked the much younger Tola why her lower lip was trembling. Eldridge lost touch with Tola for a few years after Junktown—after the terrormonger incident—but every so often, they managed to find a hardline and send a quicktalk to one another. Tola kept him posted on her efforts to become a cop, and he lied to her about how well his life was going.

Relaxing on his bunk in the jailhouse, Eldridge closed his eyes and shook his head. More music wafted down from Tola's bedroom—twangy, high-energy stuff that they found out was called "blue grass." He heard a squeak and a scratch, and she switched disks. A low, playful series of notes pranced around the jail. A smile popped onto the redhead's face. He liked blue grass and classical music fine, but he preferred music with words. He liked to close his eyes and imagine the world where those words had first been sung. This particular song was about an incredibly old man. "Will you still need me, will you still feed me when I'm sixty-four," went the words. Sixty-four! What an age! Eldridge was pushing 40, which made him an old-timer. The oldest guy he knew was Yasim, who was almost 50. He had no idea how old Clovis was. The rumortrysts held that Odds like Jeb Goldmist lived well into their 50s, but to imagine someone, *anyone*, living into their 60s—incredible. And more than that, the words of the song made it sound like people would live *together* until they got that old. They'd even take care of each other. The thought brought out deep-true smile lines that the redhead didn't even know he had: a crease under his nose; twin flares of wrinkles under his ears; a dimple on one side of his chin. Thinking about the time before Deadblast frustrated him sometimes, but when he heard songs like "The Sixty-Four Song" (as he and Tola called it), he found himself trying to imagine how they got the music onto those disks. In his imagination, Eldridge saw a white-bearded fellow sitting next to a young woman who tooted on an elaborate hookah-looking musical instrument (that's what made the goofy-sounding notes at the beginning of the song). The white-bearded guy sang the words while the woman played the music. Meanwhile, a third man—a master craftsman and the role that Eldridge assigned to himself in these fanciful escapes—speed-whittled the song onto the black plastic disk. Only the finest speed-whittlers had the skill to record a song in realtime, of course. Other, less worthy artists would have to ask the musicians to play the song over and over. Not Eldridge. He would record it all in one go and play it back for the musicians right away.

And without even realizing he had closed his eyes, Eldridge fell asleep and had the weirdest dream. His cell only had one small window—a square of inch-thick glass that looked out on the surrounding desert. During the night, frost covered it, and it was that same frost that emerged as the chief image in his dream, which began with three *knocks.*

Knock, knock, knock.

Eldridge stirred, dimly surprised that he had allowed himself to sleep deeply enough to have a dream. Where had the knocks come from? Eldridge's brain chewed on a few numbers before he noticed something on the window: four faint smears. *Knuckle* smears. He rose and cupped his hands over his eyes, peering through the tiny opening, but because it was frosted on both sides, he couldn't see anything besides the knuckle smears.

Then the letters appeared.

He jerked back from the window, afraid that something was going to break it, but when no crash came, he leaned forward again and watched as a fingertip traced out three words. These three words caused Eldridge to press both of his hands against his forehead and take a few steps back from the window. He closed his eyes and shook his head. When he opened them again, the words were still there. *Nope, not a dream.* After a moment, he stepped over to the window again and re-read the words, which revealed a shocking truth.

Who would even know that? he thought. *Nobody. Nobody would know it.*

Except one man.

The redhead considered the clock. The attack from the unknown knight would come the following morning. His meeting with Hagan was set for the early dawn hours before the attack. So in that time, Eldridge had to round up rook-worthy firepower to fend off the attack—all while staying within the 100-mile radius of Dedrick to be eligible for the attack. Fortunately, the constable's jail was inside the Zone of 64, as Xiang aficionados called the gaming area. But in light of the three words Eldridge had just read, he found that he suddenly had a need to venture to the farthest reaches of the Zone.

He had to visit the Narsyans.

Eldridge banged on his bars. "*Zor! You gotta let me out of here!*"

• • • • •

"JUST RUN."

The constable was standing with a hand propped on a doorjamb in the jail's garage. The door led to a tunnel-tube that connected the jail and the garage. Eldridge straddled his bike and zipped himself into his cold-weather gear. After receiving the mysterious message, he had pleaded with Tola to let him out early so he could make an emergency trip before his battle the next morning. The constable reluctantly agreed.

The garage door stood closed, keeping the room safely sealed from the weather. In response to Tola's admonition to run, Eldridge shook his head.

"I can't run from this, Zor," he said.

"Make for another remnant. Someplace where Goldmist can't find you. If you're outside the Zone of Sixty-four when your move comes, you'll just forfeit the square."

"Yeah, and the money. The only chance I've got is to ride this thing out to the staledate. Win enough squares."

"What about the billion you laid down on the fourth? You think Kaleb's just going to forgive that debt?"

"Honey, it ain't Kaleb I'm worried about, and it ain't Goldmist I'm worried about."

"*Who?* Who is it? Who do you owe all this money to?"

He shook his head. "What does it matter? I owe the money, and if I don't deliver, me and my family are dead."

Tola shook her head. "What family? You have kids?"

Eldridge shrugged. "Something like that. They're out there, and I gotta do right by them."

"Them? How many do you have?"

"Enough."

"Then *find* them and take them someplace where this Odd can't find you."

"And where is this magical place?"

The temperature of Tola's eyes rose in concert with her frustration. "I don't fucking know. Penticton. Hemming. Port Stafford. Someplace by the coast. Maybe see if you can make a run across the ocean."

Eldridge laughed openly at that. The oceans had retained some of their pre-Deadblast majesty by virtue of their sheer size, but anyone who ventured more than a few miles offshore would find themselves enslaved by nonhuman marauders who lived in reverse-skyscraper-shanties—fathoms-deep hovels that floated on the surface and extended their crooked limbs to the ocean floor. There, under thousands of pounds of pressure-per-inch, the marauders learned to breath an O2-rich respiro-paste that they fed into their lungs with giant pumps they kept bolted to their chests. Cut off by the marauders, the remnants of this half of the world—Eldridge's half—could only speculate about what was happening on the other remaining landmasses. Rumortrysts, bright and shiny with hope, sprung up to sing songs about these far-off places where the weather made sense and where the Odds held no sway. But they were nothing more than *somnioms*—dreams that hovered on the horizon like a mirage and kept people like Eldridge running until they were dead and dry.

Tola scowled at him. "So I guess you're off to Yasim's to load up for your big fight tomorrow morning?"

"Later. I'm headed up to Burbage now."

Tola frowned. "You haven't been there since ... well, since you left. Is everything OK?"

"Is everything OK?" he said, harder and louder than he wanted to. "No, everything is not OK. *Nothing* is OK. But I have to go see Marko."

Despite her six and a half feet, Tola shrank. "I'm sorry. Why do you need to see Marko?"

Eldridge wrapped his two bandannas around his head and mouth, then pulled his goggles over his eyes. With shining black goggle-oculars, he said, "Because last night, someone told me I might have to kill him."

In a better world, Eldridge would have been able say those words, fire up his gas-powered bike, and roar out of the garage. But because he lived post-Deadblast and rode a hydrocell-powered bike, he had to wait an awkward minute while Tola opened her garage, and he powered up his bike. As the garage door rose, powerful fans blew a sheet of warm air across the opening to block the deadly subzero temperatures outside. Tola didn't say anything for that minute while the door rose. Instead, she waited until he was about to hum out into the desert on his all-but-silent motorbike before she spoke again:

"You're the dumbest motherfucker alive, El."

He couldn't deny it, so he rode out into the desert.

• • • • •

EVEN THOUGH HIS HYDROCELL denied him a grand exit from the jail, it had the added advantage of powering a separate cooling system that ran on Freon gel. During the day, that's what kept his jacket inflated with freezing air. Also, because the hydrocell's fuel was the most abundant element in the universe, it had limitless range. Only mechanical failure could stop it. That worked to the redhead's advantage on the long journeys he took between remnants. The notion of a home had little meaning to him, but around Dedrick he felt its strongest pull—partially because the town was home to old friends like Yasim and Hagan; partially because it was home to Oksana and Tola; but mostly because of the Narsyans.

To the north rose a range whose sky-profile Eldridge knew well—the Oasis Mountains. He had ascended its peaks hundreds of times and hunted suprafelines in its caves, all under the tutelage of the Narsyans and his mentor, Marko Marinus. Marinus had since ascended to the equivalent of the Narsyan throne, which wasn't so much a throne as it was a ceiling-suspended fuck-swing from which the Narsyan chieftain could impale as many of his acolytes as he could in between endless blurry bouts of powerlifting and extended megamarathons through the mountains and desert. Only the Narsyans lived without fear of the elements. By contrast, they embraced the wild fluctuations in temperature, sometimes sleeping during the middle stretches of the day and night so they could train in both the cold and the hot while the sun rose or set.

As he rode north on the highway through the desert toward the Oasis Mountains, Eldridge spotted old landmarks that took him back. He passed a charred patch of land that marked the turn-around point for his 50-mile sprints. A ruin marked the old home-base for a mobile training fortress that six Narsyan men and women would carry on their shoulders litter-style and deposit in the deep desert. The fortress contained hundreds of weightlifting implements—lead spheres, iron beams, steel bars—that the Narsyans would distribute across the blinding sand and lift until lactic acid shut down their bodies. But if they passed out in the desert, that didn't mean they got a free ride back to the Narsyan mountain lair. No, after everyone passed out, another team of Narsyans would megamarathon out to the lifting area and carry back the equipment. Everyone left behind would awake hours later, their skin simultaneously fried and freeze-dried from the hot and cold. Once awake, they had to forage for enough sustenance to fuel their return megamarathon back to the mountains, which they had to complete at a five-minute-per-mile pace or face expulsion from the order. Eldridge remembered wrestling one of his fellow Narsyans for the right to eat a prickly dried cactus. He lost that wrestling match, but still managed to make it back to the lair on a stomach so empty it was consuming itself.

He adjusted his course to the left—slightly northwest—where he knew the road up to the Narsyan village of Burbage awaited, along with the first of three checkpoints. Although he realized that they could have moved the checkpoints in the intervening years, he figured they had left the first one where he remembered—right behind a pair of 20-foot stone totems that vaulted over the roadway. Eldridge pulled up to the leading edge of the arcing moon-shadow cast by the totems and powered down his bike, his breath misting before him. He removed his goggles and bandanna.

Already shivering, he said, "*Citius.*"

Two pairs of legs pinwheeled into view from behind the rocks, their momentum carrying along two Narsyans—one female, one male. Both were covered in sweat, and both wore the bare minimum required for survival in the desert: thin bodysuits that kept their core temps within a 70- to 114-degree range for extended hitches on guard duty. Both guards had bodies that could have stood on a thousand pedestals of old, although neither of them could find work as trixies. Despite her Narsyan training, the woman's fundamental genetic profile kept her body in a perpetual pear shape, while the man had been doled a heavy brow and thin lips at birth. They also both bore the same vertical forehead scar that marked all Narsyans, but unlike Eldridge, their scars remained unblemished by the tiny, perfect circle that defaced the redhead's. Both of them stood several inches shorter than Eldridge, but the redhead knew they could both run 100 miles while maintaining a heart rate of 60 beats per minute. The reason why Eldridge had seen their legs emerge first from behind the rocks was because they had been doing air-pushups to stay warm.

Eldridge sized them up. His megamarathoning days were a decade distant, but he had kept up a level of training over the years that would break the average dreg. All the same, he figured he would lose a megamarathon to these two, but if it came down to a fight, he would win. *Most* people would win.

Thanks to the Inculta Wars. But more on that later.

Eldridge repeated, "*Citius.*"

They chanted in unison, "*Altius, Fortius.*"

The woman said, "You're Eldridge, aren't you?"

"Yeah."

The man said, "You left the order."

"That's right."

The woman: "What do you want?"

"I want to talk with Marko."

The man: "Why would Marko want to talk with a dreg like you?"

The woman: "You're dead to Marko unless you're *Alive.*"

Eldridge rolled his eyes at the unctuous swell that bore the capital-A *Alive* out of the woman's mouth. According to deep Narsyan mythmaking, only the order members were truly alive, hence the capital A. Those born outside the order were lower-case A *alive*–their bodily functions carried on, but they didn't really "count" in the Narsyan sense. Those who left the order dropped even lower in this imaginary caste system–and Eldridge could see the word for this caste taking shape on the man's nonexistent lips, which pressed together in anticipation of the letter M.

Eldridge cut him off: "*Macta.* Yeah, yeah, yeah–I know. I left the order, so I'm *macta.* You wanna personal apology? A hug? I'm giving away hugs, y'know. I'll hug anything. I'll hug a *wall.* Just escort me up to Burbage. Marko and I go way back."

They looked at each other. The woman nodded.

"He asked. We have to do it. I'll take him."

"I 'asked'?" Eldridge said. "What're you talking about?"

She looked over. "Marko said to bring you up if you ever came and asked. Even though you're *macta.*"

The man said, "Won't do you any good. He's gone."

"He doesn't need to know that," the woman said.

Eldridge asked, "Where'd he go?"

"It doesn't matter," the woman said, then turned to the man. "I'll take him up. You stay and stand."

"Very well," the man said and ran back up into the rocks.

"Wait, wait, wait," Eldridge said, thinking of the clock. "Where'd Marko go? If he's not up there, forget about it."

The woman said, "Marko said to bring you up if you came and asked. He didn't say to do it twice. You've got one visit. You want it or not?"

Freezing air blasted between the stone totems. Eldridge thought about turning around, but then he saw the woman smirking at him.

"What?" he said.

She adopted a mocking maternal tone: "Do you need a blankie?"

Eldridge realized he was rubbing his arms. He shook like he was straddling an angry faultline. Once again, the three mysterious words he had read the night before popped into his head. He dropped his arms and forced himself to stand still.

"Oh, *fuck off*. And take me to Marko."

The woman turned and crouched into a running stance. "Ready?"

Eldridge waved his hand. "Oh, that's OK. I'll ride up. You can run alongside."

"That's cute," she said. "I'll run *in front* of you and your *macta* toy."

• • • • •

SURE ENOUGH, SHE DID. As Eldridge's motorbike ascended the mountain, the Narsyan woman maintained a dead sprint all the way up a rocky dirt road that wound its way through gray and blue stone. As they passed an elevation marker that told them they were 1,000 feet above sea level, Eldridge started to sense the lower saturation of oxygen in the air, but the woman's pace didn't falter, not even when the road vanished into a dense cluster of jagged outcroppings and her legs disappeared up to her knees in the drifts of snow. As they passed through the second and third checkpoints, the redhead found himself the subject of a series of glowering-hard stares from Narsyans young and old. Eldridge's bike handled the terrain fine, though his engine actually increased in volume from a hum to a thrum as the pathway got steeper and steeper and the wind came whooshing harder and harder through the rocks.

Eldridge knew that dozens of Narsyans were waiting behind them to erase any trace of their path. He also found that he remembered more of the mountain than he thought he would. The woman seemed to be taking random turns around every crag, but Eldridge would have been able to find his way to Burbage alone. The trip took less than half an hour, which was fortunate. The moon—a jaundiced half-circle—had already risen, and Eldridge figured he had less than half an hour before he would have to turn around and race back across the desert to make it to his meeting with Hagan in time.

The sudden appearance of a person on the trail interrupted his thoughts—and saved his life. A hunched figure, female, clutched a blanket around her shoulders and caused Eldridge to veer to the left, but as he made the course-correction, his tires dislodged a 10-square-foot patch of snow that fell *into* the mountain itself. The redhead laid down his bike and jogged to a stop.

"*Damn,*" he muttered to himself. He had completely forgotten about what the Narsyans called the Callis Oubliette—a deep cavern whose entrance yawned in the middle of the primary path, right in between two giant stones. Once he found his footing, the redhead looked over at the stranger. She was naked below her blanket.

And even though they had never met, he knew the score.

"You all right?" he asked.

Over the sound of the wind, he heard sobbing. The sobs sounded female. Eldridge looked up the mountain and saw that the female guard had stopped and was looking back at him. The wind kicked her hair into a succession of wild manes. Her face twisted around the words she screeched over the wind.

"Don't talk to that!"

The sobbing woman's shoulders flinched and fell even lower than before. Eldridge opened one of the saddlebags that hung off his bike and pulled out an extra pair of hiking boots. He hopped through snow drifts down the path until he got in front of the sobbing woman. She stopped. Eldridge held up the boots.

"The left one's got a hole in the sole, but they ought to help."

The woman bore all the marks: Pronounced cheekbones. Zero body fat. When she gripped her blanket, muscles bulged from her forearms. And down the center of her forehead ran the tell-tale vertical scar. But at the midpoint of the scar, Eldridge saw a circle of bone, and he knew that not an hour earlier, one of the Narsyan chieftain-prosecutors had taken a needle and used it to dig out a circular cross section of skin that left a centimeter-wide patch of cranium exposed. Eldridge remembered how the sound of needle scraping bone had echoed in his own head so many years ago.

The woman looked up and wiped tear-crystals from her cheeks. Blood had frozen in a circle around the hole in her forehead. But she wasn't shivering. Not yet.

"I wasn't strong enough," she whispered.

Eldridge lifted the bandanna that covered his forehead.

"Me, neither."

She looked at his scar, long since healed over—and started crying harder.

He said, "Hey, I'm sorry. I didn't mean to—"

Up ahead, the guard yelled, *"Leave that or I leave you here!"*

"Why don't you shut your *face?!*" Eldridge yelled just as the sobbing woman pushed him out of the way and jumped into the Callis Oubliette. The redhead made a try at catching her. He didn't even get her blanket. She was all gone. He stood by the edge of the pit and looked into it. Then he put his hand on his forehead.

The clock, the clock. Coming up here had been a mistake.

But he couldn't stop thinking of those three words someone had written on his prison window. If true, those three words meant that the longstanding grudge between him and Marko Marinus had come to a head at an undetermined point in the past. The words also meant he might have a few more people to kill before he was through. They were insane, the ramifications of those three words—but it all made sense in the redhead's mind. He climbed back onto his bike and powered it up. The guard gave him a nasty smile.

"You two make a cute couple."

"You look like you've put on weight. It suits you."

She sneered and sprinted on up the mountain. Eldridge followed her underneath a stone wall that leaned over the path at a 45-degree angle. Moments later, the wall fell away, and the village of Burbage jumped into view along with a 180-degree panorama of the desert below. The Narsyan lair comprised a few score steel buildings that perched on the edge of the cliff, all of them forming a giant staircase up the mountainside that shone in the amber moonlight. Although the Narsyan buildings composed most of the village, a small, symbiotic cottage community had sprung up in the hills above the lair to provide the Narsyans with the millions of calories of food they wolfed down every day. As he rode up to the largest of the Narsyan buildings, known as the Fulcrum, Eldridge spotted a few of the swarthy cottagefolk who hid among the rocks above the Narsyans and slaved over cauldrons of protein-rich slop day after day. A woman wrapped in rawhide slid behind a rock and peeked over it. She hooked her thumbs and waggled her fingers at him—a gesture Eldridge remembered as an unthinkable vulgarity among the cottagefolk, who hated the Narsyans with a mania that reduced them to howling banshees whenever they saw a member of the order, which was every day. The cottagefolk had also elevated poison-brewing to a high artform, and they spent most of their waking hours huddled in chattering circles around beakers and bowls of toxins deadly enough at the parts-per-million level to wipe out entire cities. They synthesized these toxins into delectable spices and broths that rendered the poisons undetectable. Over the years, the typical cottagefolk recipe came to be made up *entirely* of poison. All of this sat well with the Narsyans, naturally, whose training included the fortification of the body against foreign agents. A Narsyan raised from birth typically had a constitution stout enough to subsist entirely on ground glass and oil slick for a month. Pregnant members of the order injected old automotive antifreeze and other sundry abortifacients into their uteri—"Just to toughen the kids up before birth."

Years earlier, when the Narsyans discovered an infant Eldridge mewling in a garbage bag on their front doorstep, they instilled him with his earliest (and among his most vivid) memories by feeding him pear sauce laced with scorpion venom. Looking back on that memory, which crackled like a distant bonfire in the recesses of his mind, Eldridge remembered how the venom tinged his sight with dancing red spots. The memory also stood out because it was the first time he saw the aquiline nose and sunken chin of his old friend, Marko Marinus. Marko was only two at the time, but his skin had already shrunk around his muscles, and his vasculature already stood out across his body—a vein along his temple, a river-delta of vessels across his chest. The Narsyan leadership tasked the youngest members of the order to care for infants during those harrowing first years, which were all the more challenging for Eldridge because he wasn't born to the order. He didn't have the advantage of being able to emerge from the womb with nine months of pretraining to his name. He had to play catch-up from that first taste of venom, and Marko held him the entire time.

Eldridge dismounted his bike and rolled it to the side of the Fulcrum, which rose from the snow like a pile of bones held aloft with mirrors. Thin columns of white stone formed the building's superstructure, while stainless steel walls made up the rest. Eldridge caught his reflection in the buff-shined steel wall. Moonlight cast him in shadow and filled his eye sockets with a black ink that seeped into his crowsfeet.

He looked away.

As he rounded the corner of the building, he saw more cottagefolk waggling their fingers at him, and farther up the mountain, he saw a pack of Narsyans—all of them wearing the same minimal bodysuit as the two guards—sprinting up an 80-degree incline on the mountainside. The female guard was waiting in front of the Fulcrum, which looked blank at first glance, but when the light hit the surface, it brought a six-foot-by-three-foot square—the front door—into relief. Eldridge could already hear the racket inside. The woman placed a hand on his shoulder.

"Do you need to rest up before we—"

"Shut up now," Eldridge said with a smile. "Just open the door."

Eldridge let the woman open the door because he honestly wasn't sure if he could still do it. The door was a foot-thick slab of solid steel set into the earth on a lead hinge. Every Narsyan trained for months to open the door—a technique that called for incredible hand strength, as well as the agility to properly flick the door and jump out of the way before getting crushed between it and the building. The female guard executed the move as she had hundreds of times before. Eldridge jumped out of the way and found himself knocked back into the snow, though it wasn't the door that knocked him over.

It was the Narsyans.

Blinding light erupted from the doorway in an unstoppable rectangular polyhedron piledriver. Sounds followed, all of them blended together into a noise as white as the light. Eldridge picked himself up and saw that the woman was already throwing herself at one of her fellow Narsyans—a male in this case. Sexual orientation had lost a lot of its meaning since Deadblast, and among the Narsyans, the idea of preferring one gender over the other would sound as hostile and foreign to them as the concept of naps. The female guard gave the man—a towering, hairless hulk—the standard Narsyan greeting: a skull-cracking headbutt that was the origin of the vertical forehead scar that distinguished all members of the order. Headbutt complete, the woman drove her shoulder into the anonymous male Narsyan and slammed his back against a wall, which was covered with 200-pound blocks of stone and steel. As the enormous man spun her around and thrust into her, dozens of other Narsyans sprinted from one station to the next, all of them deadlifting or snatching or power-cleaning or free-squatting or pull-upping one weight after another. A 500-pound weight rocketed across the room on a straight line. Eldridge reverse-traced its trajectory and saw a kid not older than 10 standing bent over with his flattened palm extended before him—the final pose of an expert shot-put. Across the room, a girl about the same age plucked the weight out of the air like a feather and heaved it onto a holding shelf on the steel wall behind her.

Absolutely everyone was lifting, fucking and screaming.

The shot-putting boy emitted a *yawp* in honor of his prowess. The female guard howled as her huge Narsyan partner powerfucked her from behind. The ceiling was aswarm with order members whose tensile strength was so strong that they could cling to a sheer surface using only their fingertips. They performed upside-down push-up pull-ups, all of them screaming. Down a hallway, a chocolate-skinned woman clean-and-jerked a half-ton cement cylinder with enough force that it slammed into the ceiling. She caught it on its way down and slung it at the head of a toddling Narsyan infant, who wasn't strong enough to catch the beam yet, but the little fucker jumped on top of it and kick-rolled it back to the woman, squealing all the way.

Meanwhile, the dinner bell sounded. Or rather, the Narsyan equivalent of the dinner bell: An ear-killing klaxon rendered the room eerily silent for five seconds. Of course, the room wasn't actually silent; the klaxon was so loud that it flash-deafened everyone inside. Eldridge couldn't see outside the building, but he knew that the klaxon had probably caused an unexpected treat for the Narsyans training on the mountainside—an avalanche.

The female guard apparently decided that her powerfuck session was complete, so she gripped the elbows of the huge man, propped her feet on his quadriceps and propelled herself into the air. Skyborne, she tucked into a ball, rolled, and ripped off a few backhandsprings on her way over to Eldridge, where she whipped upright before him, misted with sweat, her eyes agog.

"Do you miss it?" she asked.

He cocked an eyebrow and said, "Who wouldn't?"

"Follow me," she said, then spun and broke into a sprint. Eldridge followed suit and chased her through the main hall, all while everyone else stopped what they were doing and packed in alongside Eldridge and the female guard. They all crowded into a narrow passageway. Narsyan children scrambled onto the shoulders of adults and danced along the jumping human surf down the hallway into the mess hall, which was already packed with livid cottagefolk, all of them howling and brandishing ladles full of steaming toxic swill. As Eldridge followed the guard through the mess hall, cottagefolk cackled with glee in anticipation of the mass murder they thought they were perpetrating. One Narsyan child inhaled a bowl of the black sludge and attracted the attention of a half dozen cottagefolk. They all leered at the child, confident they had finally discovered a poison strong enough to fell a member of this illustrious order. But the kid shattered the bowl against the table and screamed for more. Furious (but not cowed), the cottagefolk shook their fists at the kid and continued to serve.

Another passage forked off from the mess hall. The guard took it, and Eldridge followed close behind. Steel walls melted into stone as they passed into the inner sanctum of the Narsyans. Eldridge knew the place well from his waning days with the order years ago. The guard looped around a corner and brought another door into view—this one a wood slab lined with wrought iron. The woman yanked on a heavy iron ring to open it and admitted the redhead into the epicenter of all things Narsyan.

The room was a rectangle about 45 feet across and 30 feet wide. Curving around the periphery of the space was an elliptical stone pathway. Eldridge stood at one end of the ellipse, which rose on a gentle slope toward the far side of the room before looping back down to the doorway. A second door, crafted from steel, stood at the top of the pathway, directly opposite the redhead.

About 30 feet across the room, within the ellipse, a glass tube descended from the ceiling and terminated into the floor. The tube divided the room into proportions that equaled the fabled golden ratio, the redhead knew. He also knew that had the room been a diagram of the solar system, the tube would mark the position of the system's star.

Hence why Narsyans called it the room's "solar-center."

Icons filled the room, all of them arranged on the sloped surface of the rising ellipse. Eldridge remembered them well from his last days.

When they drummed him out.

The icons included prosthetic legs, eyeglasses, and steel walkers. But strange implements Eldridge *didn't* recognize were also included. Tiny blades glinted at him from the wall, all of them hung in ascending order of size. Yellowing old pictures of pre-Deadblast people hung from the walls, their faces divided up with dotted black lines like meat for a butcher. Eldridge didn't know what most of these things were, but he knew that the Narsyan chieftains surrounded themselves with what they hated.

"Maintain the rage," they always said.

But one icon stood out: A giant needle glittered at the end of a plastic tube that fed into a rolling white plastic pedestal that housed a clear plastic reservoir tank. Dried blood encrusted the tip of the needle, which Eldridge knew from experience was a tiny circle. For a moment, Eldridge felt himself pulled back to the last time he stood in this chamber. It had been years ago, the day he was drummed out of the order. Chief among his prosecutors had been one of his old friends, Marko Marinus, who at the time had already ascended into the upper echelons of the Narsyan hierarchy, leaving his redheaded friend behind. Marinus himself had cast the vote that expelled the redhead, and it was Marinus himself who had used that bloody needle to dig a divot out of his forehead and forever mark him as a failed member of the order. The long walk down the mountain followed—called the Circle Walk for the scar imprinted on all washouts.

"A circle has no solar-center," went the Narsyan adage, part of a life-philosophy that exalted ellipses as the most hallowed of shapes.

But Eldridge hadn't been alone that night. No, another of his old friends had joined him on the lonely trudge through 15-foot drifts of snow.

A friend who *wasn't* a Narsyan.

Eldridge's mind returned to the present. He was still staring at the glass chamber, and once again, he thought of those three words he had read on the window of his jail cell the night before. The elder members of the order used to regale initiates with tales of this glass chamber and how it held one of the order's Great Challenges. The life of a Narsyan was one of constant attrition. Dozens, scores, and often hundreds of initiates made the Circle Walk every week, but those who hung in with the order for enough time earned the right to stand in that glass chamber for as long as they dared. Simply standing in it for a moment was triumph enough, but only those who could stand in it for longer than an hour could join the council of Narsyan chieftains. Marko Marinus had stood in it for a day. That achievement helped make sense of the three words Eldridge had read the night before.

He turned to the guard.

"So where is he?"

"I told you he might not be here."

"So where is everyone else? The rest of the brass? They around?"

The guard's eyes narrowed at Eldridge's use of the word "brass" in reference to the council of chieftains, who weren't actually called a council. Eldridge had come to call them that himself, but the Narsyans abhorred the idea of hierarchy or centralized leadership. The chieftains, so the story went, made no decisions; they merely divined the order's life-mission from the ebbs and flows of the universe.

Or some such bullshit.

"So?" Eldridge asked.

Clank. The steel door opened. Heat and steam surged from the steel door and warmed Eldridge's face. A face from the redhead's past emerged. It wasn't Marko Marinus, but another of the Narsyan chieftains. He stood about the same height as the redhead and dried his sweat-glistening skin with a black towel. Rubbery red scar tissue coiled around his right leg and spread a lightning bolt across his chest—a burn wound from his pre-Narsyan days. Like many Narsyans, he buzzed his hair short and carved intricate designs into what remained. The man took note of Eldridge and walked down the sloping ellipse toward him. Naked, he stopped and looked down at the redhead.

The man said, "You can leave, Sipho."

The guard, Sipho, nodded and left. The man stared at Eldridge and sucked his teeth in thought. His fingers traced a course along the dark downward V of his groin muscles. Eldridge's eyelids fluttered in psychosomatic fear that the man was about to piss in his face, but instead of urinating, the man continued to towel himself.

"A few years ago, Marko Marinus gave a standing order," the man said. "He said that you could and should be admitted into these halls if you called at our first checkpoint in the foothills. What do you think of that?"

"I don't think anything about it, Pell. Where's Marko?"

The man, Pelagius "Pell" Yannick, ignored him and continued: "I actually didn't object. You're not the first *macta* to walk these halls. Some of us have family beyond here. Some of us *build* families here, and not everyone born to this life is meant for this life. I don't begrudge Marinus for asking that of us."

Eldridge felt the tension of time tighten around his chest. If he left right away, he might make it to his meeting with Hagan. But he exhaled and settled in to listen to the rest of Pell's spiel:

"However, Marinus asked one thing more of us. He asked that if you so requested, we should allow you to rejoin the order. What do you think of that?"

Eldridge frowned. Marko wanted him *back in* the order? He couldn't make sense of it, so he stalled and asked, "What do *you* think of it?"

"Oh, I thought it an outrage most heinous, and I challenged him to single combat and was defeated and disgraced—disgraced, of course, because he allowed me to live. Marinus let a lot of us live the day he gave you a second chance to be a Narsyan."

"That's great. So where is he?"

"He retired to the apex-peak of the mountain to undergo one of our Great Challenges."

Eldridge's eyebrows hopped. "The conventuary? Really?"

Pell nodded.

"Huh. How long's he been up there?"

"Many months."

Eldridge frowned. Had Clovis Wine been full of shit? "When's he due back?"

"We don't expect him back anytime soon."

"Let me put a question to you: Besides those orders he gave about me a few years back, has Marko said anything else about me?"

Pell stared at him. "Can you be more specific?"

Eldridge thought of those three words again. "Oh, I dunno. Has my name come up?"

Pell scratched his genitals and gave his balls a pull. "Marinus mentions your name from time to time. You and he were friends in years past, as we've heard over and over and over and over. Shall I recount one of your exploits, or do you have an actual question you'd like to ask?"

Time. The clock. Eldridge had another question—one he wanted to ask straight out—but he was out of time. Plus, if he asked the question, then he ran the risk that Pell would tip off Marko that Eldridge was onto him. The redhead mumbled his thanks and hustled his way through the Fulcrum and out to his bike, which he powered up and rode down the mountain as fast as he dared. As he rode, he thought about solar scales.

When he was a kid and training with the Narsyans, their teachers used to give them boxes of objects to balance—but they weren't allowed to use a standard two-sided scale. Instead, they used a solar scale, which had 11 scales—a sturdy prime number. The 11 scales flared out from a central stand, each of them teetering on a support of a different length. Seen from above, a solar scale looked like an ellipse. In order to balance the 11 random objects on the scale, Narsyan youths had to bound from one side of the scale to another, objects in hand. A skillful youth could drop all 11 objects in their proper places almost simultaneously.

It was the one thing Eldridge did well.

But when he considered the objects that composed his current predicament, none of them balanced. Clovis Wine told him that he had made odds with Marko Marinus. But no Narsyan ever made odds with anyone. On top of that, Marko had gone up to the Narsyan conventuary—a temple-retreat carved out of the very peak of the mountain, and Pell just told him that he had been up there for months. The hatred between Pell and Eldridge went back years, but the redhead didn't think he was lying. That left three more objects to balance.

The first object was Marko's standing order to re-admit Eldridge to the Narsyan order. Given the age and depth of the grudge between them, the contrite nature of that gesture didn't balance when placed alongside the second object, which was the glass chamber that sat at the solar-center of the Narsyan icon room. Known as the Typhoid Maiden, the chamber held enough contagions to wipe out every last remnant on this side of the oceans. Narsyans worked to master their bodies—*all* of their bodies. They started with the easy systems: muscular, cardiovascular, and skeletal. But as a Narsyan initiate moved higher in the order, they worked to master their involuntary systems as well, and that included their immune systems. Those who wanted to join the council of chieftains had to brave the Maiden. It was one of the Great Challenges. Those who conquered the Maiden not only joined the council, but they also emerged with immune systems powerful enough to thwart any illness in history.

A drop of blood from a Narsyan chieftain could cure anyone. Of anything.

And that explained the final object, which was actually three objects; three words that an unknown, shaking finger had scrawled on his prison window; three words that described the scope of Marinus' treachery against Eldridge:

MARINUS CURED YOU.

• • • • •

TOLA WAS RIGHT, ELDRIDGE thought to himself as he raced across the desert to meet with his friend Boris Hagan and get a look at his balls—his "balls" of course being the full lineup for the Xiang tournament. Eldridge and Hagan had settled on the codeword years ago when the redhead first stood in for that liar Clovis Wine, who had gotten himself in over his arid head as a Xiang rook. Speaking of which, by his current clock, Eldridge *was almost certainly* going to be late for his meeting with Hagan. The clock read 3:00 a.m., and even a hard run from Burbage to Dedrick usually took about two hours. Stars streaked by overhead as he pushed his bike harder and harder down the highway and through the night-frozen desert. As 4:00 a.m. came and went, he again thought to himself, *Tola was right. I am the dumbest motherfucker alive.* Dumb to have risked a trip out to Burbage in the first place, and even dumber to have gone all the way up the mountain when those two guards *told him that Marko wasn't there.*

As the clock spun around toward 5:00 a.m., Eldridge's chest felt heavier and heavier as he breathed harder and harder. What was his plan? Walk into the Narsyan headquarters and kill their leader in cold blood? Had he actually expected to kill Marko and get out of the Fulcrum alive?

Nope. You didn't.

And he didn't. In the moments before Pell Yannick walked into the icon room and told him his old friend had ventured to the top of the mountain to undergo one of the order's greatest Great Challenges, the redhead had been ready to kill—even though an attempt on Marko's life—successful or not—would result in his own death. And Eldridge knew what that meant. A death sentence for his family.

But back to the idea of balance. When Yannick told him that Marko had been at the mountaintop conventuary for "many months," Eldridge took that information and figured that Clovis Wine had been lying when he said he made odds with the Narsyan leader—but now he wasn't so sure. Eldridge knew all too well in what low regard the Narsyans held oddsmaking, but how else could Marko have found out about his deathday wager? How else could Marko have delivered his almighty *fuck you* from afar unless he knew that Eldridge absolutely *had* to die on that upcoming July 4? Eldridge thought of the last words he had exchanged with Marko before he began his Circle Walk down the mountain, and an array of feelings beset him—chest-deflating regret over that last exchange; grief that his former friend had harbored a grudge against him for so long; and hard-hot rage that his friend had chosen to endanger both him and his family.

A quarter after 4:00 a.m., and he was still motoring across the star-blue desert, trailing a wake of sand as he rapidly approached a horizon over which ghostly mesas hulked. The more he thought about it, the angrier he got. Marko *knew* he had family, because he was the only one Eldridge had told—a part of a foolhardy effort to make amends a couple of years earlier. Those days, unless you were an Odd, having a family was an insurmountable challenge, but dumbass Eldridge had managed to knock up the first girl he laid within weeks of his dismissal from Burbage—an impressive feat for a 15-year-old. He kept close track of the kid over the years, and he thought Marko might like to hear he had managed to father a child. The redhead didn't dare make the trip up to the Fulcrum, so he sent him a hardline, which he knew would eventually be delivered to him by one of the Narsyan mercurials—order members who ventured into the remnants. It took months, but Eldridge finally heard back from Marko via a written message hand-delivered from a mercurial who looked at him like—well, like he was a *macta*. Which he was. The message was doubly insulting:

"I trust your son is as big a cunt as his father."

The night before, when Eldridge read the three words written on his prison window, he had a hard time imagining that Marko would endanger the life of an innocent just to get back at him, but when he thought of that message, the idea didn't seem so outlandish.

He checked the clock: 4:30 a.m. Eldridge considered bypassing his meeting and heading straight down to Yasim's to arm himself for his 5:30 a.m. Xiang battle, but he decided that it was more important to get a look at the Xiang lineup, despite the risk he was taking with his polycharge. Five years earlier—the last time he had competed in a tournament—his polycharge had glowed red through his neck when Hagan had shown him the lineup for *that* game, but it didn't explode.

About half a mile before he reached the ramp down to under-Dedrick, Eldridge turned off the road, heading south toward his and Hagan's usual meeting place: a small gully that slashed into the desert earth. He steered his bike down the gully and slalomed around boulder after boulder on his way down to their pre-arranged meeting spot. He and Hagan had always held their secret meetings at the end of this gully, and when he reached the spot, his clock read 4:58. He had made it.

But Boris Hagan hadn't. The gully was empty.

Part Three

THEORETICAL NOVELTY

BORIS HAGAN HAD NEVER missed a chance to show Eldridge his balls.

Over the years, the two friends had set many such secret meetings out in the desert, and never once had his sandy-haired friend missed one. His friend's absence filled him with dread, but he had the clock to worry about. It read 5:15. His battle was due to begin at 5:30, and he was about 15 minutes away from Dedrick and all his weaponry.

Eldridge propped a pivot foot on the ground, spun his bike around and gunned it out of the gully, his mind working overtime to consider a plan of action if he should get attacked before he could get back to under-Dedrick.

Knight takes Rook.

In his last Xiang tournament, the one where he subbed for Clovis, Eldridge had successfully defended against an attack from a knight. In that case, the player he took out was a ponytailed-and-musclebound northerner named Kamara Masego. For Eldridge, anything north of

Burbage and the Oasis Mountains qualified as "the north," and any dregs he met from the north invariably reminded him of a Narsyan, even though they claimed that life was easier up there.

"It's always daytime," she supposedly said, though Eldridge never heard it firsthand. Boris Hagan told him that she also claimed that there was a temperate area near the planet's pole—a small strip of land with normal temperatures that encircled the globe. She apparently even told Hagan she lived outside, under the stars and sky. It sounded like a fairy tale, but then a lot of things did after Deadblast. Nevertheless, as a Xiang knight, Masego had distinguished herself with her ingenuity. She constructed her own flying machine—a single gliding wing that she had retrofitted with a pair of booster jets.

But back to the redhead's present troubles. As it stood, he was motoring west toward the ramp down into under-Dedrick, and the clock on his fuel tank told him he had two minutes until the attack.

Stupid, stupid, stupid. You just had *to go all the way up to Burbage, didn't you?*

Whether he did or not, it didn't matter because the sun was rising on his first day back in a Xiang tournament. The redhead attached his cooling tubes to his jacket and activated his Freon system. Superchilled air filled his jacket as the sun erupted over the horizon. The clock continued its inexorable march toward 5:30 a.m., and the only weapons he had on himself were his twin scatterguns and whatever rounds he had left in his saddlebags. His strategy—whether to make a run for Yasim's or just stand and fight—would depend on whether his opponent was flying or not. All of this would have been so much simpler, Eldridge knew, if he had just stayed in Dedrick until now. A battle against a flying assailant would be much easier to manage among the hectic streets and jagged skyline of under-Dedrick.

At 5:30 a shadow passed across the sun.

Eldridge's internal sensors kicked in alongside his instincts. He wheeled his bike off the road and immediately started drawing Z's in the sand with his path. His attacker had obviously built a flying machine, and he had already made his first blunder by casting a shadow across El's line of sight. Four years earlier, when he fought Kamara Masego, he had been trapped outside in the daytime as well, and he knew that for whoever was pursuing him up above, the desert sand looked like a giant mirror; high ground wasn't always an advantage.

But missiles were.

The first one struck a few dozen yards to his right and scooped up a block of earth that surged into the air on a sphere of flame. Eldridge course-corrected around the explosion and aimed his bike at under-Dedrick, not even daring to look in the sky; he wanted all of his senses trained on his immediate surroundings, lest an ill-timed skyward glance cause him to drive over a sinkhole or into a cactus.

Unfortunately, his opponent had a vested interest in keeping him topside, so he tracked Eldridge all the way back to the ramp into under-Dedrick—and showered it with missile-blasts. The redhead made five attempts to run down the ramp, even going so far as to consider a long-distance jump into the lowest part of the ramp, but a missile landed next to him and blew him off his bike. He hit the ground while his unattached cooling tubes whipped back and forth, spraying chilled gas everywhere. He finally ventured a look up.

"Who the hell is *up* there?!" he muttered as he blocked the sun with his hand and peered through his goggles into the sky. He saw nothing but the standard whiteout haze that anyone saw when they looked at the daytime sky, but after his vision adjusted, he spotted a nimble-looking dark spot in the air. It looked like an insect at first—it changed direction with incredible agility—but when it turned back Eldridge's way, he got a better picture of his opponent.

The flying machine looked like a robotic bird. His opponent sat in an open-air seat in the middle of the craft, which sported a wingspan of about 20 feet. Missile launchers were mounted over the pilot's chair. Eldridge didn't get a good look at the pilot himself, but he appeared to be wearing full-body armor of some kind, including an old-timey motorcycle helmet. From a console between his legs, the pilot controlled the craft's wings, which fluttered in every direction—along all three axes—and afforded the pilot total control over his roll, pitch, and yaw. Someone inside Eldridge's memorybanks held up an old chestnut from Boris Hagan:

"It's called an ornithopter, El. I read about 'em in a pre-Deadblast novel that took place in a very post-Deadblast world. They're flying machines that act like birds."

Whatever it was, some serious engineering had gone into it because in an instant, it altered course and dive-bombed the redhead, strafing him with machine-gun fire. Bullets dug pockmarks in the sand like hundreds of footfalls dancing around the redhead's bike. He covered his head and hoped to Crom that his hydrocell would escape this volley unharmed. It did. The aircraft passed overhead and launched into a soaring loop, firing a pair of missiles along the way. They arced through the sky, trailing smoke. Eldridge deactivated the Freon system and stowed his cooling tubes as he mounted his bike and rode down the ramp toward the revolving door into under-Dedrick.

His senses didn't even accept the input that the revolving door had been stopped until he was about to drive into it at 70 mph. Some deep-seated survival instinct kicked in and forced him to squeeze the brakes on his bike, but he still laid it out and skidded on his side into the halted door. He jumped to his feet and pounded on the blank wall.

"Hey! Hey! Get this thing going! Come on!"

Rocks rained down on him as a nearby blast halved his hearing and sent him staggering away from the revolving door. His opponent sliced through the air overhead along the same parallel as the ramp—and gave Eldridge a clear look at the underside of his wings. Bold red letters scrolled by:

THE LARRY MERCURY MACHINE.

Entirely on reflex, Eldridge curled his thumb over his two middle fingers and extended his index and pinkie fingers. He raised his impromptu devil's horns at the sky and yelled, *"Larryyyyyyy! Whoooo!"*

Some background: The last time Eldridge had seen Larry Mercury in the flesh or otherwise, the redhead had been standing between his friends Boris Hagan and Stewart Kaleb, his arms hooked around their necks, the three of them having indulged themselves into a hallucinatory stupor—"My hand has transformed into solid booger!" Hagan yelled at one point—and rocking out to the stylings of the Larry Mercury Machine, the hottest rock band in the southwestern desert.

The Machine had brought its might to the streets of under-Dedrick at the command of Jeb Goldmist himself, who demanded that the power-trio lay out their licks at the foot of his tower.

So now Mercury was trying to kill him. Eldridge yanked his devil's horns out of the air, righted his bike and maxed out the accelerator, reattaching his cooling tubes and reactivating the Freon system. He knew under-Dedrick was a no-go, so he had to try plan B. Luckily, the redhead had already rehearsed his backup plan four years earlier when Masego ambushed him in the open desert. He rode his bike back up the ramp, then turned right and headed west down the road. A few miles later, another road appeared—this one leading north and west. Eldridge took it. His destination lay a few clicks in that direction. He just had to evade his favorite rock star's attacks until then.

Maybe I can get his autograph before I kill him.

Blinding desert landscape rolled by as the redhead pushed his bike faster and up the road. To the west, the horizon stretched into nothingness. He knew another ocean waited out west. After all, his last trip to the coast had yielded the mountain of debt that currently engulfed him. In any case, after a quarter-hour's worth of zigzagging through the sand, Eldridge pulled a hard right up into rockier terrain, where his trump cards awaited: The first was a rock quarry. The second was a cave.

Years earlier, when he had to evade Masego, he rode out to the quarry—a 500-foot-wide hole that sank about 1,000 feet into the ground. An access road coiled around the inside of the quarry, and Eldridge rode his damn bike all the way down that spiral until he reached the bottom, where a cave awaited.

That's when the rules of Xiang suddenly switched to his advantage.

Once a Xiang battle began, so did the clock. The competitors' polycharges—the explosives embedded in their neck that tacitly enforced the game's rules—were also equipped to keep time, and the clock always favored the piece playing defense, because once an attack began, the guy on offense had two hours to make the kill. After 120 minutes, their polycharge would detonate and award the square to the opposing player. Four years earlier, Eldridge hid in that cave and waited. Once Masego exhausted her ammunition, she was forced to climb down to the bottom of the quarry and fight the redhead one-on-one. He prevailed that time, but he didn't relish the idea of taking out one of his idols. Another thought occurred to him—one that had to do with Stewart—but he suppressed it and rode ahead, cruising over rocky terrain and toward the quarry, which appeared a few hundred yards ahead, its interior walls glistening in the omnipresent sunlight.

Oh, shit.

Glistening. Quarry walls shouldn't *glisten*. He rode his bike up to the edge of the quarry. The top of the spiral access road lay just to his right. He peered over the edge of the gigantic hole, and when he saw what was inside, his chin sank into the collar of his jacket.

Water broke against the inside of the quarry's circular wall. Somehow in the last four years, thousands of gallons of water had flowed into this quarry. *Flowed*, Eldridge knew, because there was no way *any* amount of water could sit under the desert sun and not evaporate. The redhead checked the sky and saw Mercury's flying machine approaching from the east. He considered making another run to the north—toward the Oasis Mountains—but he dismissed the idea, yanked the cooling tubes out of his jacket, and jumped off his bike.

Heat enshrouded him instantly. He pulled off his jacket and boots, then fumbled with his belt as the distant reports of Mercury's advance strafing-fire grew closer and closer. He shimmied out of his pants, his body already covered in sweat, and paused next to his bike.

As Mercury's aircraft approached, Eldridge closed his eyes and cast his thoughts back to one of his final days as a member of the Order of the Narsyan. The order had many challenges for its initiates to undertake, and before his expulsion from Burbage, the redhead had attempted—and accomplished—the 30-Minute Whoop, so named for the giant *whoop* of breath that the order members took before holding their breath for half an hour, which was the bare minimum required to remain a member. (Elder chieftains could hold their breath for days, but that's another matter.) Eldridge kept up his training over the years, but he hadn't tried holding his breath for any more than a few minutes.

Plus, there was the matter of *assumptions*.

The redhead was *assuming* that the cave at the bottom of the quarry—which he had never fully explored—would lead to a chamber with air. He was also assuming that his body could withstand the pressure of a 1,000-foot dive. Was there a record for deepest dive by a human? If the oceans weren't clogged with marauders, the Narsyans might have given it a shot. Failing that, it might as well be a disgraced Narsyan to make the attempt.

Gunfire started to rain down on the rocks close behind him.

"All right, Marko," he said. "This is gonna suck."

In one motion, the redhead squatted ass-to-ankles, wrapped his arms around his motorbike and sprang out into the quarry, the bike in his arms. The water-level lay about 30 feet below, and as he fell, he inhaled an almighty *whoop* of air into his lungs, taking in oxygen until the instant he hit the water, whereupon he clenched his eyes and mouth shut and expelled a precious burst of air to keep water from rushing into his nose. The first 50 feet of water retained the heat of the sun and burned his eyes and skin, but soon after that, he passed a threshold into cold. He figured the water temp was in the 60s—not freezing, but cold enough to be plenty deadly. The weight of his bike carried him deeper and deeper. Somewhere above him, he sensed a dim flash of light and felt a rumble-shockwave pass through the water. A few errant rocks shot past him, undoubtedly dislodged by one of Mercury's missile blasts. He felt another rumble, but by that point, he had descended to a depth whose darkness and silence rivaled that of a sensory-deprivation chamber. His thoughts sounded loud inside his head:

Do I even remember where *this cave is?*

That realization spurred his hand to action. Taking care to maintain a strong grip on his bike with his left arm, Eldridge slid his other hand along the fuel tank and up onto the handlebars, where he clicked on his headlamp. He saw purple as the bluish halogen lamplight shone through his eyelids and gave him a close-up view of their vasculature. Just then, a chill rushed through his form as he passed into a deeper—and colder—layer of water. He figured he was currently submerged in near-freezing fluid, and when he tried opening his eyes, he had to snap them shut against the searing cold. But in that instant, the redhead could see that his bike's headlamp was losing its fight to illuminate the depths of the quarry—he saw only a hazy sphere of light that sparkled with floating bits of dust and dirt. He couldn't even see the wall.

So he called on his memory to remind him of where his salvation lay.

He knew that when he parked his bike at the top of the quarry, the access road lay immediately to his right. Casting his thoughts backward, he remembered that the entrance to the cave was located directly across from the top of the access road, so if he dove straight across the diameter of the quarry, he should find the cave. But when he dove in, he hadn't considered any of that. Had he spun around as he sank through the water? What if he got to the bottom of the quarry and couldn't find his bearings?

Such considerations vanished from his mind as the weight of thousands of gallons of water started to crush him. He initially felt it around his ribcage, naturally, as the water pressure sought to compress the largest empty cavity in his body. Bubbles spurted out of his nose and seeped out of the corners of his mouth. He clenched his teeth and pressed his lips together. His Narsyan training was staving off the effects of oxygen deprivation for the time being, but if he couldn't hold in the majority of the breath he originally took, he was screwed. That said, he took a chance and started kicking his feet. Thinking back over his fall through the water, he hadn't *felt* like he had been spinning. Plus the bike's weight should have acted as a kind of ballast, helping him maintain roughly the same attitude as he dove.

Whatever. He kept kicking his feet. The pressure continued to build.

Other memories and packets of knowledge started to emerge from the depths of his mind. Boris Hagan's brain had the biggest store of trivia that Eldridge knew, but Constable Tola was pretty smart, too. She used to read any and every book that she and the redhead uncovered in Junktown. Once Eldridge lost track of her among the endless dunes and mountains of trash. He ran from outpost to outpost and described her to everyone he saw, holding up a flat palm to mark her height. When he eventually found her, she was reading a book about these guys called *scooba* divers. It said that the deeper these divers went, the more problems they faced. What symptoms should he expect to feel?

In so deep he's got the bends.

That was it. She had said it earlier. On the ride out to the jail. But what were the *bends?* And was that a problem for divers or something else? At that moment, the redhead's face imploded.

Or *felt* like it—it felt like someone was closing a vise around the bridge of his nose while his brain simultaneously swelled from within. *Where the hell was the floor of this quarry?* A bright agony flared in his eyes so suddenly that he lost the grip on his bike and found himself flailing in the deep dark, his joints aching, his chest crushed, his brain on fire.

The whole thing was a *mactatrox.* At least that's what Stewart Kaleb would have called it. The guy was an expert on *mactatroxes*, for better or worse, and he shared his vast experience with troxes both good and *macta* with Eldridge and Boris Hagan during their more formative years. For Eldridge, the escape that the troxes of the world provided was too much of a temptation in the aftermath of the terrormonger incident, when he parted ways with Zora Tola. After that near tragedy, Eldridge arrived back in Dedrick with a long face and a blank gaze fixed on a distant point in a strange galaxy. Hagan introduced him to Stew Kaleb, who spent most of his time skulking in the back of Fiachra's and getting blacklisted by trixies.

And Eldridge and Hagan loved him.

The kid took after his dad, and although he was far less insane and much better-looking than the Odd, as a member of the Kaleb clan, he would always have to contend with hanging jowls. Stew's were already hanging and jiggling before he turned 20, and he also shared the same black tongue as his father—"A side-effect of tasting one too many infected honey-pots," he said with a cackle one night at Fiachra's—and most important, he was never without some kind of exotic trox.

The night of the Larry Mercury Machine concert, Eldridge, Hagan, and Stew convened in the back of Fiachra's. Stew showed up late, naturally, while Eldridge passed the time fussing over a trixie named Oksana, and Hagan propped up his feet and puffed on a pipe. The old man was wearing his usual brown sweater, green vest, and silver-rimmed glasses. As always, he had neatly trimmed his graying beard and hair to the same close-cropped length.

Finally, the smoke of Fiachra's expelled the striding form of Stew Kaleb, who was wearing his usual: one of Hagan's pre-Deadblast T-shirts ("SOUTH CAROLINA GAMECOCKS"), shorts, and steel-tipped, thigh-high boots that Hagan had helped him enhance with extra pockets, hilts, and straps. Stew kept all kinds of goodies and gadgets in what Hagan called his "utility boots."

Stewart straddled a chair and laid out three small syringes on the table. Two were filled with iridescent liquid, the other empty.

A nimbus of blue flame glowed around his eyes.

"It's time to pre-party. The Machine demands it."

Eldridge picked up one of the syringes. "What *is* this stuff? What's up with your eyes?"

"It's called tyke. It's from a remnant across the oceans."

"Bullshit," Eldridge said.

"Do it, believe it," Stew said as he drew little patterns in the neverending smoke of Fiachra's. "I'm already on it. You put it in your spinal fluid."

Hagan took his pipe out of his mouth. "Of *course* you do."

"Behold." Stew whipped his leg over his chair and spun around to give the other two a view of the back of his neck, where a small plastic stopper plugged an opening. He turned back around. "Had it installed last week. I asked the doc, but he wouldn't do it, so I went out in the desert."

Hagan sat forward, touching his gray temples with his fingertips. "One of the deep-desert sawbones? Stew, are you insane? You know what those guys do, don't you?" Hagan pointed up—and they all knew what he was pointing at: catwalk city, home of the psychoskags.

Everyone knew to stay away from catwalk city, as it was thronging with psychoskags and the occasional half dreen, all of which clambered around the catwalk in a constant swirling loop. None of them really knew what a psychoskag looked like. The rumortrysts held that most psychoskags had attempted to replace their heads with computers—a process that mostly worked. The "deep-desert sawbones" that Hagan mentioned supposedly helped the psychoskags accomplish this feat. These physicians lived a hundred clicks from the nearest outpost and specialized in forbidden sciences that involved buzzsaws, soldering irons and buckets of leftover connective tissue.

In response to Hagan's question, Stew gave a dismissive wave. "I had protection."

Eldridge frowned. "You had 'protection'? For a run into the deep desert? *Who?*"

Stew popped the stopper out of his neck and picked up one of the full syringes of tyke. "You can squirt this stuff in your eyes, too, ya know. It's not as good a hit, but it'll do for tonight."

Hagan sat forward. "Stew, who provided the transpo?"

Crius Kaleb's son squeezed a few drops of tyke into his spinal fluid. The blue nimbus around his eyes flared for an instant, then settled into a brighter glow than before.

He leaned back and squeezed his eyes shut in ecstasy. His eyeballs shone purple through his eyelids. Finally, he leaned forward and answered. "Goldmist."

Eldridge and Hagan: "*Goldmist?*"

Stewart said, "Well, he didn't escort me out there *personally*, but he loaned me a few oddments for the trip."

Hagan: "Stew. You *have* to know he was up to something. Your dad's an Odd."

Eldridge was already nodding. "And your pop's been racking up more jenta lately. A lot more."

Stew's lower eyelids quivered. Eldridge couldn't tell if they were quivering in pleasure or annoyance.

Stew: "So?"

"So Goldmist had a reason for helping you out. Later on, you won't know when, but he'll cash in that chip."

Looking back at that night from the depths of the quarry, Eldridge knew that Goldmist had no intention of currying any favors when he helped out Stew Kaleb.

But five years earlier, on the eve of the Larry Mercury Machine concert, Eldridge picked up one of the syringes full of tyke and shook it. A liquid rainbow swam around inside it. An image flashed before his eyes: Zora Tola waving goodbye as he rode his motorbike out of Junktown, leaving behind a woman who was no longer a girl. He squeezed a few drops into his eyes, which immediately started to glow blue from within, but not with the same strength as Stew's. Hagan disapproved of trox in general, but he watched the redhead's troxing with interest.

"So?" Hagan asked.

For the redhead, the tyke's effects were twofold. First, the hit delivered a pleasure payload that tracked a course through his nervous system and detonated near his prostate. Second, his perception of the room shifted. His friends vanished. Fiachra's vanished. Everyone vanished; everyone except Stewart, that is. In his troxing vision-state, the redhead perceived Stewart standing in the middle of a strange desert next to an old internal-combustor. And he was missing an eye. Where his eye had once been, a bloody-empty socket remained. And they weren't alone. Oksana sat in the car. A tall man Eldridge had never seen was next to her. He had bluish skin and sunken cheeks like two bowls of shadow-soup under his blue eyes. The tall man held up a small module that bore a single button. He pressed it.

Eldridge vanished.

Back in Fiachra's, the redhead sucked a harsh breath, as if waking from an unpleasant dream. The vision faded, but a ghostly outline of it remained, overlaying the redhead's vision. As the vision faded, the pleasure increased. Eldridge smiled.

"You gotta try this, Bor."

Hagan cocked an eyebrow and stroked his beard.

"Is it safe?"

Stewart: "Absolutely not."

"Bring it on."

The redhead hit his head. His mind returned to his present predicament. He was still swimming in the frozen blackness of the bottom of the flooded quarry, but he caught a break. His efforts to swim across the diameter of the quarry had led him to the entrance of the cave. He dared to open his eyes an instant and spotted the distant glow of his bike's headlamp a few yards to the right of the cave entrance. A sudden downthrust of water pressure squeezed his chest and forced a spurt of bubbles out of his mouth. *What the hell was that?* No matter; he started swimming the length of the cave, his limbs numb from the cold and from what he knew were his body's efforts to consolidate its heat around his vital organs. Narsyans knew all about hypothermia.

He swam, once again calling on his Narsyan training to combat another sensation that beset anyone who wasn't capital-A *Alive* under these kinds of circumstances. For most people, a situation like being trapped under 1,000 feet of freezing water and pursued by a killer would cause time to dilate, but any Narsyan youth knew that such a distortion of the senses could hasten the arrival of death. As always, Narsyans taught their initiates how to subvert this phenomenon with *balance.* The words of Marko Marinus sounded in his ear:

"Under duress, your mind will do everything it can to look back in time. It will want to look back to a time when you weren't under such duress, when your muscles weren't screaming with the pain of a 100-mile sprint. We Narsyans call that 'the Time Before.' Don't be tempted to think about the Time Before. Cast your mind forward, and your efforts will help balance the passage of time."

Swimming through the inky ice, Eldridge looked ahead a few moments in time, when he would find a chamber with air. The chamber would lie a few meters ahead, where he would discover a secondary passage that took a 90-degree turn straight up. Eldridge saw himself swimming up that vertical passage toward a glimmer of light, and when he reached it, his head would break above the surface of the water in an onrush of sound—mostly the howl of wind blowing into the passage through a snaking crevice in the earth. Light seeped in through this crevice, as well, giving the redhead a moment's reprieve before the effects of hypothermia started to overcome his body's defenses.

And it all came to pass.

Moments later, the redhead was dog-paddling at the top of the small vertical tunnel, his world suddenly five feet wide and eight inches high. Eldridge spread his legs and used his feet to wedge himself into place at the top of the tunnel, where he forced himself to take normal, measured breaths. Again, the words of Marko Marinus sounded in his mind:

"Don't hyperventilate. Saturating your blood with oxygen will only make you lightheaded and increase the chances of a blackout."

So the redhead breathed, his limbs like lead, his genitals having contracted as far as they could. He hugged himself, and as his body finally started shivering, the past once again exerted its pull on his mind and placed him at the foot of Jeb Goldmist's tower, his arms wrapped around two of his best friends. The crowd was growing restless before the empty stage. All three of them were in the midst of a tyke-fueled trox, their eyes a sextet of glowing blue pinpricks among the vast crowd, which packed the streets of under-Dedrick. Light towers had been erected all over town—some of them alarmingly close to the walls, and by association, catwalk city—while Goldmist had ordered a C-shaped stage built around the foot of his tower. An extension thrust from the center of the C out into the cheering crowd. Every light source in under-Dedrick had been extinguished in anticipation of the concert.

And that made the redhead think about Tola.

While he waited for Larry Mercury and his Machine to take the stage, Eldridge remembered the future constable's grief over Junktown's indifference to her record player, and he almost bolted. He almost left his friends at the concert alone, the sudden onset of guilt too much for him to process.

"No one listens to recorded music anymore," he once tried to explain to her.

And no one did. Besides a select few like Tola and Eldridge, no one even understood what it was for. The dregs of the post-Deadblast world only understood jenta, blood, and spectacle.

Luckily for Eldridge, Larry Mercury took the stage before he could abandon his friends—lucky, because if the redhead hadn't seen the Machine in concert, he and Boris Hagan would have never befriended the psychoskags.

It had his leg.

"Fuck." Eldridge's body tried to shout, but all he could produce was a strangled whisper in the tiny chamber that sat at the top of the

flooded tunnel at the bottom of the quarry. Somehow, the rest of his body still had strength, and he kicked something that had bumped into his leg. The meager light from aboveground flickered along the water and brought into focus the outline of a human form. And even while freezing his ass off, Eldridge could see that the person below him was floating face-down.

A moment later, the body of Larry Mercury himself bobbed to surface of the water and flipped backward, bringing the redhead face-to-face with the frostbite-blue visage of his rock idol. The redhead's eyebrows made a steeple. He touched Mercury's face. It was already cold. He sighed.

"Damn. You really gave it a shot."

The last time Eldridge had been so close to Mercury was five years earlier when the post-Deadblast world's first rock legend finally took the stage. A single spotlight cut through the darkness and landed on the frontman, who stood, microphone in hand, before all of Dedrick, as well as thousands of dregs who had trekked across the desert. He wore white slacks and a white vest. As always, his clean-shaven head glittered in the lights. He stood glaring at the cheering crowd until an airborne virus of silence made a geometric progression across the audience. When the only sound was the hum of the lights and the thrum of the circulation fans high above, Mercury spoke.

"I am about to commit mass murder."

A few dregs laughed. He hissed into the mike:

"*Shut the fuck up.* Attention, scumbags of whereverthefuck: I and the Machine are about to fill this city with rock so fantastically stupendous that you're all going to shit blood for a week. There is absolutely no difference between witnessing our rock and diving headlong into a wood chipper. *None.* No difference. You are all about to die. I suggest that *everyone* leave the city now. Commence evac. Now. *Now!*"

This went on for about half an hour. Alone onstage, Mercury implored everyone to leave, and when finally no one budged, he shook his head in disgust.

"You fucking monsters. *One, two, three!*"

Thousands of lights flared across the city and blasted the stage with an onslaught of rainbow shades while Mercury and his bandmates thrashed their way through their set, and once again, Eldridge felt the pangs of guilt. He only called it a "set" because Tola had told him that rock bands used to play "sets," or a succession of single, discrete songs. No more. Now everyone from the Machine to Klara Kira simply roared their way through a single, improvisatory song-blob that had no discernible beginning or end. They just rocked. Every so often, Mercury would yargle something into the microphone—"*Satan, Satan, tits, Satannnn!*"—but after an hour of it, Eldridge had forgotten about Tola and was simply enjoying his friends' company. Or at least he was enjoying it until the *mactatrox* hit.

Over the course of the evening, the tyke had been pinging his brain's pleasure center, but one hour into the Mercury concert, a new vision besieged him: In rapid progression, the redhead watched Dedrick fall to pieces before his eyes. Every building melted, every support strut and joist vanished, catwalk city disintegrated, the brick ceiling above fell away and let loose a torrent of earth that filled the city—and trapped Eldridge inside, buried alive.

Darkness, silence.

The tyke had already disabled his brain's capacity to quell panic, so the redhead's first course of action was to flail as hard as he could. His first round of flailing saw him cup his hands behind his friends' heads and crack their skulls together. The music drowned out their yelps, and the redhead kept convulsing, his arms and legs striking everyone around them. Other concertgoers started to throw punches back, and Hagan belted a denim-and-corduroy-clad dreg in the mouth.

Shaking out his hand, Hagan yelled, "What's happening to him?!"

Smiling, Stew started to answer, but the denim-and-corduroy guy tackled Hagan and sparked a brawl in the middle of the concert floor.

From the stage, Mercury heaped praise on the participants: "Dudes! You dudes fighting down there! Make sure you kill each other!"

His eyes still fire-glowing with blue light, Stewart brought one of his steel-toed utility-boots up into the groin of the denim/corduroy dreg. That done, he elbowed another screeching dreg in the nose, then leaned down and hooked his elbows under the wailing redhead's shoulders.

"We gotta get him out of here!" he screamed at Hagan, who was fending off another attacker with his fists. He skipped around on the balls of his feet and fired powerful jabs into the dreg's face, causing his nose to blossom red. Stew rolled his glowing eyes and yelled, "Quit fucking around, Hages!"

Onstage, Mercury sang: *"Bloody vagina farts!"*

Hagan dipped his hips and launched his fist into a driving, crushing arc that started below his waist and ended above his head. Midway through the arcing motion, a hapless dreg's face got in the way. The dreg hit the ground. Hagan called the punch an "upper-cut." Hagan turned to his friend.

"I'm ready to leave now."

They each took a shoulder and hustled Eldridge through the crowd, leaving behind a perfectly respectable mini-riot. While they carried the redhead, he continued to yowl and buck and struggle in their grasp. The crowd packed the streets for block after block, but eventually, they turned down an alleyway that was empty. They forced the redhead to sit down and pinned his arms against his sides while his legs continued to kick.

Mercury, onstage: *"Mighty stupendor!"*

"Thanks for the great trox, Stew," Hagan said with asperity, but the Odd's son couldn't stop giggling.

"This happens sometimes, Hages. You know that. It's a just a *mactatrox.* Macta, macta, macta."

"Shut up! We need to get him over to Dr. Enki's—see if he can, if he can—"

"What? Give him a full blood transfusion? An eyeball transplant? He just needs to ride it out. He'll be fine, I promise—"

Although Eldridge hadn't been maintaining the same level of Narsyan training over the years, his strength trebled that of his two friends. In a sudden bunching of pectorals, he slung them both into the crumbling stucco walls across the alleyway and took off at a dead sprint back toward the concert. Hagan and Stew rubbed their heads, looked at each other and gave chase.

Mercury, onstage: *"Skullfuck-kablooie!"*

The redhead weaved through the crowd, tracing a rough L through the jumping mass of people. Their eyes still glowing, Hagan and Stew shoved their way through the uncooperative audience, striving to keep Eldridge's red hair in sight.

"There he is!" Hagan yelled as he jabbed his finger at one of the steel towers that had been erected for the concert. The redhead scrambled up it, then leapt from one tower to another, then another, then another, and within moments, Hagan could see that he was about to leap right into–

"Catwalk city!"

That alarmed even Stew, who forearm-shoved a few dregs out of his way and followed Hagan through the crowd while Larry Mercury and his Machine continued to shell Dedrick with rock. They fought their way through wave after wave of headbangers and chest-bumpers while Mercury's bassist launched into one of his trademark, hour-long solos. A platform rose from the stage on an ascending column and lifted the bassist into the air above the crowd, where he finger-mashed his guitar under a hundred multicolored spotlights. While the bassist played, Mercury dropped to his knees and began a 10-minute yell of the word "fuck."

"Fuuuuuuuuuuuuuuuu–!"

Meanwhile, Eldridge mounted the top of the easternmost lighting tower, which stood a mere 50 feet from some of catwalk city's lowest platforms. Rusty steel ladders and moss dangled from the suspended walkways, while the flat faces of a few score psychoskags reflected the light of the concert. To the horror of his friends, Eldridge made the flying leap across the divide–and a dozen psychoskag faces turned his way.

Hagan and Stew reached the easternmost lighting tower and started climbing. Hagan ventured a look up toward the lower edge of catwalk city, where Eldridge was tangled in a mass of vines and moss.

"Hurry up!" Hagan yelled.

Moments later, they reached the top of the flashing tower. Mercury continued to bellow nonsense at the foot of Goldmist's fortress, while thousands of dregs boogied in the streets below. Eldridge's screams floated over the havoc of the concert.

Hagan and Stew paused. Their chests heaved from the exertion, while the blue glow in their eyes faded completely.

"How the hell're we gonna get over there?" Stew asked.

But Hagan was already kneeling. He unstrapped a small, shining device from Stew's utility boots and stood. The device looked like a silver jenta stylus that had a long wire cable wrapped around its tip. Hagan stood, pointed the device at the catwalks, and pressed a small button on its side. It flashed and launched the wire across the 50 feet of open space, where it attached itself to the catwalk platform immediately above the redhead. Hagan bent over and affixed the stylus part of the device to one of the lighting tower's struts.

"I've had that this whole time?" Stew asked.

Hagan shrugged. "Magnets and science, in action. OK, watch what I do."

Boris Hagan sat down and lowered himself out onto the magnetized cable, where he hung out over one of Dedrick's side streets, which thronged with Machine fans. He called back to Stew: "Come on!"

Stew gawked at the cable and shook his head.

"No way!"

"He needs us, Stew! Get your ass out here!"

Stewart kneeled and stood, kneeled and stood. "I can't. I don't want to make an urbit out of my dad."

"If you don't help him, your dad might as well *be* an urbit!"

Stew backed away from the edge of the tower. "I'm sorry."

Hagan glowered at him, then turned his attention to following through on his admittedly stupid plan. He traversed the cable, hand-over-hand, each swing prompting the cable to make a stomach-churning bounce. His heart skipped a few beats, but minutes later, he hooked his leg over one of the steel struts and lifted himself into catwalk city—just in time to meet his first psychoskags face-to-face.

They all looked like someone had chopped up a half-dozen dregs and stacked random cross sections on top of each other until they assembled a full human form, their flesh a zebra pattern of varying tones and textures that piled up to a head that was a head in name only.

And the rumortrysts had been right about the heads—they had all attempted to replace them with computer monitors, but the operative word was *attempted.* Some of them had full monitors in place of their heads, while others had only been able to encase their human heads *inside* of an old monitor. Light reflected off a nearby steel roof and flashed across the grotesques that hid inside—faces stripped of skin and covered with boils that dripped abscess. All of them resided in a nether-zone between human and machine, their bodies interlinked with crisscrossing wires and conduits, while their mismatched stacks of flesh bled constantly.

Five of them crouched on the catwalks above, staring down at Hagan and a catatonic Eldridge, who was foaming at the mouth and bleeding from his eyes. Boris Hagan pulled his attention from the redhead and looked up at the largest of the psychoskags facing him. An ancient flatscreen monitor was wedged behind his collarbones.

Nobody moved for a moment. Then, clamor:

Someone crashed onto the platform next to Eldridge and Hagan, knocking the bearded man to the catwalk. The psychoskags vaulted up a few levels in response to the racket. Hagan looked up to see Stewart Kaleb standing over him, but he didn't look quite like Stewart. Every vein on his body stood out in pulsing relief, while his muscle mass had somehow doubled. He stood, feet spread, fists clenched at his sides, and roared:

"Stay away from them."

Clicks and *whirrs* sounded all around them. The psychoskags descended, and they brought reinforcements. Dozens of shining monitor-faces surrounded them, while a few others crawled out on the naked brick below using strange hand- and foot-claws to hold onto the wall. The flatscreen psychoskag dropped onto their platform and approached them. Words scrolled across his blank face:

HIS BODY BELONGS TO US

WE TOLD YOU TO STAY OUT

Stewart: *"You'll have to go through both of us."*

Again, the psychoskag said:

YOU TWO GO

HIS PARTS OURS

Stewart: "*Never!*"

But then Hagan broke in: "What if I could offer you something better?"

A pause, then the psychoskag said:

LISTENING

And as Eldridge later heard, the psychoskags *did* listen to Hagan's offer—which they accepted—but years later, when he was floating in freezing water next to the corpse of Larry Mercury, he had to dispense with the looking backward and focus on how to get out of that cave. With his feet still wedged in place on the walls, he peered down through the water, which faded into darkness below him.

Hm. If Dr. Enki doesn't have to amputate my dick after this, I might just use this cave for all my Xiang battles.

And that's when he got flushed down the toilet.

The water level dropped out from under him with such sudden speed that both he and the late Mr. Mercury remained suspended in mid-air for an instant before they fell down the vertical shaft. Ice-cold water enveloped the redhead, as did the sensory blast of thousands of gallons of rushing fluid, all of which carried him back down to the main tunnel and deeper underground, where the original cave took a few hard rights and lefts before it opened out onto a blinding blaze of light. An instant later, the redhead shot out of a giant pipe over the red-hot desert on a cascade of near-freezing water. Mercury's corpse followed close behind, as did the redhead's bike.

Eldridge rolled to a stop against a sand dune. Still shivering, he just lay there for a moment and savored the sun's rays. He knew that in seconds, his body would start to cook in the 160-degree heat. He struggled to his feet and hobbled over to his bike on shaking legs. He activated the bike's hydrocell and rode over next to the body of the fallen Larry Mercury. He had landed on his back, the force of the water's blast having buried half of his form already. A south-blowing wind was carrying more sand their way and quickly concealing the rocker's body for all time. Dressed only in his soaking wet underwear, Eldridge saluted him.

"I'm sorry it came to this, man."

The redhead spun his bike around and looked at the huge, steel pipe that had just spat him out of the quarry. The pipe sat inside a 1,000-foot wall, the other side of which was the quarry. The gush of water had slowed to a mere flow of fluid. He shook his head. He knew he didn't have time to dawdle, but he scanned the surrounding area. There was nothing but desert. No crops, no animals—nothing that would require this much water. Someone had filled the quarry with water only to dump it out onto barren wasteland.

Two pains hit him: His sinuses exploded again, and the sun's heat penetrated the top of his skull and singed his brain. He hit the accelerator and began the long ride around the enormous wall.

• • • • •

THE REDHEAD STARTED THE short trip back to Dedrick—even though he had no idea how he would get back *into* the city if the revolving door was still stopped.

Well, he knew of *one* other way back in, but he didn't relish the idea of taking it.

He could ride the Old Mine.

Unbeknownst to everyone but Eldridge, the ancient roadside attraction actually served as a back door into Dedrick, and if anyone was willing to brave an entire underground maze full of dreens, they could use it. It worked like this:

Under-Dedrick sat hundreds of feet underground. In fact, it was so far underground that a hundred feet of earth lay between the under-Dedrick ceiling and the aboveground surface. Meanwhile, the Old Mine itself was located a few clicks to the northeast, but the track for its ride snaked through the underground all the way down to Dedrick, where it passed directly through the layer of earth that sat on top of under-Dedrick.

The trick, of course, was *getting to* that section of the track, seeing as how from the perspective of your average denizen of under-Dedrick, the only way to get to it was through the ceiling, which was inaccessible—both because it was hundreds of feet in the air, and because the only possible route to it would be through catwalk city.

Eldridge had a way. That was another of his secrets. But more on that later.

About 15 minutes later, he rode down the long ramp into Dedrick. Naturally, the stupid revolving door was working again, and he motored out of the boiling sun and into the cooler confines of his hometown. Once he was safely sequestered from the elements, his mind came alive and started trying to make connections. The question remained: *Who cured me?* And for Eldridge that question had several *possible* answers but only two *likely* answers. In the "possible" category were the likes of Constable Tola, Boris Hagan, and Oksana—all people who cared about him and might not want to see him croak. By contrast, Clovis Wine hated his guts and would delight in Eldridge losing his deathday wager. But none of them were *likely* to have cured him because of the advanced stage of his cancer. They just didn't have the medical know-how. When he first diagnosed Eldridge, Dr. Enki had told him it was terminal, inoperable, and incurable.

But that automatically put the doctor into the "likely" category with Marko Marinus, because only those two had the *means* to make his cancer go away.

And Marko was the only one who had both the means and the long-deep hatred of Eldridge to *want* to make it happen. That made him the prime suspect.

That said, why had Boris Hagan stood him up this morning? Was he afraid to face the redhead after betraying him? Eldridge knew that Hagan's lifelong dream was to become a big-time Odd. Was fucking over Eldridge part of his plan?

Eldridge knew that once a Xiang battle was complete, the results would take a while to get reported. Each competitor's polycharge also monitored their vital signs, and whenever the vitals for a player flatlined, tournament reps tracked down the dead body and reported the results, which would be relayed to the general public at Nix's. Eldridge wanted to get a look at how the game was playing out so far, but he was more concerned about getting his fingers, toes, and junk checked out, so he headed toward Goldmist's tower and Dr. Enki's.

He also had some questions for the good doctor.

On his way up Sinister Street, he passed the spinning neon sign of Nix's, where he heard hundreds of cheering dregs, no doubt obsessed with the latest Xiang results. Eldridge also saw some good, old fashioned Xiang mayhem on his way to over to the doc's:

As he rode around a traffic circle, an old-school big-rig truck came smashing through the diameter of said circle. The competitor behind the wheel had outfitted the front of the truck with a giant, triangular plow. Hagan had shown the redhead a picture of an ancient steam-powered train that bore these plows.

"They were called cow-catchers, for some reason," Hagan said.

The cow-catching truck was most likely a rook on the attack, Eldridge figured. A mohawked woman sat behind the wheel of the truck, her earlobes stretched around three-inch, black decorative disks. She screamed through black lips as she rammed her truck into another building, which expelled a gaggle of scattering dregs as its walls caved in.

But one of the dregs—a wiry brunette wearing camouflage—climbed up the cow-catcher, both of his hands full of a rusty ancient broadsword that was as tall as he was. Standing on the hood of the truck, he raised the sword—just as the mohawked driver pulled a gun.

Eldridge closed his eyes in anticipation. He knew what was coming.

The moment the woman leveled her gun at her target, the side of her neck glowed red from within—and exploded. The polycharge expelled her severed head through the truck's windshield. It bounced off her target's chest and rolled down the street. The victorious pawn stood panting for a moment. Then he dropped his sword and sat on the still-steaming hood of the truck, holding his face in his hands. The redhead rode by, knowing that a lot of dregs were about to lose a shitload of jenta because a pawn had just successfully fended off an attack from a rook. In addition, the rook had been mortally penalized for trying to use a gun—rooks were only allowed to use ground vehicles, ballistics, and explosives—and he knew that all kinds of side bets were placed around who might try to cheat in a Xiang tournament.

Eldridge touched the bump in his neck that marked the location of the polycharge. It felt warm. He wondered if they had improved the technology in the last five years. Would sneaking a glance at the lineup "count" as cheating in the "exploding neck" sense of the word?

He rounded the traffic circle and merged back onto Sinister. He heard (and felt) the *thud* of other explosions around town. As he approached Goldmist's tower, more and more black-clad oddments filled the streets. As before, one of them stopped the redhead, but he explained his intentions and rode up to Dr. Enki's office, where he parked his bike and walked right in.

The office was empty.

The redhead's first thought was that the doctor was in trouble. After all, the legless physician hardly ever left his office, and he always traveled *with* someone, typically in their arms. The doc wasn't a coward, but as he was nothing but torso, head, and arms; he wasn't terribly mobile. Eldridge scanned his office and found everything in order, as far as he knew. All of his old anatomy and medical textbooks were on their respective shelves, and all of his equipment was in place. The only thing *out* of place was the strange photo on the wall by the door—the cauliflower-jabbed-on-the-end-of-a-ladder image—which was crooked.

Eldridge straightened the photo. As long as he had known the doctor, he had this picture, and from their first meeting, the doctor had treated the unusual image like a riddle. The redhead remembered that first encounter. He had gone to visit the doctor to see if he could remove the scar on his forehead. The doctor responded with instant dubiety.

"Explain why you want to change your appearance."

The redhead tried to explain that the scar reminded him of a rotten time from his past, but that only made the doctor more cantankerous.

"That's exactly the reason why you shouldn't change it. A fixation on the past, as well as an unhealthy attitude about your appearance—even a small aspect of it—are both avenues to becoming a dreen. It's why I tend to decline all cosmetic work."

That's when Eldridge noticed the weird photo. He asked what it was, and instead of telling him, Dr. Enki made him a deal.

"If you can guess what it is, I'll remove the scar."

Eldridge had never been able to figure out what it was, but in the interim, his desire to remove the scar had abated, although not faded entirely. He touched it with his fingertips, then had a thought. He crossed the room to the doctor's hardlined computer and brought up a window that let him check his own hardlined messages.

He had one. From Boris Hagan. It read:

```
Sorry missed you.

Meet tomorrow 0500.

The game's afoot.
```

• • • • •

The game's afoot.

That meant trouble.

Eldridge and Hagan had more goofy codes than a pair of brain-spliced identicals. As he rode his bike southwest through town—away from Dr. Enki's (and Goldmist's tower) and toward Yasim's—the redhead considered what those three words might mean. He hadn't ruled out the possibility that Hagan had betrayed him, but the more he thought about it, the less likely it seemed.

And right at that moment, the White Queen decided to make her second appearance in the tournament.

The redhead had just swung his bike around a curve when a small hut exploded from the inside, revealing the enormous, callus-armored White Queen. Debris from the exploding hut knocked Eldridge off his bike. He nearly got run over by a passing internal-combustor that chugged along, but he rolled out of the way and watched while the White Queen surveyed the scene. Eldridge looked at the remains of the tiny hut.

How the hell did she fit into *that?*

She was still armed with her gigantic blade and miscellaneous bazookas, but she was also cradling something in her arms. Against her hugeness, it looked about the size of a baby and was wrapped in black sheets. When she moved, her layers of callus-armor scraped together with the gravelly wet sound of a hit-and-run victim being crushed under the wheel of a giant truck.

She spotted Eldridge.

The redhead froze. His jad hadn't printed out notice of a move, so there was no way the Queen was about to attack, but nevertheless, she kept *looking* at him for a full few moments. And then she sprang away. She leaped in the direction of Goldmist's tower. Did she have business over there? No matter–Eldridge had to get to Yasim's. He climbed back onto his bike and immediately stumbled off of it as his neck caught fire and his jad started spitting out new instructions from Xiang high command.

`Black Rook captures White Pawn`

The jad printout also listed a series of coordinates that indicated where his target could be. It looked like whoever this white pawn was, he or she was hanging out topside–in the desert. Fine by him. He'd get periodic coordinate updates via jad transmission until the attack, and as an offensive player, his clock broke down like this:

He had 24 hours to deliver notice of his move to his target (also via jad-trans).

Once he delivered notice, as a rook, he had to give his target 30 minutes to prep.

Once the battle started, he had two hours to make the kill.

But for now, he had 24 hours to sufficiently arm himself to take out a mere pawn.

"Piece of pie," as Boris Hagan would say.

With that in mind, he felt the need to retain Oksana's services again. Once again, the redhead climbed onto his bike and rode through town against a backdrop of random explosions until he reached the rickety plywood ramp that led up to the roof of Claude's. He parked his bike and somersaulted through Claude's window. Once inside, he saw that someone had blown a hole through one of Claude's walls. A family huddled on the other side of the hole, the whites of their eyes shining in the dim light. Eldridge shouted a greeting to Claude, then made his way into Yasim's.

Which was no more.

To be sure, the *room* was still there, as was Yasim himself, but a crater sat in the center of the room where his illustrious hyperglobe had once spun. Dozens of Yasim's underlings worked to clean the place with brooms, mops, and dustpans. Carpenters also hung from the remaining rafters and worked to put support beams back in place. A few dregs sat around the remains of the bar, drinking. The drought spigots had somehow emerged from the mayhem unscathed.

Eldridge spotted the once proud Odd off to the side of the room, turbaned head in hand. He sat in his throne, which had somehow been detached from the giant hydraulic arm that used to hold it aloft. The remains of a wooden booth surrounded him. Eldridge walked over. A glaze covered the Odd's eyes.

"Hello, El."

"Hey. What happened?"

"Fucking *Xiang* happened."

"Who?"

"How should I know? Queen. Knight. Two of them came through here. This is what's left."

The redhead sat on the slanted surface of the shattered booth's seat. "Do you have another?" He nodded at the crater.

"Of course I have another. I have *three* more hyperglobes. But this is it."

"What do you mean?"

"Critical mass. Goldmist took notice. Decided I had too much jenta."

"But you've always competed with him."

Yasim unwound his turban and set the pile of silk in his lap. "What a pleasant tryst to rumor myself with in the quiet hours of the night. Too bad it came true."

Eldridge nodded. He looked at his lap for a moment.

Eventually he sighed. "Yasim, I have to ask–"

The prospect of impropriety dispelled some of the Odd's grief. He jumped to his feet and said, "Of course, of course. What do you need?"

"I need arms. And a bed. And Oksana. And a *drink*."

"You shall have all this and more. *Chloe!*"

One of his underlings zipped down from the rafters on a line of black rope. She wore six-inch black platform shoes, a tank top, and a tattered red silk skirt. She jerked her chin at the bar and crossed behind it, grabbing a drink jar along the way. She flashed some greeny-green eyes at the redhead and flicked a lock of her own red hair out of the way. Eldridge grinned and sidled up to the mostly empty bar, but as soon as his rear-end touched stoolseat, slumber overtook him. His forehead hit the bar.

A rough hand shook him awake. It was green-eyed Chloe, shoving a drink under his chin.

"Special order from Yasim," she said. "Enjoy."

Fwip.

Eldridge took a sip. A thousand red-hot needles stabbed his face and neck—only they weren't red-hot needles; they were shards of glass. Specifically, *drink-jar* glass, and only then did he realize that he had heard a muffled *fwip* from the doorway just as he was taking a drink. One moment he was drinking, the next he was holding his fist next to a jar-shaped drought of grog that sat frozen in midair. Splattery entrance and exit wounds spewed out of either side of the grog-shape, both connected by a tunnel. Shattered jar-glass surrounded the grog-shape.

Eldridge staggered back from the bar, still holding the glass handle to the shattered jar. Glass shards and grog covered him. His eyes burned. A familiar voice screamed from behind:

"*Hey, buttwad!*"

He looked, and it was Oksana, standing spraddle-legged in the doorway, a silenced pistol smoking in her hand, her eyes alight. She pointed at Chloe.

"El! The bitch is a *bish!*"

As his polycharge started to heat up, Eldridge turned to green-eyed Chloe, but all he saw was the sole of her platform boot as she vaulted over the bar and delivered a kick to his face. He fell back another few steps, his vision already blurring. While Yasim watched from his fallen throne, Oksana came running across the bar, but the redhead held up his hand and waved her off.

"No," he wheezed. "No help."

But even as the trixie backed off, his polycharge kept getting hotter. He swallowed a mouthful of steaming saliva, his fingers tugging at his jacket collar, his face turning red. Green-eyed Chloe bounced off a nearby post and landed another kick across his face—one that spun him around and sent him on an arm-pinwheeling plunge to the floor, where he skidded across more broken glass, splintered wood, and stale grog. He rolled onto his back and struggled to sit up, but green-eyed Chloe was already upon him. Her platform boot cracked him across the cheek. Fortunately, his polycharge had cooled down—Oksana had retreated to Yasim's side—but whatever poison Chloe the green-eyed Xiang bishop had introduced into his system was working fast. His insides felt like they were liquefying. A pair of hot, smelly streams ran down the inside of his pants as his bowels gave way. Fluid started to flood the tissue around his eyes, threatening to squeeze them shut. He somehow managed to jump to his feet as green-eyed Chloe pulled a pair of blades—big, serrated ones—from the back of her belt. She advanced on him in the ruins of Yasim's, swiping the blades through the air so fast their tangs sang.

Eldridge went for all he had: his scatterguns. He ripped them out of his cargo pants, *flicked* the bayonets to the ready, and aimed them at her chest. He almost pulled the triggers before his deep memorycenters flashed to life and sent a screaming missive to his brain reminding him that *Xiang rooks can't use firearms!* Instead he swung one of his bayonets in a great, upward, swooping arc. The blade caught hold of green-eyed Chloe's pug nose, tore the chunk of cartilage from her skull, and sent it flying. The mess splattered against the ceiling and dripped. She howled with her suddenly skeletal face and hooked a blade at his throat. He backward-bent at the waist, feeling the blade hiss-slice through the air above him, and then he bulled his shoulders behind his bayonets and charged. Both blades penetrated her chest. He found strength in his rapidly numbing legs and drove her back, back, back until he double-impaled her against the far wall. The bayonets formed an X through her torso. The redhead reeled backward. Chloe remained stuck to the wall.

Grimacing, the redhead turned to Oksana.

"Punch me as hard as you can!"

As ordered, she ran to him and punched him in the stomach over and over while he stuck his fingers down his throat. Finally, Eldridge—who was already well into a healthy shitting of himself—uncorked his gorge. Hands on knees, Eldridge puked all over Yasim's floor until he dry-heaved.

A moment of silence followed this outburst. Yasim, Oksana, and everyone else gaped at the redhead. Eldridge stood up, woozy. He raised his hands.

"No, please. Hold your applause."

He lurched into the bar and held himself up with his arms as his legs lost feeling entirely. Oksana stomped over and caught him under a shoulder.

"Tell me what to do, old man," she said.

With one eye swollen shut, the redhead said, "Get me to my room."

Oksana started to carry him out of the bar, but Yasim got in their way.

"El, El! I didn't know. Chloe was new!"

The redhead nodded. "It's OK, man. This game got us all."

Yasim stood holding his unwoven turban and watched Oksana carry Eldridge away.

• • • • •

BY THE TIME HE woke up, he was already late.

"Eldridge! El! Wake up!"

It was Oksana, jumping on the bed and using her foot to bounce his body up and down, her tiny downward kicks knocking gusts of wind out of his gut. He finally came to with a jolt, sitting up so fast his head hurt.

But his eyes weren't swollen, and his bowels felt fine. He jumped out of bed, then realized he was naked.

"Why am I naked?!"

Standing arms-akimbo on the bed, Oksana said, "Because I raped you. *Because I had to clean all the shit off your legs, buttwad! It's 4:45!"*

Eldridge lunged across the room and checked the computer. Sure enough: 4:46 a.m. He spun on the trixie. "Why'd you let me sleep so late?!"

"*Let* you sleep late? I've been jumping on you for the last *two hours!* I thought you were dead!"

The redhead held his head, then noticed that his clothes were cleaned and folded on the foot of the bed. As he dressed, he started to do the math. He turned and looked at Oksana, who had crossed her arms and settled into a pout. The redhead zipped his pants and held out his hands.

"Did you do all this?" he asked.

She didn't look at him. "Maybe."

"Hey," he said to draw her gaze. She looked at him. He offered his hands, which she took. He said, "And you went to Doc Enki's?"

She nodded. "He gave me some meds. I brought 'em back here."

He closed his eyes and took a breath. When he opened his eyes, something in his gaze melted her freeze-out. Her whole body relaxed. She dropped to her knees on the bed. The redhead smiled and squeezed her hands.

"I ain't like to forget this," he said. "Big time."

He released her hands and finished dressing. As he zipped up his jacket, he took stock of the weaponry she had procured from Yasim:

A few boxes of ammo for his scatterguns. That was it. And he couldn't use any of it.

Eldridge said, "Is this all?"

"Yasim had to offload some stuff to keep the lights on," she said.

"Right, right," he said, nodding. Eldridge knew he personally had another store of weapons inside the city, but getting to it took time. He checked the clock: 4:53. He didn't have enough time, so he decided to go with what Yasim coughed up. He grabbed the ammo, then found his scatterguns on the bedside table. He slipped them into his cargo pants and headed for the door.

"Wait," Oksana said.

She slid off the bed, then reached under one of the pillows. She produced a small box and crossed to him.

"I've got another weapon for you."

The redhead glanced at the box. "What is it?"

She handed it to him. "Open it–but *be careful.*"

What he saw inside the box didn't compute at first. He thought they were candy bars or ingots of lead, but they felt too light to be either of those. But when he saw the numeric keypad on one of the two objects, he almost fumbled the box out of his hands.

"*Shee-it!*" He crossed to the bed and set down the box. Turning on her, he asked: "Where'd you get those?!"

"You don't wanna know."

"No, I probably don't. Listen, I need to *win* my next battle, not…blow up…the…*everything*—listen, nobody even knows what these things'll *do* when you use 'em, and I wouldn't know *how* to use 'em if I did!"

"You only need two, El. You make the call with one. The dreg on the other end is the one who…*gets* it."

The redhead's eyebrows rose. "Well, OK then. Anything else you wanna tell me?"

"I want you to strip me naked and throw it to me before you go. For good luck?"

"Not now." He winked. "I need all my wits about me."

He looked down at the two cellphones. Slowly, he picked them up like fragile vials full of global-killing bugs. He reached into a back pocket and pulled out another bandanna, which he used to wrap up the two phones. He stowed them in a smaller pocket on his cargo pants. He smiled at the trixie.

"Just in case," he said. "And thanks, little girl."

Her mouth didn't smile, but her eyes sure did.

"You're welcome, daddy."

He crawled out the door.

• • • • •

COLDGEAR IN PLACE, ELDRIDGE rode up the ramp out of under-Dedrick with lingering questions. He still had to ask Dr. Enki if he knew anything about his cure. He was also curious about how the revolving door had been stopped. And what was up with the water in the quarry?

But as he turned off the road and headed southeast toward the gully, those thoughts vanished from his mind and in their place thronged hellish thoughts of fire and dread.

Despite his fear, the redhead grinned. Hagan must be close by. Eldridge knew that the feelings of terror originated from one of Hagan's inventions: the smallpitch. It looked like nothing more than a black tent, but Hagan had outfitted the tarpaulin with micropores that emitted a powerful pheromone that stimulated the fear centers of all mammals. As Eldridge rode his bike down the narrow gully, he saw the smallpitch come into view. Standing outside it was Boris Hagan himself.

Well, not standing. *Jumping,* more like. He was jumping up and down, holding a piece of paper that had to be the Xiang lineup. The redhead pulled over next to the smallpitch. Hagan ran over.

"El! El! You've gotta run!" he said.

The redhead checked his bike's clock: 5:21.

"What? What? What's the problem?"

"Where the fuck have you been?" Hagan snapped, holding up the flap of the smallpitch and waving him in. Once inside, the interior of the tent blocked the pheromones, but Eldridge was left with his friend's panic.

"What is it? Who's in the match?"

"Just look—many Bothans died," Hagan said as he thrust the paper into Eldridge's hand. The expression "many Bothans died" was a side-effect of Hagan's life-passion, which was the Arpa. Post-Deadblast, computer networks were limited to small, local arrays of hardlined systems, but Hagan had discovered a link to a pre-Deadblast thingamajig he called the Arpa. According to Hagan, it had once been a huge network of computers that crisscrossed the oceans. It sounded like a fairy tale, but Hagan stood by his story, even though all that remained of this magical virtual realm were fragments of code and the occasional uncorrupted graphic file. From these detritus, Hagan would spin tales of epic heroes meeting on ancient battlefields and desperate struggles against impossible odds. Eldridge liked to meet with Hagan on the roof of Nix's gaming palace and listen to his bearded friend tell these tales over drinks. It was during one of these storytelling sessions that Hagan first used the expression "many Bothans died," which had come to mean "I busted my ass for this."

In the smallpitch that morning, Eldridge snatched the Xiang lineup out of his hand and tried to read it, but Hagan was already pushing him out of the tent.

"Keep it! Burn it when you're done! *Just run!*"

"What? Why? Who am I fighting?!"

"The Minister!"

An observer stationed outside the tent would think that someone had dropped a live hand grenade inside because one side of the tent shot outward like a cannonball had been fired into it. That cannonball was Eldridge, who upon hearing Hagan's warning, sprinted into the side of the smallpitch, devil-may-care of where the actual door was. The tent untethered from the ground and spilled sideways as Eldridge clawed at the tarp in search of the door, all the while screaming, *"Fuck, fuck, fuck!"* After a minute of struggle, the redhead emerged from the tentflap and immediately slapped at his chest and jumped from one foot to the other as the smallpitch's fear pheromones once again hit him. He screamed, *"Yaaah! Yaaah! Eeeeg!"*

The name "Minister" came from the original Xiang tournaments, which took place in the far east, across the oceans. The original tournaments centered on a different board game: XiangQi, also known as Chinese Chess. In XiangQi, the game's Kings must remain within a nine-point grid known as the Palace. Two other pieces guard the King in the palace: Ministers. Playing as a Minister was widely regarded as a deathwish, as the Palace and its King were under constant assault. Over the years, only one man had ever played as a Minister and survived. This same man had gone onto play as a Minister in dozens of XiangQi tournaments—surviving them all—and somehow, this same master warrior had braved a trip across the ocean to play in multiple Xiang tournaments as a pawn. Eldridge knew the name because not only was this warrior the only pawn to ever advance to the eighth rank and be promoted to Queen, he was also set to potentially reproduce the feat if he captured Eldridge's square.

Qi Li. The Minister.

Hagan struggled out of the smallpitch in a cloud of desert dust, plugging a small, blinking device into his neck—a doodad that canceled out the smallpitch's effect. Overhead, black clouds rushed in from the north, their interior flashing white. Eldridge pointed at the smallpitch.

"Would you shut that thing *off* already?!"

Hagan crouched and pinched a button on his shoe, then stood.

"They're onto me, El. I have to stay topside for a while."

"Wait, what? Who? Who's onto you?"

But Hagan was already shooing him away. "You need to run. *Read the lineup.* Read all of it, and—"

Thoom! Titanic hands struck a giant bass drum and silenced Hagan's next warning as the first flashes of lightning licked at the desert floor miles distant.

Eldridge shouted, *"What?"*

Hagan said: *"Be sure to read the rest of the list! You're not gonna believe who's—"*

Ka-boom came the next beat of the drum. The morning sky darkened. Eldridge powered up his bike.

"You need a ride?!"

Hagan shook his head. *"I don't wanna be anywhere near—"*

An array of sensations accompanies the impact of a nearby lightning bolt. Crius Kaleb used to brag that he had been struck by three lightning bolts, but Eldridge never believed him until that morning when a column of white light spontaneously emerged from the air a few yards to their left. The column was about the width of a building, and from Eldridge's perspective, it seemed to fire *up* into the sky—as a child, he had always imagined lightning moving downward. Of course, he heard no thunder, because the explosion that immediately followed the lightning-strike would echo across the desert as thunder moments later. The only things the redhead *did* hear was a crackling of static electricity that surrounded him and the pesky, lame pulse that his heart beat against his sternum. The lightning knocked him onto his side, and when Hagan tried to help him up, a mini-bolt of electricity snaked between his hand and the bike's fuel cell—*krazzakt!* Hagan yelped and staggered back. Eldridge pulled himself out from under his bike, righted it, and helped Hagan up. He jumped on his bike and took off.

As the walls of the gully fell away and Eldridge rode into the open desert, the redhead got the sensation that he was traveling back in time—back, specifically, into one of those old motionshows that didn't have any color. A duststorm swirled on the horizon and turned the sun into a white disk that hovered in the distance and sucked all the color out of the land as those lightning clouds gathered overhead and descended slowly like a giant, mighty death-trap. It was a shooting gallery. Seconds earlier he had borne witness to his first lightning strike, but now he was seeing his second, third, fourth, fifth, and more. Bolt after bolt struck the earth and forced him to slalom back and forth, each impact heralded by the sudden standing-up of every hair on his body.

You're not gonna believe who's...

What had Hagan meant by that? He wasn't going to believe who *else* was in the tournament? Hell, the tourney already had Qi Li among its pawns—who could be more frightening than the most fearsome pawn to ever play the game?

The White Queen.

Of course. Hagan's lineup included everyone in the game, which meant he knew who was responsible for that *thing* that was the White Queen. As another volley of lightning bolts rained down around him, Eldridge—in spite of his better judgment—fished in his pocket for the list and held it flat against the fuel cell between his legs. He spotted Qi Li's name instantly as White's G-pawn, which put him in a perfect place to crash across the board and threaten to capture Eldridge's kingside rook, which began the game on the H-file. He spotted his own name—Eldridge, W.—but when he checked the name of the White Queen, he almost wrecked his bike. Lightning continued to flash all around him, but he ignored it, his focus coalescing around the flapping paper between his legs. He had heard the White Queen's name before because just about everybody in the world had. It didn't matter what remnant you called home; if you had a pulse and a properly functioning libido, you had had heard this name.

White Queen | Feruccio, Shanta

"Shanta Feruccio?!" Eldridge shouted as a lightning bolt slammed into the earth before him and heaved up a shivering wall of dirt. He wheeled his bike around the wall and crammed the list of Xiang competitors back into his pocket. *That thing in Yasim's was Shanta Feruccio?* Madness. Not possible. In the days since Deadblast, celebrity had yielded to notoriety—very few people were famous anymore, only notorious. But a select few managed to become famous in spite of the world they lived in. Klara Kira, the prepubescent pop starlet whose pesky reproductive system had thwarted the oddsmaking of Clovis Wine, had emerged as a celebrity on this side of the world. But *Shanta Feruccio*...her legend spanned the continents and trumped all. She originated from one of the eastern continents, where she posed for a local hardcore hardline. (Boris Hagan had also told Eldridge that the Arpa used to be the source of untold visual pleasures, but after Deadblast, porn had become purely a cottage industry, a phenomenon that championed its own local heroes.) Feruccio had emerged from an obscure far-eastern remnant not as a hardcore mistress, but rather as a plain old nude goddess.

"They used to call 'em pin-ups," Hagan once said.

Pin-up or hardcore hardliner, Feruccio boasted a genetic profile whose sheer perfection put her existence at odds with the idea that she was human. Nowhere was this truth more apparent that at the perigee of her tiny waist, which was the star of her first so-called pin-up. That first picture had made her an intercontinental, post-Deadblast sensation. You couldn't even see her face. Instead, the photographer had simply aligned the camera vertically and snapped a shot of her naked midriff, which swooped in and out of the frame like a sine wave. Mist rose from her skin, giving the impression she had just stepped out of a hotbath. Faint light accentuated details along her flesh—the teardrop contour of her navel, a dusting of peach-fuzz along her flat stomach. But the *pièce de résistance*—or *pieces de résistance*—however, appeared at the top of the frame, where the bottom hemispheres of her breasts hung just within view.

Years ago, that picture hit the hardcore hardline of that tiny far-eastern remnant, and within days, rumortrysts had sprung up on every local hardcore hardline telling tales about the impossible new beauty from the far east, and every horndog, pervoid, and tollo was clamoring to see her. Mere hours passed before hundreds of moto-express messengers were dispatched to the antipodes with that photo in hand. A day later, a cadre of mighty Odds descended on the tiny remnant and demanded audience with Feruccio and her photographer, who was summarily executed for having the temerity to exist inside her personal sphere. Feruccio herself was spirited away to the coast, where an emissary from the land of undersea marauders met her on bended knee and escorted her across the ocean on a private cruise-liner. The rumortrysts held that Feruccio was the only landlubber to have seen the central city of the marauders, which sat at the bottom of a miles-deep abyss and required all visitors to undergo a fortnight's worth of decompression to survive the voyage. After holding court with the marauders, Feruccio arrived on this side of the ocean as a worldwide star based on one photo. And when she started taking *more* photos, she transcended celebrity and entered the realm of high myth. Parents spoke of her in hushed tones to their little ones, imploring them to rewire their DNA to be more like Feruccio's. Not surprisingly, her name became a synonym for perfect beauty, and even the theocrazzies exulted in her by copy-pasting her visage over the face of their almighty.

"We always knew he was a feruccio," said Rene Rosaire, supriest of the Church of the Ancients.

So suffice it to say that when Eldridge found out that the most beautiful woman in the world had somehow appeared in his Xiang tournament as an eight-foot-tall bazooka-wielding golem, it didn't balance—but he temporarily forgot about it when he activated his jad device to request the coordinates of his target, the great Qi Li. It spat out a piece of paper that the wind instantly carried away. He muttered a curse and started to make the request again, but he stopped when he saw a beam of white light streak across the desert; a beam of white light *that wasn't lightning*. No, it couldn't have been lightning because lightning couldn't fly horizontally, hovering a few feet above the ground. For a few moments, Eldridge watched the beam of light slash around sand dunes before he realized what he was looking at—or more specifically, *who* he was looking at. Another bolt of lightning smashed into the ground in between Eldridge and the beam of light, and for an instant, the redhead could see the blinding cyclone of Qi Li's legs as they churned through the sand and propelled him across the land at 70 mph. The storm continued to boil overhead, and for a moment, Eldridge thought his luck had changed when a blinding bolt blasted out of the heavens at Li, but the redhead's face fell when he saw the XiangQi master use one of his ancient blades to split the bolt in twain.

"Holy Crom, he just chopped a fucking lightning bolt in half," Eldridge said as he squeezed the accelerator and sped up to 80 mph—way, way faster than he liked to ride across sand, which had the nasty habit of clogging up his bike's machinery as well as providing zero traction. His bike kicked up a pair of arcing waves of sand and grit. The beam of light—or rather, Qi Li—altered course directly at him. Eldridge noted the time: 5:30 a.m. Rook takes Pawn. It was on.

By his estimation, Dedrick was still a mile away, which meant he was a mile away from under-Dedrick and its intricate streets that he knew so well. No matter—if he was going to stay alive until the staledate and provide for his family by proxy, he'd have to figure out a way to slay the deadliest pawn to ever set foot in a Zone of 64.

On cue, Eldridge noticed that Li had slowed down and pulled up next to him. They looked at each other. Eldridge could hear the audible *chucks* of his feet as they chewed through the sand. Li wore a white robe—one of two he always wore for Xiang play; the other was black—while his feet bore simple, black slippers. Black leather straps made an X across his chest and held secure a pair of sword hilts on his back. His face looked like the cratered surface of an asteroid. His black hair had grown over a fist-sized divot that sank into his skull, while scores of scars turned his skin into corduroy. Other craters marked the ruins of old features—his chin, a nostril, one half of his brow. Only his eyes had survived the rigors of his life unmarred, and they regarded Eldridge with bored calculation.

The redhead smiled. "Howdy!"

Li's remaining eyebrow rose in acknowledgment. And then he struck.

As with the bounty-merc Quillig, Eldridge didn't wait for Li to strike. He assumed the attack was coming and so had already swerved out of the way just as Li's two swords swiped through the air where his head had been. That set off a half-mile chase that put Eldridge on a course away from Dedrick. The redhead's left knee skidded along the sand as he banked hard and cut a huge, arcing path through the storm-dark desert with Qi Li inches behind him. More black clouds clustered together overhead and tommy-gunned the land with bolt after bolt, and as Eldridge negotiated the electrified landscape, he began to sense—or *think* that he could sense—where the next bolt was going to land based on the erectile state of the hairs on his body. That, in turn, gave him the idea that he could somehow lead Qi Li into the striking path of one of those bolts. Eldridge got a lot of similarly kooky ideas when he was under duress or otherwise fearing for his life, and in this case, he was almost on target. He felt his hairs stand up, and he steered his bike directly into a burgeoning dark spot on the ground.

It was quicksand.

Luckily, his bike didn't plunge into the muck, but instead skimmed over it at 90 mph and flipped forward end-over-end, slinging him headfirst across hundreds of feet of sand. He pitched onto his side and rolled to a stop with the sound of Qi Li's superhuman footfalls echoing in his ears. No slouch himself, Eldridge used his forward momentum to carry himself to his feet and land upright with both of his bayonet-adorned shotguns in hand. His fingers started to trigger-squeeze, but his whipcrack memory blared:

Xiang rooks can't fucking use firearms, dipshit!

"All right, all right," he mumbled, hurling one of scatterguns like a spear at the charging Li. The Minister changed directions like an electron jumping from one shell to another—one instant he was charging at Eldridge, the next he was retreating along a diagonal vector.

For an instant, Eldridge considered using the cellphones, but after a few lightning-quick rounds of inner debate, he dismissed the notion. Given the grim scope of the Cellphone Edict, he figured that the explosion—whatever it may be—would be huge enough to take out Li, but he didn't want to be caught in it himself. Plus, Li was a moving target, a *rapidly* moving target; and he didn't want to waste such precious ammo. A distant voice in his mind told him he might need it later.

Back to business. The excitement had jacked the redhead's body-temp a few degrees, but the subzero early morning chill was already freezing his sweat to his face and seeping in through his clothes. He knew the cold wouldn't last, though. Through the black clouds, he could see a shining pinprick on the horizon: the rising sun. When it rose, the desert would instantly convert into a pressure cooker. He had to get someplace cool–

The redhead lowered his guns and stared at his bike, which lay on its side 100 feet away.

Someplace cool.

He grinned, impressed with his own stupidity, and broke into a hunched-shoulder sprint at his bike. Meanwhile, the white streak that was Qi Li looped back around and tracked a course directly toward him. The race was on, though the finish line was unclear: Eldridge raced for his bike while Qi Li raced to decapitate him. The redhead slid through the sand just as the sun crested the horizon and flooded the land underneath the clouds with red-hot rays. The clouds acted as insulation and promised to hold in every kilojoule of energy until the sun disappeared behind the black murk above. The redhead's eyes dried out instantly when the heat hit, his face clenching in a sudden squint. Fortunately, Qi Li wasn't immune to heat or light. The explosion of luminance across the basin hit him dead-on and brought his feet to a tentative halt as he raised his forearms to block the light. That delay gave Eldridge time to reach his bike, then grip the bike's fuel tank and pull it open, revealing both his hydrocell and a blue packet of gelatinized Freon. The glop powered his bike's cooling system and was designed to last for decades. Eldridge tore the pack out of his fuel bloc and hurled it at Qi Li, who had already righted himself and was sprinting toward the rook, his legs once again a pair of elliptical blurs. Eldridge waited until the pack of gel had flown the distance between them, and he raised his remaining scattergun.

And fired.

The redhead decided to make the gamble in an instant. Xiang rooks couldn't use firearms, no, but Eldridge wasn't aiming at Li when he fired his scattergun that morning. He was aiming at the Freon pack, and as he pulled the trigger, he focused all his thoughts on that distinction–*I'm not shooting at Qi Li, I'm not shooting at Qi Li, I'm not shooting at Qi Li*–hoping against hope that the sketchy technology housed in his polycharge would detect the technicality and opt against decapitating him.

It worked.

The Freon pack flash-expanded into an explosive, icy blue sphere. In a pair of fleeting instants, the sphere engulfed Li, then vanished. Li's momentum continued to carry him forward, even when frozen solid. His frosty form dug a trench through the sand and came to a stop. His life ended in action–poised in a full sprint, swords in hand. The only indication that he saw what was coming was a slight pursing of his lips and squinting of his eyes; a wince in the moment before he died.

Eldridge jumped to his feet and tried to run over to Li's body, but the 160-degree heat reduced his run to a plod. Every breath burned his lungs. Sweat seeped out of every crease of his clothes. When he reached Li, he was shuffling from one foot to the other, his head hung back on his neck, his arms hanging by his sides. Panting, he raised his scattergun and fired a round into Li's face. The frozen statue of Qi Li shattered along and around vectors and vertices that appeared at his shoulders, hips and knees. The greatest pawn to ever play Xiang fell to pieces in the middle of the desert at the redhead's feet.

Eldridge dropped to his knees and forearm-wiped sweat from his brow. The sun had already passed above the clouds, which were boiling away underneath its heat. A few random lightning bolts struck miles away, the thunder distant in the redhead's ears because of the pounding of his heart in his head. Still on his knees, he scrabbled around in the sand in search of the Freon pack. He found it buried underneath one of Li's feet. A few drops of gel remained, but the pack lay in transparent tatters.

But when he grabbed the Freon pack, his fingers had also closed around something else in the sand; something that had been buried underneath the Minister's dead feet: a folded-up piece of paper. Eldridge unfolded it, read it, smiled, and collapsed to the ground.

Black.

The next thing he knew, he awoke to find himself lying on his side in the sand, which had risen to bury the left half of his body. A glaring white sky had pushed away the storm, which hung over the land many miles to the south. Eldridge tried to gauge the time of day by the position of the sun, but he couldn't find it—the whole sky looked like sun. He inhaled a hot breath dusted with sand and coughed. A spark of fear ignited in his chest, but it wasn't related to the possibility that he might die from exposure. It was related to the game. He couldn't see Li's body. *Could he still be alive?* The fear animated him long enough to dig himself out of the sand and cast his gaze around. He exhaled sharply when he saw Li's still-frozen hand sticking out of the sand nearby.

He crammed the folded piece of paper into his pocket.

"Okie-dokie," he rasped.

He performed a slow, deliberate scan of the surrounding area until he spotted his bike buried up to its fuel cell a few yards away. He put a foot on the ground and propped a hand on his knee. A minute later, he pushed himself upright and slogged through the sand over to his bike, but instead of trying to pull it out of the sand, he dropped to his knees and pulled at the one unburied saddlebag on his fuel cell.

"Oh, boy, I hope I put it..." He trailed off and opened the bag. A smile passed across his face as he pulled out another shell casing medicine-holder tube. He popped it open and swallowed four remkillers—the same anti-sleep pills Oksana had taken the night before. They hit his system fast. He leaped to his feet, eyes wide and fully aware that he didn't have long before he keeled over from dehydration or cardiac arrest. Moments later he was powering up his bike with no memory of how he had been able to pull it out of the sand. After retrieving his other scattergun, he pulled on his goggles and twin bandannas. Reflexively, he tried to plug in the eight thermally lined tubes that connected his jacket with his bike's cooling system, but then he remembered it was gone. He dropped the tubes and made for Dedrick as fast as he could.

He rode through an oven. The white sun had already filled the sky, and now it filled every inch of space between him and Dedrick. As he rode through the endless expanse of white-hot sand and sky, his vision kept flashing white as the remkillers delivered their time-delay payload of caffeine and a synthetic adrenaline invented by none other than Dr. Enki. Eldridge looked like he was sucking on a lemon, but only because the insides of his cheeks had dried out and stuck to the sides of his tongue. Every breath felt like flaming sand. By his estimate, Dedrick wasn't more than a mile away, but the trip stretched out into a hallucinatory run through a desert overrun with gigantic dreens who strode along the horizon, their enormous forms rendered a light, transparent blue by the atmosphere.

He was almost crushed by the giant revolving door into Dedrick.

But by then, he was traveling too slow to be at much risk. Although his engine was still running, his hand lay limp around the accelerator so that his bike simply rolled down the ramp that led underground. He listed to the right and stopped against the wall. One of his feet hung in the air, while the other held himself and the bike upright. As the revolving door swept past, cool air gusted onto his face. He perked up slightly at the stimulus. He waddled the rest of the way into the revolving door with his bike wedged between his legs. The door scooted him into the under-earth area where he rolled forward a few feet, came to rest, and collapsed on the cobblestone street. Somehow, his foot caught the kickstand on his way down and kept his bike upright.

A shaking hand and voice woke him.

"El! El! El! Wake up!"

He tried to ignore the voice, but it kept imploring him to *wake up*, so he did, his red-rimmed eyes creeping open to reveal a jigsaw puzzle of crumbling flesh encased in flaking burlap and enshrouded with flecks of dust. Eldridge squinted into the light.

"Clovis?"

"El, you gotta help me. I'm the Black King, and I've gotta castle with you."

Part Four

L'ESPRIT de L'MONTAGNE

THE CASTLING MOVE WAS one of the last formal changes to the ancient game's rules. All of that happened before Deadblast, of course, but Boris Hagan occasionally passed down little packets of wisdom from his research into the Arpa. The castling move always appealed to the long-dead child inside Eldridge, the wide-eyed moppet who the Narsyans never allowed to exist. When he first saw a chessboard as a rebellious child who sprinted down to Dedrick to hang out with his ne'er-do-well friend, the redhead immediately wondered if the king could hide out inside the little castles at the corners of the board. He was right.

When the king castles, he moves two spaces to the side, and the rook leaps over him. Hagan told Eldridge that the pre-Deadblast oddsmakers added the rule to speed things up.

"It gets the rook into play a lot faster," Hagan said.

In a Xiang tournament, however, castling was a lot more complicated. On the board, the move still worked the same, but post-Deadblast oddsmakers had modified how the rule applied to the avatar-warriors (including the King) in an effort to slow the game *down*. Longer Xiang tournaments meant more money for everybody, so castling became a very rare occurrence—mainly because most of the players who acted as Xiang Kings were total cowards. It worked like this:

The two Kings played a chess match via correspondence. Every time they captured a piece, two avatar-warriors would battle to the death over the square. Things got complicated when a player tried to attack the King. In pre-Deadblast chess, putting the king in check meant that the player had to get out of check somehow; usually by capturing the attacking piece, blocking the attack, or moving the king. In Xiang, a checking move typically led to another battle. If a King had to capture or block to relieve a check, then they could dispatch any of his other players to fight the avatar battle in their stead.

That's where the castling rule change came in.

If the King chose to castle, they forfeited the privilege to ask others to fight for them and would have to fight their remaining battles themselves under pawn controls. That meant they would have to give 36 hours notice before attacking and only fight with hand-to-hand melee weapons.

But that's not all. The post-Deadblast elder-Odds added some sweetener to the mix. In pre-Deadblast chess, the King couldn't use the castling move to get out of check. In post-Deadblast Xiang chess, they could, no questions asked, no battle fought.

Which is exactly what Clovis was doing.

"You're fucking *castling?*" Eldridge rasped, still sprawled on the ground next to his bike.

Clovis discharged little clouds of dust with each rapid breath he took. His clothes crowded around his joints in great folds of crackling corduroy and burlap.

In response to the redhead's question, he nodded. "I have to. *She's* after me."

Eldridge pushed himself to a sitting position. "So you know who the White Queen is?"

Skin cracked around Clovis' mouth. A frown.

"The White Queen? Why would I?"

"You called her a 'she.'" Eldridge said. "Crom, can you get me some water? Do I *not look like* I just staggered in from the desert, dying of thirst?"

Clovis ran off for a few minutes and emerged from a nearby dreg shanty with a jug of water. He shuffled over, trailing a squat, screaming dreg who wore gingham overalls and shook its little fists in protest of the aquatic theft. The redhead held up one of his scatterguns to scare it away. He upturned the jug over his face, chugged and barfed a few times, then started sipping. Finally, he looked at his dry friend.

"Clovis, you called the White Queen a 'she.' Haven't you heard who it is?"

"No. I called her a she because, y'know, it's a Queen. Queens are she's. Right?"

"Oh. So why the hell are you castling this early–"

Clovis took a knee. He had that quartz gleam in his eyes again. "Why? I haven't tried to capture her yet. Who *is* the White Queen?"

Eldridge shook his head. "You wouldn't believe me."

"Who? Who?"

"You ever hear of Shanta Feruccio?"

Upon hearing her name, Clovis shrank like an invisible hand was crumpling him up to throw in the trash. He drew his arms and legs close to his chest and buried his head between his knees. He raised his head and peered at the redhead through crinkles of arid eyelid flesh.

"You don't say?"

Eldridge swallowed another mouthful of water. "You know her or something?"

"No!" Clovis said. "No, no. I don't know her. But have you seen her? Now?"

"Yeah. I watched her capture one of your bishops. By the way, you know that White almost captured me and promoted a pawn this morning, right?"

Clovis nodded.

"And you're castling to escape a check by the White Queen?"

Clovis hung his head.

"Right. So where'd you learn to play chess, Clove? In the fucking *dark?* You're gonna get us all killed."

The dry man looked up and shook his head. "El, you've gotta help me. You've gotta hide me. She can't find me. No way she can find me. I'm castling with you. I don't care. You have to hide me if you know what's good for you, and I know you will because it's too important to you. You told Nix you have family, and you can't leave them in the church."

"Leave them in the *lurch.*"

"That, too. C'mon, El. Hide me!"

Clovis' repeated requests to be hidden sprang from Xiang's Byzantine rules and traditions. Although avatar-Rooks were by no means required to hide a castling King, it was in their best interest as competitors to put their King in a well-fortified place so the King could play the rest of the match—and fight the rest of their battles—from as strong a position as possible. Eldridge shook his head at his poor, dumb friend. Meanwhile, the water was seeping into the redhead's system and slowly recharging his fuel cells, so he attempted to stand up. His joints quivered, but he managed to force himself upright. He swayed in place for a few moments.

"OK, Clove. Let's get you to my safehouse."

"You have a safehouse?"

"I have a house that is safe," El said. "Climb on."

They mounted the bike. The redhead gunned it before Clovis had a grip, causing the dry man to swat at the sky to regain his handhold.

"Shit, El! Watch it!"

"Shut up and *spill,* Clove!" Eldridge called over his shoulder.

"Spill what?"

"Spill *what?* The last time I saw you, I kicked you *out* of this tournament. Now you're a King? What happened?"

They rode in silence through the twisty streets of under-Dedrick until they reached the far-eastern wall, where Eldridge turned north. Along the ground, shanties built from mudwater and dogshit glommed onto the cobblestones like giant hornets nests, their insides lit from the occasional dreg's fire. Emaciated faces glared at them with eyes twice too big for their skulls. Other structures clung to the lower walls of

Dedrick—wooden stilt-shacks that gave the hunger-crazed inhabitants a great view while their bodies learned to digest muscle tissue. Brick cube-houses, held aloft with cracking mortar, stuck out from the wall like books on a cluttered shelf. But none of these dreg-built structures dared to reach *too* high, lest they disturb the residents of catwalk city: the psychoskags.

Finally, Eldridge spoke again. "Well?"

"You *know* why, El. I need the money. I owe Jeb Goldmist and Marko Marinus big time."

"OK, enough: I'm calling *macta* on this Marko Marinus bullshit. You haven't made any odds with him."

"But, El! El, man! El! I totally did! I made the odds with him up in the mountains!"

Eldridge stopped his bike so fast, Clovis' forehead rapped into his back. He parked next to an altar built from a trash heap. He turned around.

"*Where* up in the mountains?"

Clovis' head sank into his collar. He whimpered, "A place-y place."

"What place? *Tell me.*"

"It took forever to get to. I had to pay for a guide. One of those Narsyan maniacs. It was all the way up at the top. Like a monument. A building. They had cut it right out of the stone of the peak, all the way up there."

The redhead's jaw flexed. "The conventuary."

"Is that what it's called?"

Eldridge ignored the question: "Anything else you wanna tell me?"

Clovis looked around for help. He saw only a gray-skinned man whose hands had been bone-boiled up to the elbows. He supplicated them from his knees and extended his skeletal hands. Finally, Clovis' head elevated out of his collar, his lower lip poking out like a dried crust of bread.

"I may have lied about something else."

Eldridge held up his palms. "Holy Crom, *what?* Do I even want to know?"

"I didn't make odds with Marko about Klara Kira."

"So what *did* you make odds about?"

"You."

Eldridge dismounted his bike and got in Clovis' face: "What?"

Clovis covered his face. "I'm sorry, El."

"How did you make odds about me?" Eldridge asked, though he already knew the answer.

"Your deathday. Marko bet it wouldn't happen on the Fourth."

Eldridge put his hands on his hips and looked at the ground, where maggots and centipedes squirmed and swarmed. Clovis kept blathering about something, but all Eldridge heard was a voice inside his head that told him when he was being an idiot, except this time, it was saying *Marinus cured you.* He looked up and revealed that he finally believed Clovis by asking a simple question.

"So you're running odds for Crius Kaleb now?"

Clovis nodded. In oddsmaking, some bets you had to make face-to-face, while others you could make with virtually anybody who could get to a hardline. Eldridge had to make his deathday wager face-to-face with Crius Kaleb, but anyone could make ancillary bets on his deathday wager with virtually anyone else.

Silent, Eldridge climbed back on his bike and took them to the far corner of Dedrick, where the bottom platforms of catwalk city descended low enough that someone standing flat-footed could jump up and grab one. He parked under one of the lowest platforms and jumped off his bike. Clovis stayed put and watched while the redhead scrabbled around in a pile of garbage packed against the wall. Eventually, he pulled out a 10-foot pole capped with a hook, which he used to reach up to the platform above to pull down a steel ladder. The ladder fell into place with a *clang* and drew the attention of a half dozen psychoskags up above. They halted their swarm pattern to aim their monitor-faces down at Eldridge. Clovis shifted in his seat.

"*Eldridge.*" His whisper sounded like Styrofoam rubbing together. "What the hell're you *doing?*"

But as soon as the dry man had spoken, the psychoskags up above nodded at Eldridge and returned to what they were doing. Eldridge turned.

"It's OK. I'm kind of a folk-hero in psychoskag circles. They sing songs about me, but you wouldn't wanna hear 'em."

Eldridge hid the hook back in the trash, then secured his bike in place with some nanocords. He then rummaged around in his saddlebags and produced a set of clanging metallic instruments that looked like torture devices—two pairs of sharp claws that fit over their wrists and ankles. The wrist-mounted devices included hand grips that, when squeezed, would contract their claws. The ankle-mounted devices were roughly analogous, with foot pedals that activated the device, but instead of contracting, the ankle-mounted devices would spit forth a quartet of hooked spikes.

Clovis gawped at the devices. "What are *these* for?"

"They're the keys to my safehouse."

Eldridge started to climb the catwalk, but Clovis grabbed his coattail.

"Wait!"

Eldridge stopped, his foot propped on the ladder's lower rung.

"What?"

"Where's your safehouse?"

The redhead pointed out to the center of Dedrick's ceiling, where the fungal expanse of catwalk diminished into tributaries of steel and wire, leaving nothing but exposed brick.

Clovis cowered. "We have to climb...out there?"

Eldridge grinned. "Yeah! Ain't it great?! Now, come on, stupid. I need to get you up there before your jad prints out another check on your ass."

With that, the redhead climbed up the catwalk for the first time in a year. As he climbed, rust flaked off the old steel grating and pipes and stained his callused palms. It brought him back to the last time he visited his safehouse. He had just made his deal with Dr. Enki—the deal that should have ended with his death on the Fourth of July, but had instead ended with him competing in one of the deadliest Xiang tournaments in history.

Eldridge seemed to be equipped with an anti-psychoskag magnet. Every time he swung through an opening or pulled himself up to a higher level on the catwalk, all the psychoskags in their vicinity drew back, some of them even precariously hanging off the side of the catwalk to make way. Others cleared out all of the half dreen that watched Eldridge and Clovis with gland-hungry eyes.

But one of the half dreen got past the psychoskags. It dropped 30 feet through an opening in the catwalk and slammed onto the grating before them. No two dreens were alike. Everyone had a different reason for becoming a dreen, though no one ever started the process *wanting* to become a dreen. Most of the first dreens were ragers–muscle maniacs who wanted to get bigger and bigger, so they fucked with their testosterone levels until their internal ecosystems spiraled out of control and they transmogrified into hulking masses of muscle tissue that could barely move. But once they got ahold of someone, they could crush them into paste.

The half dreen that landed on the catwalk, however, wasn't a rager. This one looked like a tary-fairy. Eldridge knew the look. In their pre-dreen existences, tary-fairies ran screaming from mirrors. Otherwise, they wept at what they saw. That's how they'd start down the road. They'd wet-hack into their pituitary glands to rewire their DNA so they could look in the mirror, but it never worked, not entirely.

The tary-fairy that braced them on the catwalk had a face out of a motionshow and plumbing out of a hardcore hardline, but the rest of his body looked like someone had grilled it. Black hashmarks crisscrossed his flesh, while livid scars ran along the insides of his arms and around his neck.

He rasped at them: "You can still hear after your head's chopped off. I listened to my own blood gushing from my neck. It was the best pleasure to end all pleasure. But it didn't end."

And Eldridge knew it didn't, at least not easily. Once you went dreen, suicide became a well-nigh impossible proposition unless they found the nerve to swallow a hand grenade or jump into a vat of molten lead. Eldridge knew the only way to kill them was to neutralize the heart and the brain, but the redhead could tell that the tary-fairy crouched before him had tried to behead himself only to find that his body remained animated long enough to stitch its own head back on.

Needless to say, the concept of dualism had enjoyed a resurgence in the wake of headless dreen bodies running around the deep deserts. Rene Rosaire's Church of the Ancients made its home in the center of an endless expanse of desert some thousand leagues to the northeast of Dedrick, and it was there that he first encountered the living headless.

"Souls inhabit us all, and our souls inhabit *all of us,*" the theocrazzic leader told his faith-hungry flock, all of whom had braved the deep-desert journey in search of an old man named God. What they found instead was a huckster in gold lamé who told them he had a hardline to the almighty because he had seen a decapitated body sprinting through a sandy ravine with a head tucked under its arms.

At least that's what Rosaire told Constable Tola when she came looking for her husband, Milos.

Hunched on the Dedrick catwalk with Clovis behind him, Eldridge looked into the beautiful, crazed eyes of the tary-fairy and thought back to the happy-sad times he had with Zora Tola. The redhead thought back to their time in Junktown, and he thought back to the time she sent him a moto-express to tell him she was getting married and if he was disappointed.

"Disappointed in what?" Eldridge asked the next time they got together, which was at Yasim's some months later.

"Well, aren't you disappointed I didn't ask you to marry me?"

In both time periods, Eldridge shook his head and smiled.

The tary-fairy on the catwalk said, "What's funny?"

"Nothing," Eldridge said.

Clovis rustled. "El, don't talk to it, man."

"Shut up, Clove," Eldridge said, then turned to the half dreen and said, "If you want, I can put you down."

The half dreen used its sparkling eyes to weep. "I can go back."

"Nobody goes back," Eldridge said, though he knew it was a lie. "I give you two, three months before you're in the desert with all the rest."

"I don't *want* to ride the Old Mine," the tary-fairy said.

"Buddy, no damn body wants to ride the Old Mine, but if I don't put you down, that's your ticket."

The half dreen pulled at his lower lip. "Tell me I'm pretty."

Eldridge winked. "The prettiest."

He smiled. "OK."

The redhead pulled out one of his scatterguns and shot the half dreen, taking care to liquefy the head. That done, he pressed the gun against the tary-fairy's still-beating heart and pulled the trigger. The gore from both shots spewed through the grating and splattered some psychoskags a few levels below. They howled in protest and scrambled up the catwalk to them, but when they saw it was Eldridge, they backed away. The redhead nodded his thanks and turned around to see Clovis sling a handful of cat food off the side of the platform. Eldridge smirked.

"What're you doing with cat food?"

Clovis glared back. "Wasn't cat food. I just shit myself. Let's *go.*"

Eldridge chuckled and continued climbing up. Dedrick simultaneously shrank beneath them and expanded before them. Ramshackle spires jutted up from the landscape, which included rooftops made from slate, tile, stucco, skin, and wood. Chimneys of a thousand different diameters peppered the rooftops; some of them long steel pipes, others square brick columns. Smoke rose from some, while others belched forth a frothy black bubbling sludge that spread from rooftop to rooftop in an ever-expanding slick. On the opposite corner of town, the red neon letters of Nix's joint glowed around the steeple of an old church. Meanwhile, Jeb Goldmist's tower rose from floor to ceiling, a pillar among the rabble. Eldridge looked down and caught Clovis staring at it.

"See anything you like?" the redhead asked.

Clovis looked up at him with hate in his eyes. "Just get me to your safehouse."

Without another word, they climbed the final hundred feet of the catwalk and came out onto a five-foot-square platform that stood just under one of the giant fans that pumped purified air into Dedrick. The sound of the fan had been growing as they climbed higher, and now it drowned out their voices while also rattling the catwalk two feet in every direction. Heretofore, they had moved *vertically* through the catwalks—straight up along the wall—but now that they had reached the ceiling, the catwalks led *horizontally* out along the ceiling in a maze of steel grate platforms that hung from metal poles bolted to the bricks above. Clovis dropped to his stomach and clung to the steel grate, while Eldridge gyrated his hips to maintain balance.

"Follow me!" he yelled at the dry man, then started the walk out toward the center of the ceiling as dozens of psychoskags ran to and fro and occasionally gave them an encouraging pump of their fists. Under-Dedrick was *big*–almost five square miles–so it took them about 45 minutes to reach the end of the catwalks.

Over time, the psychoskags had laid claim to the walls and ceiling of under-Dedrick, but even they didn't dare build their catwalks too close to Jeb Goldmist's tower, which rose from the ground below and met the brick ceiling half a mile away. About a quarter of a mile away, just barely visible through a bank of mist that hung near the ceiling, was a small wooden trapdoor that led up *into* the ceiling. Eldridge pointed at it.

"There's my safehouse, Clove. Time to–"

When he looked over, he saw that the dry man was cowering on his hands and knees, dust dancing around his hyperventilating form. He looked like a busy anthill.

"Get up!" Eldridge shouted over the fan. "Time to spider-walk!"

With that, he affixed the climbing claws to his wrists and ankles, then bent at the knees, jumped and caught the ceiling with his handclaws. He kicked his legs back, swung his feet forward and latched the footclaws to the ceiling's brickwork. Once he had a grip, he moved like a spider and scurried around the ceiling with ease. Upside down, he called down to Clovis.

"It's easy, man! Once you get a grip, you can't go wrong! Just don't fuck it up, or...y'know! You'll plummet!"

After a moment, he looked up at Eldridge, whose face was already red from hanging upside down. The dry man fished the climbing claws out from among the folds in his clothes and attached them to his wrists and ankles. Shivering, he eased his way to his knees, then to his feet. Eldridge nodded.

"That's it! Now jump!"

Clovis did indeed jump, and one of his claws snagged hold of the ceiling. Unfortunately, at the same time, the ceiling fan emitted a gust that kicked his legs out from underneath him. He shrieked and swung his other hand-claw around. It caught, and Clovis found himself clinging to the ceiling with his hands outstretched to his sides.

"*Eldridge!*"

"You're doing fine! Now kick your legs out and grab the roof with your feet!"

"I will do no such thing!"

"Believe me! Once you get a grip with your feet, it gets easy!"

Clovis swung back and forth a few times, then slung his lower half forward and caught the ceiling with his foot-claws. His face was pressed flat against Dedrick's brick ceiling. The dry man craned his neck and looked at Eldridge.

"This better be worth it!"

Eldridge laughed and scurried around so he was facing the center of the ceiling. His movements came quick and easy at first: right hand, left foot, left hand, right foot. He called instructions back to Clovis as he crawled upside down farther and farther out along the brick ceiling, which was overgrown with moss, mold, and the occasional flash of grass. Eldridge let his vision soft-focus so he could pretend he was crawling along the ground and not hanging 500 feet in the air about to pass out from dehydration or plunge to his death because his hands were shaking and he couldn't keep a grip on his claws. He pressed on, though, as the occasional fist-sized spider skittered over his hands and miniature weather patterns drifted by underneath. Clovis whimpered all the way out to the center of the ceiling, where a wooden trapdoor was set into the brick. When they arrived, Eldridge used one of his hand-claws to pull open the door, which swung open and away from them. A small rope ladder was attached to the door's interior. Eldridge turned himself around and backed up to the trapdoor. He looked Clovis in the eyes.

"Watch what I do," he said, his voice normal because the fans were farther away.

The redhead unhooked his feet and hung from the ceiling. As before, he swung his legs forward, but this time, he caught hold of the rope ladder, unhooked his hand-claws and grabbed hold. He climbed up into the trap door and stuck his head down.

"Come on! This is the easy part."

But the redhead was already prepared to snatch Clovis out of the air if he should screw up and fall, which is exactly what happened. Despite the pounding in his head, Eldridge snagged the dry man's flailing form and hoisted Clovis into the safehouse.

They both fell on their butts on either side of the trapdoor, which Eldridge pulled shut and secured with a metal rod. Darkness. Eldridge stood, stumbled through the room and pulled on a cord of metal beads. Light pushed the dark away from one corner of the 20-square-foot room, which had brick walls lined with faded woodwork. Eldridge stood next to a bookshelf that had been built into the wall. An ancient brass lamp stood on the shelf and cast light through a cracked green shade. The light made Clovis' pupils get small while the contents of the room made his eyes get big.

Box upon box of canned food was stacked on the shelves lining one of the walls, while a row of water coolers stood along another in front of a stack of 10-gallon water jugs that stretched to the ceiling. The third and fourth walls held the weaponry—boxes of bullets, rifles, handguns, rocket launchers and a dozen different kinds of land mines and explosive devices. Some boxes were steel, others cardboard, and dozens of them lay strewn about on the hardwood floor. A cot sat in one of the clear spaces, neatly made.

Eldridge flumped down on a green easy chair. The chair exhaled a year's worth of dust as it absorbed his weight. After a moment's rest, he spoke. "All right, Clove. Hand 'em over."

"What?"

"Your claws. I can't have you sneaking out of here before the match is over."

Clovis lurched to his feet and looked around, his mouth hanging open. The inside of his mouth looked like a magnified view of red sandpaper.

"You want me to *stay* here?"

"Sure. There's enough chow for months and a head in the back." He hooked his thumb at a narrow door set into the bricks. "Whaddaya say?"

Clovis handed the redhead his climbing claws.

"What *is* this place?"

Eldridge hooked a leg over an armrest, sat back, and blinked owlishly as the remkillers started wearing off. "Well, look up there." He pointed at one of the doorframes. The doorway had been bricked over, but the frame remained, and carved into it was the word STACKS. The redhead said, "A buddy of mine told me this used to be a part of a library."

"Why was there a library up here?"

Eldridge opened his eyes and shook his head. "There wasn't. Back before Deadblast, this was ground level. Then everything got buried, and we all went *under*ground. Dedrick got built up underneath...well, underneath whatever used to be here. But this room was still around."

"How'd you find out about it?"

Eldridge shrugged, his eyelids drooping. "I looked up. Spotted the trapdoor. Figured I could do something with it."

A distant scream seeped through the walls. Clovis whipped around and showered the floor with dust. Eldridge, his brow dark, pushed himself out of his chair with a grunt and poured water into a tin cup. Clovis scuttled over and grabbed his arm.

"What was that?"

"A dreen."

"What? Where?"

"Through that wall," he said, stifling a yawn. "You ever hear of the Old Mine?"

"That old thing in the desert? The ride?"

"Yeah," Eldridge said as his eyes dropped, though not because he was exhausted. He drained his water, grit his teeth and said, "We're right next to the track."

Clovis groaned and backed away. "I can't stay here."

"No, you can't. I'd move if I were you." Eldridge pointed at the dry man's feet. Clovis looked down and saw he was standing on the trapdoor, which was bowing under his weight. He yelped and hopped onto the floor.

"You call this a fucking *safe*house?"

Eldridge poured two cups of water and offered one. "Look at the door. Bricked over. There's at least ten feet of stone between us and the Old Mine, and no dreen has the attention span to dig through it. I think." He drained his water. "All the same, I've never liked hiding out up here. The screams get to me."

On cue, another dreen howled, this time with a voicebox that hit a deeper register. Clovis flinched and threw the cupful of water down his throat. "How long do I gotta stay up here?"

"The way I see it, you should stay up here as long as you can. Even if Feruccio comes after you, I don't think she's got a jetpack. You'll be able to see her coming up the catwalk. You've got plenty of firepower up here. You ought to be able to handle any fight that comes your way." Eldridge took a step closer. "And you *better* handle any fight that comes your way. I just need to win one more square and ride this thing out to the staledate to make back the money I need."

Clovis tilted his shoulders away and grinned off a few more chunks of face-flesh. He had that quartz gleam in his eyes again. "About that."

Eldridge sighed. "What now?"

"Did you go by Nix's on your way over here?"

Eldridge rolled his eyes. "You were *with me* the whole time, so no."

Clovis pulled a red stylus from his folds and scribbled some smart characters on a nearby wall. They were *jenta* characters—and a lot of them. They scurried toward Eldridge, who produced his own red stylus and collected them. His eyes bulged as he totaled the sum of money Clovis had just given him.

"What the hell is this for?"

"Oh, that's your tip."

"For what?"

"Winning me all this money."

Eldridge dropped his stylus, grabbed the nearest gun he could—a revolver—and stuck it under Clovis' chin. "Tell me what you're talking about or I end this tournament with a pull of the trigger."

Clovis wheedled: "El! Elly—you didn't see it! You didn't see the play you gave me when you left Nix in my hands after Dr. Enki's. The doc scrambled his brains so much, he tried to go outside! *Outside!* I couldn't resist, El. I couldn't!"

"Resist *what? What the fuck did you do?*"

"I'm you, El. Or you're me. Point is, Nix was so out of it, he'd do whatever I wanted. I asked him to put in *my* name for all of *your* fights. No problem. That way, any time you won, I'd get your money. I wanted to be the Black King. No problem! He just put me in under another name."

Eldridge shoved Clovis against the wall. "You fucking...you *son* of a—*Do you have any idea how important that money is to me?! What I need it for?!* Who *I need it for?!*"

Clovis' eyes turned to slits. They looked like the cross sections of ancient burial chambers wedged among excavated strata of stone and earth. He drywashed his hands, which would never be clean.

"I guess only *Eldridge* needs money. When his friend Clovis needs to pay off the biggest Odd in town, it doesn't count. But when *Eldridge* needs money, it counts. He's the only one who needs anything."

"Clovis, I will end you right now if you don't put this right."

"But you still don't see the play, do you? I'm the Black King. *And* I'm you. If Black wins this match, I'm set for life, and that means I just might maybe-possibly have enough jenta left over to help out poor Eldridge with his insurmountable debt."

Eldridge's gun wavered. "Clove—"

Clovis said, "Did you know that the F-file is open and clear?"

Eldridge's shoulders sagged. An "open" file in chess meant a vertical row that had no pawns on it, but Clovis said that the F-file was *open and clear,* and although that wasn't a term of art, Eldridge took it to mean his piece, the kingside rook, was in position to make another capture.

"And?"

"Indeed it is. Thanks to a few captures by Qi Li, both the black and white kingside rooks are staring at each other." The dry man's cracked-fingernail teeth came out to party as his face shattered around a full smile. "It's Black to move, El, and I need you to capture White's Kingside Rook."

"Clovis, are you fucking kidding me? I'll report us both. Get us both sent to the Chain for frauding up a Xiang tourney. To hell with my family. If you don't right this–"

"You don't mean that."

"You don't want to find out if I do. We're all alone up here."

"You might change your mind when I tell you who White's Kingside Rook is. I believe you and he already know each other."

A crackling-cold sensation spread across the redhead's skin. His eyes snapped open. "What? Who is it?"

"Marko Marinus."

Eldridge stood still, processing. His expression fluctuated–frown, wince, smile–but as soon as his brain absorbed the impact, he yanked the Xiang lineup out of his pocket and checked it. Sure enough:

```
White Rook Kingside | Marinus, Marko
```

Nothing balanced anymore. Clovis Wine had outsmarted him, and Marko Marinus was making odds and entering Xiang tournaments. But even though his world had lost its solar-center, the redhead looked at Marinus' name and thought about the move Clovis had just given him. He remembered what he said to Tola outside the jail.

Someone told me I might have to kill him.

And he thought back to the night years earlier when his best friend betrayed him.

"Clove, how do I *know* you'll pay off my debt after the tournament?"

"Really, El–who cares?"

"Who *cares?*"

"Yes," Clovis said, his eyes widening to reveal glinting shards of silicon. "I say 'who cares,' because right now, I don't think you care about the debt."

"And why wouldn't I?"

"Because you *want* to kill Marko Marinus."

A flash of insight spurred Eldridge into tipping his hand: "You wrote those words on my prison window."

The dry man's face shifted downward like a wall of refuse settling into a landfill. "Come again?"

Eldridge blushed. The redhead didn't consider himself a great reader of faces, but the instant Clovis responded, he knew the dry man hadn't written the three words. Worse, the redhead knew he had made a tactical blunder. Clovis pounced.

"*What* three words?" he cooed with the same shit-happy grin he had been grinning since he revealed his treachery.

Eldridge tried to wave it away. "Nothing. No three words. How'd you know I had a beef with Marko?"

Clovis made a sound like a cinder block breaking. A chuckle. "You're joking, right? Who *doesn't* know of the legendary grudge between Eldridge and the leader of the Narsyans? Who doesn't know that you used to be a Narsyan until you got kicked out in disgrace? Who doesn't know that Marko Marinus betrayed you? And who doesn't know that the whole thing happened because you were trying to help your friend—"

"That's *enough,*" Eldridge said, fidgeting. "Crom. I didn't think *everybody* knew about it. I thought me and Marko had kept it pretty quiet over the years."

"You didn't. When I made the move to capture him, his identity was revealed to me, naturally. I was delighted to pit you two against each other."

Eldridge stepped forward, his brow heavy. "Don't sound so fucking happy about it. I've gotta go kill my best friend."

Clovis aped a wide-eyed expression of grief.

"Oh, no," he said. "You two are still friends. How tragic. But not. Because you're not. *Friends* anymore, that is."

Eldridge once again raised his gun and stuck it in Clovis' face. "I can still end it all. Right now."

"I know you can," Clovis said. "But I don't think you will, because I've given you a gift, El. I've given you a perfect moment. How many people—before or after Deadblast—can point to a perfect moment in their lives? How many people can say that they got a chance to right an old wrong or live the spirit of the stairway?"

"The what of the what?"

Clovis touched his lips. "Oh! Whoops. I guess I should tell you: I'm older than Deadblast."

Eldridge made a face. "*What?*"

"It's true. I'm the oldest man alive. But that's not important. Here's what is: Before Deadblast, I lived on the far side of the ocean in this place where they had the most beautiful language. I can't think of the name of either—the language or the land. But the language had a phrase: *esprit de l'escalier.* There's no way to translate it, because the actual translation is nonsense: 'spirit of the stairway.' It means that feeling you get when you think of the perfect thing to say after you've already left the room—or as you're walking down the stairs. I can tell you this, El: Most everyone lives their lives on the stairs. Before Deadblast, after Deadblast—it's all the same. Everyone thinks of perfection after they've missed their chance. Everyone. But not you. You and Marko have some old odds to resolve, and I've given you a perfect time and place to do it. Eldridge and Marko Marinus will battle to the death atop a mountainpeak, inside the Narsyan conventuary—and those old odds will finally be paid in full, one way or the other." Clovis bowed, then added, "You're welcome."

Eldridge hung his head for a moment, then replaced the gun and picked up a rocket launcher. And another rocket launcher. And another. He kicked open a footlocker that lay on the floor against the wall and pulled out a series of leather harnesses that he used to secure the weaponry to his back. That done, he started stuffing gun after gun into every free pocket he had. Clovis looked on, a faultline of glee bisecting his face. The redhead crossed to the trapdoor, crouched, and lifted it. He paused.

"Hey, that old language you spoke—how do you say 'mountain'?"

Clovis raised an eyebrow. "*Montagne.* Why?"

Eldridge put a foot on the rope ladder and said, "Because Marko's about to feel the spirit of the *montagne.*"

• • • • •

BORIS HAGAN ALWAYS SAID Eldridge was from a place called Missouri. The redhead didn't know what the hell his old friend was talking about, but Hagan always assured him that before Deadblast, there existed a place called Missouri where no one believed anything unless they saw it. That's when the bearded pre-Deadblast historian would point to a metal plate on his wall that was embossed with random alphanumerics, as well as the name "Missouri," and the words, "Show-Me State."

"Miss, Sour, Ree," Eldridge said the first time he saw the plate.

"No, no—it's 'Miz-*er*-ee,'" Hagan said as they sat in his domicile years earlier, which he had furnished and decorated with pre-Deadblast relics—posters for old motionshows, plastic cups decorated with the logos of old sports teams, ancient books and a slew of other Hagan-specific treasures that no one else gave a shit about. In fact, it had been Hagan who presented Eldridge with a stack of T-shirts that celebrated the achievements of pre-Deadblast sports teams, including the fabled Utah Jazz. Hagan gave Eldridge the gift as thanks for one time when the redhead saved his life.

But back to that place called Missouri: Hagan started saying Eldridge was from Missouri when the redhead demanded to see the Arpa. Hagan had been drunkenly blathering on about it on top of Nix's one night, and Eldridge called *macta* on his ramblings.

"Show it to me," Eldridge said, and Hagan did, also informing Eldridge that he was from Missouri.

So after Eldridge left Clovis Wine up in his safehouse, he immediately climbed down the catwalk—ushered down by a few psychoskags, of course—and rode his bike west through town and directly over to Nix's where he could check on the latest results of the Xiang tourney and confirm whether Clovis had been telling the truth. Given the amount of money the dry man "tipped" him, his story seemed likely to be true, but all the same, the ancient land of Missouri demanded his allegiance.

Of the major haunts in Dedrick, Nix's satisfied another spatial requirement—Fiachra's hid inside one of the walls. Yasim's lurked underneath a massive clot of houses and huts. Nix's by contrast, sat astride an old A-frame building that (legend had it) had fallen from the ground level into the under-earth area when Deadblast happened. Hagan said it had once been a church—like Rene Rosaire's—but for a different god. The church merely served as the foundation for Nix's main establishment. Its A-frame roof remained intact, right up to a tapered tower that held a swinging bell. But underneath the A-frame, the remainder of the building sat in a crumpled heap of splintered two-by-fours and shattered stained glass. In the years following Deadblast, dregs of all iterations constructed various hovels on the church's carcass, but Nix came along with a stylus full of jenta and the wherewithal to demolish the cluster of hovels and replace them with his own neon emporium.

Approaching Nix's joint brought a slow increase in volume as the chattering, shouting, cheering and weeping combined into a cacophony of noise that hovered just underneath the white level. An equalizer display of the joint's sound output would look like a smattering of red lights dancing across a solid matrix of yellow and green.

As a weapons-laden Eldridge pulled up to Nix's on his bike, he swerved around a half-dozen dregs—some clad in leather, others in denim, others in steel—who came stomping down the front stairs of Nix's (formerly the front steps of the ancient church), all of them grousing about the latest results from this or that sporting event. Eldridge managed to smile at their anger. *If they only knew.* A red neon sign curled around the top of the old church steeple, reading, NIX'S. The redhead bounded up the front steps two at a time, his quadriceps burning from the added weight of ordnance on his back. He strode through a set of double doors—a pair of stained-glass images of unknown saints from a forgotten era—and beheld Nix's.

Like most Odds, Nix's chief currency was information. Yasim's information poured in from a thousand different sources, all of it intended to clarify the state of the current global map. Nix's information shared some DNA with Yasim's. Like his fellow Odd, Nix was forced to collect his information on sporting events through low-tech means: moto-express, hardline messages, and oftentimes a combination of the two.

But like Yasim's, Nix's oddsbroking included a hefty amount of fudging, rounding up, rounding down, and outright dishonesty—all of it dedicated to suckering dreg after dreg out of their hard-killed jenta. The results of Nix's dishonesty shouted down from motion-displays and streamed across old electropanels in animated red letters. All of this electronic equipment hung from the ceiling, which (like Nix himself) was adorned with a thousand shining banners that proclaimed the superiority of every sports team known to the remnants.

Old sports made the transition through Deadblast and metastasized into deadlier versions of their old selves. An old game called footbomerico made the leap and brought with it all of its trappings of warfare: armor, helmets, a battle for territory. But post-Deadblast footbomerico made the war metaphor literal and invited the bombing of opposing locker rooms before games. This meant that only about 70 percent of games ever made it to the field, and it sparked the genesis of the most important position on the team: bomb-sniffer.

Another old game called balimpsest involved a lot of tall guys chucking a ball through a hoop. Post-Deadblast, the game had gone back to its roots of being played inside cyclone fencing, all while raising the height of the hoop to 100 feet. This turned the game into a mad, climbing scramble from hoop to hoop, as the rules dictated that each team take the ball down to ground level every time possession changed or a hoop was scored.

Another game called baseball also made the leap and remained largely unchanged, save for the dominance of ragers on every team's roster. For all of these sports, Nix provided his patrons with results that were at least comparable with what happened on the field, but he and his retinue never reported the results so accurately that they lost money.

That wasn't the case with Xiang.

Xiang stood in contrast to the other team sports in that it was far harder to fudge the results of a tournament. No less than Jeb Goldmist oversaw the local tournament, and other tournaments held elsewhere attracted the caretaking attention of only the mightiest Odds. No one was quite sure why Xiang attracted the most money and the most ardent followers, but it did, and the evidence of this was standing all around the Xiang booth in Nix's—scores of fans, all of them thrusting red styli in the air and screaming for the results. One of Nix's oddments, a slow-thinking but quick-talking dreg named CiCi, balanced herself on the aluminum railing that ran around the bar, her hands filled with a pad of smartpaper and a red stylus. She wore simple overalls and one of Hagan's pre-Deadblast T-shirts ("ATLANTA FLAMES"), but some years ago, she asked Dr. Enki to permanently encase her feet with steel. That's how she balanced on the narrow beam so easily—it was magnetized. Speaking of narrow: CiCi had narrowly avoided becoming a dreen around the same time—specifically, a tary-fairy dreen—but Dr. Enki had covered her actual face with a series of strategically placed tattoos that altered her appearance enough so that she could look in the mirror without incident.

Eldridge negotiated the crowd and made his way over to the Xiang bar, where CiCi was standing with her legs spread wide, her hands in her pockets. A pair of pigtails bounced around her head as she giggled at a scowling dreg below her.

"Sorry, sir! You lost that move! Tee-hee!" She actually said "tee" and "hee."

The scowler spat on the floor and stormed off, leaving a space for Eldridge to shoulder his way up to the bar. A few dregs complained when the redhead's rocket launchers bonked them on the head, but they quickly grew silent when he shot them a dead-hard look. A grid of nine old televisions stood behind CiCi and in front of a curved mirror that covered the back of the booth. Results from the current Xiang tournament were listed on the TV, and even though the results (by the very nature of the game) only trickled in every few hours, the size of the crowd remained constant, as did the sleepy smile on CiCi's face. One of the TV's displayed the current state of the board, which indicated that White was massacring Black. The board displayed more information than just the current position, though. The lower-left corner of each square displayed one (or more) of three characters: X, U, or D.

An X indicated that a standard capture had taken place according to the rules of chess and Xiang, meaning that a stronger piece had captured a weaker piece.

A U indicated that an upset had happened, meaning that a weaker piece had defeated a stronger piece, regardless of who was capturing whom.

A D indicated that a piece had successfully defended its territory, meaning that a traditional capture had been thwarted.

Eldridge checked the square for Black's Kingside Rook but saw no letter in its corner yet. Neither did he see his own name, Clovis' name or the names of any of the other combatants, which raised the question of how dregs knew what piece to bet on. The answer was a combination of rumor, hearsay, and observation. Despite the best efforts to conceal the list of combatants, someone always leaked the list to the general populace, and odds were made based on that intel. But not everyone had access to the list, and for those unlucky dregs, they simply had to watch the board to see what pieces did better than others.

For example, in the case of Qi Li's pawn: A lucky few knew of Li's presence in the tourney and made gigs of jenta by wagering on him in early battles against far superior pieces. But everyone else had to watch the board and figure out that the avatar-warrior playing as White's H pawn was invincible, and as Li cut a swath through the Black camp, wagers on his success went up higher and higher. When he took out Black's Queen—an aging field marshal from the first post-Deadblast war—the odds in favor of him defeating Black's Kingside Rook and achieving promotion leapt skyward.

Eldridge knew it.

He waved over CiCi, and she crossed the booth with three loud *clonks* of her steel bootfeet. She crouched so her tattooed face was inches from his.

"Hey there, cutie-pie," she said while a pair of dregs screamed into her ears.

"CiCi! Do you have anything for me? Any news?"

Her eyes shifted in density from serene to bemused, but she kept smiling and shook her head. "Not that I know of, honey-pie," she said, then stood up straight and extended her hands over Eldridge's head. A messenger had just run in bearing information about the Xiang tourney. The shouting increased in volume. Snippets of commentary reached the redhead's ears:

"He's got results!"

"Who won the H1 square?!"

CiCi took the piece of paper, read it, smiled and shook her ass at the crowd.

"Tutti-frutti!" she said, and the place fell silent. Despite the stress he was under, Eldridge grinned. CiCi always said "tutti-frutti" when she had big news, and in this case, he had an idea what it was.

She continued, "Gents! Ladies! Freakazoids! We have an *upset that's not an upset!*"

Mayhem. Everyone knew what she was talking about. In any normal Xiang tourney, a Rook defeating a Pawn wouldn't be an upset, but seeing how White's H pawn, aka the supreme badass motherfucker Qi Li, had left a trail of U's in its wake, the D that appeared in the lower-left corner of the H1 square sparked howling protests from the entire joint. Dregs leapt up to the rafters and slung mugs of grog to and fro while the occasional hopped-up wannabe rager punched a hole in the wall. No one believed it—and everyone wanted to know who the hell Black had as its Kingside Rook.

On instinct, Eldridge shrank away, but he froze when the stream of whispers gave him the answer he sought. Two dregs caught his ear with their convo. The first dreg who spoke was a lanky hunchback who looked like a giant C.

"It's Wine, McDragg. It's fucking *Wine.*"

The second dreg, a bemonocled blusterton in a pith helmet and an evening gown whose name was apparently McDragg, responded, "You have just taken a shit in my brainpan, good sir. Wine? As in Clovis? As in Mister No-H2O? Balderdash. The H pawn was Qi Li. *The* Qi Li. I respectfully submit that the premise 'Clovis Wine is the Black Kingside Rook' is poppycock."

The giant C said, "But CiCi doesn't lie, and Goldmist signed off on this tourney. Wine must've picked up some skills."

"Or gone half dreen."

They both nodded sagely. Half dreen entering Xiang tourneys wasn't unheard of.

The cross-dressing blusterton said, "Though I'd be surprised if his body had enough moisture to power a working endocrine system."

Eldridge lost track of their words. Once again, he toyed with the idea of killing Clovis, but the idea of killing Marko Marinus seemed so much more delightful right now. As he thought about killing Marinus atop the Narsyan's own mountain, Nix's joint melted away and left him with a view of the Narsyan central chamber. Years ago, he stood alongside a friend and begged for the largesse of the Narsyans, only to have Marko dig a circle of flesh out of his forehead—all while condemning his other friend to life as a freak.

The redhead remembered holding hands with another of his childhood friends that night as they faced the Narsyan council of chieftains. This other friend was the only friend Eldridge had outside the order, and as he stood in Nix's that day in a fugue of rage, Eldridge remembered how his friend had once looked: blond hair, green eyes and a smattering of freckles. He and Eldridge had come to know the streets of under-Dedrick together during the redhead's impromptu jaunts down from the Narsyan sanctuary to the city.

Back then, this friend of Eldridge's didn't have to talk through a speechmouth or view the world through synthetic oculars. His skin didn't hang around his body, and his paralyzing fear of orifices was still just a nascent phobia. Eldridge's friend had yet to retreat into the back room of his casino.

The young Eldridge looked over at his old friend, Crius Kaleb, so many years ago. Years before he became an Odd. Years before he took the redhead's deathday wager.

A hand landed on Eldridge's shoulder and brought him out of his reverie. He blinked. Nix's and all its myriad clamor had returned. Someone was shaking his shoulder. It was CiCi, her pigtails bouncing. (CiCi always seemed to be in a perpetual state of bounce.)

"Hey, cutie! There's a nice gentleman who wants to see you."

"OK," Eldridge said, but she just stared at him. He looked around but saw no one. CiCi kept bouncing. He said, "Um, is he here?"

"Oh! Yeah. He said he's out back and that he wants to show you his balls."

A microscopic needle passed through the redhead's heart. "Got it, CiCi. Thanks."

He was out the door, rocket launchers askew from his rush. He sidestepped a few dregs on his way down the stairs, then circled around to the back of Nix's, which hid in an alleyway made dark by the overhanging balconies of a few nearby shanties. Steel trash collectors were set into the rear walls, directly underneath windows above. Trash in the form of half-eaten food and various crumpled detritus periodically rained down from above and clattered into the collectors. The trash collectors led into an elaborate underground network of tunnels and incinerators, Eldridge knew, having seen them firsthand with the man he was trying to find.

"Boris?" he whispered.

One of the trash collectors, which had been sitting closed, opened a few inches. Eldridge recognized the golden glint of his friend Boris Hagan's spectacles. The redhead smiled and tiptoed over, throwing a glance at the sky to check for any watchful eyes. He saw none and sat on an overturned crate next to the collector. They spoke in hushed tones.

"Boris? What're you doing?"

"El, what happened?"

"You mean with Qi Li or with Clovis?"

The glint of recognition in Hagan's eyes told Eldridge that his bearded friend knew everything. Hagan nodded and said, "Both."

"I killed Li. My bike's cooling system is shot, but I killed him. And Clovis is me. He's getting all my jenta when I win squares. I killed a rock star last night, the revolving door's trying to kill me, and someone's wasting a *lot* of water in Dedrick. Boris, what the hell's happening?"

"What rock star?"

"Larry Mercury, man."

"No shit? Good thing Stewart's not around, or he'd be distraught."

The mention of Stewart Kaleb darkened the inside of the redhead's mind. Boris was checking the alleyway for intruders and didn't notice.

Instead, he asked: "What was all that about water and the revolving door?"

"I had a knight battle, right? So naturally, I get stuck topside come gametime, and when I tried to get back down here, the revolving door was stopped."

"Did you go to the quarry?"

Eldridge gave him a look. "How'd you know?"

"It was probably full of water, right?"

"Yeah."

"So how do you think the revolving door works? Magic?"

Eldridge: "Um."

Hagan sighed. "There's an old hydroelectric generator underneath the door. The quarry's connected to it. Sometimes Goldmist vents off water to generate a few more kilowatts for the city. I don't know all the details, but the door'll stop sometimes. Man, you *have* been gone for awhile, haven't you?"

"Apparently. So, why are you hiding?"

"They're onto me."

"You said that before. Who?"

"Goldmist. I don't know how, but I think someone blabbed that I snuck you the tournament lineup."

"The lineup always gets leaked."

"Yeah, I know. I'm the one who always leaks it, but there's something different this year."

"You said 'the game's afoot.' What did that mean?"

"I think you already know."

Eldridge nodded. "Marko."

"So what's next?" Hagan asked.

"Clovis is sending me to kill him. It still doesn't balance—Marko in a Xiang tournament. But you already knew he was in it, didn't you?"

Hagan nodded.

"But you *didn't* know about Clovis, did you?"

"Nope. When I got the list of avatar-warriors, his name wasn't anywhere on it. The Black King was one of our usual monarchs. How did Clovis say he did it?"

Eldridge rolled his eyes. "Well, he had some help. I strong-armed my way into the tourney by forcing Clovis out. But Nix had already put him on the ledger, so I strong-armed *him* to switch us out."

Something metallic clattered above them. Hagan closed the trash collector's lid, and Eldridge squatted against the wall and cast his gaze about. When all looked clear, he tapped the lid, and Hagan reappeared with a question:

"I'm sorry, El—can you unpack the verb *'to strong-arm'* for me? What exactly does that mean?"

"Well, I may have stabbed Nix in the stomach. And I might have accidentally asked Dr. Enki to rewire his brain so he wouldn't remember switching us out."

Hagan held his head. "*El—*"

"Hey, you know I need the jenta—"

"Right, right, right. You're in this huge hole, and you need to do right by your family. So you asked Dr. Enki to hack into an Odd's brain and delete your shenanigans?"

"Right. And the *good* doctor did such a *good job* that Clovis got Nix to switch the names back."

Hagan shook his head. "No."

"What do you mean, no?"

"Nix takes down names and records the lineup for the tourney, but Goldmist—listen, he does more than just *oversee* the tournaments. He's a *fan.* When he's not porking his way through gaggles of nubliites, he's obsessing over the latest tourneys. He gets results from trans-oceanic XiangQi tourneys delivered to him. *He pays maniacs to cross the oceans so he can follow Xiang.* I don't know how Clovis could have pulled this off unless..."

"Unless what?"

"Unless he's in league with Goldmist."

Eldridge shook his head. "It doesn't balance. Goldmist makes jenta whether I get fucked or not. Why go out of his way for a dreg like me?"

"It *doesn't* make sense—unless you figure in Marko."

"What does he have to do with it?"

"You know the rumortrysts. They say Goldmist has an old, old grudge against the Narsyans."

The redhead's thought-centers activated. He looked at the balconies above while he crunched some numbers and facts. Finally:

"You're saying Goldmist gamed the tournament? Why? To take out Marko?"

"Yeah."

"Why?"

Hagan rolled his eyes and trotted out one of his kooky sayings: "El, you need a slide rule to figure that out? You know very well what the blood of a Narsyan chieftain is capable of. A universal cure? For anything? The Odds only traffic in jenta and chance. There's no comparison."

"Yeah, yeah, I *get* that. But Marko's not even their leader. They don't have one. You kill Marko, and the order'll just go on like nothing happened. And besides, the Narsyans don't know their pisshole from a sucking-chest wound. If it isn't lifting or cleaning or squatting or circle-jerking its dumb fucking cock, they don't give *one good fuck about it. Fuck them, and fuck Marko Marinus.*"

Unbeknownst to himself, Eldridge's face had deepened in tone until it matched the reddest hair on his head, and spittle flew from his lips with the utterance of each plosive consonant as his whisper increased in intensity until it was a strangled hiss. His sandy-haired friend reached out of the trash collector and touched his hand. The contact silenced Eldridge mid-sentence.

Hagan said, "Listen. I'm as sorry as anyone for what he did back then. For what he did to Cri. But don't do this. *Run.*"

"You know I can't."

"You'll find another way to pay it back."

Eldridge glared at him with an incredulous smile. "Do you *know* the hole I'm in?"

Hagan looked him in the eye for a full moment, and his shoulders sagged.

"It's actually true, isn't it? What the rumortrysts say? You're really in that deep?"

"Yeah. Marko's gotta die, and I'm the man to punch his ticket."

"How do you feel about that?"

Such questions were why Eldridge loved Boris Hagan. Since Deadblast, questions about *feeling* seldom delved deeper than the nerve endings that inhabited the skin's dermal layer. Hagan, however, had developed sensitivity for knowing when to probe beyond.

Eldridge considered the question, then said, "Boris, Marko cured me."

Hagan took a few seconds to absorb that statement. "*What?*"

"He did."

"How do you know that?"

"Someone told me."

"'Someone'? Who?"

"When I was in jail last night. Someone wrote it on my window. Marko's the one who cured me."

"El, what does that even *mean?* Who would go to the trouble of telling you that? Why would anyone even care? No offense."

"None taken, but–"

"And doesn't it make *more* sense that–oh, I dunno–you read Dr. Enki's instructions wrong?" Hagan had objected to Eldridge's deathday wager on principle, and at the time, he also argued that the doctor's idea to keep Eldridge alive with meticulously measured doses of meds was foolish.

"I didn't read them wrong."

"Are you sure?"

"*Yes,* I'm fucking sure. And it balances. Marko curing me. It balances. You know it does."

Hagan looked up and weighed his next words. "He knew about...well, he knew about your kid?"

There it was. The length and breadth of Eldridge's family. A single offspring.

The redhead nodded. "He knew, all right. And you said it: He's a Narsyan chieftain. His blood can cure anything. All he had to do was find a way to get one drop of his blood into me, and my cancer would go away. What better way to fuck me–*and* my kid–than that?"

"But how could he have known about your debt?"

"Everyone else did, didn't they? When I was back in the order, we heard about what was happening in town. Hell, we *loved* getting gossip up there. Kept *me* sane, at least."

Hagan's next logical question hung in the air for a moment before Eldridge pre-empted his friend and asked it himself:

"Do you think the doc helped him?"

Hagan pondered. "It would follow. Enki was in a position to make it happen. But do you have any *memory* of him helping you?"

"You mean, like giving me an injection of Narsyan blood? I think I'd—"

"Don't be dense. *Think.* Think back to a moment that didn't compute over the last month. Some dead time in Enki's office. You'd wake up with a sore spot on your arm. Something like that."

Eldridge thought. "I was out all last night, but the—"

"Why were you unconscious last night?"

"Xiang fight. I killed a bishop, but not before she poisoned me some."

"Of course she did."

"Yeah, *that* happened. But that's not when I got cured, because the doc told me I was cured right after I got into town. Right after he gave me a full-body scan—oh."

"What?"

"I don't remember the scan. I fell asleep."

Hagan looked at him. "Are you sure you *fell* asleep?"

Eldridge nodded. "Right." He stood. "You know what I'm going to do? I'm going to kill Marko Marinus, and then I'm going to ask the good doctor if he had anything to do with it."

"How do you plan to kill Marko?"

The redhead smiled, reached into his pants and produced two small rectangular objects that he had wrapped in a bandanna. He unwound the fabric and showed the two cellphones to Hagan, who covered his face.

"You want my advice, get rid of those now. You don't want to mess with that kind of firepower."

Eldridge ignored him and said, "I need you to do two things for me."

Hagan sighed. "What?"

"One, give me your smallpitch. Two, cross your eyes."

"What?"

Eldridge scratched his head. "What's that old thing they said? For good luck?"

"Oh, cross my *fingers?*"

"Yeah, that. But cross your eyes, too. Just in case."

"Will do. The smallpitch is in my apartment. You know where." Hagan started to lower himself back into the garbage tunnels. "El?"

The redhead stopped.

Hagan: "Last chance. Don't do this. Please."

The redhead gave his friend a hard look, then walked away.

• • • • •

AFTER A QUICK STOP by Yasim's to win some jenta—the intel from Qi Li's corpse came in handy—Eldridge bought a brand-new pack of supercooled blue gel. Ten minutes later, he was hunched over the innards of his bike in a private garage he maintained in a small shack that hid in a circle of buildings surrounding Goldmist's tower. He worked on his motorbike to the accompanying gouty howls of Goldmist's hoverbike-riding oddments, who swooped through the sky outside. Inside the garage, Eldridge had covered the walls with corkboard and hung hundreds of tools. In the corner sat a plastic table that held one of Constable Tola's record players. A scratchy rendition of a song about an artist obsessed with the color black floated out of the speakers. The new Freon pack fit right in, and as he was shutting the housing to his bike, someone knocked at the open door of his garage. It was the constable. Her lanky, bow-legged form blocked off most of the exterior light.

"I heard you're capturing Marko?"

Eldridge turned and held up his palms. "Oh, for the days when Xiang moves were actually kept secret. Does every damn body know?"

"No, just me. I was breaking up a fight over by Fiachra's when Boris pulled me into an alley and begged me to talk you out of it."

"I can kill Marko."

"I know you can. But you shouldn't."

Eldridge ignored her and started securing the rocket launchers to his bike with bungee cords. She followed him around the bike as he worked.

"You shouldn't, El. What he did—it happened so long ago. Forget about it."

Eldridge stopped and rested his palms on his bike. He stared at it for a moment, then glared up at Tola. His eyes burned at first, then softened as a glaze appeared over them. He crossed to her.

"Did Hagan tell you he cured me?"

"Boris cured you?"

"No. Marko. Marko cured me."

Tola placed a hand on her sidearm. "How?"

Eldridge shrugged. "Beats me. But he did." He looked at the ground. "No lie–I'd like to kill him for what he did to Kaleb back in the day. But this...making me better? When he knew I wanted to die? *Had* to? It balances. If I kill him, I can win it all back. Get even with the house again. But that's not enough. If I didn't have family, I'd be dead by now. I'd have given my body to the desert. Just wasted away. But with my kid floating around out there, I can't. I gotta do this. Simple as that."

Tola's brow wrinkled. "You have a kid? How old are you?"

"Not so old, but I had her when I was really young. Fifteen."

"Where is she?"

"Doesn't matter. If I don't get even, the Odds will find her."

Tola did the math in her head. "If you were fifteen...then she'd be twentysomething right now, wouldn't she?"

Eldridge nodded.

"Who's that trixie you're always seeing?"

"Oksana? Zor, that's gross–"

"I know you don't sleep with her," the constable said. "But she's about that age, isn't she?"

"Zor, *you're* about that age. But that doesn't make you my daughter, and it doesn't make Oksana my daughter, either. My daughter...she's nowhere near here, thank Crom."

Tola thought, and just as she was about to ask another question, Eldridge stood his bike upright and climbed on.

He said, "Come on, I gotta get moving. It's a long ride out to the mountains."

"Wait, wait–how do you know Marko cured you?"

"I don't. Well, not really. Someone wrote it on my window last night."

"What? At the jail?"

"Yeah."

"Who would do that?"

Eldridge sighed. "Listen, I have to get going."

She touched his arm. "Wait. Boris told me something else. Something about *cellphones?*"

"You gonna try to talk me out of using those, too?"

"No, but–you need to use them in tandem, right? You'll need someone to plant one somewhere. Let me do it."

Eldridge, instantly: "No."

"You can't do this on your own. Let me–"

"I know I can't do it on my own. That's why I'm going to retain the services of my favorite trixie. But you can help me another way."

"OK, how?"

The redhead walked to the back of the garage, where an old vinyl slipcover concealed...something. Eldridge pulled off the covering and revealed a device that resembled an instrument of torture. A heavy metal arm made an L shape over a target area. The tip of the arm was capped with a thick needle. A stool sat under the machine, next to a footpedal that apparently powered the contraption.

Tola's face lit up.

"You never told me you had a *sewing machine!*"

"Well, I was saving it for your birthday, but seeing as I need your help now..." Eldridge reached into his satchel and pulled out Boris Hagan's smallpitch. "Do you think Oksana would look good in black?"

• • • • •

IF ANY SATELLITES HAD remained in orbit the day Eldridge rode out to the Oasis Mountains to face off with Marko Marinus, they would have recorded *two* people traveling north along the highway through the desert, not one. The redhead rode alongside Oksana the trixie, who sat behind the wheel of an old yellow hatchback internal-combustor that herked and jerked its way through the sand, clouds of exhaust billowing out the back. Eldridge and Tola had labored for the better part of a day over the sewing machine in the redhead's garage, which prevented him from departing until much later. The desert sun began its descent toward the horizon to the west.

Eldridge glanced over at Oksana, who extended her middle finger at him. Behind his bandannas, he smiled and returned the gesture. They rode for an hour longer before the sun started to vanish and the temperature began its precipitous drop. The Oasis Mountains were growing larger before them, and once they got within striking distance, Eldridge signaled to Oksana to pull over behind a rocky hill that lay to the side of the faint desert road. Once they were stopped, the trixie got out of her car—but she wasn't wearing her usual attire. In place of her corseted dress, she was wearing a black, full-body suit. Oksana herself provided the black suit, which was merely the foundation for a series of shining black panels that Tola had sewn on.

The panels had once been part of Boris Hagan's smallpitch.

Tola sliced up the smallpitch to match the pattern of Oksana's bodysuit, and both Tola and Eldridge collaborated on the rewiring of the getup, which they nicknamed the "pitchsuit." The finishing touch was a small panel on the wrist of the suit that held the on/off button. When Tola completed her sewing, she pressed the button—and instilled terror into all their hearts. She switched it off.

"Sometime, I need to show you something that Boris and I built together," the constable said, smiling.

"Maybe some other time," Eldridge said.

But later, out in the desert, the redhead waved Oksana back into her car so they could keep warm by its surprisingly robust heating system. They slammed the doors and rubbed their hands as the sun set and the windows frosted over.

"OK, El. Why am I wearing this, and what's the plan?"

"All right—here's the plan. I'm fighting Marko way up at the peak of the mountain, at the conventuary. Now, here's a little secret: There are actually *two* paths up there. The Narsyans only use one of 'em, but they patrol them both."

"Which one am I taking?"

"The main one. You'll have to be crafty, but the pitchsuit should give you plenty of cover. About halfway up the path, you'll see two huge rocks, right next to each other. *Be careful.* In between those rocks is a bottomless pit that cuts into the mountain. It's called the Callis Oubliette, but who gives a shit. You'll need to drop this into it."

He held out one of the phones. She took it and gave him a look.

"Don't these things have, like, codes or something? How're you gonna *call* it?"

"When I swung by Hagan's place to get the smallpitch, I hopped on the Arpa and figured out how to get the code."

Oksana gasped in awe. "You...*pressed the buttons?*"

"I sure did. And if you'd been there when I figured it out, you'd have seen a grown man shit his pants. Well, you would've seen a grown man shit his pants *again.*"

She giggled. "What do I do after I drop it?"

"Run like hell."

The trixie nodded. "Let's go."

They got out of the car and split up—Eldridge due east, Oksana on a more northerly course toward the main path. As he ran through the frozen desert toward the secondary path, he thought back to the day he discovered it.

It was the same day he got drummed out of the order.

He was about 12 years old at the time—very few people knew their own age in those days—and he was planning to sneak out of Burbage and down to Dedrick for the hundredth time. The young redhead had been executing a half-ton hack-squat when he decided to sneak out of Burbage for the hundredth time. A dozen fellow Narsyans sat atop the order's hack-squat rig, which looked less like gym equipment and more like the roof of a mausoleum that Eldridge pressed skyward with his bulging quadriceps. One of his fellow order members, a flinty nine-year-old girl named Yamuna, perched over him while he ripped off his 300th repetition.

"You're not going to sprint to the city again, are you?"

Sweat broke across the redhead's brow. He nodded.

Yamuna said, "You shouldn't. You should stop going down there. Gonna get the circle, El." She tapped the middle of her forehead, which bore the tell-tale vertical scar of all Narsyans. Eldridge thrust his legs upward and sent the dozen Narsyans sitting on the rig flying off it while he slammed the rig's safeguards in place and stood up, his legs tingling.

He winked at Yamuna.

During his next sleep cycle—which was three days later—he slipped out of Burbage the same way he always did: He said he was training.

No Narsyan elder would stop a young member from squeezing in a few extra sprints instead of allowing himself the one hour of sleep out of every 96 that order members usually took. Of course, "sprint" in Narsyan parlance usually meant a sustained run of 30 miles or more. In Eldridge's case, it meant a full-tilt sprint across the desert in the middle of the night. None of the Narsyan chieftains had noticed yet—but his days missing were starting to add up.

The preteen redhead slowed to a jog as he approached the giant revolving door that led into his favorite place in the world: the shitty under-earth area of Dedrick. Back in those days, Jeb Goldmist's tower was little more than a stump that stood over the rest of the skyline, while Nix's hadn't even been built yet. Constable Tola wasn't around, either, because she had yet to be born. Eldridge arrived in town wearing the severed skins of various suprafelines, all of which he stripped off when he got into town. He typically dumped them with the first freezing dreg he saw, confident that his preternaturally muscular, youthful body would be enough to win him some replacement skins from a lonely Dedrick citizen—Narsyans taught their young the virtues of powerfucking at an early age. But he had all night to play, and he retraced an imaginary dotted line that led him on the shortest route through the city to the building that would one day house Yasim's, except back in those days, the building—a small house—had yet to be consumed by the hundreds of houses that would bury it in the years to come. Neither had Yasim and his hyperglobe appeared on the scene yet. No, in those days, Yasim's was simply a restaurant called Jaagup's.

But for Eldridge and his friend Crius Kaleb, it was absolute fucking paradise.

Crius hung out at Jaag's virtually every night, and as always, he was waiting for Eldridge when he appeared in the doorway, misted with sweat from his sprint. Crius ordered two beers, which arrived at their table on an elaborate slide system that Jaagup had built into the walls of his joint, which glisten-gleamed with neon and old-style electric light fixtures that hissed and sparked in tune with the surges of power that came from a gas-powered generator that whirred behind the bar. Eldridge had been coming down to Dedrick for about a year by that point, and in that time, Crius had already begun to deteriorate. The skin had started to sag around his face, and his complexion had faded to a paler shade than usual. Everyone was pale because no one really went outside, but Crius' appearance stemmed from the side effects of an anti-psychotic, anti-anxiety injection he had started giving himself as his fear of orifices–and everything else–grew. This fear manifested itself as a perpetual glaze of terror that covered Crius and only abated when Eldridge was around, and they were drinking beer. They drank a lot of beer at Jaagup's, sitting in that rear booth and dreading the sunrise.

As soon as he sat down, Eldridge said three words he'd said a hundred times before:

"Let's do it."

Crius shrank into his corner of the booth. His jowls quivered.

"Next time."

It was a common refrain, "Next time."

Eldridge pressed him: "Why not *this* time?"

Crius repeated the same question he always asked: "*How* are we going to get up there again?"

"We'll klep a ride. I'll drive, you'll ride in back. We'll get something with a sidecar, maybe. And a roof."

His frail friend wept a pair of fear-tears. He wiped them away and stared at the table. "El, I don't know if I can. It's such a long way out there. And the one time I saw the sky...I still have nightmares about it."

"Don't you want to be better?"

"I *am* better. Than I was. The shots help."

Eldridge never asked where Crius got the injections, and he didn't care to know.

He said, "Cri, this will work. I found another way up to the peak. It's safe."

Crius asked another question he had asked many times before: "Why do I even need to come? Can't you just bring it down with you?"

"You've got to be there or it won't work. Besides, the trip will be good for you."

The balance between their two opposing viewpoints had remained undisturbed for the previous five months, and Eldridge saw no sign of that changing.

So he gave Crius something that his future friend Boris Hagan would have called "a mickey." Eldridge slipped it into Crius' drink. He carried his unconscious friend out of Jaag's and across town to where he found an old internal-combustion motorcycle parked outside Fiachra's. Using knowledge he had picked up on the under-streets of Dedrick, Eldridge cracked open the engine and spliced a few wires together to start the bike.

Crius woke up halfway out to the mountains. He didn't stop screaming all night.

Those screams stirred Eldridge back to the present day, where he sprinted past one of the starting lines that the Narsyans used for their deep-desert sprints. Eldridge hated his time with the Narsyan order. He hated the work, hated the endless days of exertion, but when he sprinted through the desert in the dead of night, his body a transportation system, his heartrate the only thing holding back the cold, he appreciated the hours he put in alongside Marko.

But years ago, when he spirited a sickly Crius Kaleb up to the mountain peak, he had nothing but a heap of stolen animal hides to keep him and his trembling friend comfortable as they rode through the night. But upon arrival at the mountains, the redhead's plan, almost by necessity, would lurch to a halt and shiver to pieces under its own weight.

He hadn't even thought about how he was going to get Crius up the mountain.

The Narsyans had taught him a lot during his formative years. They had taught him self-reliance. They had taught him unparalleled survival skills. They had taught him how to powerfuck any lifeform within an inch of its life. They had neglected, however, to teach him how to fucking *think*, which led to the derailing of his plan at the foot of the mountains when the elements beset them on both sides—the sun on the eastern horizon and the impenetrable snow on the mountains. After screaming his voice away, Crius had passed out some miles back. At the foot of the mountain, Eldridge dismounted the bike to survey the scene. The redhead picked up his friend and slung him over his shoulders.

Years later, on the threshold of his battle with Marko Marinus, a grown-up Eldridge stood in the exact same spot where he once hoisted Crius Kaleb over his shoulders and looked up the mountain path that led to Burbage. The first Narsyan checkpoint was still some miles ahead on the main path. Eldridge thought back to that awful night years ago, when he noticed something that none of his fellow order members had seen before.

A second path up the mountain.

It was little more than a slight difference in color among the rocks to the right of the main path. As a child, Eldridge knew about the checkpoints, of course, and like the rest of his stupid plan, he hadn't considered how he was going to circumvent them. The second path appeared to solve that problem. So he took it, Crius still slung over his shoulders—and he climbed and climbed and climbed. High above, he knew that the council of chieftains—even though they weren't a council—had convened for one of their thrice-annual love-ins ("vision-odyssey," in Narsyan parlance) where they would go spend a solid 170 hours smoking and powerfucking atop the mountain, all in an effort to determine a course of action for the order. Like all pubescent Narsyans, Eldridge had heard tales of the council's retreat told in hushed tones. Even among Narsyans, it sounded decadent; decadent, because by the end of the weeklong bender of sex and high-powered drugs, the council actually fell into a deep sleep that lasted *another* full week.

A full week of uninterrupted sleep. The idea of such slothfulness would enrage the average Narsyan, but for the council, the week of sleep offered up the most vivid waking dreams possible due to the stratospheric level of toxicity in the venom-crystal they smoked. The Narsyan resistance to most poisons also translated to a resistance to a wide spectrum of hallucinogens, so in order to induce a visionquest among the council of chieftains, they special ordered a thermonuclear strain of venom-crystal crafted by the aquatic marauders that lived at the bottom of the ocean. The marauders tasked their most brilliant and foolhardy scientists to cultivate the venom-crystal from a deadly primordial sludge that bubbled up from a sea-floor vent. They infused the crystal with radioactive isotopes whose half-lives would post-date the heat-death of the universe. The marauder-scientists had to invent a hermetically sealed supercontainer just to ship the crystals. The cargo arrived at the Narsyan camp accompanied by a team of land-faring marauders who held the decagram of crystal on 10-meter-long pikes, all of them buried in prophylactic gear that not only provided them with the respiro-sludge they needed to breathe, but would also protect them from contamination if the supercontainer's hull should be breached. The Narsyan chieftains themselves didn't dare open the supercontainer until they reached the conventuary, where they could be sure that none of their younger charges would accidentally inhale the smoke given off by the burning of the crystal.

But the young Eldridge didn't know if the smoke would be gone by the time he reached the conventuary. No matter. He continued to climb, and as his younger self carried Crius Kaleb to the conventuary, the elder Eldridge slogged up the same secondary pathway he had discovered as a child. His feet cut deep troughs through the snow, still weighed down by the rocket launchers, guns and other weapons he took from his safehouse.

Of course, he had his primary weapon—the cellphone—in his pocket, but he brought everything else, too. Just in case. He paused on the path and considered the time. The rules of Xiang dictated that he give his target 30 minutes advance notice of his attack. He figured he had that much climbing time left. He pressed a few buttons on his jad device, felt a quick surge of heat in his polycharge, then continued his ascent.

He was environed in a sea of snow and rock. The path was little more than a wide spot of snow that cut higher into the crags that hovered in the mist above. Wind blasted him from all sides at once. Snow stabbed at his cheeks like a frozen sandstorm. He lowered his shoulders and marched on, the weight on his back reminiscent of Crius Kaleb's dead weight on his shoulders so long ago.

When the young Eldridge emerged at the top of the secondary path all those years ago, this is what he saw: the Narsyan conventuary lancing through the clouds like a spike in a bed of cotton. The original mountain's peak had been far more rounded, of course, but the Narsyan craftsmen who carved the conventuary had honed the stone into a point as fine as sharpened graphite. The secondary path spilled out onto a small, rocky clearing that hovered above the clouds about 20 yards east of the conventuary. It was oddly free of snow, probably due to the altitude. At the time, Eldridge had no idea how he was going to get across it. Crius still lay unconscious across the redhead's shoulders. He lowered Crius to the ground and sat down. Across the cloudy clearing, he saw what he hoped he would see: a slew of unconscious Narsyans, all of them strewn about the conventuary, which looked like a giant, serrated bullet lined with featureless, smooth columns. Eldridge stood and crept down to the cloudline, where he lowered his foot into the mist—and found purchase. Slowly, he slid down under the clouds until he found himself on a small path that led across the divide. Moving inch by inch, he made his way over to the conventuary, holding his breath the entire way. (Eldridge was years away from taking his first crack at the 30-Minute Whoop, but even young Narsyans could hold their breath for 10 minutes at a time.) Once his head rose above the cloud level again, he looked around and recognized several of the Narsyan elders, though there were many he had never seen before. As he approached, Eldridge saw that although they were asleep, they were not motionless. Those that had fallen asleep in groups lay still, but those that lay in the freezing cold alone had curled into fetal positions, their hands clasped before them, their bodies shaking in a rigid, unchanging pattern. All of them held bowls, pipes, and hookahs that bore the ashes of the deadly crystal.

Eldridge had yet to take a breath since reaching the mountain's peak.

The redhead looked around for any sign of the crystal's smoke, then shook his head. He didn't even know what the smoke would look like. Or *smell* like, for that matter. So he opened his nose and mouth and inhaled until his lungs were full.

He didn't die.

The redhead exhaled and looked around. For what he needed to do, any one of the Narsyan chieftains would suffice. And like his older self years later, the young Eldridge also had something hidden in his pocket. He pulled it out and held it glinting in the diffuse, high-elevation sunlight. At a glance, it looked like a syringe, but closer inspection would reveal that it had no plunger—it was only a small glass tube affixed with a needle at one end. Eldridge removed a plastic protector that covered the needle and turned to check on his friend. Crius continued to slumber on the rocky clearing across the clouds. The redhead kneeled next to the nearest Narsyan chieftain and held his breath, this time out of anticipation. He recognized the chieftain as one of their long-distance sprinting mentors. His name was Mill, and he slept in the arms of a fellow (and much younger) chieftain whose face was hidden.

They both lay perfectly still.

Eldridge surveyed their sleeping forms in search of a prominent blood vessel to tap. He knew that if he could transfer the blood from the Narsyan chieftain into Crius in less than a minute, it would cure his friend. Mill slept with his arms curled up close to him, but his sleeping-mate had fallen asleep with his arms outstretched, and the weight of Mill's shoulder resting on his arm had caused the younger Narsyan chieftain's vessels to rise out of his arms in quarter-inch relief. Eldridge gripped the Narsyan's forearm and prepared to slide the needle into his vessel. But an instant before he did, he noticed something familiar: a birthmark on the inside of the Narsyan's forearm. The snaking pattern of the birthmark stirred memories inside the younger Eldridge—memories familiar enough to make him frown—but he cast them aside and slid the needle into the younger chieftain's arm.

Years later, Eldridge emerged onto the same rocky clearing, only this time he bore weaponry on his back instead of a friend. Stars sparkled overhead, accompanied by a bright, round moon. He half expected to discover an ambush waiting for him atop the mountain, but he only found what had been reported to him by Clovis Wine and Pell Yannick: the conventuary, deserted except for one man.

Marko Marinus.

But contrary to what Pell had told him, Marko wasn't there to complete one of the order's Great Challenges. Well, that's not *all* he was there to do.

Marko had apparently hidden his intentions from the Narsyan order by *telling* them that he had retired to the mountainpeak to undergo a Great Challenge, when in reality, he was merely using the mighty

Narsyan conventuary as the greatest fortress in the storied history of Xiang. A balimpsest fan would've called it a "home-cage" advantage. Marko had outfitted the great stone spike with various mortar cannons that he had fixed into porthole-like openings around the base of the spike's circumference. In addition, he had also fortified the conventuary in another way.

Eldridge spotted the device just inside the conventuary. It looked like any number of gas-powered generators he had seen in his time, but he recognized the blue-luminescent steady-state workings of a force field generator. Like the redhead's bike, they ran on a hydrocell, which meant that Marko had encased the conventuary in a half-sphere of invisible, impenetrable plasma.

But like a good Narsyan, Marko wasn't allowing himself any spare time, instead filling his idle hours atop the mountain by carrying out one of the order's Great Challenges. The Narsyans had hundreds of such challenges, but one of the greatest was to survive with no food, water, or air for a fortnight—also known as the One Way challenge. Eldridge figured that Marko was deep into the challenge because he was also ankle-deep in his own shit. Narsyans were allowed to pass food *out* of their bodies—hence the One Way nickname—but no food could enter. Besides the huge pile of shit around his ankles, Marko looked about the same: His head still resembled a trowel, with a pronounced, hawklike nose and sunken chin. He stood naked, every muscle on his body as prominent and well defined as an anatomical chart. Narsyan training had boiled away the fat on his body so that even the coloration of his muscles and tendons stood out from each other under his leathery skin. He looked like he was wearing a red mask with white highlights that encircled his mouth and eyes. The top of his skull shone through the millimeter of flesh that encased his head. Marko stood perfectly still, his eyes closed, his fists clenched and outstretched at his sides.

But what attracted the redhead's gaze wasn't the freakish appearance of his old friend. No, instead it was the inkvine scar that ran along the inside of his forearm.

At a glance, someone might mistake the scar for a birthmark.

And years earlier, when the young Eldridge inserted a needle into the arm of a slumbering Narsyan chieftain, a sudden shriek drove the redhead back onto his rear-end. His friend Marko Marinus, who for some reason had joined the Narsyan chieftains on their retreat, stood from behind Mill. At first, Marko's scream rousted none of the chieftains—he simply stood amidst dozens of still-sleeping Narsyans and howled a warning to the skies, his finger leveled at Eldridge, whom he appeared not to recognize. Finally, Marko dropped to a knee and delivered a crushing blow to the side of the chieftain Mill's head, which brought him sputtering back to consciousness.

"Wha—what? What's happening?"

Marko screamed, "Invader! Invader! Inva..." He trailed off as his mind processed the impossible: His friend Eldridge was sitting on the ground before him, holding a blood-sampling tube. "El?"

The redhead didn't have time to respond because the rest of the Narsyan chieftains were already rising up from their slumber. The sounds of chattering and yelling echoed across the mountains as dozens of naked Narsyan chieftains surrounded Eldridge. One of them stepped through the throng: Pell Yannick. He glared at the redhead.

"You're Eldridge, are you not?"

The redhead nodded.

"And what is that in your hand?"

Eldridge held it up. Pell took it and examined it. Blood dripped from the needle. His eyes narrowed.

"What did you plan to do with this?"

Another voice: *"Over here!"*

Eldridge's chin sank against his sternum. Across the cloudy divide, a few Narsyans had discovered Crius Kaleb's unconscious form. They carried him over and deposited him at the ground next to the redhead. Pell Yannick kneeled and lifted a lock of hair away from Crius' face.

"Is this is an outsider?"

Eldridge held his face in his hands. "Yes."

"From the city? Dedrick?"

Head in hands, Eldridge nodded. Murmurs of disapproval filled the air as the chieftains processed the news that one of their own had absconded down to Dedrick—an expulsion-worthy offense. Pell's inquisition marched on:

"You carried him all the way up the mountain?"

Nod.

"With the intention of injecting him with the blood of a Narsyan chieftain?"

Nod.

"And you are well aware that such an infraction is worthy of immediate expulsion from the order?"

Eldridge's head snapped up. He spat: "And I'm *also* well aware that any order member has the right to face the council of chieftains before expulsion."

Pell's lower eyelids quivered. "We're not a council."

"Then I have the right to face the *whatever* of chief—"

A firecracker exploded inside Eldridge's head. His vision flashed white, a *crack* sounded in his ears, and his head rocked back on his neck. When his eyesight cleared, he shook his head and saw Pell Yannick glowering at him, his lips curled. The Narsyan chieftain rubbed his right hand in response to the blow it had just delivered. His voice rumbled with rage:

"You *will* meter your tone when you speak with me, future-*macta.* And you'll get your audience with the chieftains. *Posthaste.*"

Years later, as he stood in the rocky clearing on top of the mountain, Eldridge looked at his old friend—the friend who had betrayed him—and he fingered the cellphone in his pocket. He knew it had a twin; a twin that Oksana had (hopefully) deposited into the Callis Oubliette.

He stood and called across the cloudy divide:

"*Marko!*"

His friend opened his eyes and searched for the source of the sound. When he spotted the redhead, Marko Marinus frowned and stepped out of his own shit. He took his first breath in weeks—an enormous, gasping gale that inflated his torso—and he squinted into the moonlight that gleamed off the rocks. He pressed his hand against the side of his head and closed his eyes. He teetered on his feet as oxygen raced back into his system, and when he opened his eyes, he looked at the redhead again—and smiled.

"El? Is that you?"

"It's me, Marko."

"How are you feeling, my friend?"

Eldridge winced at the words and shouted back: "I'm not your friend. And you know exactly how I'm feeling."

Marko frowned. "I don't understand. But there's no time—you should get out of here. It's dangerous."

"And why is that?"

"I entered a Xiang tournament, believe it or not. And I'm due for an attack any minute."

"Right," Eldridge said. "That'd be me."

Marko frowned. "You're the rook?"

"I'm the rook."

"Wait, but—why did *you* enter the tournament?"

"Really, Marko—what the fuck do you care, after what you did to me? After *everything* you did to me?"

"Eldridge, you should withdraw from the tournament immediately. I know what a deep hole you're in—"

"Fuck you, Marko. You know why I'm in this tournament."

Marko shook his head. "No, I don't."

"Because you *cured* me!"

"Of course I did!"

Everything suddenly balanced. Even though Eldridge was expecting the answer, he still reeled from it, his ears pounding from the revelation.

"Why?" the redhead asked. "Why'd you do it? I already knew you hated me. Why fuck with me *and* my daughter?"

"El, listen to me! You don't understand."

"I understand *everything*. I know you hate me, but why get my girl involved?"

"Your girl? Your daughter? No, Eldridge, I cured you to *help* you, I—"

"You *knew* I had to die! Holy Crom, Marko—if you hate me so much, why not just let that happen? Let me out of this shitty world? At least my girl could've been even with the house again, but you—"

Marko's face reddened. His tone darkened: "Look at yourself, Eldridge. What happened to you? You could have been the greatest among us."

"Rook takes rook, Marko."

"No, no, wait, Eldridge, let me explain—"

"No. *Look.*"

Eldridge pulled out the cellphone and held it up.

"You know what this is."

Marko dropped back a step. He knew exactly what it was. Everyone did, and anyone would.

Years earlier, a few hours after Marko Marinus blew his cover on the mountaintop, Eldridge entered the Narsyan central chamber—the same elliptical room that held all of the order's most treasured (and reviled) icons, and the same room where he would meet with Pell Yannick years later—for the first time in his life. A shivering Crius Kaleb followed him into the room and was immediately ushered to the side by a guard. Another guard escorted the redhead to the room's solar-center. The Typhoid Maiden retracted into the ceiling, leaving a single black circle on the floor. Eldridge stood in it. The council that wasn't a council of chieftains filed into the room and stood facing the redhead. They had clothed themselves in standard Narsyan garb: minimal wraps and straps that seemed to cover random parts of their bodies. The usual regions of modesty remained exposed on half of the chieftains. Pell Yannick, wearing only a pair of black straps that encircled his chest, stood directly across from Eldridge.

Marko Marinus stood next to him.

Pell cleared his throat. "We convene today in the wake of our tri-annual vision-odyssey to inquire into the matter of order member W. Eldridge, who has—if the evidence balances—betrayed our trust and the trust of all order members. Speaking for the chieftains, I eye-witnessed enough evidence to support his immediate expulsion from the order, but as order member Eldridge has invoked his right to face the chieftains personally, we must grant him that right. What have you to say for yourself?"

Eldridge, instantly: "Why'd you punch me in the face, you fucking pussy?"

Pell's spiral leg scar turned purple. "What?"

"You gotta answer my questions. Them's the rules."

"I struck you because you're an insolent cunt and always have been. Do you have anything else to say?"

Eldridge laughed. "Do I have anything else to *say?* Don't the rest of you fuckheads wanna know why I was trying to steal some of your blood?"

Pell: "Oh, I've already informed them."

"And?"

"And we agree that you deserve to be expelled immediately."

"You're kidding, right?"

Pell stared at him for 10 seconds. "I assure you we are not."

Then someone else spoke. Marko.

"Why would you even ask that?"

Eldridge shot back: "Why are *you* even *talking* to me? You're not a chieftain."

Pell said, "Not yet, but young Marinus was to brave the Typhoid Maiden as soon as we returned from our vision-odyssey. For the purposes of this inquisition, you have to answer to him, too."

Pell put his hand on Marko's shoulder. The young Narsyan's chest swelled. He looked down at the redhead and repeated, "Why would you even ask if we're kidding?"

"Because we're a joke. This whole world is a joke. I've been down to the city, and I know."

Marko said, "What do you know, exactly?"

"Down in the city, I've asked—*what* happened at Deadblast? No one knows. No one can even guess. That's how fucked we are. The world ended, and no one knows how. No one remembers. And then there's us. Hey, assholes: We're wasting our time up here. Have any of you morons thought about that? What if the Order of the Narsyan dedicated itself to—oh, I dunno—*growing some fucking food?* Or helping poor folks? Or helping *anyone?* You see my friend over there? He's got a parasite in his brain that's making him crazy. The physician *iacios* they got down there can't figure it out. Don't have any idea what's wrong. Hey, come here." Eldridge waved Crius over, but he didn't move. The redhead walked over but stopped midstep. Crius had put his head between his knees and was massaging the backs of his ears. A puddle of water was expanding around his head. Eldridge kneeled next to his friend.

"Cri?"

He looked up, and Eldridge saw that the fluid on the floor wasn't water but *saliva* that was running nonstop out of Crius' mouth. The front of his shirt was soaked. He kept rubbing the backsides of his ears.

Looking back at this moment years later, Eldridge would reflect that the parasite in his brain wasn't the only thing that drove his old friend mad.

The redhead took his hand, helped him to his feet and walked him to the center of the room. Still drooling, his friend trembled before the sight of all the mighty Narsyan chieftains staring down at him.

Still holding Kaleb's hand, Eldridge continued: "Listen to me: *One drop* of blood from any of you dipshits could make him normal. But *no.* You've got to build a wall around us while we sit up here in one big circle-jerk until we die."

Pell exhaled. "Are you finished?"

"Yes."

"Very well, the chieftains—"

Eldridge: "Wait! One more thing: Fuck you."

Pell's lips pursed. "Very well. The chieftains have held audience with you, and we will now vote on the matter of your expulsion. All those *opposed to* expulsion."

Roughly half the room screamed at the upper limit of human possibility. Pell looked at them in shock, his narrative of unity against the redhead instantly undone.

"All those *in favor* of expulsion?"

Once again, roughly half the people in the room screamed their asses off. But one of the chieftains remained silent: Marko Marinus, who was staring at the ground. Pell squeezed his shoulder.

"You cannot abstain, Marinus. If you *oppose* expulsion, sound your voice. If in favor, do not."

Marko looked up. He looked at Eldridge with soft eyes that recalled their times together in early training. But over the next minute, his gaze grew harder and harder until suddenly all feeling drained out of his eyes, and he was looking at Eldridge like a stranger. He shook his head. Pell grinned down at Eldridge with dark eyes.

"It is thus."

Years later, Eldridge brandished the cellphone given him by Oksana and shouted across the cloudy divide to his old friend.

"It's got a twin, Marko! Deep inside the mountain! If I press this button, I bring it all down!"

"Eldridge, wait, please!"

"*Shut up!*"

"El, *please!*"

In the next instant, three things happened:

Eldridge pushed the "send" button.

Marko said, "I entered the tournament for you."

And a dark feeling crossed the redhead's brain.

Something didn't balance. But it was too late. When he called the other cellphone, the sky flashed an instant blinding purple as the ground slurped a bolt of pure energy out of the heavens. The giant purple bolt blasted through the conventuary (and its force field), plunging into the earth toward the cellphone Oksana had dropped. Stone and earth heaved upward as a thunderous crash erupted out of the sky and sent a flattened Eldridge sliding down the secondary path on his back. The rocket launchers he had toted up the mountain skittered down the path alongside him and disappeared off the side of the mountain. When the noise of the explosion faded, Eldridge found himself a few dozen yards down the far side of the mountain and under a neverending rain of dust and small stones. He struggled to his feet and climbed back up the path, his ears ringing from the explosion and with the words of Marko Marinus.

"I entered the tournament for you."

It didn't balance, of course, but then again, not much was balancing anymore. Eldridge mounted the top of the path and saw what

Oksana's gift had wrought: A smoldering black shell marked where the great Narsyan conventuary had once stood. The primary path up the mountain had been shattered. Great slabs of stone and huge piles of crushed rocks and rubble lay everywhere. The sky over the mountain, still a bright shade of purple, crackled with leftover energy. A sheet of boulders untethered and slid down the mountain.

Facts started to pour into the redhead's mind. He thought of Marko's standing order that he could rejoin the Narsyans at any time. He thought of Marko's last words. He thought of Marko's admission that he had cured him.

The redhead sprinted across the cloudy divide—and fell.

The explosion had incinerated the middle of the path, but luckily, the redhead merely fell about 10 feet onto a slope of loose stones and rubble, which gave way and carried him down toward the ruins of the conventuary. He slammed into one of the structure's former walls and stopped, coughing on dust. His coughing slowed to a wheeze that was quiet enough to allow another sound into his ears—the sound of breathing. Eldridge spun and called into the ruins:

"Marko?!"

The redhead leaped to his feet and started pulling rocks off the pile, pausing only to wince at the occasional roar of pain in his legs and back. After a quarter-hour of digging, he finally revealed a bloody hand. Moments later, he moved a rock and revealed the face of his old friend.

He was smiling.

Eldridge dropped to his knees and held Marko's hand.

He said, "You entered this tournament for *me?*"

Marko hacked up a bloody clot. "Yes. Word arrived in Burbage that you were in need of capital. Of jenta."

"And the cure?"

"A drop of my blood. I had never traveled to the city before. It was quite...colorful."

"When did you do it?"

"My friend, please. My lifespan is suddenly measured in moments."

"Oh, my—holy Crom. Marko, *why?*"

Marko Marinus, the unspoken high chieftain of the Order of the Narsyan, looked into his friend's eyes and spoke in the simple, singsong cadence of a child, his voice a full octave higher.

"Because my friend was sick." His voice returned to normal: "And I thought...I thought...if I can *cure* him, I can take a step toward making amends for failing him all those years ago."

"Oh, my god. Fuck. *Fuck*. Marko, if you were sorry, why didn't you just *tell* me?"

Marko's spirit surged: "*I am a Narsyan*. The day I express my contrition with *words* instead of *actions* is the day we pull down this great conventuary stone by stone."

Eldridge surveyed the scene around them. "I think I may have beaten you to it, old buddy."

Marko gave a bloody chuckle. "So it seems. My friend, I would consider it a high honor if you would absolve me before I depart."

Eldridge blinked owlishly at him.

Marko smiled. "Forgive me?"

Eldridge slapped his forehead. "Of course. You're forgiven. I forgive you."

Marko's eyes lost focus. "I can't see." He inhaled sharp enough to suck his lower lip into his mouth. When his lip came back out, it was quivering. Tears beaded at the corners of his eyes. He spoke one last time: "El, I would gladly trade the life I've lived to spend one more day with you, even if it meant I would only live one more day."

His hand fell limp. Eldridge set it on his chest and stood.

• • • • •

THE DRY MAN WAS a believer.

At the same time Eldridge made his ascent up the Oasis Mountains to face Marko Marinus, Clovis Wine, aspiring Odd and unlikely Xiang King, sat in the redhead's safehouse and listened to the wail of dreens through the wall. He was full of mirth and fear and plans within plans.

Plans within plans, he repeated to himself, casting his gaze back to the wall of static that rose up from the road to the past. The wall had been growing stronger, more opaque in recent years. He had been having more and more difficulty looking beyond it into the time before.

But the age that came *after* the wall of static, he could remember *that* just fine.

And that was exactly why the dry man was so important to Jeb Goldmist. They both remembered everything. That was one of the reasons why Clovis was a believer in the ways of Jeb Goldmist. They had so much in common.

When Clovis patrolled the streets of under-Dedrick, he spent half his time making odds and the other half simply *listening.* He listened to the stream of whispers that ran from remnant to remnant. He listened to the grumbling of the dreg masses as they filed in and out of Nix's. He listened to the all the rumortrysts, bright and dim, and kept a sharp ear open for word from the mountains.

Goldmist had been closely watching the Oasis Mountains for many years, and word had come down from the Narsyan stronghold that a charismatic chieftain had...*distinguished* himself.

"They *believe* in him," Clovis told the mighty Jeb Goldmist at the pinnacle of his tower. "And he just might unite the Narsyans in a way never seen since the days of the Inculta Wars."

The Inculta Wars. The first–and only–direct conflict between the Odds and the Order of the Narsyan. The wars happened when the Narsyans lived in the desert; before the Narsyans retreated to their mountain home–*retreated* because of their catastrophic defeat at the hands of the Odds, who were led by a young Jeb Goldmist–who was known by a different name in those elder days.

Like many such conflicts, the passage of time had concealed the reasons why they happened. Some said the Odds struck first. Others said the Narsyans did.

Only Clovis Wine remembered the truth.

He remembered because had once been a Narsyan himself.

And as the dry man ran sat in the darkness of the safehouse, a smile split his head asunder, like a giant pod suddenly cracking open to unleash its deadly, insidious spores on an unsuspecting host.

Little does Eldridge know that we've both made the Circle Walk.

Indeed, ages ago, not long after the wall of static appeared in the landscape of his mind, Clovis Wine was drummed out of the Order of the Narsyan. And *he* was known by a different name back then, too, just like Goldmist–*another* reason why Clovis was a believer.

He pulled a burlap wrap close around his shoulders. He could never seem to stay warm. Not like in the deep desert, where the Odds and the Narsyans once fought for supremacy. Clovis squinted with glee at the cause of the war.

Babies.

Having been a Narsyan infant himself, Clovis knew that the survival rate for children born into the Order was close to 50 percent. Those were great odds for an Odd to make. But the Order took offense that the Odds were using the deaths of their own to make such sport, so they made war with the Odds near their desert home.

If anyone had been in the safehouse with him, they might have mistaken the dry man's laughter for the crackling of a nearby fire.

Clovis himself had seen the ruin wrought by the Odds. Goldmist and his oddments had smashed the Narsyan front lines with a combination of overwhelming numbers and superior firepower–none of which they even needed. Clovis remembered the sight of the Narsyans swinging their primitive weapons at the oddments and missing wildly. Had more of the Narsyan warriors been able to land a blow, they would have knocked their foes to pieces. A few of the Narsyans got lucky. The results included an oddment whose decapitated head flew 200 yards. Another oddment got in the way of a swinging Narsyan pike and watched his entire midsection vaporize.

But such results were rare on that battlefield, whose permanent residents included thousands of Narsyan dead.

The Order's humiliation pleased Goldmist as much as it pleased Clovis, and in the intervening years, Goldmist was content to build his tower and count his jenta. But when Clovis brought him word of this charismatic new Narsyan leader, he resolved to delete him from the world.

The Narsyan's name: Marko Marinus.

And Clovis wanted Marinus gone, too.

After all, the dry man was a believer.

Clovis sat in the safehouse and waited. Until someone knocked at the trapdoor.

• • • • •

BACK AT THEIR HIDING place near the foot of the Oasis Mountains, the moon continued to sweep through the leftover purple sky-plasma from the cellphone call. Eldridge saw that Oksana's car was waiting for him, running, though he saw no one in the driver's seat. He looked closer and found the brunette trixie buried under some animal hides in the back seat, asleep. He knocked on the glass. She stirred and cracked the window.

"Did it w–?"

The expression on the redhead's face cut off her question. His glazed eyes stared at nothing. His lips curled into a succession of failed sounds. When she saw him, Oksana pulled a hide around her shoulders and stepped out of the car.

"Did it work?"

He nodded, his gaze somewhere else.

"Then what's wrong?"

"It balanced. It always balanced. I was just too stupid to see it."

Oksana took his face in her hands. "Did you win?"

Eldridge seized her in an embrace so sudden and so strong that her spine cracked and she gasped. He fell silent. She hugged him back. The nighttime wind whipped around them, carrying with it a sharp chill. After a few minutes, he spoke.

"I blew it. I had one chance to make this right, and I blew it."

"I don't understand. What happened?"

Eldridge released her. "It doesn't matter what happened. It just matters what's *going* to happen."

"What's that?"

"I'm going to kill *the shit* out of Clovis Wine."

Part Five

the QUEEN and the KING

CONSTABLE TOLA COULDN'T STOP looking at Stewart Kaleb's face.

Sitting in her tricycle on the north side of under-Dedrick, she sipped a mug of coffee and looked at the photo of the deceased dreen. Something about his death had lodged in her mind, burrowing into her doubt-centers. She had heard Eldridge talk about him a lot—particularly how much trox he did.

Didn't he have an extra orifice of some kind?

Many future dreens would add extra in-ports to their bodies to facilitate the injection of endocrine cocktails. But where had Stewart's been? Tola flipped through the rest of her photos of the body and paused on one—a profile shot that also showed the dead dreen's neck. She was leaning in for a closer look when a column of smoke rose across town.

She could see the commotion from half a city away. The black smoke was forming a cloud over the city block surrounding Nix's gaming palace, and the racket echoed off the ceilings high above and reverberated throughout the entire subterranean realm. Behind the controls of her gigantic tricycle, the constable downshifted and roared down Sinister Street, weaving around dregs who sprinted in front of her vehicle, as well as other cars, motorcycles and rickshaws that darted out from every block.

Nix's got louder as she approached.

Her tricycle rose onto one wheel as she rounded a corner and brought Nix's into view, but all she could see of the establishment was the neon sign that revolved at the top of its steeple—everything under that was *people*; squirming, punching, fighting, struggling people who had swarmed onto the ceiling, some of them lighting fires, some shooting off firearms into the sky. Tola brought her tricycle to a skidding stop. She hopped up, grabbing a bolt-action shotgun and a riot helmet. She climbed up the small ladder to the tricycle's hatch and climbed on top. Standing astride the invisible central sphere, she fired her shotgun into the air.

No response. The riot surged on. Then a voice rose above the chaos.

"*Zor!*"

She turned and saw the vest, slacks, and glasses of Boris Hagan. He was leaning out from behind a nearby shanty, his face streaked with grime. The constable locked the tricycle, jumped down to street level and ran over to him, her shotgun at the ready.

"Boris! What the hell's happening?!"

But he was already screaming at her: "*You didn't stop him, did you?!*"

She fired back: "Hey! He does his own thing. You know that!"

"But he *listens* to you! And you fucking know it! He *cares* about you."

"He cares about everybody. Now, what's happening in there?!" She jerked her chin at Nix's.

"What do you think happened? He killed Marko. So Goldmist aced the tournament."

Tola's charred eyes popped big. She lowered her shotgun. "Oh, no."

Steel heels clacked against cobblestones and heralded the jackbooted arrival of a few score oddments. Hagan's face stretched in horror. "I gotta run. You—*find El! Keep him out of Dedrick, no matter what! Goldmist wants him!*"

"Wh—what?"

"Find Eldridge!"

Hagan turned and sprinted down an alleyway as the oddments arrived and surrounded the constable. One of them stepped forward and poked her in the chest with a splatter-iron rifle.

"Constable. Was that a Mr. Boris Hagan you were just conversing with?"

Zora felt like her heart was filled with sand.

"Um–"

He stepped close enough to bump her nose with his face shield.

"Which way did he go?"

Zora looked in the oddment's blank face, and when she saw her own reflection, the moment dilated as her focus narrowed around her crispy eyelids. An earnest voice spoke from within: *Why* were *you and Eldridge living together in Junktown, anyway?*

The constable smiled.

"Have you ever heard of the 'Sixty-Four Song'?" she asked.

"What?"

But by the time he spoke, Zora had fallen on her back and fired her shotgun directly up into his groin. He screamed. Reflexively, a few oddments fired off wild shots of splatter-iron. Blood blossomed from bodies all around her. She pumped the shotgun and fired again. A knee exploded, and half a leg fell sideways while its owner remained standing. *Pump.* She fired again, and an oddment crumpled at the hip.

Pandemonium.

The constable did a reverse headroll through the legs of one of the oddments, planted her feet, and leapt upright. A few more wild rounds of splatter-iron spat into the sky. She shot one more oddment in the back, then turned and ran for the tricycle.

Find Eldridge, Hagan said. Goddamn right I will.

• • • • •

ELDRIDGE PUSHED HIS BIKE to the limit.

The implications of killing Clovis weren't lost on him. If one of the sides in a Xiang tournament lost its King–whether by legitimate capture or other means–that side automatically lost the game. And of course there was the matter of his enormous, epic, outstanding debt to a mysterious, shadowy figure. If he killed Clovis without resolving the identity-switch he had pulled, he'd get nothing.

Fuck it. If he wasn't going to die anyway, he might as well avenge the death of Marko Marinus. He'd find another way to pay off his debt to the Man.

The Man Across the Oceans, specifically.

But despite his admission to Oksana that everything balanced, the redhead hadn't been telling the entire truth. As soon as he figured out that Marko had been trying to help him all along, one object fell *out* of balance:

Clovis Wine.

A number of images occurred to Eldridge as he rode through the desert back to Dedrick and considered Clovis' role in Marko's death. The redhead thought of that look Clovis got in his eyes when he said he knew Marko; the dry man's eyes gleamed like a sprinkling of quartz in the earth.

His eyes gleamed like that every time he mentioned Marko.

Then there was Clovis' bullshit about making odds with Marko about when Eldridge would die. And then Clovis showed up in the tournament as the Black King and pitted Eldridge against Marko—and *relished* it.

"I was delighted to pit you two against each other."

Slowly and incrementally, Clovis had tipped his hand, Eldridge thought. There was a connection between him and Marko Marinus. Eldridge was going to find out what that connection was.

But first, the killing.

Eldridge and Oksana raced toward Dedrick, the sky fading from purple to the normal dark blue of the night. The moon emerged from behind the plasma and shot shadows across the land. Oksana's shit-shaking car rumbled up next to him. She beeped her horn and waved. Eldridge waved back—just in time to spot something white that flashed in the distance.

A muzzle flash.

Reaction, instant: *"Look out!"* Eldridge yelled.

She slammed the brakes just as Eldridge sped up. Some kind of projectile whistled between them and struck *another* vehicle that had crept up behind Eldridge in the darkness. The unknown vehicle exploded in a jagged ball of flame. No matter–a pair of distant headlamps flared to life, accompanied by the rumble of wheels spinning through loose sand to the north. In the corner of his eye, Eldridge spotted Oksana's car wheeling around to the south, back toward Dedrick.

Good girl, Eldridge thought. *Stay safe. I can fend for myself.*

But her car tilted onto two wheels, making a hard turn back to the north. She was headed straight for the mysterious new vehicle that was threatening them.

"Goddammit, Oksie! Stop!"

She roared past, forcing him to squeeze his brakes. Oksana's shit-shaker backfired its way across the sand toward the undoubtedly better-appointed attacking vehicle–which didn't attack. It simply slowed to a stop before Oksana's car, its blinding headlamps casting her ride in silhouette against the desert landscape. Eldridge righted his bike and sped over to find Oksana already jumping out of her car, screaming.

"Come on! Come on, you buttwad! I'll take you by myself!"

As he approached, Eldridge said, "Oksie! Knock it the fuck off! Don't–"

His words and his bike both stopped. There was no third vehicle; only three huge wheels that were seemingly attached to an invisible chassis. A tricycle.

Eldridge yelled, "Zora?!"

The tricycle's hatch opened, and Constable Zora Tola stuck her head out the top, pulling a pair of goggles over her eyes.

"El! I found you!"

"I'll say you did. You almost killed us!"

"Oh, quit whining, you big baby. I blew up one of Jeb Goldmist's oddments for you," Tola said. "El, I'm here to warn you: *Stay out of Dedrick.*"

"What? Oddments? Who? Huh?"

"You killed Marko, didn't you?"

Eldridge rubbed his brow. "Yeah. I take it the word's out?"

"Yeah. El, Boris was right. Goldmist wanted him dead. He aced the tournament. It's apeshit in there. I had to shoot my way out. I'm sorry."

Eldridge leaned on his handlebars, his shoulders slumped, his breath steaming before him. Oksana walked over and put her hand on his shoulder.

"You needed the money from the match, didn't you?"

Eldridge squeezed her hand, realized what he was doing, and jerked his head up at Tola. He took his hand away. He said, "Well, *I* didn't need it. But someone else did." He looked at the constable and said, "Zor, you know the trouble you're in, don't you? Killing oddments? Warning me? Where are you gonna go?"

"Right back home. Goldmist and his goons don't scare me. If they wanna come fire me, they're welcome to it. But, El?"

"Yeah?"

"I'm sorry you're still in your hole."

He nodded his thanks. "There's always an escape hatch." With that, he wheeled his bike around toward the north and the jail.

Tola waved him down before he could take off. She said, "You giving me an escort home?"

"Nope. I'm on my way to ride the Old Mine."

• • • • •

RATHER THAN TRY TO talk him out of another harebrained scheme, Tola simply absorbed the news, nodded and asked him if he had time to drop by the jail before he visited the Old Mine. Eldridge agreed and turned to Oksana.

"You have to get out of Dedrick," he said.

Her dark eyes shone. "Why?"

"If Goldmist is looking for me, they'll be asking around. That means they'll ask you, sooner or later. And I can't have any more blood on my conscience. The rumortrysts are already gonna have a field day with my antics this week. They'll plug you into a pain amplifier or hold up your severed head and make you watch them serve food off your body. I know it sucks, but you gotta run."

"El, I can't leave you."

"This isn't a question."

Tola broke in: "El? She can stay with me till it blows over. I've got a little hidey-hole she can squat in."

Eldridge rolled his eyes. "Great. Two more people I'm in hock to."

"Don't sweat it, stupid," the constable said. "Hey, trixie! Can that *pessum* you're driving make it up north a-ways?"

All attitude, Oksana propped a hand on her hip and said, "Uh, *yeah* it can. And beat your dumb ride, too, Miss Big-tough Constable." She addressed Eldridge: "Hey, buttwad." And then she hugged him. "Thanks."

Eldridge shrugged out of her embrace. "What the hell are *you* thanking *me* for?"

"Nothing. Thanks for thinking of me."

"Well, thanks for saving my life," the redhead said, then held up his palms. "Hey! Let's see if I can make it to the jail without killing any more of my best friends!"

They rode out there together, passing the Old Mine along the way. When they arrived at the jail, Eldridge left his bike out in the cold in case he'd have to make a fast getaway or a grand exit. Tola showed them inside. They stopped immediately inside the door.

"OK, El. So what's in the Old Mine?"

"I have to kill Clovis Wine. He's in my safehouse."

Oksana: "You have a safehouse?"

Tola: "Yeah. It's up in the ceiling down under."

Eldridge: "Just tell her *all* my secrets, why don't you?"

The constable elbowed him and said, "Isn't there a secret *you* want to tell her?"

The trixie's eyes got that big, shiny look again.

Eldridge sighed harshly. "There's no secret to tell her, Zor. But OK, listen–I have to kill Clovis, and, yes, he's in my safehouse. Now that Dedrick's off-limits, the only way to *get* to my safehouse is through the Old Mine."

"You know what's in the Old Mine, don't you?" Tola asked.

"A flajillion dreens?" he said. "Oh yeah. Don't worry; my asshole's already puckered up in anticipation."

"Dreens?" Oksana said.

Tola touched her shoulder. "Don't worry, trixie. Eldridge does *macta* shit like this all the time." The constable adjusted her body armor and slapped Eldridge on the shoulder. "All right, El. Looks like you're gonna have to kill every dreen in Dedrick to get at Clovis. You wanna dip into my armory?"

Eldridge's eyes lost focus. He didn't respond.

Tola said, "El?"

The redhead looked at her and nodded. "Thanks."

Tola directed Oksana to a secret door in the back wall of her office and told her to stay quiet. That done, she guided Eldridge down a dark, wood-paneled hallway lined with old brass oil lamps that held flickering candles inside.

"Aren't those a fire hazard?" Eldridge asked.

"I think they're pretty. El, what happened up there?"

They arrived in a small room with more wood paneling on the walls and shiny cement floors. Several wooden cabinets with metal-latticed glass doors stood against the walls, all of them packed with weaponry. Tola unhooked a ring of keys from her belt and unlocked a few of them.

"You killed Marko, didn't you?"

Eldridge nodded.

"So why aren't you happy?"

The redhead pivoted backward on a heel and fell against the wall, coming to rest against his shoulders. He slipped his hands into his pockets and looked at the floor.

"I was wrong about him."

"What?"

He looked up. "I was wrong."

"I don't understand. So he didn't cure you?"

"No, he cured me. And he entered the tournament to win the jenta I needed."

Tola's breathing stopped, and then she exhaled for a long time.

She whispered, "I'm so sorry."

Eldridge nodded. She hugged him for a while. When he released her, she was smiling.

"What's so funny?" he asked.

"Come on. Let me show you something."

She waved him over to another paneled wall, this one seemingly blank. After searching through her ring of keys, she unhooked one that was merely a one-inch length of flat metal lined with three black bars along the length of the key. She slid it into a small slot in the wall and gave it a hard turn. A seam appeared in the paneling, part of which popped out to reveal a secret door. Tola grinned over her shoulder at the redhead.

"Don'tcha just *love* secret passages?"

And indeed they did, having installed a secret passage in their junkshack years ago. The young Tola had insisted on it. But as the night that Marko Marinus died wore on toward morning, Tola led the redhead down another secret passage that led directly into the stone hills that rose to the north of Dedrick. She had installed more brass lamps in the walls of the secret hall, which wound deeper into the earth and somehow managed to be hot and cold at once; hot from an unseen heat that radiated from below, and cold from sharp subterranean winds that slashed by them.

"Where are we going?" Eldridge asked.

"Do you remember when you taught me how to fight?" she asked.

"Sure. It was back in Junktown."

"Right," she said and ducked under a low-hanging entryway. "Remember how you'd take me out onto those mountains of junk and teach me balance and how to keep my opponents *off* balance?"

"Sure."

The constable led him through another small stony room and into a pitch-dark room. She clicked open a cigarillo lighter and lit a pair of candles set into the wall. The light revealed the room. Planks of wood shored up dirt walls. A wooden rocking chair sat in the middle of the room, next to a small table that held another candle, which Tola lit. A book sat on the table, open to its middle. A torn strip of paper was wedged in between the pages.

But the redhead wasn't looking at the table.

Standing against the far wall was what *looked like* an ancient protective suit, but it wasn't. Boris Hagan had told him tales about giant rubber outfits worn by soldiers who had to go into irradiated areas. Those suits had a funny name—"maz-splat suits," or something—but the apparatus Tola presented to him wasn't one of these.

"Remember when I told you that Boris and I had built something together? This is it."

Tola and Hagan had built a wooden skeleton-frame that they reinforced with three-inch-thick springs, pulleys and servos. A round device that looked like a model of the solar system sat in the equivalent of the apparatus' pelvic cavity: a gyroscope. A rubber suit that was capped with a rubber headpiece/mask combo was stapled to the wood frame. Thick rubber gloves hung off the ends of the wooden frame's arms, while bulky rubber boots sat next to the apparatus.

"What is it?" the redhead asked.

"Let me show you," Tola said, and stepped into the apparatus. She slid her limbs in between the slats of wood that lined the frame. She didn't bother to put on the headpiece, boots or gloves for the demonstration. Instead, she tapped a button on the inside of the apparatus, which activated a small, shiny black cylinder located along the inside of the thing's left thigh. Eldridge recognized the hum of a hydrogen fuel cell. Wearing the apparatus, Tola took a tentative step toward him.

"Watch," she said, gripping the lapels of his jacket. Servos spun and hinges creaked all across the apparatus, and she hoisted him skyward. Setting him down, she asked, "Think this'll come in handy down in the Old Mine?"

Eldridge straightened his lapels and nodded. "Thanks, it will."

"The hydrocell will attract the dreens, so you'll have to—"

"Zor, I've got to be honest with you—"

She held up her hand. "El, it's OK. I know I won't see it again."

"That's not what I meant—"

"I know that's not what you meant."

She climbed out of the apparatus and leaned it against the wall. Eldridge looked around the room, then checked the cover of the book she was reading. It was called *Midnight Mushrooms.*

"Never heard of this book," he said.

"Yeah, I know. I wrote it."

Eldridge smiled at her. "When?"

Tola shrugged. "Here and there. I got some dreg in town to print it up for me. Cost a lot, but it was worth it. We don't see new books anymore. I remember back in Junktown I found an old magazine about the guys who used to write books. They'd go to these beautiful places where people would go to spend time together and buy things. The writer-guys, they'd sit behind tables and inscribe books for their fans. I can't have that, but I wanted to have a book of my own."

Eldridge glanced around. "Why's it back here?"

"Oh, you know. This is a 'last stand' kind of room. I wanted to have my most special stuff with me if it all ever came down."

"What's your book about?"

"It's about a guy who doesn't want to have any kids."

Eldridge smirked at her. "I don't want to have any *more* kids. Believe me, if you ever met my daughter, you'd know she was enough."

"That doesn't sound nice. You don't like her?"

"No, no. I love her. But she was a boatload. A lot to handle."

"Whatever happened to her?"

Eldridge thought for a moment. "She...got hurt. Bad. And it was my fault. We haven't really spoken since."

"Ah, OK. Well, anyway, the book's not about you. It's about a guy who lives before Deadblast."

Eldridge raised his eyebrows. "Really? That sounds inventive."

"It's fun to play pretend. But you need to hustle if you're going to kill Clovis. You sure I can't talk you out of it?"

Eldridge shook his head. "Sorry."

Tola's eyes fell. She looked back up. "OK, then. Let's hit the armory on the way out. And then we'll get this contraption loaded onto your bike."

• • • • •

THE TIME FOR RAGE had come—both on offense and defense.

As Eldridge motored south along the desert highway with Tola's apparatus strapped to his back like a lanky, undead passenger, he recalled an old Narsyan saying: "Maintain the rage."

And although Eldridge stood in opposition to the Narsyans' entire worldview—if it could even be called that—he saw sense in it as he rode through what remained of the night that Marko Marinus died. He'd need the rage if he intended to fight his way through the countless shrieking dreens that awaited him in the Old Mine. That was the "offense" side of it. But even more than that, he needed the rage to stave off the water-knife of guilt that threatened to swipe across his midsection and slice him in half. That was the "defense" side.

With the rage fully maintained, Eldridge reached into his saddlebags and took out a few remkillers. Each pill would keep him in a state of jittery, sweaty-eyed super-consciousness for about an hour.

But how long will I be down there?

The Old Mine was located about five miles from town. Traveling aboveground at a Narsyan-caliber sprint, Eldridge could make it from the Old Mine to Dedrick in about 25 minutes, but he wasn't *going* to be traveling aboveground. He was about to make an *under*ground hike through dreen-infested passageways.

He could be down there for days.

He popped all the remkillers he had left.

A shake of his head halted the incursion of terror into his mind. He needed the rage as well as the 75 pounds of weaponry given him by the constable. He still had several handguns left over from his semi-aborted battle with Marko Marinus, but he had lost all of the rocket launchers from his safehouse in the cellphone energy-blast. The constable had been happy to equip him with a pair of rocket launchers as well as a few hundred more rounds for his twin-bayoneted scatterguns. But the cherry on top had been the gleaming black cylinder of destruction she had bequeathed him—a minigun. His bike listed side to side under the weight of all that shit, but he counted on the Tola/Hagan apparatus of doom to be able to tote it all through the twisting caverns of the Old Mine.

"Hm," Eldridge muttered to himself. "Tola/Hagan apparatus of doom. The tolahagan. The *tolhagan*." And so the apparatus became the tolhagan just in time for his arrival at the Old Mine. As it had for decades, The Ancient Sea and the Old Mine sat half-buried in the sand to the northeast of Dedrick, roughly halfway between the city and Tola's jail. The sand concealed most of the building's superstructure and created the illusion that it was little more than an outhouse, but when Eldridge rode up to it, he could see the outline of the larger building swelling up underneath the sand. The same cartoony viking (or spiking) squinted at an unseen horizon on a sign that stood on a man-made hill nearby, and a square black hole sat in the center of the seeming outhouse. As the redhead approached on his bike, he saw that an old wooden door lay smashed just inside the entryway, one of its remaining planks still held to the jamb on a gnarled hinge. He stopped his bike, dismounted, and felt the rush of freezing air washing down from the Oasis Mountains to the north. He wondered if any Narsyan training teams were in the area. He pulled his scatterguns from his cargo pants, flicked the bayonets to the ready, and approached the door.

A volley of the testicle-shriveling *wails* came howling out of the door, forcing Eldridge to scuff to a stop and close his eyes. A gust of hot air accompanied the wails emerging from the earth and passed over the redhead's face. Sweat rose from his forehead, and he looked back at the tolhagan. *It's gonna be hot down there.* He flicked his bayonets back into place and secured them in his pants. *It's gonna be hot, but Clovis needs killing.*

The redhead returned to his bike and outfitted himself. First, he pulled a black burlap cylinder out of his saddlebags and unfurled it across the sand to reveal a line of glittering chrome tools that he used to secure the minigun to the tolhagan's right leg. He had given some thought to how he wanted to deploy the weapon, but as badass as it sounded to attach it to his forearm, he wanted to be able to use his hands. Instead he bolted the gun to waist-mounted swivel, so he could turn the gun toward the earth when he wasn't using it. He also affixed a pair of handled flashlights to the tolhagan's shoulders.

The rest of his arsenal included the twin scatterguns; a half-dozen half dreens; four 9mm handguns with three 17-shot magazines for each; a pair of Bowie knives; an old black baseball bat, smooth and shiny with age, that bore the number 14 on the end; and finally, a small tube of boompaste that he'd use to blow his way into his safehouse. He kept these weapons in various places—some guns in his pockets, some bullet magazines strapped to his chest, the bat strapped to the side of his left thigh—and then he started the 15-minute ordeal to ensconce himself inside the tolhagan, hoping all the while that a dreen wouldn't interrupt the process. He pulled on the protective rubber suit first, then hopped around until he landed inside the tolhagan's superstructure. Once he was interlocked with the suit, he pulled on the rubber helmet, gloves, and boots and secured them in place with heavy-grade zippers that were sewn into the apparatus. That done, Eldridge teetered in place for a moment before he fired up the tolhagan's hydrocell.

At first, he felt like he was floating. The tolhagan instantly extended and amplified his strength, erasing the burden of all his weaponry. The minigun still threw off his balance slightly, so he'd have to watch that down in the Mine. The redhead tested his newly augmented strength by using one hand to lift his bike into the air.

"Righteous," he said, then carried his bike around to the back of the Old Mine, where he buried it in the sand, hoping no dreens would discover (and feast upon) the vehicle's hydrocell. He'd have to hope that the hydrocell on the tolhagan would be distraction enough.

His bike hidden, Eldridge lumbered around to the front of The Ancient Sea and the Old Mine and took one last, long look into the black opening—and then he plunged in.

The smell inside reminded Eldridge of a far-off region in his past—a time when he found himself duking it out with some half-rager dregs who threw him and Boris Hagan down into the elaborate system of garbage tunnels that ran under Dedrick, where it smelled simultaneously of sawdust, mildew, and rotting fish; a smell known to the redhead only because of a brief time he spent near the eastern ocean, which radiated the stench of long-dead aquatic life a hundred miles inland. Legend had it that the undersea marauders still farmed fish in the deep trenches that remained unaffected by Deadblast, but Eldridge couldn't imagine how anything could have escaped the world-changing event.

But back to those Dedrick garbage tunnels: He and Hagan fought their way to safety that day, but as the redhead made his way through the entryway into The Ancient Sea and the Old Mine, he countenanced the feeling of solitude that surrounded him. And that was when he saw a thousand eyes staring at him.

Gray. Gray filled his vision as a frightened outburst of breath fogged up the tolhagan's plastic face shield. The redhead listed to the right, the minigun's weight taking advantage of his loss of balance. He slammed into a wall and struggled to unzip the rubber helmet, which remained fogged. Once he got it off, he righted himself and crossed the room, his rubber boots sounding light *plomps* on the floor's scattered stone tiles. Across the room, the redhead saw hundreds of small photographs of families that had visited The Ancient Sea and the Old Mine—but the photos on the wall before him weren't taken *at* the old roadside attraction. They were taken everywhere *else.* Dozens, scores, *hundreds* of families waved at the camera from these pictures, all of them wearing an Ancient Sea/Old Mine T-shirt or sweatshirt or hat. All of them stood in an endless string of wondrous places Eldridge had never heard of, not even in the most fantastic, far-flung reaches of his dreams: New York. Chicago. Atlanta. Places filled with buildings too tall to be believed. Another family stood in front of a hulking steam engine in a place called Chattanooga. Air seeped out of his mouth—first as a natural exhalation, but as he looked at more and more photos, their weight settled onto his chest and forced an audible sigh out of him. He stood frozen and forgot to breathe. One fat family waved to the camera in front of something called the Hanging Gardens of Babylon. Another picture showed a single man submerged up to his eyes in opaque, steaming water, an Ancient Sea/Old Mine hat on his head. He was in a place called Hot Springs, Iceland. Still another family stood in a more familiar place—a desert—and hooked their thumbs at a trio of gigantic triangular structures that hovered on the horizon. Still another family stood in a sea of lights in a place called Las Vegas, Nevada.

Nevada. Eldridge squinted, looking looked closer at the picture, and saw that one of the shining buildings was a casino, just like Kaleb's.

Is that what it used to be like?

One family stood in front of a magnificent and elegant steel tower in a place called Paris. Something in the corner of the Paris photo caught the redhead's eye. A small sign on the base of the tower displayed a white arrow that pointed up a stairway. A word on the sign read ESCALIER. Something clicked in the redhead's mind. He thought of Clovis' words:

I lived on the far side of the ocean in this place where they had the most beautiful language. I can't think of the name of either–the language or the land. But the language had a phrase: esprit de l'escalier.

Eldridge pulled down the photo and pocketed it as he continued scanning the wall. He thought back to his time with Marko Marinus and wondered what honor befell the proprietors of The Ancient Sea and the Old Mine to have received so many wonderful images. And then he noticed a sign to the right of the mass of pictures that read, "Take a picture of yourself wearing an Ancient Sea Tee, and if we've never seen the city, you get in for free!" Part of Eldridge wondered if people used to conduct commerce with photos before Deadblast, but an old admonition from Hagan chased the fanciful notion out of his mind.

"They traded jenta for blood like everyone always has, El."

The redhead felt a sudden urge to cram every last photo into his pockets and forget about Clovis Wine. He'd deliver the photos to Boris Hagan's door and leave Dedrick for good. He'd take his chances with the Man Across the Oceans, the mysterious party who held him in such an insurmountable debt.

But no. The Xiang tournament was over, and he was still in all that debt. Only now, he was a creditor, too, and Clovis was the debtor. Mr. Wine owed the redhead for the wrongful death of one best friend. Eldridge turned away from the wall of photos and aimed his lights deeper into the lobby of the old roadside attraction. He pulled out his scatterguns and flicked the bayonets to the ready. The scattered rock tile floor led him between the musty remains of a gift shop (more T-shirts and hats strewn among torn clothes, shattered glass, and decomposed fingers and toes), and a restaurant (overturned tables and smashed chairs interspersed with broken plates and the furry, blackened, long-rotted-away remains of a fatty pre-Deadblast meal). The redhead's foot bumped against something metallic. He looked down and saw the crushed remains of a red aluminum can that had the word "Coke" on the side.

Another volley of shrieks and howls froze him in place. He waited a minute for them to die down, then continued. The stone tiles led him past a scale model of the surrounding desert—largely a blank yellow expanse, except for the mountains and the same streak of black highway that brought him to Dedrick. Educational pictures and text covered the walls and told him all about The Ancient Sea: "Largest subterranean body of water in North America." *North America.* He made a mental note to ask Hagan about that. More text read: "Native Americans discovered The Ancient Sea while hiding from Union Cavalry." Finally, he spotted a pair of signs that read, THIS WAY TO THE ANCIENT SEA and THIS WAY TO THE OLD MINE.

A red arrow pointed toward the Old Mine. He followed it. The scattered-tile floor gave way to hardwood. He walked down a hallway lined with stone walls. The ceiling arched overhead. Tattered red velvet ropes lay on the ground alongside brass poles. The hallway ended in another smashed wooden door. Eldridge stepped over the wooden remains and entered the loading area for the Old Mine. The room was round, with two exits—one directly ahead, the other to the left. A train track curved through the room from one exit to the other. Cobwebs and dust covered a long-dark control panel next to the door. One of the ride's cars—a stylized mine cart with the name "Jethro" stenciled on the front—sat on its side next to the track. Statues of human miners, frozen in a permanent wave good-bye, stood next to the entrance to the ride. Over the entrance to the mine were the words "Help wanted! New miners needed!" The miner statues stood on patches of fake sand in front of a mural that depicted the sun setting over a desert landscape.

Voices, suddenly and everywhere: *"This way, kids! This way, kids!"*

Eldridge's reflexes activated, both to piss himself and to blast the head off of one of the statues, which had suddenly sprung to life and started waving to him with a pair of crimson eyes that glittered in the center of its skull. The redhead paused and saw lights blinking under the inch of dust that covered the control panel. The train tracks seemed to be moving, too, until he looked closer and saw that a single chain was running down the middle of the tracks, carrying along more mine carts that each bore a different name: Cletus. Homer. Fred. Hoot. Each cart had two rows of seats. The redhead watched more carts pass by before he heard more wails from down below. He had an idea, and he scanned the stone walls. Most of the walls were splattered with dark spots—mostly blood—but the redhead knew that dreens had found ways to projectile vomit, shit, spray, or otherwise disperse any fluid ever secreted by man.

In any event, he found what he was looking for: a map. It hung on the wall next to the control panel. The map was mostly for show—another cartoon, like the spiking (or was it *viking?*) outside—but it looked to be approximately to scale. The ride's logo stood in the upper right corner. Next to it snaked a red circle that traced the course of the Old Mine ride. Eldridge knew that the entrance to his safehouse was located at the far end of the ride, but as he had never seen the other side of the wall, he had no idea what to look for. How the hell had the basement of a library wound up next to an underground scare ride, anyway? No matter. Eldridge read the map and its yawn-inducing list of *macta*-fied scary names: The Hellhole. The Dark Passage. The Miner's Graveyard—*wait.* That was it. The Miner's Graveyard lay about halfway through the ride. Maybe the entrance to his safehouse was near it.

Eldridge turned toward the mine track, trying not to think of the stories that Marko and the gang used to trade about the Old Mine when they were kids, but the more he tried to block out their voices, the louder that fucking roboghoul miner kept yelling.

"This way, kids! This way, kids!"

Then the ride stopped.

The robot miner's eyes faded from red to black as his limbs froze back into place. The mine carts stopped. Shrieks died down from within the ride. Eldridge checked the control panel and found the two largest buttons. One red, one green. He gave the green one a rattle and found it was loose. Casting his gaze about, he found a rock and wedged it onto the green button. The ride reactivated, as did that fucking miner. The redhead blundered his way into one of the carts, the tolhagan transforming him into a giant. He discovered he could sit down if he rested his feet in the front row and his butt in the back row. As he rode into the Old Mine, Eldridge raised a scattergun and blew off the remaining roboghoul's head. Marko's words followed him into the ride:

The proprietors of The Ancient Sea, they met with the eldest Odd, a man named Uzziel, and he got them both to sell him their souls. In exchange, he built them the Old Mine. But Uzziel tricked them.

The cart carried him around a bend where more roboghouls told a story. A family sat around an empty dinner table, useless forks poised in the air. The patriarch, a black-bearded miner with red eyes, pleaded with his gingham-aproned wife. The kids wept. Everything smelled like earwax and sawdust and sweat. Heat radiated from somewhere ahead and below, but Eldridge couldn't get a fix on the source.

A voice with an unfamiliar accent intoned, "*Times sure were tough back then. Poor old Cletus couldn't hunt no more bison, the desert done run dry.*"

Eldridge pulled his attention away from the stupid roboghouls and focused on the tunnel ahead, where more lights twinkled in the dark distance. Screams floated up from below. *Where are they coming from? How did they get down deeper?*

Another scene emerged from the darkness. Poor Cletus stood in a long line of roboghouls, all of them waiting to sign their names on an endless scroll of paper being held by a rotund roboghoul who wore upscale clothes: red fabric tucked into his collar, a long-tailed coat, bits of white paper on his shoes like the ones Hagan sometimes wore. (He called them "spats.") The evil, fat, rich roboghoul devoured the line of miners with his eyes and directed them into the entrance behind him—a cave marked with a wooden sign that read "The Old Mine"—which is exactly where the mine cart carried Eldridge.

And that's when he heard the rumble from below.

Scores of roboghoul miners trudged along a pair of paths that ran alongside the train tracks, which dipped suddenly when entering the mine, jarring Eldridge out of his seat and onto his side. He scrabbled for a grip just in time to see that the rumble from below was a huge grist mill that had been running dry for decades. It powered a crank that lifted the mine carts up a hill that ascended into a shrieking black void that swallowed the twin lines of roboghoul miners. Eldridge struggled to right himself in his seat before he reached the top of the hill—but it was too late. His faux mine cart rattled over the crest of the blind hill and hurtled down into a flaming pit that was packed with the most dreens the redhead had ever seen in his life.

On the way down, he passed a sign that read THE HELLHOLE.

Fortunately, it wasn't *really* a flaming pit; only a simulacrum of one. True to form, the Old Mine ride followed the twin lines of pathetic, desperate miners as their roboghoul forms, all clad in overalls and flannel, rolled down a slippery slope into hell itself, which was a literal hell for Eldridge. At least two-score dreens were feasting on a fallen comrade, each of them a genetic mistake of the highest order. One was all limbs, its torso and head shrunken into a coiled ball of perpetually bleeding flesh with teeth where its navel should have been. An eyeball blinked from its left shoulder like a gawking epaulet. It turned Eldridge's way and squealed. Five others turned their visages his way—none of them had eyes in the classical, homosapien sense—but most of them had eyeballs growing out of some nightmarish part of their body. One had eyes for teeth; another had eyes wedged in its nostrils. Still another apparently had an eye for a head—huge and pendulous and dangling from a thigh-thick optic nerve that sprang from between its collarbones. All of them moved as a unit, the news of the arrival of newflesh spreading among them via some kind of body language or telepathy.

Whatever the case, the redhead struggled to his feet astride the plummeting mine cart and leveled his twin scatterguns at the mass of dreen—just in time for the ride to slam to a halt.

His feet flew over his head as he pitched headlong into them. Without the tolhagan, he probably would have been screwed, but with it, he was a battering ram. The first dreen exploded in a splat of dreenjuice on contact, but five others clamped their superstrong claws around the redhead's limbs and yanked. Fortunately, the tolhagan was equipped to yank *back*. Eldridge slung a pair of dreens—one for each arm—into each other and smashed their swollen skulls together. A sphere-shaped dreen clutched at the redhead's feet with its tiny hands, and Eldridge spent a scattershot to turn it into a dreenjuice doughnut.

Then he ran. Good timing, too, as the smell from the tolhagan's hydrocell had just hit the crowd of dreens. Hydrogen had no odor, of course, but the steady-state workings of a hydrocell emitted a faint, exhaust-like aroma. Humans barely noticed it, but to a dreen it was pure crystal, a first hit of heroin after a year on the wagon. When the smell made contact, a chorus of giddy shrieks bounced around the cavern's walls behind Eldridge as he loped around smoke emitters and floor fans outfitted with yellow lights and red cellophane. A small workpath led back up to the track. He clambered up a set of iron steps to where the mine carts lay dormant.

"It's a funny experience!"

"Fuck!" Eldridge screamed, wheeling toward a dreen that scrambled down the wall like a spider, its limbs growing out of its back. An instant decision prevented him from spending another round of scattershot. Instead, he shoved his bayonet in between the spider-dreen's eyes—all 16 of them—and rammed his boot into its belly, sending it flying back into the oncoming rush of skittering, swarming dreen.

Dreens can talk?

The question echoed from a distant corner of his mind as he spun and ran, each step in the tolhagan a heavy, hurdling stride that spanned 10 feet. *Clump, clump, clump!* He ran alongside the train track, his plastic face shield fogged again. He unzipped it and tucked it into the wood frame around his face, his breaths coming hard and fast. A voice inside his head thanked Marko Marinus for training him so hard back in the day, while another voice questioned the need to avenge his old friend's death. *He wouldn't really want you to run headlong into this room full of dreens, would he? I mean, he's not* that *dead!*

Room full of dreens. It wasn't a joke.

There aren't many times in a man's life when he has occasion to think, "Boy, I sure am glad I brought this minigun," but the redhead had occasion to think it the night he invaded the Old Mine and stumbled onto a room full of dreens. A room full of dreens looked less like a room full of people and more like a valley full of severed body parts during an earthquake. It was also a perfect target. Eldridge grabbed the minigun and opened fire. Despite the years that had passed since the weapon had last been called to action, it still matched its pre-Deadblast output of roughly 3,000 shots per minute. Each bullet uncorked a gout of dreenjuice, some of which sprayed upward, some laterally. By the time the redhead had exhausted his supply of bullets, the toxic orange lifeblood had drenched everything.

And there were still a few left.

The grenade appeared in his hand before he could think. He chucked and ducked. A *whoomp* thudded through the cavern and shook dirt from the ceiling. A light fixture tinkled somewhere ahead. A wave of steaming dreenjuice broke against the tolhagan's plastic—and started burning holes in it.

The redhead jumped up and started running. Side note: Not *all* dreenjuice was acidic. By definition, a dreen's endocrine system had gone completely haywire, so the chances of its bloodstream being an acid or a base were about even. Eldridge slopped through the juice and kicked aside still-bucking limbs. A dreen that was nothing more than four legs arranged in a six-foot X dug itself out of the muck on the wall and ripped off a series of handsprings (footsprings?) to block the redhead's path, where its central flesh-blob unfolded like a dozen labia and spewed forth a fluid was that most *definitely* boiling acid. Eldridge was already jumping to the side, but unfortunately, a dreen that was permanently holding its severed head over its torso was waiting for him. It slammed its shrieking face into Eldridge's head. The redhead fell on the train track just as the lights returned, casting ghostly, flickering light across the ceiling. The space leapt into instant relief in the faint glow, every inch writhing with stunted dreenlings—the unholy spawn of who the fuck knew *what* was living down in that cavern.

"Them durn fool miners din't know that the Old Mine was a secret passageway for Old Scratch to get back earthside and find him some mischief."

The narration squawked from an unseen speaker as a pair of dreens—one an eight-footer with thorny, willowy limbs; the other a human spiral whose torso hung upside down over its legs like a *mentari* jack-in-the-box—blitzed him full-force. Still on his back, Eldridge swung a tolhagan'ed arm around in a great arc that caught the jack-in-the-box in the jaw and smacked it right off its face. It spun on its heel. Eldridge ripped a scattergun from his pants and impaled the willow on his bayonet. Meanwhile, a mine cart rattled down the track right at his head. Eldridge squeezed the trigger. The willow split in two. He rolled out of the way of the impending mine cart and grabbed hold of the chain that ran down the center of the tracks. It yanked him away from the surviving parts of the willow and the jack-in-the-box, all of which were already struggling to right themselves amidst pools of their own dreenjuice.

The chain drug Eldridge along on his stomach. The ride rolled on and wrenched him around a sharp corner where the track dove into a clattering darkness whose blackness was only interrupted by a rainbow-array of dancing demons that bubbled from the walls. Hagan might've called them "jell-oh molds." Light from within the wall-mounted jell-oh molds made them glow like giant, primary-color blisters. An increase in the room's racket banished all extraneous thoughts from his mind.

Something was churning ahead. He *had* to see what it was.

He gripped the cart's rear seat, his legs dangling off the back and dragging in the dirt. The cart sped down an endless black tunnel that terminated in the distant form of a naked woman. She stood with her back to Eldridge, whose eyes bulged inside the tolhagan's helmet.

There she was. There *it* was.

Marko's words whispered through the din:

She had her back to you. And all the way down that tunnel, you knew she was going to turn around when you got to her. And as soon as you thought that—as soon as you knew it—you lost your mind.

Marko had been right about the length of the ride, and the bulk of it was in that tunnel, where the mine cart hurtled along so fast it shook, an army of jell-oh devils flanking the track. Eldridge figured the tunnel alone carried him half a mile. As he approached the naked woman, her form took shape. A seam bisected her from crown to rear. A *plastic* seam. Unskilled hands had adorned her body with squiggly red and blue lines. Caucasian-toned paint had been peeling off her for years, revealing crumbling white plaster underneath. Eldridge shook his head and chuckled. *I've been afraid of* that *for all these years?*

But a few dreen-free moments later, Eldridge's mine cart passed before her, and an ancient spring-coil spun her around for an instant, revealing a little secret: Something had replaced the woman's *plaster* head with a *human* one. Some kind of embalming agent had preserved her head in the deep, moist cavern, but her skin had still retreated from her eyes and mouth to leave her in a perpetual state of grin-glare. As she spun back around, chunks of her scalp flew off her head, spattered across the redhead's rubber suit, and started smoking.

Eldridge shrieked like a little girl.

When he was done, he actually looked over his shoulder to see if anyone had heard him. The tunnel was empty. The redhead shook the bits of scalp off his suit and turned his attention ahead. He had already made his way past the Hellhole, and the mine cart carried him through the Dark Passage (he assumed). Now all that remained between him and the entrance to his safehouse was the Miner's Graveyard—and there it was. The cave opened up into a domed room. Patches of formerly fluorescent green turf covered the ground, which was pockmarked with faux graves—some open, some closed. The train track wove a twisted path through the graves, all of which were packed with dozens of dreens, of course.

"Of *course,*" Eldridge muttered.

They writhed in their holes, some of them faceless, eternally screaming monstrosities that breathed through giant slits in their chests. Others sat in place, their bodies too malformed to move due to hands growing out of their mouths or entire biological systems lying on the outside of their skin. One dreen's circulatory system hung around its form like a thousand delicate, dangling necklaces, all of them twitching with blood that the poor thing's heart struggled to pump. Another clawed endlessly at its own perfectly clean skull, having long since scraped off all its flesh. Still another lay next to an open grave that held its gigantic, distended cranium. It moaned from time to time.

Eldridge pulled a grenade from his suit and considered throwing it to clear a path, but he decided against it. Only a few of these dreens could even move, and none were attacking. He rode the mine cart through the graveyard, and as he beheld tableau after tableau of sorrow, his ears picked up on a stream of whispers that flowed through the room.

"I wonder how her head would look on a stick."

"If I got out, I'd feel obliged to get even."

"I haven't blocked out the past."

"They're daring to kill me again."

A pair of faux-wooden double doors sat at the far end of the graveyard. They opened to admit Eldridge's mine cart. He knew he was close to his goal. He instantly recognized the red brick wall that composed the remains of the old library that stood above his safehouse.

And there wasn't a dreen in sight.

He hopped off the mine cart and landed on dry, cracked earth. He paused and reloaded his scatterguns, one of which he stowed and replaced with a 9mm. Fully loaded, he crept along the still-running train track as stealthily as the tolhagan would allow. The brick walls revealed more and more clues that he was getting close. He passed by shelves still laden with soggy books, thick with moisture. The sight baffled him. He had always figured that the library over his safehouse had been buried during Deadblast, but apparently its interment had predated the event by enough time to allow for the construction of a subterranean dark ride alongside its ruins. An old sign bolted to the brick wall read, THIS WAY TO STACKS. He checked behind him for any pursuing dreens and saw none. His foot got stuck. Looking down, he saw a dark boundary that marked where dry earth gave way to sopping muck. His boot *popped* out of the muck, and he continued *popping* his way down the moist path as empty mine carts continued to chug along by him.

Mostly empty mine carts.

It had a dozen arms and reeked of piss. He smelled it an instant before it locked hold of him from behind and tried to pull his head off. It only managed to rip off his protective helmet, which it cast into the muck as Eldridge spun around and faced off against a dreen whose urinary system had grown out of control. Its three-foot cock had merged with its left leg, which was capped with a thumbless six-fingered hand. It had an abundance of arms—eight—but only three of them worked. The rest dangled from the thing's torso, which throbbed with hundreds bulging bladders, all of which leaked parabolas of urine that streamed from pinprick wounds that peppered the dreen's body. Its head was inverted—a lipless mouth snarled atop a wide-set nose that snorted air through mucus-clogged nostrils. A pair of eyes sat in an irregular pattern and glared out from where the thing's chin should have been. Green bile and yellow piss gushed from its mouth. Eldridge raised the scattergun and the 9mm, but before he could fire, a crushing grip closed around his right arm and pulled him backward. He jerked back like someone had tied his wrist to a speeding car. Something *popped* inside his shoulder. *Dislocated. Great,* he thought as an unimaginable force pulled him backward like a corpse; pulled him so hard he left his boots standing in the muck; pulled him so hard his vision dimmed.

He found himself dangling a dozen feet off the ground, his dislocated arm stretched above him, his guns gone, his face exposed. Somewhere in his peripheral vision, he saw his goal—the brick archway that led to his safehouse. It bore carved letters that read: STUDY ROOM 104. So this entire chamber used to be the stacks, and on top of that, Eldridge's safehouse was located less than 20 feet away from the colossus that was now holding him skyborne like a pesky insect.

The thing looked like a dreen-mountain. Over the years, limbs and body parts and viscera and brains and gore had gathered into a dark corner of the Old Mine until one day it achieved sentience. An appendage with a half-dozen joints jutted out from the center of the mass of flesh and held Eldridge with stubby, taloned digits. As Eldridge hung there, he noticed that the surface of the flesh-mountain was changing—a quartet of slits sank into it, three of which disgorged spheres of eyeballs that blinked in an unending strobe that reminded the redhead of Yasim's hyperglobe. The fourth slit sank deeper and deeper and opened wider and wider—a maw webbed with steaming mucus. The maw emitted a low-pitched warble that reverberated across the cavern and summoned a chattering, clicking, shrieking wave from both directions on the train tracks. Thousands of dreens hunched into the old library's former stacks, scrambling over one another in a madcap struggle of limbs and red-hot perspiration. They fell before the dreen-mountain that held Eldridge captive, and the dreen-mountain spewed forth thousands of tentacles from its massive jaws. The appendages slithered among the horde of dreens, all of which grabbed onto them and—using whatever approximated a mouth—started sucking. Eldridge finally noticed the raised nubs that lined the tentacles. The nubs were leaking a green fluid that smelled like antifreeze. All the dreenlings cradled the tentacles in their arms and sucked on the protruding flesh, which meant one thing.

They were nipples. And that left no doubt about the identity of the creature.

It was the motherfucking dreenqueen.

As her dreenlings fed, the dreenqueen turned one of its eye-spheres on Eldridge and examined him head to toe. Another crooked appendage slurped out of its mass and ripped the tolhagan off Eldridge's body. It dropped the apparatus into its maw and shuddered with a swallow. The tolhagan was gone—but his pockets were still stuffed with another 9mm, some grenades, and the boompaste. Meanwhile, scores of blinking eyes regarded the redhead, who finally spoke.

"Y'know, seeing as how this is the scariest thing I've ever seen in my whole life, you'd think I'd be screaming right now."

The eye-sphere rotated clockwise.

"Did you jab that lady's head on the dummy back there? I squealed at that, and *that* wasn't a half-jenta as petrifying as this."

The eye-sphere rotated counter-clockwise.

"Maybe I'm in...whaddaya call it? Shock?"

Hundreds of eyeballs rolled toward the ceiling as the dreenqueen lowered Eldridge into her maw.

"Hm. You're about to eat me alive. I should really be yelling my ass off right now, but—"

Another voice interrupted. "Eldridge?"

His descent stopped. All three of the dreenqueen's eye-spheres rotated to the right and looked down at the side-rear of the queen's flesh-mountain, where a single head peeked up out of the slippery, carbon-based glop. Eldridge could also see the faint outline of shoulders underneath the head—but no neck. It was a man, buried up to his chin *inside* the dreenqueen. His head had been separated from his body. Recognition dawned for Eldridge, but his mind couldn't quite make it all balance.

"Have we met before?" Eldridge asked.

The head smiled, its mandible buried in the queen's flesh. When it spoke, the entire upper half of its head flapped back and forth.

"Yesss. It'sss meee. Milosss."

Milos. Milos Tola. Husband to a certain Dedrick town constable. Long since missing, and last seen sprinting through the deep desert with his head tucked under his arm out near Rene Rosaire's Church of the Ancients. Now, here he was, glommed onto the side of the queen of all things dreen.

"Um," Eldridge said. "How's it going?"

"Dazzleglow," he said. "Sheen on everything."

"Oh. Kay. Can you tell her to put me down?"

"I can *ask.* I don't tell...*her*...to do anything."

Milos drizzled affectionate honey all over the word "her." His eyes rolled back into his head as his breaths heaved in and out of his mouth. The dreenqueen's side inflated in tune with her parasitic husband's breaths. He was speaking to her.

She set Eldridge down. He immediately sank up to his ankles in the muck. He took a moment and popped his shoulder back into place.

"Mighty fuck!" Once the pain subsided, he addressed Milos: "Thanks. So...I take it you remarried?"

Milos' eyes twinkled. "Yesss. Goddess. She is goddessss."

Eldridge nodded. "She misses you. A lot. Zora."

Milos closed his eyes. "I...missss...her. Too. But she can't understand. *This.*"

Eldridge looked at the dreenqueen. "No, I guess she can't."

Zora Tola's ex-husband looked at him and said, "Why are you... *here* in the Old Mine?"

"I was actually trying to get through there," Eldridge said, pointing at the bricked-over passageway to study room 104. "I need to get back into Dedrick."

"Ssscenic route."

It took Eldridge a moment to get the joke, but when he did, he gave an honest laugh. "Yeah. I took the scenic route. Milos, listen. I don't expect that you and your kind are much accustomed to visitors, right?"

"No."

"And I'm gonna hazard to guess that you wouldn't be amenable to letting me go, right?"

"Silly."

Eldridge pulled a grenade from his pocket. "Ha, ha! I thought so, too! But here's the deal, Milos. I've got this grenade." He popped the pin. "There. Pin's out. And if I release this handle, then you, me, and the missus go blammo."

Hisses sounded from everywhere. Thousands of dreens hissed all around him, including the queen, who hissed through a pair of yonic slits that sliced open across her midsection.

Milos hissed, too. "Nooo."

"Hey, I don't wanna die down here either, OK? So, let's have a confab. I need to kill a man, and he's right behind that wall."

Milos wheezed, "You are fodder."

"Right. I am fodder. I bet I'm tasty fodder, too, but your main squeeze there already ate the hydrocell I had in my supersuit, so her tummy ought to be full right about now. And let me tell you something else, Milos: This man I have to kill? I'm doing it for Zora."

"For...*Zor?*"

"For Zor."

Milos' eyes spun in their sockets until they turned white again. He breathed deeply into the dreenqueen once more. Finally, he looked at Eldridge.

"You will have thirty of your pulsebeats. After that, we come."

"Milos, thank you."

"Twenty-nine."

"Oh. You started already. OK, then."

The dreen-legion disengaged from the nipple-tentacles, which retracted into the queen's maw. One of the tentacles whiplashed around the redhead's ankle and drew blood. He ignored the sting and slopped over to the door to his safehouse, where he pulled the tube of boompaste from his pocket and used the sharp edge of a rock to slice it open. He stuck it to the base of the wall, then ran back across the room, dodging in between dormant dreens that were simultaneously rising and awaiting the go-ahead from their mistress.

Still Milos counted down: "Twenty-one. Twenty."

Once he reached a safe distance, the redhead took aim, hurled the grenade at the boompaste, then dove facefirst into the ground. The explosion shook the cavern and buried him even deeper in the muck. A pair of dreens—one that was nothing but joints, the other a red-hot walking insulin factory—fell onto him, but didn't attack. They wouldn't attack until Milos' countdown ended.

"Fifteen. Fourteen."

The redhead elbowed both dreens off of him and yanked his arms out of the muck. He pressed his hands against his knees, pushed himself upright and began a horrific slow-sprint through the knee-deep bog that surrounded the dreenqueen; a nightmare made literal as he tried with all his might to run but found himself unable, all while a spectral voice counted down to his doom:

"Ten. Nine."

But there was light ahead. The boompaste had scattered the bricks everywhere and left a blinding white-bright opening to his safehouse, into which Eldridge lumbered with his mud-heavy limbs. Instantly, he pulled off his jacket and lunged for his wall of ammunition. It was empty for some damn reason. Fucking Clovis must've been attacked a dozen times already to have gone through all his stores. No matter: Eldridge kept an emergency stash of goodies under the floorboards. He pulled the shelf down, dropped to his knees and yanked up the floorboards. Behind him, something rolled along the floor and dropped through an opening. Eldridge ignored the sound and found his stash: two .357 Magnums, some grenades, and most important: more boompaste. Inside the Old Mine, Milos concluded:

"One. Zero. *Feed.*"

Wails of ecstasy rolled through the opening as a thousand dreens converged on the tiny doorway. Eldridge ripped open the boompaste, hurled it at the ceiling, and shot it with the 9mm.

He wondered if he'd ever be able to hear again.

The explosion in the small space had the same effect as a pair of icepicks jabbed into his brain. He fell backward, clutching at his head. The ceiling came loose and rained down like a miniature avalanche. When the dust settled, his head was rattling with the ceaseless drone of an imaginary alarm klaxon. But the passage was closed, even though he could still hear the shriek of a thousand dreens a few feet away. Eldridge looked himself over. The tolhagan was gone. He was covered in quickly congealing dreen-slop and crusted with brick-dust.

"All right, Clovis—"

And his safehouse was empty.

A column of light shone up through the center of the floor where the trapdoor had once been. Eldridge stood up and surveyed the room. He checked the bathroom, found it empty, then returned. Not only was Clovis gone, but the whole room echoed the look of his ammunition shelf—*bare.* Continuing his search, Eldridge found nothing but clean spots among the dust where his food, water, and weaponry had once been. Even his water bottles were gone, and those had been a monumental pain in the ass to haul up here. (A team of friendly psychoskags had erected a temporary scaffolding to help him get it done.) Maybe Clovis had simply been raided by someone (or something) with the resources to clean out his safehouse. Or maybe Clovis had more resources at his disposal than Eldridge thought.

It wouldn't have been the first time he underestimated the dry man.

Crunch! Brick chips rained from the wall that blocked the entrance into the Old Mine as a thousand dreens continued to pound and dig at the barrier. Eldridge took stock. As for weapons, he still had one of his scatterguns, as well as what he had stashed under the floorboards. If the dreenqueen and her legion breached the wall, they'd swarm all over Dedrick, and the redhead didn't feel like murdering an entire city. He checked his secret stash and found one last tube of boompaste.

He examined the ceiling. A pre-Deadblast artisan had built it out of hundreds of interlocking stones, including one keystone that sat at the center of a radiating hub. Eldridge slung the boompaste at the ceiling, where it stuck in a splat of white. He took a moment to find homes on his person for his scattergun, the 9mm, the rest of the grenades (three of them), as well as the two .357 Mags.

More stones fell from the barrier into the Old Mine. The white noise shriek of a thousand dreens filtered through the debris. The redhead started to lower himself through the trapdoor before he realized he was missing something: his climbing claws.

"Holy *Cromshit.*" He checked his pockets and found a tear in his cargo pants where they had once been. They must've fallen out when the dreenqueen grabbed him. *Crunch, crunch!* Bricks and chunks of rock were sliding down from the barrier in earnest, so Eldridge stuck his head out the trapdoor and did a dance with his toe-tips so he could get a 360-degree view of the airspace in under-Dedrick. He had one chance to pull this off, and it all hinged on the dumb-luck appearance of one thing.

And there it was.

It chugged through the air with an engine that sounded like an old man with a chest full of phlegm. Its exhaust pipe leaked black sludge that fell on the city in putrid sheets. Standing astride it was one of Jeb Goldmist's fearsome oddments, clad in spiked black armor. If he flew *directly beneath* the trapdoor, Eldridge might have a chance; if not...well, let's just say that a forearm had just smashed through the barrier, its livid flesh covered with infected ingrown fingernails. Eldridge watched the oddment blunder through the air until he corrected his course and tracked a new vector, one that would take him directly under the trapdoor. Another limb smashed through the barrier, this one a twisted gnarl of leg. More shrieks. More wails. The oddment was a few dozen yards away and closing. Eldridge pulled the 9mm. The barrier gave way, and a pair of goggling dreen faces tried to force their way through the opening. The redhead ignored them and concentrated on his task. He sat down in the open trapdoor and held himself up with his arms and legs. He peered between his legs and saw the oddment nearing his position. Just as the hoverbike was about to pass underneath, Eldridge relaxed his body. He slipped through the trapdoor at the same moment the dreens broke through. As he fell, he aimed at the boompaste stuck to the safehouse ceiling—and for the third time in 10 minutes, he struck what Boris Hagan would call a "bull-zay." Smoke and fire burst from the trapdoor's opening as Dedrick's under-ceiling rumbled. A shockwave slammed through the redhead, who crashed back-first onto the passing oddment's hoverbike, flipping it into a barrel-roll. Exhaust-sludge scattered in a midnight arc around the bike. Dropping the 9mm, Eldridge grabbed onto the side of the bike and held on, while the oddment—whose feet were strapped to the bike—simply held onto the handlebars and rode it out. Once the oddment righted the hoverbike, he turned his attention to Eldridge, who held on with one hand and waved with the other.

"Sup!"

The oddment looked at Eldridge with its blank black face and grabbed a handheld commlink that trailed a coil of black wire from the receiver.

"I found him, sir."

"Hey!"

The oddment looked down.

Eldridge said, "Catch!"

A small, round object arced through the air. Reflexively, the oddment snagged it before he realized it was a half dreen. As he bobbled it out of his hands, the redhead unfastened his foot-straps and shoved him off the hoverbike. He fell. Eldridge climbed to his feet, grabbing the grenade out of the air on his way.

The pin was still in it.

Eldridge pocketed the grenade and watched the oddment crash through a corrugated steel roof. He then steered the faltering hoverbike skyward to check on his seal of the safehouse. Rocks completely filled the trapdoor's opening. Righteous. Time to get the hell out of town. The redhead had never piloted a hoverbike before, but its controls echoed those of a motorcycle: accelerator on the right, brakes on the left. Trailing a wake of black sludge, the redhead swooped through town, keeping his eyes peeled for any other patrolling oddments. He saw a few, but none noticed him. He aimed himself at the giant revolving door out of town and didn't even notice the bright red light that flashed from the streets below. He might have made it if he had just looked down, but instead, his body seized up as his entire nervous system went into a superhot hard-freeze. The hoverbike fell away underneath him and left him floating in the air for an instant before three horrible hooks yanked him earthward. He slammed into the cobblestone street, flat on his back. He struggled to move, but his limbs wouldn't obey. Something had tinged his vision an electric red.

A man clad in a red Kevlar three-piece suit stepped into his line of sight. In his gloved hand he held a gun that sprouted three electrified spikes that generated a trio of red-hot chains that had implanted themselves into his nervous system—a mortarchain rifle. A patch of plaid fabric covered the man's face. A black ocular device jutted from his brow and fixed its electronic gaze on the redhead.

Quillig, bounty-merc for the Chain of Tears, chuckled.

"Gotcha."

• • • • •

THE DEAL-MAKING BEGAN THE instant Quillig captured the redhead—only the redhead didn't know that a deal had already been struck.

"Quillig, Quillig, man! Hey! You don't have to take me to the Chain!"

The bounty-merc was leading Eldridge along the cobblestone streets out of town, giving the mortarchain a jerk now and then.

In response to the redhead, the bounty-merc said, "I'm not taking you to the Chain."

"Wha—" Another jerk of the mortarchain cut off his words and dropped him to the ground. Dregs drew away from the horror of a future resident of the Chain. Windows slammed shut in the shanties above the street. The redhead struggled to his feet and said, "What?"

"The Chain is many leagues distant, Eldridge. I couldn't have recharged my rifle so soon. I have a new client now."

That's when Eldridge noticed Quillig wasn't leading him *out* of town but *deeper into* town. In fact, a certain central Dedrick landmark was growing in their vision as the bounty-merc drug him straight up Sinister Street. Eldridge finally figured it out.

"Goldmist."

"The mighty Jeb Goldmist himself retained my services to help his legion of terror troops bring you in. Congratulations on attracting the attention of such an eminent Odd. But then he's *nobody* when compared to your primary creditor, is he?"

"Don't even say it, Quillig."

"Why would I need to? You know who you owe."

Actually, Eldridge didn't. Everything he knew of the Man Across the Oceans was included in his cryptic title: He was a man, and he lived across the oceans.

Nothing more was said for the rest of the trip. As they approached Goldmist's tower, two things started to build up inside the redhead: dread and curiosity. He had never seen Goldmist in person, and he knew of no one else who had. He and Quillig passed the small roadway that led up to Dr. Enki's office and proceeded toward the portcullis that blocked the main entranceway into Goldmist's tower. A pair of oddments hunched next to the gateway, both of them armed with splatter-iron rifles, which they leveled at Quillig as he approached.

The bounty-merc said, "Delivery for Goldmist." He jerked the chain and deposited Eldridge at their feet. One of them laughed behind his black faceshield and kicked the redhead in the stomach. The other spoke into an ear-mounted commlink. The portcullis dropped into the earth and admitted them into the largest room Eldridge had ever seen. The entire tower was one big atrium. A single wrought-iron staircase spiraled around a central elevator shaft that shot up through the center of the room. Small railed pathways radiated out from the staircase toward the tower's different floors, which encircled the outer wall.

In addition, the redhead took note of a pair of 100-foot steel columns attached to the inside of the tower. They reminded him of the minigun he had bolted to the tolhagan, except that these were 100 times as large and manned by oddments who sat in control consoles mounted on the rear of the giant columns, which weren't actually *columns* at all so much as *giant cannons.* Vast steel doors sat to either side of the cannons, ready to open up onto the city.

The tower was silent. Eldridge had expected Goldmist's tower to be one giant orgy or an odds-broking palace of the highest order. Instead, thousands of oddments lined each of the floors and stared down at Eldridge and Quillig as they entered.

Right away Eldridge noticed that the spiral staircase was the only way to reach these different floors because the elevator only stopped at the top and bottom levels, each of its trips heralded by the powering-up of an unseen dynamo. The churning-up of the dynamo culminated in a *boom* that sent the elevator barreling up or diving down. Moments after their entrance, the elevator dropped down to meet them. It had no door; only an opening in the central tube that allowed admittance. Eldridge had stopped struggling.

"You wanna turn me loose of this thing? We're surrounded by assholes. I'm not going anywhere."

A shaft of light accentuated the bounty-merc's sneer through his plaid mask.

"Your suffering makes my phantom cock twitch, El."

"I'm touched."

They stepped into the elevator. The dynamo churned up. *Boom,* and the elevator rocketed skyward. Floor after floor of oddment terror-troops flew by. The redhead's ears popped. He swallowed. Steam evacuated from around the elevator as brakes kicked in to halt its ascent. Another opening greeted them, and here the redhead's original expectations were met. Outrageously proportioned women slunk around the room; their eyes, lips, breasts, butts, and hips all expanded, exaggerated and idealized beyond human possibility. Some of them wore trixie overalls, but most didn't. Their huge eyes glinted at Eldridge, his body surrounded by a crackling nimbus of red electricity. The room had no furniture, only a vast assemblage of super-squishy pillows. Hundreds of viewscreens displayed the results of a thousand different odds-makings from around the continent, while others displayed distorted video footage of various sporting events. More output arrived via glass-domed tickertape machines that spewed forth endless strips of white paper, while still more arrived through oddment-drones who sat holding ancient phone-receivers to their ears, their faces twisted with the strain of listening to tinny voices that delivered news of events distant.

But the windows.

Eldridge had seen Goldmist's tower often enough to know it only had one window, but this room had *three* giant picture windows that each displayed a different spectacular view. One depicted a body of water that Eldridge didn't recognize because of its goofy blue color. The water broke against what looked like a desert, but the redhead knew it was a fantasy because he had seen the ocean—it was black and only ever broke against volcanic glass. Another window displayed something more familiar: a forest. But again, it was a fantasy. This forest swept on and on over hill after hill. When he and Tola lived together in Junktown, they had seen expanses of trees, but most of them were dead. The third window overlooked a view of outer space—a planet with a ring system, specifically, that floated near a titanic swirl of stars and interstellar dust.

All three of these windows were viewscreens, of course, and as phony as the women who lounged around the room. The one real window stood across the room, overlooking the city.

Eldridge said, "All right, already. Let's get this over with. Where is he?"

Two voices, both familiar: "*El!*"

He winced before he even saw them. Both Constable Tola and Oksana stepped out from behind a mass of oddments, both of them bound at the wrists. That dumbass Clovis was with them, but his wrists weren't bound. Tola was already babbling.

"El, I'm so sorry, I didn't know!"

"Relax, Zor. I've got 'em right where I want 'em."

"But, El—"

Eldridge addressed Clovis: "Hey, Clove! Remember when you tricked me into killing my best friend? That was awesome."

Clovis made a sound like two bricks scraping together. Laughter.

"You want to see something more awesome, El?"

"Sure! I'm gonna kill you here in a coupla minutes, but you go ahead and show me that awesome thing you've got."

The dry man touched his face, then dug his fingers into his flesh, which fell away like musty, age-old mummified bindings. Dust coughed up from his form as he pulled and scraped away the endless chunks of dried flesh that clung to...*something* underneath. He pulled off his clothes, too, revealing what looked like a sausage-man; as if someone had filled translucent tubes with Caucasian-toned meat-glop until every tube swelled at its corners with volume. When he finished scraping away all the dry detritus that had covered his face, he stood naked before them and stared at Eldridge with eyes that couldn't blink and a mouth that was frozen in a permanent half-grin. When he spoke, his lips barely moved.

"What do you think?"

Eldridge shrugged, kicking up a storm of red sparks. "Great disguise, Clove. Now where's Jeb Goldmist?"

Tola rolled her eyes. "He *is* Jeb Goldmist, you moron!"

Eldridge gawked at her, then at Clovis/Goldmist. He put a hand on his hip. "Right! I knew it was him all along. The constable and I made odds about it. Back me up, Zor."

But when he looked over at her, the giant, magnificent woman with black eyes grimaced as she bared her teeth and heaved heavy breaths. It took Eldridge a moment to remember that her encounter with the terrormonger in Junktown had cauterized her tear ducts.

"What's wrong?" he asked.

She couldn't answer, but Goldmist could.

"Your friend is dead," he said with a squeal. "The one with the gray hair."

"Boris?"

The Odd nodded. Eldridge yelled, "*Why?*"

One of his cartoonishly proportioned attendants wrapped Goldmist in a microfiber robe. He ignored the redhead's question and flopped onto a pillow, where a trio of toon-babes beset him in a jiggling mass of flesh. He giggled.

"Eldridge, how would you like to pay off that last bit of debt you have hanging over your head?"

The redhead stood silent.

Goldmist said, "I have one final task for you. You've already been good enough to kill poor Marko. Now I need you to complete one final move in the Xiang tournament. Capture the White Queen."

"You aced the tournament."

The head of an attendant bobbed in his lap. "Did I now? Well, no matter. If you dispose of the White Queen, I shall settle your debt with this *interesting, interesting* person who holds you in such thrall. The Man Across the Oceans."

"Why'd you want Marko dead, you fucking pussy?"

"Oh, what does it matter? He was making my ass itch. But let's turn our attention to the White Queen. She and I have some old odds to settle."

Eldridge frowned. "What're you talking about?"

Goldmist continued: "Like you and Marko Marinus, an old grudge stands between me and the White Queen."

"Between you and Shanta Feruccio?"

Everyone looked at Eldridge. Goldmist's face, which had been lolling backward in pleasure, snapped up. His expression moved a few millimeters in the direction of rage. Eldridge's eyes got big.

"Awww. What happened, Jeb? She wouldn't touch your dinky?"

Eldridge would remember the following events in reverse order, his brain never able to reconcile them: He held a bleeding Tola on the ground. He tossed her up onto her feet, where her chest vacuumed her blood back into itself. A bullet flew back across the room into a smoking barrel. Goldmist hid the gun under his pillow and screamed.

But after Goldmist shot Constable Tola, time snapped back into place.

Eldridge howled over the bleeding form of the constable as an island of red expanded from the center of her chest. Oksana kneeled next to him, her face blank. As blood pooled in her mouth, Tola looked up at Eldridge and spoke.

"El? Listen. The...dreen you killed."

"Zor, baby, don't talk. I'll get you out of—"

She shook her head, smiling. "It's over. But the dreen. His neck."

"What?"

"His neck. It was fine."

Quillig jerked on the mortarchain, but Eldridge struggled against it, screaming a single discordant note of grief. Red lightning licked from his body as he strained against the triplex of chains. Still holding the revolver, Goldmist lurched to his feet and stomped across the room.

"Hey, Eldridge!" He fired in tune with his words: *"Dead! Dead! Dead!"* Bullet holes burst open on the constable's neck. Her face fell into bloody fragments. Eldridge screamed again. When his gun was empty, a wheezing Goldmist turned to the redhead.

"I bet I can guess how you got back into Dedrick, El."

The redhead's screams had settled into silence.

Goldmist said, "You went through the Old Mine, didn't you?"

Eldridge's eye contact confirmed it.

The Odd continued: "You fought your way through all those dreens to get a chance at killing me. You were willing to take that kind of risk to avenge the death of your friend."

The redhead growled, "Get fucked, Goldmist. You just gave me nothing to lose."

"Oh, Eldridge. You know why I picked you to help me rid the world of Marko Marinus, don't you?"

The redhead glared at him.

Goldmist's eyes narrowed. "Before Deadblast, we'd have called you a mark. Today we just call you a *relic*. An *antique*. An *anachronism*. You love more deeply than anyone I've ever known."

"Wait. Lemme guess–and it's my greatest weakness."

"Hardly. It's the reason why I'm going to shoot you in the head and throw you out that window. Quillig?"

In one smooth motion, the bounty-merc pulled a handgun, pressed it against Eldridge's head and pulled the trigger. The redhead fell limp. Oksana remained silent. Quillig holstered his gun and drug the redhead's body across the room to the window, where he swung him in a giant circle and disengaged the mortarchain as he drew even with the opening. The redhead's body flew out.

• • • • •

HE WORE A HOT tiara.

As the vaulted brick ceiling of under-Dedrick fell away from him, the redhead felt a burning-hot tiara on his head. The tiara fit like a headband and cut a red-hot line over his scalp from temple to temple. Quillig's shot had deafened him for the time being, but he was pleasantly surprised to find that he wasn't dead. At least not yet. As he fell, he saw a second body get pitched out of Goldmist's tower above him—the curvy form of Oksana. He wondered if she was wearing a hot tiara, too. He expected his vision to flash black and blank at any moment, but it didn't. Instead, he *saw* something. It rose from the Dedrick skyline on a column of smoke capped with a fireball that exploded into a perfect, blinding white sphere that engulfed the city. Smiling, Eldridge wondered if he was having his own vision-odyssey like the Narsyan chieftains. He finally understood something that had been bugging him for years.

So that's what that picture is, he thought.

But instead of smashing into the ground outside Goldmist's tower, a mighty, callused arm broke his fall. Another such arm caught Oksie before she hit the ground, too, and in the moments before he finally blacked out, Eldridge saw the White Queen for the third time that week—only now, she was cradling both him and Oksana in her giant arms.

Black.

When he woke up, he was buried under a blanket on a comfy bed in a dark room lit by a single candle. Oksana was cuddled up next to him, warm and soft.

He was no longer wearing the hot tiara.

Oksana spoke: "Eldridge, when you said Goldmist had given you nothing to lose, what did you mean?"

Despite his clouded senses, Eldridge picked up on her wounded feelings. "Aw, girl," he said. "Of course I still have *you* to lose. I didn't mean it like that."

"What did you mean?"

Sleepiness overtook the redhead as the remkillers he had swallowed hours ago finally wore off. His eyelids were metal, the floor a magnet. As he drifted off, he squeezed Oksana.

"I meant it like...well, the constable. Zora. She was my daughter."

If Oksana reacted, he didn't hear it because a door opened into the room. Another candle floated in, borne by an unseen figure who glided across the room, seemingly on a dark cloud. A face appeared in the darkness; the face of a goddess, with two eyes as true-blue as the faux-blue of Goldmist's phony ocean, and with skin as flawless as a snow-drift on a lonely starlit walk.

But something didn't balance: her chest. Giant plates of callused armor covered it, and as Eldridge lost consciousness, those giant plates shrank and faded away, leaving nothing but silky white flesh underneath.

He slept.

Part Six

the URBITS

THE RUMORTRYSTS HAD LIED about Shanta Feruccio.

It wouldn't be the first or last time the trysts would lie about someone, but in the case of the world's most beautiful woman, they had done her a particular injustice by decreasing her station in life by a factor of 100. The stories Eldridge had heard about Feruccio over the years—the same stories Boris Hagan used to regale him with—held that Feruccio was but a humble resident of a nameless remnant across the ocean.

The real Feruccio, who sat across from Eldridge and Oksana in a small, wooden room with black curtains hidden somewhere in under-Dedrick, told her new friends that she had in fact been the rector of that far-off land. Admittedly it was more of a *people* than a *land*, as she ruled over a mobile tribe of far-eastern wanderers that had retained a good deal of its history and culture through the horrors of Deadblast. But just like the scattered refugees who inhabited this side of the ocean, no one in her tribe knew exactly what Deadblast *was*.

She looked thinner than Eldridge had imagined. He had only seen one or two images of her, and in both she swelled with perfectly proportioned curves. That array of perfect curves also included the top of her head, as Feruccio had always appeared with a shaved one. By contrast, the Feruccio who sat before them with her legs crossed and sipping tea had white hair that hung to her mid-back and looked at least 30 pounds lighter than the images Eldridge had seen. Then again, she was also *two feet* shorter and a *thousand pounds* lighter than the *last* time he had seen her, so how could he even trust his own memory?

Whatever. He was still alive and in the same room as Shanta Feruccio, who had apparently just saved his life.

"May I offer you some tea?" she asked.

Eldridge, who had never been offered tea by the world's most beautiful woman, responded with a confused, nonsensical syllable that approximated, "D'errr."

Oksana punched him in the arm. "We'd love some tea."

Feruccio nodded, rose, and appeared to glide across the room.

"Are you wearing roller skates or something?" the redhead asked.

"No," Feruccio said. "I'm trying not to bounce when I walk, otherwise the pain in my spine will cause me to scream uncontrollably."

Oksana mumbled, "Nice question, buttwad."

"*You're* a buttwad," he whispered back.

"Great comeback."

Feruccio poured two cups of tea and brought them over. After retrieving her own cup, she sat before them again.

"How is your head?"

Eldridge's head was wrapped vertically in gauze. He touched the top of his head and winced.

"It's OK, thanks. Where *are* we?"

"Near the northwestern walls of under-Dedrick. After I caught you outside the tower, I brought you to this house. I've been making my home here during the tournament."

Eldridge crossed to the window and pulled back the curtains to reveal one of a thousand anonymous Dedrick back streets. The skies overhead swarmed with Goldmist's oddments. A pair of patrolling oddments passed by the window. Eldridge snatched the curtains shut and turned back to Feruccio.

"Thanks for saving us. How'd you even know to be there?"

"I saw Goldmist's men take all of you captive one at a time. I didn't have the strength to extract you from the tower alone, but I suspected that he might opt for the grand gesture of a defenestration."

"I didn't understand anything you just said."

Oksana broke in: "El, how are you not *dead?*"

Feruccio said, "Your skull stopped the bullet, but it still grazed around your head and cut you to the skull from temple to temple."

Eldridge shook his head and sat down. "What're the odds?"

Feruccio sipped her tea. "Indeed." For a moment, the world's most beautiful woman regarded Oksana. The trixie twined her fingers in her lap and at first returned the gaze with a polite smile, but as Feruccio stared at her longer and longer, Oksana's attitude slipped into defiance. She threw up her hands.

"*What?*"

"What is your name, trixie?"

"Oksana. You wanna make something of it?"

Feruccio ignored her and addressed Eldridge. "You would do well to court this woman. She loves you with fierce tempest. With thunder and earthquake. With so much of her heart that there is none left to protest. With–"

Eldridge held up a hand. "OK, OK! Crom. I'll take her in a manly fashion."

Oksana blushed and instantly said, "I'm not blushing. You asshole." She punched Eldridge in the arm again.

Feruccio smiled and shifted in her seat. "Good."

Eldridge shook his head. "If Boris were here, he'd say something like, 'Dames!'" He fell silent for a moment. Oksana put a hand on his knee, ready to speak, but he cut her off with: "What's the *odium* between you and Clovi–I mean, Goldmist?"

Wrinkles appeared between Feruccio's eyebrows like a rose blooming in time-lapse. "A million deaths are not enough for that *macta.* I first met him when he tried to pledge himself to the Order of the Narsyan."

Eldridge slowly lowered his cup of tea. "Why am I not surprised? When was this?"

"Many ages ago. Shortly after Deadblast, before the Narsyans trekked across the ocean; before the world fully reconstituted itself; before the Odds."

Oksana's eyes got wide. "How old are you?"

"Older than Deadblast."

Eldridge said, "Just like Goldmist."

Feruccio nodded. "Yes. He and I can remember some of what came before, but only fragments. I cannot fathom why fate has ordained that we should live so long, but nevertheless–live we must."

"So what happened with the Narsyans?"

Feruccio rolled her eyes. "Goldmist–he actually had a *different* name back then–joined the order. A month later, he tried to supplant our leader. The council of chieftains–"

Eldridge jabbed his finger at her. "*Ha!* I knew you guys called it a council!"

The two women stared at him.

He sipped his tea and said, "Inside joke. Please, go on."

Feruccio said, "The council of chieftains split on whether to drum him out of the order. Some applauded his audacity, while others respected the chain of command. I cast the vote that dismissed him. I didn't see him again until years later, after I had left the order and taken control of my own little nomadic remnant."

Oksana: "What happened?"

"Goldmist stood on a wall while my family begged for help from underneath a sheet of burning gel. My son reached for my hand and cried out, 'Mother, it hurts.' I tried to pull him to safety. His arm detached at the elbow. I watched him melt. But Goldmist didn't drop the flaming gel on my land. He merely revealed our position to a rival remnant, who took advantage of the intelligence to wipe us all out. All but me. It was years later, while living alone in the far east, that the hardlines discovered my pleasing shape."

Eldridge and Oksana nodded. They all sipped their tea in silence for a few moments.

Finally, Eldridge slapped his knee.

"Hey! I know what we can talk about next. Remember when you were a giant monster that shot bazookas? You wanna tell us about that?"

Feruccio lowered her eyes. "I thought you'd be more interested in how I knew that you were cured by Marko Marinus."

The redhead fumbled his tea cup. "I got it!" It shattered on the ground. "Um." He picked up the shards. "These weren't, like, an heirloom or anything, right?"

Feruccio said, "I would put their age at approximately five hundred years."

Oksana: "Way to go, butterfingers!"

"Sorry," Eldridge mumbled as he carried the shattered remains over to the dresser that held the rest of the tea set. He returned to his seat and addressed Feruccio: "You were the one who wrote on my window. At the jail."

"Indeed I was. I apologize for not being able to do more, but I was busy trying to ascertain the identity of my old enemy. My intelligence had led me to Dedrick, but I didn't know who he was until he revealed himself by switching identities with you, Mr. Eldridge."

"How did that blow his cover?"

"It was just the kind of subterfuge he employed when I first knew him. It's just the kind of subterfuge he's *always* employed—misleading others into carrying out his despicable acts."

"So how did you know about Marko? Or *me*, for that matter?"

Feruccio's expression course-corrected around a smirk and settled on a neutral smile. "I saw him cure you."

"You saw? How?"

"The rumortrysts speak loudly, and they spoke of the great feats of Marko Marinus, so when I saw him wandering the streets of under-Dedrick, I took notice."

"Wha—? Where'd you see him?"

"A few days ago, near Goldmist's tower. He was walking away from the office of a physician, Enki."

"Don't tell me you know the doc, too?"

"Indeed I do, and my relationship to him holds one more revelation."

Eldridge pressed his palm into the side of his head and grimaced, both from the gunshot wound and at the mind-blowing network of connections that was slowly revealing itself.

"You can tell me in a minute," he said. "So ... Marko must've found a way to inject his blood into Dr. Enki's leech."

"Indeed. As for yourself, Mr. Eldridge—"

The redhead held up his hand. "You don't have to call me mister. Just Eldridge is fine."

Oksana bumped him with her shoulder. "I call him El sometimes. Or buttwad."

"I like 'old man' better," Eldridge said, smiling at Oksana with sad eyes.

Feruccio shook her head. "Your loss pains me."

Eldridge blinked, unable to follow her thought-jump. "What?"

"Goldmist maneuvered you into murdering Marko, did he not?"

Eldridge opened his mouth, closed it, then nodded.

"Mister—well, Eldridge, I don't know your entire story, but here is what I know: The rumortrysts hold that you owe an outlandish sum of jenta to an unknown party."

"Right."

"Furthermore, you made deathday odds in an effort to satisfy this debt."

"Right."

"But when Marko cured you, you felt compelled to enter this latest Xiang tournament."

Eldridge closed his eyes. "Is this going somewhere?"

"I can only assume that Marko never revealed his intentions to you?"

He shook his head.

Feruccio pressed on: "So given the facts you knew, it seemed that an act of kindness was actually one of retribution?"

Elbows on knees, Eldridge held his head in his hands. "Hey, I've got an idea. Let's pretend like I already feel like shit, and we don't have to talk about it anymore."

"Forgive me."

Eldridge looked up. The world's most beautiful woman was weeping. The sight instantly drove Eldridge and Oksana to their feet.

"Whoa, whoa," they said in unison.

Oksana said, "You can't cry. Don't cry."

"What're you crying about?"

"Please make her stop crying." Oksana covered her eyes. "Tell me when she's done."

Feruccio said, "I did not know."

"Didn't know what?"

"I did not know ... what I was doing. I thought that telling you of Marko's good deed would comfort you."

Eldridge looked at her for a long time. He put his hands on his hips and sighed at the ground. Finally, he spoke: "OK, so we're both kind of morons. What're we going to do about it?"

Oksana, still covering her eyes: "Is she done crying yet?"

"Yes," Eldridge said.

The trixie peeked through her fingers, then lowered her hands. "Please don't cry anymore."

"I shan't."

Oksana covered her mouth and giggled. "She talks pretty. Where'd you learn to talk so pretty?"

Eldridge rolled his eyes. "Oksie, can you stop flirting with the world's most beautiful woman for two seconds while we plot some revenge?"

"Right! Revenge!" She punched him in the arm.

Eldridge rubbed his arm. "First order of revenge: One hundred percent less punching of Eldridge in the arm during our attack."

Feruccio managed a smile. "Attack?"

"Well, yeah. *You* want to kill Goldmist. *I* want to kill Goldmist. We have so much in common, we oughta hang out some time, killing Goldmist. Besides, you owe me for the message at the jail."

Feruccio: "I agree on all counts, but we're only three people. How are we supposed to challenge the mightiest Odd in Dedrick?"

Eldridge smiled. "All we gotta do is maintain the rage. I've got a plan coming." He tapped his temple, then winced. "Ouch. Ahem. Anyway, you never answered my question."

"You're no doubt curious about my alter ego."

"I'll say. She might come in handy in a fight."

"Quite so. Unfortunately, she won't be able to join us for the rest of my life."

"Why?"

"It was a serum Dr. Enki provided me with. It only works so many times. You were there when he administered my most recent–and final–dose."

Eldridge thought. "On the street. You smashed out of that little hut. Scared the crap out of me. Was that the doc in your arms?"

"Indeed. He was kind enough to make the trip across town, so I brought him back to his office."

"You said it was the last dose. Can't he make more?"

Feruccio shook her head. "No, it isn't that I ran out. My body is physically unable to withstand the rigors of transformation another time."

Oksana elbowed him in the ribs. "That's why her back hurts, dummy."

"I got it, I got it. Well, that makes my unstoppable plan for revenge a little more stoppable, but we'll make do. For now, we need to get out of Dedrick."

"It is more prudent that you should leave me behind. I can remain here."

Eldridge crossed to Oksana and said, "Hey, you hear that? She thinks we're going to leave her here after she saved our lives."

"Funny!" Oksana said as she raised her fist–then lowered it.

"See? See how easy it is not to punch me?"

"It'd be easier if we were fucking right now."

"We'll fuck when Goldmist's a chalk outline."

"A what?"

"Something Zora says." Eldridge caught himself. His eyes glazed over. "Fuck it. Let's go interface with the psychoskags."

• • • • •

THE SUGGESTION TO INTERFACE with the psychoskags was a product of the police-protectorate that Goldmist had made of Dedrick. A blitz-out would be impossible, as Goldmist had deployed platoons of oddments everywhere, presumably to find and capture Feruccio, Eldridge, and their confederates.

But seeing as how Feruccio's safehouse was located so close to the walls—and by association, catwalk city—the redhead figured it was time to finally ask the psychoskags for a favor.

"What *is* it with you and them, anyway?" Oksana asked as they stole down an alleyway that led to the western wall.

"Oh, I hooked 'em up to the Arpa. Well, me and Boris did."

"That pornobox he was always yakkin' about? That's it? Now you're their hero?"

"Hey, it was either that or get chop-shopped for my organs."

They reached the wall, but they couldn't reach catwalk city. At that point, the lowest catwalk platform was 30 feet overhead.

"Shit," Eldridge said. "I'd climb it if I had my claws."

Suddenly, voices from behind: *"Hey! It's him!"*

The three of them turned around and looked down the alleyway, which had grown dark with the invasion of a squad of oddments, who were all running their way, splatter-iron rifles at the ready. Eldridge spun around and looked above, where he saw a psychoskag clamber by.

The redhead shouted, *"Flarg-barg!"*

Oksana stared: "What?"

The psychoskag turned its face floorward, spotted Eldridge, and instantly started howling and pounding on the catwalks all around it. Still the oddments approached, but just as Goldmist's jackbooted thugs reached the end of the alleyway, a jabbering horde of psychoskags instantly beset them from above. They rained from the catwalks and tackled the oddments. One by one, the psychoskags dispatched with the oddments with a variety of methods. Some used their hands or teeth to tear open throats, while others simply hugged their targets close and used their techno-hybrid bodies to electrocute them in a whirl of sparks and lightning.

Once the oddments were properly disposed of, the psychoskags turned to Eldridge and bowed. A few of them reeled off salutations on their monitor-faces—`HI, ELDRIDGE! GREETINGS!`—while the others (the ones who didn't have monitor-heads) simply howled their hellos.

Oksana squeezed the redhead's hand. He shook her off.

"If you wanna hold my hand, you can just hold it, Oksie. You don't have to pretend like you're afraid of these guys."

"Maybe *you're* afraid, buttwad."

He winked at her. "I am."

The redhead laid a hand on Feruccio's shoulder and stepped in front of the two women to meet with the dozen psychoskags who stood before them. Some of them sported the fruits of successful head transplants, but the one who appeared to be the leader was one of the unlucky ones. His head merely glared out from within a grimy and warped old monitor. Eldridge held up his palms and addressed him.

"Blarg boogity bog bloof!"

It responded, *"Flargity boggity boog!"*

Oksana: "Are you kidding me?"

Eldridge: "Hey, this is a very tricky dialect. *Boof! Barg-barg Goldmist-oog boof! Oog-boog-blarg!"*

Three psychoskags, including the leader, squatted in front of them, offering a piggy-back. Eldridge indicated Feruccio and continued: *"Boooooog. A! Boggity-boof-boof."*

The psychoskag, who was apparently the leader of the platoon, nodded its craggy face sagely.

"Booga."

Without so much as a *barg* or a *boof*, the psychoskag dropped to a knee and offered its bloody, stitched-together arms.

The world's most beautiful woman didn't budge.

"What does this creature want with me?"

Eldridge said, "I explained your situation to them. He's going to carry you up to their nest or headquarters or whatever."

The kneeling psychoskag, whose head bore the word MAGNA, looked up at Feruccio and said, *"Arg bargle barg-barg blarg!"*

Feruccio: "Translation?"

"I gave them a little of your backstory. He said it would be an honor to bear a queen in his arms."

The kneeling psychoskag, Magna, barked at Eldridge: *"Barg-barg!"*

Eldridge nodded. "Excuse me. He said it'd be an honor to bear *such a beautiful* queen in his arms."

Feruccio touched her heart. "You told them I was a queen?"

"Of course."

"But I wasn't. I was merely the rector of my wandering state."

"Hey, this tournament isn't over yet, and until it is, you're my queen."

Feruccio smiled and sat in Magna's scabby, bloody arms like it was a golden litter. While Eldridge and Oksana rode piggyback, Magna carried Feruccio with one arm as he scaled the wall. Once they reached the catwalks, the psychoskags let Eldridge and Oksana dismount and climb the rest of the way while Magna handled Feruccio. They scrambled up the catwalk in pursuit, occasionally receiving a helping boost or a passing *booga* from a supportive psychoskag. Ten minutes later, they arrived at a reverse-delta in the catwalk that spilled into the western wall. Hundreds of guardrails all converged on a dark opening like a black hole had opened up in the side of under-Dedrick. Eldridge turned and looked out over Dedrick. Nix's neon sign glowed across town, partially obscured by Goldmist's tower. The redhead sensed a dimming of lights all around him, a sudden feeling that Dr. Enki's most recent diagnosis had been wrong.

"Hey, old man!"

Oksana's voice helped the feeling to pass. He turned and followed her into the black cavern that sank into the outer walls of under-Dedrick. Inside, the metal beams from the catwalk continued to stretch into the darkness beyond, where they subdivided and crisscrossed each other in a dense network of grids that shored up the tunnel. Eldridge spotted a glimmer of light ahead. The silhouette of a Magna-borne Feruccio passed before the light. Eldridge and Oksana hurried ahead until they arrived in a chamber about 20 yards wide. Technology covered every square inch of wallspace—monitors, digital readouts, keyboards, circuitboards, and hundreds of other devices unknown to the redhead. Set against the wall were scores of electronic thrones. Each of the psychoskags sat carefully into one. Once seated, they all reached into the walls next to them and plugged four-pronged interfaces into their heads, whereupon the digital displays of their faces vanished. Magna stood remained in the entryway, still holding Feruccio, who he set down. Eldridge and Oksana stood next to her. Magna ran over and sat in one of the remaining techno-thrones, where he plugged himself in.

That's when the room started shaking.

Eldridge fell on his ass, Oksana on top of him. Feruccio's frail body had apparently instilled her with a preternatural sense of balance, because she remained upright. The middle of the room started moving. Hundreds, *thousands* of tiny cross sections of floor rose and fell in an undulating wave of transistors, circuitry, and steel. The thousands of cross sections parted in the center and gave rise to a 10-foot-wide cylindrical interface that included at least 20 input-ports. As soon as it rose and stopped in place, the outer walls sprouted mechanical arms that detached the monitor-heads of the psychoskags—even organic heads like Magna's—and plugged them into the central cylinder. A six-foot monitor on the front of the cylinder activated. Glowing letters rolled out across the monitor. Eldridge, Oksana and Feruccio stepped close enough to read.

The first words read:

```
HELLO, ELDRIDGE
```

Eldridge looked around for a keyboard, then spoke. "Um...hello, big psychoskag computer thing?"

```
HELLO
```

"Hello."

```
HELLO
```

"Hello."

Oksana: "El. Come on."

"Sorry," he mumbled, then addressed the computer: "So, you...*all of you* heard my request?"

```
YES. WE WOULD BE HONORED TO HELP YOU ESCAPE
DEDRICK

BUT

WE CAN'T OFFER ANY FURTHER AID
```

"Why not? You guys don't like Goldmist any more than I do."

OUR WORK HERE IS TOO IMPORTANT

BUT

WE CAN OFFER A SAFE HIDING PLACE FOR THE QUEEN

YOU HONOR US WITH YOUR PRESENCE

Feruccio crossed her ankles and dipped at the knees.

"If it please you," she began. "What *is* your work here?"

The psychoskags said: LET US SHOW YOU

A small hatch opened in the cylinder. Inside sat a headpiece outfitted with dozens of small contact sensors. Feruccio took it out and examined it.

The psychoskags said: PUT IT ON

Eldridge stepped forward and touched her arm. "You sure that's such a good idea?"

"You count these creatures among your friends, do you not?"

"Yeah. All the way."

"Then they are my friends, as well."

The world's most beautiful woman put on the headpiece–and crumpled. Eldridge and Oksana fell to their knees around her.

"Hey! *Hey!*" He jumped up and yelled at the monitor. "What did you do to her?!"

The monitor read, ONE MOMENT

On the ground, Feruccio's eyes fluttered. She sat up, her gaze distant. Eldridge kneeled next to her.

"Are you OK?"

She nodded, then took the redhead's hand. "Do you know what they're doing here?"

"No. What?"

"They're creating paradise."

She removed the headpiece, but as soon as it left her head, her body seized like someone had tied her head to her ankles and was pulling them together. She shrieked. Eldridge looked at the psychoskag's monitor and was about to yell something when he read this:

REPLACE THE HEADPIECE

The redhead dropped to his knees and put the headpiece back on. Feruccio's body relaxed. Her breathing slowed. She stood up, trembling.

"Thank you," she said.

The psychoskags said:

THE PLEASURE IS OURS

BUT

YOU MUST REMAIN IN THIS CAVERN

FOR THE PAIN-CANCELING AFFECT TO WORK

"I understand. But if I remain, may I also indulge in...all of the rest?"

The monitor printed: OF COURSE

Feruccio did that crossed-ankle/knee-bend thing again, then turned to address them.

"I shall remain here. I may even remain here for all time. Or what time I have left."

Eldridge nodded. "The serum?"

"It's ruined me. But your friends are close to perfecting paradise. I may be able to enter it before my body expires."

"I didn't understand anything you just said, but it sounds great. Thanks for saving our lives. So how are we getting out of here?"

"They'll explain everything," she said. "But, Eldridge? One more thing."

Seemingly from nowhere, Feruccio produced a small black bottle capped with a dropper. Eldridge had seen Dr. Enki use them before to administer tiny doses of medicine (or otherwise) to his menagerie of experimental subjects. He took it.

"How much is left?"

"Enough for one more transformation. Each dose lasts approximately 24 hours."

The redhead pocketed the serum. "Thanks again."

"Thank you, Mr. Eldridge."

"You don't have to call me mister."

"Don't you think you deserve to have a name?"

Eldridge wrinkled his nose and smiled. "That one went over my head, too. But thanks." As he turned to leave, a few psychoskags disengaged themselves from the giant interface.

Feruccio said, "Remember your promise."

"You got it. The next time you see us, Goldmist'll be dead."

"Well, that too, but I was talking about her."

Oksana, who had been standing politely to the side, looked to her right and left, fidgeting under the sudden attention. But she regained her composure and smiled. A dozen psychoskags (including Magna) reactivated their heads and stalked over to Oksana and Eldridge.

Magna said, *"Arg bargo-barg!"*

Eldridge looked a question at him and responded, *"Bargo-barg?"*

Magna nodded and lumbered down the tunnel in the direction of Dedrick. The others followed.

Oksana asked, "What was that?"

"It's kind of untranslatable."

"Do your best."

"Well, he said the psychoskag equivalent of 'Grab onto your butt, we're going for a ride.'"

• • • • •

THE PSYCHOSKAGS MOVED AS a unit. Along with the dozens that detached from their central chamber, hundreds more appeared from scores of dark hallways that led off from the main passageway. All of them chattered and barked and *booga*'ed their way past Eldridge and Oksana. On their way to the exit, each of the psychoskags tore a steel beam from the wall. Magna ran alongside the two humans, now their apparent liaison to the psychoskag leadership. He scooped Eldridge and Oksana into his arms and howled down the ever-brightening hallway. His fellow psychoskags parted before him, all of them armed with steel beams—but they weren't weapons. No, as they emerged onto the outer catwalk high above under-Dedrick, the psychoskags streamed out and scattered across the highest reaches of the catwalk. Some of them attached their steel beams into what looked like random parts of the catwalk, while others got to work on constructing some kind of sled for Eldridge and Oksana.

"What're they doing?!" she yelled over the racket.

"Wait and see!"

Moments later, Magna barked a series of commands at his fellow psychoskags, and they all scrambled across the catwalk to assume various positions. Eldridge looked down, and sitting before them was a steel sled. Magna carried them over and dropped them on it, pushing them down onto their stomachs. He kneeled over them and detached a pair of steel cables from his monitor-head, which he plugged into the sled. In response, hundreds of lights fired up across the vehicle and blinked. Magna screamed, and the psychoskags screamed back in response. In one fluid, coordinated motion, they all slammed their fists into the catwalk—*which detached.*

But not all of it. Only a vast vertical section fell away from the ceiling overhead, revealing an elaborate series of hinges that only a carefully trained eye could have noticed heretofore. As the track fell floorward, it groaned loud enough for the whole city to hear—and more important, loud enough for the oddments to hear. A few hoverbikes chugga-chugged their way toward the plummeting catwalk. One of them spotted Eldridge and pointed just as a foot-thick metal beam flew threw his chest. His body dangled from his upside-down bike. Other oddments took notice and flew over, but the gigantic steel track was already smashing into houses far below, sending dregs running in fear from the terror that fell from above.

Finally, Magna screamed something that activated a pair of rockets on the back of the steel sled. Eldridge and Oksana's faces stretched backward from the instant onrush of blinding-fast wind as their butts heated up from the outblast of rocket fire that propelled them down the ramp in a velocity-burst that took them from standstill to supersonic in a few fleeting instants. Dedrick blurred in a 45-degree smear. The steel track streaked by underneath. The giant revolving door quantum-leapt in front of their faces, its rotation halted by the crash of the steel track into it. Eldridge and Oksana thought they were about to splat into the side of the door, but somehow another mass of psychoskags appeared in front of them to detonate a series of small explosives that opened a howling breach through it. It was genius: The sudden change in pressure admitted an inrush of freezing air that chilled their teeth and eyes while also acting as their brakes. The steel sled's rockets kicked in one more time and carried them up the ramp that led out of under-Dedrick. A bump in the pavement sent them flying in a spinning arc out into the desert night. Eldridge, Oksana, and Magna fell off the sled. The redhead jumped to his feet and looked down the ramp.

Black figures were already amassing at the entranceway.

"*Run!*" Eldridge yelled.

"*Blarg!*" Magna hollered, pointing at the sled.

Eldridge stared at him stupidly, then slapped his forehead. "Right! Thanks!"

"How do we steer this thing?!" Oksana shouted.

"Beats me! *Fire it up!*"

They tapped on random buttons for a few moments before Magna lurched over and pounded a big, red button on the side of the sled. The sled rumbled, its rockets firing up.

"What about you?" Eldridge asked.

"*Barg barg barg!*" Magna cried, then sprinted down the ramp toward the oncoming phalanx of oddments.

"What?! No! Shit! Stop!" Eldridge yelled as the sled took off and carried them north into the desert. He screamed, "*Why do I fucking owe my life to everything that moves?!*"

• • • • •

THEY ROCKETED INTO THE desert, keeping an eye out for any oddments patrolling the over-Dedrick area. Avoiding the main highway, Eldridge guided the sled behind a rocky outcropping to evade a black car that held two oddments, but besides that, they made the trip north largely unmolested. The redhead guided the sled—which was rapidly losing speed as it expended whatever fuel it used—in a wide circle around Tola's jail, constantly vigilant for any sign of oddments. The sled finally gave out next to a rocky swell in the earth. Eldridge stopped it and held Oksana, who had been warming herself by the sled's rocket-fire but was now shaking uncontrollably.

"Where...are...we...going?" she asked.

"I've got a plan," Eldridge said. "But in order for it to work, I need to ask you for one more favor, little girl."

Teeth chattering, she looked into his eyes. He smiled back at her.

She said, "Kiss. Me. Dumbshit."

"Oh," he said. They kissed. She didn't stop shivering, but her cheeks looked a little redder.

"What's the plan?"

"Well, first, we need to get into the jail, and after that, I'm gonna have to ask you to risk your life for me again."

Oksana nodded, but her eyes fell.

Eldridge: "What is it?"

"El, why don't we just run?"

He nodded. "Fair question. You don't have to do anything else. Listen, we'll get you some transpo in Zora's garage, and you can beat it for another remnant. I'm sorry I asked."

"Why don't you come with me? Is it the jenta you owe?"

He shook his head. "No, it's like...in this world, we're lucky to have friends. Before this week, I had already lost four or five good ones. Then this week comes along, and I lose three more. One of 'em was even my kid. Now, they're all gone, and it's my fault. To hell with the jenta I owe—*that's* a debt I need to make right."

"I meant to ask—why didn't Tola know?"

"Know what?"

"That you were her dad."

Eldridge looked at the desert. "Well, you remember those scorch marks on her eyes?"

"Yeah."

"She didn't remember much after that terrormonger tried to ace her. I was bringing her up in Junktown, and by that time, she was about ready to strike out on her own."

"You lied to her?"

Eldridge nodded. "I dunno know why. Felt bad about letting her down. It was my fault the freak got into our place. I told her I saved her so she'd think I was all right."

"But you *did* save her."

"Sort of."

They sat in silence for a moment. Oksana took his hand.

"What do you need me to do, old man?"

• • • • •

HALF AN HOUR LATER, Eldridge parted ways with Oksana at the entrance to the Old Mine. Part of the redhead's plan involved the trixie venturing into the fearsome dreen stronghold, but he armed her with a figurative sword and shield.

"If my plan works, you'll be the cavalry," he said.

"The what?"

"Something Boris used to say. Here," he said and kissed her one last time.

Now the redhead, once again astride his hydrocell motorbike, zoomed north toward the Oasis Mountains and Burbage, home of the Narsyans. His plan involved them, too. He saw the same two Narsyan guards standing watch over their first checkpoint, and he flew in between them, not slowing down until the angle of the mountain pathway rose above 45 degrees. When his bike started to misfire due to the altitude, he ditched it and finished the rest of the voyage at a full, Narsyan-style sprint, ignoring the burn in his legs and lungs as he ran through a driving snowstorm. A full contingent of Narsyans awaited him at the border of Burbage. They escorted him through the Fulcrum into the central audience chamber, where Pell Yannick was enduring the Typhoid Maiden.

"Wait here," one of the guards said as they left Eldridge alone with the Narsyan chieftain, whose skin bubbled with boils for a few moments until his immune system crushed the infection. Once his skin returned to normal, he stepped out of the glass chamber and regarded the redhead.

"I assume you have an explanation for your presence here," he said.

And for the first time since he was a child—and a Narsyan himself—Eldridge cried. He fell to his knees and wept before one of his lifelong enemies. His weeping continued for a few long minutes before Eldridge realized that Pell had quietly crossed the room and sat down next to him with crossed legs. The Narsyan chieftain sat with his legs crossed. When the redhead's weeping finally slowed, Pell spoke.

"What happened?"

Eldridge said, "About a year ago, I got really sick."

• • • • •

ELDRIDGE TOLD HIM EVERYTHING. He walked him through the specifics of his debt and the deathday wager and the rules of Xiang. He told him all about Clovis and Goldmist and Feruccio and Hagan and Constable Tola. He explained how Goldmist had manipulated him, and he explained why he murdered Pell's fellow Narsyan chieftain and his own best friend. When he was done, Pell was still sitting with his legs crossed, staring at his hands with a knit brow. He stood and extended his hand to Eldridge, who he helped to his feet.

"The Order of the Narsyan stands ready to assist you."

Eldridge forearm-wiped snot from his nose. "What? You believe me?"

Pell smirked. "You may remember that I once called you an insolent cunt."

"Uh, yeah."

"Well, you should realize that your breed of insolence is blood-related to a form of arrogant honesty I've never been able to stomach. In all your years in this order, you never once told me a lie, much to my chagrin. Why would you *start* lying now?"

The very density of the air around Pell seemed to change for Eldridge, who hoped with a far-off heart that he might be in the process of replacing one of his missing best friends. He ignored the bright feeling for the time being and pressed on.

"Pell, I've got a plan to take down Goldmist, and it involves the Narsyans. All of you guys. And it's risky. There'll be deaths."

"None of which I take lightly," Pell said. "But all the same, an Odd has struck to the heart of our order, and we must respond in kind. Can your plan accomplish that?"

"If you guys do what I say, then yes."

"You can stop referring to us as 'you,' Eldridge. Marinus left standing orders that you be readmitted to the order at any time. Those orders stand in spite of his death. If you so chose, you may address us as an initiate anew."

Pell offered his forehead for a headbutt—the Narsyan equivalent of a handshake—but Eldridge declined.

"I'm not made of stern enough stuff for you guys. But I can show you how to kick Goldmist's ass."

"Then let's address the troops," Pell said, striding toward the door.

• • • • •

IN THE GREAT HALL of the Fulcrum, an extraordinary event happened: The Narsyans stood still.

Pell conferred briefly with the rest of the chieftains and sent out an order to rally every living Narsyan, all of whom made the trip back to Burbage within an hour, no matter where they were. Eldridge took note of the time and wondered how Oksana was doing with her part of the plan, but he dismissed the worry from his mind and concentrated on the sheet of paper that Pell had shoved into his hand as a thousand jittery Narsyans packed into the Fulcrum and glared at Eldridge. Some of them knew him personally, but all Narsyans knew *of* the redhead Eldridge and his legendary grudge with Marko Marinus—a grudge that had ended in an epic battle that leveled their very own conventuary. The expressions that looked back at Eldridge ranged in tenor from curiosity to outright hostility, but before Eldridge even entered the room, Pell and the chieftains spoke with them all and explained how once again the Odds had attacked the Order. When Pell was done, he brought in Eldridge, who stared at the script Pell had prepared for him. The room continued to buzz with chatters and murmurs until Pell raised his hand.

"Silence! Former order member Eldridge will now address you!"

Eldridge stepped forward and read: "Um. O great Order of the Narsyan, know then..." He trailed off, stepped over to Pell and whispered, "Do I have to read this? I feel like an idiot."

"The initiates require a measure of pomp in order to be spurred into action."

Eldridge gave him a look and turned back to the glaring crowd. "O great Order of the Narsyan! Know then that Jebediah Goldmist, Odd of Dedrick, has brought about the death of chieftain Marko Marinus..." he trailed off again. Then he folded up the paper and said, "O great Order of the Narsyan. Know then that Jebediah Goldmist, Odd of Dedrick, tricked me into murdering my best friend in the whole world. But here's the worst of it: I didn't even need to be tricked. I had spent my whole life hating him. I'd have killed him even if I didn't have an excuse to do it. I'd have killed him even though he had long since made peace with me, and even though he was trying to make things right with me. I'd have killed him anyway. That's how much of a low-down, ratfuck scoundrel I am. But it's the truth, and here's more of the same: Goldmist made me and one of the finest women I know into urbits, all over the course of his miserable, shitty life. The man needs killin', and we're the ones to do it. I've got a plan in two parts to take him down, and we're part one. I've got my favorite trixie from Dedrick taking care of part two, and if her heart's as big as I know it is, we should be just fine. But I'm gonna have to ask for some bravery and derring-do from all of you guys, and more than that, I need all of you to make yourselves a new life-choice from here on out. You Narsyans are some of the toughest dudes I know, and if we can shake things up down in Dedrick, then, by Crom, we can do it in other places, too. Other remnants."

Pell whispered, "Eldridge."

The redhead shook his head. "All right, all right. I'm getting ahead of myself. But listen: I'm going to explain my plan to the chieftains, and then they'll explain it to all of you. And guess what? When we get done, the Order of the Narsyan will have its boot heel on the throat of Dedrick. *Who's with me?!*"

Havoc. Bouts of powerlifting and powerfucking broke out across the room in celebration of their imminent triumph. The din forced Pell to escort Eldridge back into the central chamber, where he closed the door.

"Eldridge, you know of the Inculta Wars. Our embarrassing defeat at the hands of the Odds."

"Yep."

"You do realize that we're not cut out to be infantry."

"You're not going to be infantry. You're going to be *artillery.*"

• • • • •

THE RUMBLE BEGAN LOW. Anyone still outside in the arctic cold would have perceived a darkening of the northern horizon as the first morning sunbeams broke. It was like a vast, black wave washing over the sandscape. But instead of a wave, it was a massive, mobile square of people.

Narsyans. All of them arrayed into a flawless platoon that sprinted south across the desert, eschewing the need for mass transport and relying on their own legs to carry them all the way down the Oasis Mountains and clear across the desert basin that separated them from Dedrick proper, each of them pumping their arms in unison, each of them matching the top speed of whoever was the greatest runner in the moment—a title that changed almost as rapidly as they moved their legs.

And riding alongside them on his motorbike was the redhead; his head buried under a bandanna, his eyes hidden behind black goggles. He had to juice his engine to keep up with the Narsyan horde, all of whom had their marching orders, and all of whom were ready to die to avenge the death of Marko Marinus, the former unspoken high chieftain of the order.

Running next to the platoon and immediately next to Eldridge was the recently ascended unspoken high chieftain of the order, Pelagius "Pell" Yannick, whose spiral leg-scar squeaked incessantly with each of his mighty strides. As they rode across the desert, snow started to fall. The redhead looked through the snow and back many years to the moment right after Marko Marinus cast the deciding vote that dismissed him from the Order of the Narsyan. Eldridge's forehead burned from where Marko himself had dug out the circle of flesh that would forever ruin the perfection of the vertical scar. Blood spilled out of the wound and broke like a stream around his nose. He had to continually wipe his face to keep himself from inhaling his own blood as he began the long walk down the mountain that all disgraced order members had to make: The Circle Walk.

But in Eldridge's case, he wasn't making the walk alone. Crius Kaleb trudged through the snow alongside him, weeping and wailing. In the hours since Eldridge's failed attempt to procure the blood of a Narsyan chieftain, a new storm had dropped a few fresh feet of snow on the ground and concealed the path. Eldridge put his arm around his frantic friend and held him close. They lowered their heads and continued the walk, but a voice interrupted them.

"You!"

Eldridge looked up. Marko, clad in the minimal garb for a chieftain, stood in the center of the path. Deep, rapid-fire footprints in the snow led up to where he stood with his hands on his hips. The redhead tried to wave him away.

"Just move, Marko. We're done."

Marko stepped forward and blocked their path. Eldridge sighed.

"If you want to fight, Marko, we can–"

"My grievance isn't with you."

The young Marko Marinus planted his hands on Crius' shoulders and shoved him to the ground. He wagged his finger and screamed.

"Never again shall you disturb our conventuary, outsider! Never–"

Eldridge's punch sent Marko staggering to the ground. He tried to yell something, but the redhead had already fallen on him, pinning him under the snow. The redhead rained fists down on his former best friend, blow after blow, and when Marko's face was sufficiently bloody, Eldridge started to grab fistful after fistful of snow and rub them in Marko's face. This went on for 10 minutes. Finally, the redhead stopped. Marko lay in the snow, sobbing.

Neither of them knew how old they were, but they both knew how young they were.

Eldridge said, "You were always faster than me. Stronger. *Better.* But never *tougher.*"

Marko spoke between sobs: "He's an outsider. I can't look weak."

"You're twice as strong as me. But you can't take this back. You wanna be a part of that up there? Be a chieftain? *Good.* They're a bunch of weaklings, too. You'll fit right in."

Eldridge covered Marko's mouth and pinched his nose shut. Marko struggled but couldn't break the redhead's grip. After watching his former best friend struggle to breathe in the snow, Eldridge released him. Marko gulped air into his lungs amidst wet sobs. Eldridge stood and helped Crius to his feet. Marko lay in the snow, still sobbing.

Eldridge yelled, "You're lucky, Marko. I don't fucking *remember* how to cry."

The redhead and his sick friend continued The Circle Walk.

The snow stopped.

Once again, Eldridge was riding his motorcycle through the desert with Pell Yannick and the rest of the Order of the Narsyan as they descended on Dedrick for a final showdown with Jeb Goldmist.

Eldridge called over: "Are they ready?!"

"As ever!" Pell called back.

The highway sloped down into a rockier area as it drew near the giant ramp that led into under-Dedrick. As soon as they entered the rocky area, Eldridge reached into a saddlebag, pulled one of his remaining .357 Mags, and fired into the sky.

"*Now!*" he screamed.

In response, the Order of the Narsyan broke ranks; the perfect square dissolved into a scattering mass of humanity as each took up a densely packed cluster of carbon atoms—commonly known as "rocks"—but given that these were Narsyans, the rocks available to them included everything from hand-sized stones to 10-foot-tall boulders. They hoisted the rocks just as they reached the down-ramp into under-Dedrick, which was packed with oddments.

Oddments who never stood a chance.

The rocks flew, whizzed, zipped, and careened at the mass of oddments, who all raised their weapons an instant too late as the rocks smashed, crushed, slammed, bammed, and caromed into their heads, faces, and bodies. Black armor shattered, spikes flew, and fearsome trappings were cast aside as the Narsyans carried out the redhead's orders and drug the bodies out of the way and *made* way for Eldridge and Pell to lead the charge down the ramp toward the revolving door, which still lay open—but it was covered with a thick steel grate.

Eldridge leveled his .357 at the grate and howled, *"Take it doooown!"*

The Narsyans obeyed, and a dozen materialized as instant volunteers; a dirty dozen of muscular badassery that insta-teamed into a mobile battering ram that sprinted headlong into the grate and knocked it flat—*boom!* Eldridge hit the gas and zoomed into under-Dedrick, a hail of bullets already greeting him. The order saw its first casualties here in the form of exploding hearts and heads that punctuated the falls of physically perfect initiates young and old. One of the chieftains—a midnight-haired muscle-matriarch of four decades—also met her doom when a pellet of boompaste attached to her forehead and went *pow.* Eldridge and Pell took the first right turn into town, the redhead hoping to Crom that the order members would remember his orders.

They did.

Narsyans swept the streets of Dedrick, each of them taking up whatever arms they could find. Eldridge had already made sure they knew *what* arms to take up.

"Anything that normal folks *can't* lift," he said back up in Burbage.

And the order remembered. They lifted great slabs of stone, rickshaws, broken-down cars, entire small houses, all of which they hurled at the oncoming thrust of oddments who powered their way down the main streets at them, their ranks constantly replenished from Goldmist's tower like a neverending stream of dark sperm as stream after stream of black, spiked armor spurted from its gate. Eldridge slowly led them through the panicking city, which was gripped by two sources of mayhem: The attack of the Narsyans and the freaked-out response of the general populace, who all ran screaming from the endless volleys of bullets, boompaste, and load-bearing members. One Narsyan—a stocky, yellow-skinned asskicker—squatted and deadlifted a newly dropped foundation out of the deep earth. He teetered in place for a moment as he balanced the two-ton column of hardrock on his chest, but then he dropped the motherfucker horizontal like a superstrong pre-Deadblast insect—"Ants!" Hagan would have yelled in ecstasy of knowledge—and the Narsyan slowly started to spin the column around until he had cleared a city block with its unstoppable whirling radius. At just the right time, he released it and sent it soaring over the city, where it took out a half-dozen hoverbiking oddments on its way to shattering one whole side of Goldmist's tower. Oddments rained out of the wound. Eldridge and the Narsyans cheered.

Just in time to get smacked in the mouth.

Goldmist's tower, undeterred, *bloomed.* Great doors flew open all around its diameter and up and down its great height. Most of the doors spewed forth thousands more oddments, but the largest ones—the ones nearest the top—made way for the building-sized cannons that Eldridge had seen earlier. They *whirred* into place, then rotated on gigantic pivots and took aim. Eldridge and his comrades heard no reports. Only brief muzzleflashes accompanied by the disintegration of entire buildings told the story of Goldmist's secret weapons. But Eldridge kept astride his bike, which he rode up a stucco stairway and onto a rooftop, where he shook his fist.

"Keep moving inward! Those guns've only got so much range—shit!"

He gunned his bike just in time for the building underneath him to shiver apart into dust and splinters. Eldridge kept the wheels spinning and maintained his balance as he rode farther into town, capping a few oddments with his .357 along the way.

"Come on, Oksie. Come on, come on," he chanted as he led a few score Narsyans down Sinister Street, right at the tower. Nix's neon sign passed by on the right as the order members took up more weighty weapons and hurled them into the chests of attacking oddments and across the city at the tower, which continued to rain down silent destruction on them. Eldridge watched the female Narsyan guard Sipho splatter apart when one of the tower's blasts hit her head-on. But still he and Pell forged ahead, both of them sprinting straight down Sinister Street. When they neared the center of town, Eldridge turned to Pell.

"OK, we're here. You think you can hit it?"

Eldridge pointed up and to the right of Goldmist's tower, where the trapdoor entrance to his safehouse sat in the ceiling, still blocked with rocks.

"Stand back!" Pell Yannick said as he squatted down before the blackened chassis of an ancient car and lifted it into the air over his head. Once he had it skyborne, he got a running start, reared back *with one arm*, and hurled the chassis on an almost perfect 45-degree vector at the ceiling, where it smashed directly into the blocked-up entrance to Eldridge's safehouse.

Rocks and debris showered the city as the stones that had been wedged into the tiny trapdoor gave way and fell, along with the car chassis Pell had thrown. It all fell across the city, which in turn fell silent. Pell walked over to Eldridge. They both looked up at the opening.

Pell asked, "You think that did it?"

"I hope."

The silence lasted less than a Dedrick moment before the shrieks came—dark shrieks of mad joy that floated down from the trapdoor, which was suddenly full of a thousand squirming heads and eyes and legs and arms. The mass of limbs, sinew, and connective tissue broke through the ceiling and transformed the trapdoor into an all-out breach in the vaulted brick ceiling of under-Dedrick. And then they came. Thousands upon thousands of them came.

Dreens. All of them.

Eldridge screamed, "*Yes! Hell, yes!*"

They infested the ceiling in an instant, and up in his tower, Goldmist apparently had no idea how to respond to an attack from below *and* above, because his sound-cannons paused in their aim, their operators no doubt unsure of what a direct blast into the under-ceiling would do. Eldridge revved his motorbike's silent hydro-engine.

"*Let's go!*"

As Eldridge led the Order of the Narsyan directly down Sinister Street toward Goldmist's tower, thousands of dreens swarmed across the ceiling like an infection, inexorably spreading toward Goldmist's lair. Eldridge and the Narsyans reached the base of the tower just as the dreens reached the top of it, and as Eldridge dismounted his bike in front of the portcullis into the tower, he looked up and saw it.

Or rather, he saw *her*.

She fell from the ceiling like a colossus descending from the heavens. It occurred to Eldridge that Hagan might have had one of his kooky classical references on hand to mark the occasion, but who gave a shit? Eight feet tall and clad in the same callused super-armor, the new

White Queen plowed into the ground and dug a five-foot crater with her impact, which kicked up sheets of pavement and knocked Eldridge on his ass. One of her callused hands reached out and helped him up, and when he looked into her eyes, her recognized the dark twinkle of his favorite trixie.

"El, this is fucking *rad*," Oksana subwoofed.

"Tell me all about it later, Oksie! Now, get that gate open!"

Oksana twirled around, grabbed the portcullis and tore it asunder. She lowered her shoulders and knocked a queen-sized hole into the side of the tower. As she led them all inside, more gunfire rained down on them. Oksana spread her arms and shielded everyone underneath her as the dreens did their job and fanned out across floor after floor of the tower, devouring and dismembering oddments as they went.

"Hey, Oksie! I guess my idea worked?"

With her huge, callused lips, Oksana smiled. "When I showed Milos that book Zor had written, he got the queen to help us."

Eldridge nodded. "You did me proud, little girl."

"We're not done yet."

"I hear that," he said as the gunfire faded overhead. Once the gunfire stopped entirely, Eldridge nodded to Pell and looked up at the new queen.

"Meet us upstairs, Oksie!"

"You got it, El!"

Eldridge, Pell, and the Narsyan chieftains crossed to the elevator, which opened up and released a pair of screeching oddments who had dreens attached to their backs. Oksana started scaling the inside of the tower, each floor ascended with a mere sweep of her vast arms. The redhead led the chieftains into the elevator, which churned up and *boom'ed* them skyward.

Jeb Goldmist was smirking when they arrived. Behind him was one of his viewscreens, which displayed a dark silhouette. As Eldridge strode into the Odd's throne room, Goldmist hooked his thumb at the dark figure.

"Spare my life, and I'll pay your—"

The Odd's brains sprayed across the viewscreen. The dark figure didn't flinch at the violence, nor did it react to the entrance of the redhead, who was accompanied by a group of insanely muscled men and women, as well as an eight-foot giant and a gaggle of squealing dreens that sprinted back and forth across the throne room. Eldridge, who had just blown a hole through Jeb Goldmist's face, blew smoke off the barrel of his .357 and addressed the dark silhouette onscreen.

"Yeah, yeah, yeah—I *know* I owe you big-time. I'll pay you back later."

He blasted the viewscreen, which shattered and sent sparks flying everywhere. What oddments remained all fell to their knees and twined their fingers behind their heads. Eldridge stood before the very same throne room that Jeb Goldmist had occupied hours earlier. Everyone looked at him.

"Now what?" Pell asked.

Eldridge holstered his gun and took a breath. He rubbed his brow, then sat on the ground. He looked up.

"Hey, does everyone want to have a seat?"

Pell nodded to the rest of the Narsyan chieftains. They all sat down, Pell next to Eldridge. Oksana remained standing. The dreens came to a standstill and glared at them, wheezing. Eldridge started to dismiss them, but then he remembered Constable Tola's last words.

The dreen you killed. His neck was fine.

The redhead addressed the dreens: "Uh, I need you to deliver a message to the dreenqueen."

• • • • •

THE CLEAN-UP ENCOMPASSED THE city. Before his demise, Goldmist had dispatched clean-up crews to undo the damage done by the Xiang tournament, but in the wake of the pitched battle just fought, Eldridge (as the newly installed steward of Dedrick) called on the Narsyans, the psychoskags—everyone—to pitch in.

The day after the battle, Eldridge made two stops. The first was at Dr. Enki's, the second at Boris Hagan's.

At Dr. Enki's, he merely stuck his head in the door and pointed at the mysterious photo on the wall. As always, it depicted something that looked like a ladder capped with giant, glowing head of cauliflower.

"Hey, doc," Eldridge said.

The doctor was performing a handstand on one of his worktables so he could peer through his head-mounted laser-loupes at a creature he had splayed open for dissection. When he saw the redhead, he lowered himself and smiled.

"Eldridge! Congratulations on your ascendance to the ranks of Odd-dom!"

"There's no ascendance, Doc. And I'm not an Odd. I just wanted to drop by and say—" (he pointed at the photo) "—nuclear blast."

The doctor's face lengthened with surprise, and then delight.

"Quite impressive. Can you tell me the timestamp?"

"I'd say three or four milliseconds after detonation."

"Excellent. How did you figure it out?"

"Oh, I had an epiphany when someone shot me in the head at point-blank range and chucked me out a window."

Enki nodded sagely. "Ah. Naturally. Shall we dispense with that nasty scar, then?"

The redhead touched the scar and felt it with his fingers. His eyes misted over, but after a moment, he looked at the doctor and said, "Actually—yeah."

"Very well. Have a seat."

Enki pointed to an old dentist's chair. The redhead sat down while the doctor climbed one of the walls to a shelf where he kept an implement that looked like a ballpoint pen with a scalpel at one end. He crawled back down the wall and made his way to the chair. He climbed up and set the flat cross section of his torso on Eldridge's chest and settled in to perform the procedure. Before he began, he looked the redhead in the eyes.

"You're sure about this, El?"

"Yeah. It's time."

"Very well. No anesthetic, I assume?"

"Nope. Go."

Enki used the scalpel to carve away the scar tissue. Eldridge hissed in pain, but didn't squirm. The doctor dropped the tissue–which resembled the ancient Greek character *phi*–into a metal pan. He then flipped the scalpel around and activated its opposite end, which was capped with a laser that he used to stimulate the layers of dermis on Eldridge's forehead. After a few minutes, the doctor sat back up, smiling.

"All done. Have a look." He pointed to a small mirror that sat on a worktable next to the dentist's chair. He hopped off the redhead, who stood and looked in the mirror. Bright red skin in the same *phi* shape marked where the scar had been, but the inflammation was already fading. Eldridge closed his eyes and smiled.

"Thanks, doc."

"My pleasure."

Eldridge stood for a moment longer, then said: "Doc, I gotta ask...did you know that Marko had slipped some of his blood into your leech?"

Enki's eyes fell. He looked up and said, "Mr. Marinus didn't have to resort to such measures. I administered the dose myself."

"What?"

"I stand by my decision."

"But...but you *knew* the hole I was in. The jenta I owed. My daughter. And you *knew* that Marko was in the tournament–"

"I knew no such thing, and even if I did, I would've made the same choice."

Eldridge stood up. "Why?"

Dr. Enki removed his laser-loupes. "Your cancer was terminal. I provided you with the medicine needed to keep you alive until your deathday, but there was nothing to be done. When Mr. Marinus approached me, that changed."

"But you *knew*–"

"Eldridge, I will not have you lecture me in my own medical office. Yes, I was quite aware of your situation, but contrary to my trappings of mad science, I undertook the study of medicine to *heal.* Marko Marinus gave me an opportunity to heal you, and I happily accepted his offer. Even though you remain, as ever, an idiot."

Eldridge stood for a moment, looking at the photo of the nascent nuclear blast.

"But..."

Enki asked: "What is it?"

"Doc—I was starting to feel better *before* you cured me."

The doctor affixed the laser-loupes back into his eye sockets. "Well, maybe you wanted to live more than you thought."

Eldridge nodded. "Thanks."

"How is the clean-up progressing?"

"Fine. My next stop is Boris Hagan's."

• • • • •

BORIS HAGAN'S APARTMENT WAS a deceptive hovel. The first room inside the door looked like the site of a quadruple murder-suicide that involved a breach of radioactive material. Pre-Deadblast icons sat everywhere—BIOHAZARD, FLAMMABLE, DANGER, POISON—along with bucket-sized splatters of blood.

But Eldridge knew the secret way in. It was another goofy hidden door that he, Hagan, and Tola had installed. For some reason, Hagan insisted they hide the door behind an old file cabinet, which Eldridge slid out of the way so he could enter his departed friend's inner sanctum.

Inside was a 10-foot-square habitat that Hagan had built out of dozens of sliding shelves. By moving around the shelves, Hagan could reconfigure his room into hundreds of different shapes and sizes. Eldridge didn't know all of them, but he knew where Hagan kept his old computer, which he also knew was hooked into the ancient Arpa. The redhead uncovered the console, sat before it and tapped the keyboard to wake it up. A cursor appeared. Eldridge reached into his pocket and produced the photo from the Old Mine's wall that depicted the fallen city of Paris. He shrugged and typed, PARIS TOWER. The computer whirred and clicked, and after a moment, text spilled out on the screen:

```
The EIFFEL TOWER LAKM;;HHH ----1889 iron
IXUNNH&& located in Paris 4HUQEJUDR3
53EHATHA22AGUFRATU NAZAVAB2U8RA VUCE6RE
```

```
WEP 94HAQEW 3NEXAP2 built as the;---arch
for the 1889 Fair.
```

Eldridge smiled and looked at the photo. A voice interrupted him.

"El?"

He spun around, pulling both of his scatterguns, and if his senses hadn't still been heightened with leftover adrenaline from the previous evening's battle, he might have shot the bespectacled, sandy-haired man who was gawking at him. But even though Eldridge didn't pull the triggers, he still kept his weapons trained on the man while his brain calculated the results and told him the impossible.

Boris Hagan was alive.

The scatterguns hit the floor at the same instant that Eldridge wrapped his arms around Hagan and squeezed with the full force of his old Narsyan strength.

Hagan wheezed: *"Elllllllllll!"*

"He told me you were dead!"

"Who?"

He released him and said, "Goldmist!"

Hagan cocked an eyebrow. "Yeah, and he *always* told the truth."

They broke up laughing. A shriek interrupted them. Both men screamed and staggered back from the door, where a creature was standing—a creature whose incredible body heat and putrid perspiration marked it as a dreen. It crouched in the doorway in an avian pose—its overlong arms tucked into its sides. The thing's head had elongated around a jutting jawline that resembled a beak.

Hagan touched his friend's arm.

"El, what is this?"

"Bor, it's OK." Eldridge addressed the dreen: "Do you have a message for me?"

The dreen spread its three-foot-long arms and kneeled. A voicelike warble emitted from its throat like a spliced-together recording of a hundred voices that each spoke one syllable at a time.

"You. May. Come. To. The. Mine."

The dreen withdrew. Hagan stared at the redhead.

"What the hell did *that* mean?"

"It means I have to go back to the Old Mine."

"Why?"

"I forgot something."

• • • • •

HIGH ABOVE UNDER-DEDRICK, PEOPLE heard some of the explosions from the battle underneath, but for the most part, business went on as usual in the casino of Crius Kaleb, Odd of Dedrick. He sat behind his desk and counted his jenta, unaware of the carnage happening under his feet and unwilling to admit that such a subterranean realm even existed. The Odd was still counting his jenta when Reginald, the mound-man, knocked on his door, indicating that he had visitors seeking audience.

"Let them in," he said with his computerized voice.

Three dark figures entered, two of them concealed within black cloaks. The third he recognized.

The redhead.

"You defaulted on your deathday wager, Eldridge. Are you here to pay me?"

"You're an urbit, aren't you?"

The question upset Kaleb's delicate mental state. No one ever did anything but answer his questions when they had audience with him. He was an Odd. Not the most powerful Odd, but an Odd nonetheless, and his words weren't to be ignored.

"What did you say to me?"

"You lost a child. You're an urbit. You lost your son when I killed him in the alleyway outside this casino."

Kaleb tongued his speechmouth and squirmed in his chair. Casting his consciousness even as far as the region immediately surrounding his casino sparked a flame in his guts.

Finally, he responded.

"I lost my son years ago."

"I know," Eldridge said. "When he became a dreen. I wanna tell you something, Crius—I'm an urbit, too. One of you—one of the Odds—killed my little girl. Her name was Zora. You might've seen her around town."

"Of course," Kaleb snapped. "I know of the constable. She and Goldmist were to sign off on your death if it had happened on the fourth."

Eldridge chuckled. "Well, seeing as how I just killed Jeb, that's not gonna happen."

Sweat started to gather in the hanging folds of flesh around Kaleb's mouth.

"What is this all about?" Kaleb asked. "Who are those people?"

"Constable Tola was a good cop, but she screwed up sometimes. She screwed up the night I killed your son. *Thought* I killed him. The guy I killed, he was a dreen, see, so it was easy to get a false ID." Eldridge turned to one of the cloaked forms. "Stewart?"

Kaleb's speechmouth fell from his lips and clattered onto his desk, revealing the orange teeth and black tongue that hid inside. The dark form stood forward and pulled the cloak back from its head. Shiny red scar tissue covered the man from head to toe. He was younger and much taller than the redhead, and his cheeks sagged below his chin. He looked across the room with glistening eyes.

"Dad?"

The sound of his son's voice caused the room to give way all around him. The walls quivered like a silent earthquake was rumbling below. The ceiling lost opacity and revealed the stars overhead. Kaleb grit his teeth and forced himself to respond, but when he did, he dissolved into tears that he didn't even know he could still shed. He buried his head in his arms and wailed. "Son, son. I can't let you see me like, see me like–"

"Mr. Kaleb?"

The third dark figure had spoken. He stood forth, pulled his cloak back, and revealed a head covered with an elaborately shaved pattern of hair.

He said: "You may not remember me, but we met many years ago. Up in the mountains far north of here. My name is Pell Yannick."

Kaleb looked up. The ceiling had vanished, and the walls were disintegrating in slow motion. But he focused on the stately man before him.

"I remember you," he whispered.

"I was afraid you might," Pell said and lowered his gaze. "Mr. Kaleb, in lieu of the jenta that Mr. Eldridge owes you, we wanted to present you with your restored son, as well as one more gift. Eldridge?"

By that point, the casino had vanished. Kaleb's desk sat on a solitary planetoid that drifted near the event horizon of a black hole, which hung below them like a dark sphere of deafening, silent void. All perception smeared in circles around the black hole, including the three men who shared the planetoid with him. As their rate of descent approached the speed of light, Kaleb's scope of vision narrowed into a round window through which everything glowed blue at the center, while the edges glimmered with redshifted crimson light.

But he kept his eyes on his son, and as he did, he saw the redhead pull out a rubber strap and tie it around Pell's bicep. As soon as a blood vessel rose out of his arm, Eldridge produced a small glass vial that was capped with a needle. He drew a few ounces of the Narsyan chieftain's blood, then removed the vial and pressed a cotton ball into the wound. Eldridge crossed the room and stood before Kaleb's desk as the Odd continued to weep, and their fragile little planetoid inexorably fell toward the black hole.

"Cri?" Eldridge said, his voice echoing in the endless expanse. "Cri? It's OK. It's OK. It's all going to be OK. Now, give me your arm."

Kaleb sat frozen for one awful moment as they plunged toward the event horizon.

But right before they disappeared, he reached out.

About the Author

Robert J. Peterson is a writer and web developer living in Los Angeles. A Tennessee native, he graduated from Northwestern University's Medill School of Journalism. He's written for newspapers and websites all over the country, including the Marin Independent Journal, PerformInk, Space.com, the Telluride Daily Planet, and Geekscape.net. In 2004, he co-founded the pop-culture emporium CC2KOnline.com. He's appeared on the web talk shows Comics on Comics, The Fanboy Scoop, Geekscape, and Fandom Planet. He's the founder of California Coldblood Books.

His friends call him Bob.

Acknowledgments

Huge thanks go out to my beta readers, including my lovely and amazing girlfriend and partner, Lauren Rock; screenwriter and filmmaker Karl Mueller; TV producer and writer Corey Finkle; literary agent Victoria Marini of Gelfman Schneider Literary; film producer Oscar A. Torres; and communications specialist Jonathan Lipman.

Special thanks to Tyson Cornell and Julia Callahan of Rare Bird Books for taking on California Coldblood as their imprint for science-fiction and fantasy. I'm honored to be working with them and look forward to a fantastic future under the Rare Bird banner.

Special thanks to Meeno Peluce for my wonderful author's photo. You can see more of his work here: meenophoto.com

Special thanks to Ratna Pappert for her amazing rendering of Eldridge and related concept art. You can see more of her work here: curiositydrawsme.com

Special thanks to Nils Jeppe for the use of his gorgeous concept art. You can see more of his work here: enderra.com